COLD CASE FLASHBACKS

JANICE KAY JOHNSON

GUARDING COLTON'S CHILD

LARA LACOMBE

MILLS & BOON

First Published in Great Britain 2021
by Mills & Boon, an imprint of HarperCollins*Publishers* Ltd
1 London Bridge Street, London, SE1 9GF

www.harpercollins.co.uk

HarperCollins*Publishers*
1st Floor, Watermarque Building,
Ringsend Road, Dublin 4, Ireland

Cold Case Flashbacks © 2021 Janice Kay Johnson
Guarding Colton's Child © 2021 Harlequin Books S.A.

Special thanks and acknowledgement are given to Lara Lacombe for her contribution to *The Coltons of Grave Gulch* series.

ISBN: 978-0-263-28335-8

0421

MIX
Paper from
responsible sources
FSC™ C007454

This book is produced from independently certified FSC™ paper to ensure responsible forest management.

For more information visit: www.harpercollins.co.uk/green

Printed and bound in Spain
by CPI, Barcelona

COLD CASE FLASHBACKS

JANICE KAY JOHNSON

An author of more than ninety books for children and adults with more than seventy-five for Mills & Boon, **Janice Kay Johnson** writes about love and family, and pens books of gripping romantic suspense. A *USA TODAY* bestselling author and an eight-time finalist for the Romance Writers of America RITA® Award, she won a RITA® Award in 2008. A former librarian, Janice raised two daughters in a small town north of Seattle, Washington.

Lara Lacombe earned a PhD in microbiology and immunology and worked in several labs across the country before moving into the classroom. Her day job as a college science professor gives her time to pursue her other love—writing fast-paced romantic suspense with smart, nerdy heroines and dangerously attractive heroes. She loves to hear from readers! Find her on the web or contact her at laralacombewriter@gmail.com

Also by Janice Kay Johnson

Hide the Child
Trusting the Sheriff
Within Range
Brace for Impact
The Hunting Season
The Last Resort

Also by Lara Lacombe

Ranger's Justice
Ranger's Baby Rescue
The Ranger's Reunion Threat
Ranger's Family in Danger
Colton's Undercover Reunion
Deadly Contact
Fatal Fallout
Lethal Lies
Killer Exposure
Killer Season

Discover more at millsandboon.co.uk

Chapter One

Jack Cowan investigated murderers, rapists and other scumbags on a daily basis, and was glad to snap the cuffs on each and every one of them. Not having it in his power to go after the killer he wanted most to nail... yeah, that ate at him.

Today Jack walked out of the locker room at the health club and saw Ric Ortiz on a treadmill. The one beside him was empty. Good. Ortiz was Jack's single remaining connection to the murdered woman and the one witness. That made him Jack's only hope, too.

The two men ran into each other often enough, Jack didn't have to orchestrate meetings. In a city the size of Leclaire, that happened. It was somewhere in the top twenty cities in Washington state by population and needed a significant police department, yet wasn't so big you didn't see people you knew at a grocery store or, in this case, a health club. Growing up, he and Ric had been school classmates and soccer and Little League teammates, thus sharing some parental carpools—before, in different ways, their worlds were shattered.

Even though he wanted to claim that empty treadmill before someone got to it, Jack paused to take a look around the gym with a cop's typical caution. He'd hit on a good hour to be here, he saw, with the place only half-full. Lots of machines available, weight lifters letting out harsh sounds and clanging the weights back onto the racks as they released them after their reps. He saw more women than men, some in formfitting exercise getups, but no one who caught his eye.

Unsettled by his complete lack of interest, he scanned some fine-looking female bodies again, but, damn, he just wanted to get in his run and go home. Eat and fall into bed, alone. He'd hook up with someone one of these days. It had been only... Okay, four or five months since he'd parted ways with Laura. Normally he'd have been getting restless, but he'd been working long hours, as detectives often did.

Jack reached the treadmill, adjusted the speed and set his water bottle in the holder before stepping onto the track. Ric Ortiz must have been there awhile, because he'd worked up a good sweat and was really moving. Tall and lean, he'd always been a good athlete.

He glanced at Jack, who started to jog. "How's it going?"

"Good." Jack had closed a big case yesterday and spent today on the paperwork. He'd intended to run at the park or on the high school track, but the sky started spitting out sleet as he left the police station and walked to his car. This was better than nothing. "You?"

The two men chatted desultorily. Ric's breath was coming hard and fast. Jack was only half listening when Ric said, out of the blue, "You remember my sister?" Not slowing, he snatched up a towel to wipe sweat from his face.

This was why Jack always made a point of talking to Ortiz when their paths crossed.

Still, as he stepped up his own speed, Jack only grunted a response.

In fact, he knew a hell of a lot more about Gabriella Ortiz than her brother could imagine. In Jack's most vivid memories of seeing the girl, she'd been riding a hot pink tricycle on the sidewalk outside the Ortiz home when Jack's mom dropped off Ric after a soccer practice or Little League. He pictured two dark pigtails tied off with pink ribbons. Either they were always pink or he just hadn't paid attention. Later, there'd been a bike with training wheels and more pink ribbons fluttering from the handlebars. Funny he could remember that, when he couldn't have cared less about some dumb little sister.

Not then.

But now he said with pretended indifference, "I remember you have a sister."

"Yeah, once upon a time." Seemingly brooding, Ric let his pace gradually drop. It was another couple of minutes before he said, "Gabby's coming home."

Gabby's coming home.

Jack broke stride, stumbled, cursed and had to do some quick footwork to keep from falling and to regain his pace.

Fortunately, Ric's head had turned as he answered a hail from some buddy. Gave Jack a minute to hide his shock and exultation.

"To stay?" he asked.

"To stay?" Ortiz glanced his way. "Oh, you mean Gabby. Uh, probably not. This is more of a visit. We haven't seen each other since, man, she was like eight and I was eleven."

"She went to live with an aunt, didn't she?" And had grown up in a smallish town in Vermont.

Ric slowed to a cooldown jog. "Dad and I flew back to see her a few times that first year or two, but my great-aunt wasn't what you'd call welcoming. I guess…even

Dad kind of gave up." His forehead crinkled. "He thought she was better off there."

Safer, was what Ric meant. Supposedly, four-year-old Gabby had had a couple of near misses that might have been nothing, just weird things happening, but might instead have been attempts on her life. Gabby Ortiz had witnessed her mother's murder, so that made sense. Enough, at least, that Jack could see why her dad would have thought an out-of-sight, out-of-mind plan good.

Gabby now had to be almost thirty…no, she *was* thirty. Doing his research, Jack had taken note of her September birthday.

"What inspired the visit?" Jack asked.

Ric stepped off his treadmill and ran the towel over his head, leaving his dark hair sticking up in spikes.

"We've been emailing more often. With Dad gone now…" He shrugged.

Given his intense interest in the Ortiz family, Jack had noted the obituary in the local paper, too. He'd even gone to the funeral, wondering if prolonged grief had worn out Raul Ortiz's heart before its time.

"Great-Aunt Isabel died, I don't know, seven or eight years ago, too," Ric added. "One of Mom's sisters is still alive, as far as I know, but they were ten years apart in age and never close. I've barely met those cousins, and I doubt Gabby has at all. That kind of leaves the two of us."

"I know what you mean." Jack's sister was married to an army officer, and they were currently stationed in Jordan right now. Really, they were almost complete strangers. That left him and his father, and Dad was in Oregon.

Dad grieved, too. If his heart gave out, Jack wouldn't be surprised. Enraged, but not surprised.

"So… I get pissed at her," Ric said. "She should have come home years ago. Told the cops what she knows, but she didn't want to hear it. Buried her head in the sand and won't pull it out. We'd get friendly, then mad at each other and not be in contact for a year." His mouth tightened. "Not holding my breath, but I guess I'm hoping that seeing each other will mean something. You know?"

"I hope it does," Jack said sincerely, even as he was thinking about whether she'd talk to *him*.

"I gotta get going." Ric seemed to shake off his mood. "Good to see you."

"Yeah." As Ric walked away, Jack called, "Hey, when's she coming?"

The guy turned to walk backward. "Next week. Monday. We've been planning this for a while."

"Good luck."

"Yeah." The grin was kind of weak, and a minute later, Ric disappeared into the locker room.

Jack kicked up his speed and brooded. Be straight with her and ask for an official interview? That's what he should do, but what if she declined? Going undercover wasn't something he'd exactly done before, given the size of this town. Too much chance of being recognized. But she'd have no way of knowing about his obsession with her mother's murder, so it might not matter if she knew he was a cop. He could sound her out a little, find out what she was like. Why she hadn't come home, even once she was an adult and her aunt had died.

Her confused childhood memories might be gone altogether, but if so, wouldn't you think she'd have told her brother? If they were still there, in her head, why was she refusing to examine them? Maybe knowing what Jack did for a living might be a positive, if she had any desire at all to talk about the stalled investigation and whatever weird stuff surfaced in nightmares.

Or maybe she barely remembered her mother and

figured what was past, was past. She'd moved on with her life.

Well, there were people who hadn't, he thought, speared by bitterness and anger, and she owed them something. He had every intention of making sure she paid.

"RIC?" GABBY WOULDN'T have recognized the man pushing himself away from a pillar near baggage claim at the Spokane International Airport if she didn't follow him on Instagram and a couple of other sites. Not until he smiled did she see the skinny boy she'd worshipped as a kid.

"Damn." He grinned at her. "Who'd have thought you'd come out looking so good?"

She made a face and surrendered her laptop case to him. He leaned over to kiss her cheek.

"Didn't grow so much, though, did you?" he added, reminding her how much he had loved irritating her.

She sniffed. "Doesn't take mass to make quality."

His laugh followed her to the carousel, where bags were appearing. She could have packed enough in a carry-on suitcase…but on the chance she'd decide to extend her stay, Gabby had decided to bring plenty.

Feeling a certain queasiness at the thought, she reminded herself that, for all her determination to find some answers, she wasn't stuck here. She could pack up and leave whenever she wanted. Who could stop her? She just…didn't want to hurt her brother's feelings. Or close off any possibility of a relationship with him.

Leclaire was a western suburb of Spokane, almost butting up to the Washington–Idaho border. The drive from the airport shouldn't take long. Once Ric had loaded her and her bags and they got on the way, she didn't recognize a thing. She could have been on the outskirts of any medium-size city in the US, except this one was greener than most. She saw some forests and low mountains in the distance, and that had to be the Spokane River.

"Look familiar?" Ric asked.

She shook her head. "I was so young. I wish Mom and Dad had been into camping or something like that, but…" She shrugged. "I remember the house and the neighborhood, sort of, but not much else."

His dark eyes rested on her face for a minute, but she resisted meeting them. She knew what he was thinking. *Don't you remember watching Mom get butchered?*

A rush of adrenaline made childish feelings well up in her. *I don't! I don't!* But she kept her mouth clamped shut. That argument never went well. Ric must be trying, and she'd do the same. She had to face the fact that, however hard she tried to recover her memories, she might fail. She'd worked too hard to *block* those memories. To be a strong woman, how could she build on the shaky foundation of knowing, in the most terrifying way, what true vulnerability felt like?

Anyway, the murder had happened so many years ago, and she'd seen it as young child, not an adult. Kids didn't think the same. Plus her mind might have reworked the memories and even her ability to access them in order to allow her to recover and become a functioning person.

Yes, the visit would bring back memories. Enough to be helpful? She had no idea. And she didn't plan to tell Ric she was going to try to do as he asked until she found out whether she could get anywhere. Their perspectives were poles apart.

For starters, she couldn't understand how Ric had brought himself to stay in their childhood home. Since he wasn't married, it was too big for him. And Dad.

How had *he* stood living there, where Mom had been murdered? Did he have to clean up her blood himself? Why hadn't he moved? Wouldn't that have been healthier for Ric?

And maybe the biggest question was, why hadn't Dad been willing to move so he could keep *both* of his children with him?

Yeah, she had her issues.

The silence had become prolonged. Her fault. She sifted through possibilities and went with, "So, are you seeing anyone right now?"

"Not seriously," he admitted. "What about you?"

"No." She wasn't sure she could do serious. That was one of those issues. "I date, but…" She shrugged.

"Job?"

Keep it light. "I don't have much staying power." She was one dissertation away from her PhD in American History, but once that was approved, she'd be looking for a position at a university where she'd be put on a tenure track and maybe never leave. The idea made her shiver. The reasons for her procrastination on polishing the blasted dissertation and presenting it were not subtle.

Nor relevant, she reminded herself. This was a visit, that's all. Whether she could come up with any information to help track her mother's murderer or not, this wasn't home anymore. She'd get to know Ric, but not too well. His turn to visit her next. Somewhere, anywhere, besides the city and house that were bound to keep haunting her.

At the sight of a bright green highway sign that said Leclaire, Gabby leaned forward, stretching out the seat belt.

"Four exits?"

"It's grown." Ric put on the turn signal and worked his way two lanes to the right, finally leaving the freeway.

"Oh, I made a reservation at the Wilmont," she said. "I don't think it's that far from the house."

He braked at a red light and turned to stare at her. "What? You're not staying with me?"

"I… I thought it might be more comfortable for both of us not to be thrown together quite that much."

"Is it the house? Or me?"

Oh, heavens, she'd already hurt his feelings.

"Mostly the house, but…a little bit of both. I don't *know* you. Every time I think I start to, you lash out at me." She swallowed. Pride kept her voice even. "I thought some space would make sense."

"Fine." He accelerated hard enough to press her back in her seat. "I'll give you all the space you want."

"You're mad at me."

"You think?"

Of course, he was. She should have told him in advance. But why would he imagine she'd cheerfully go home with him to her childhood bedroom? Hang out in the kitchen, when he had to guess she'd look like a kid playing hopscotch to be sure she didn't step on the place where Mom's body had lain, or plant a foot in the pools of blood?

He hadn't been home. *He* hadn't seen Mom's body at all. Probably not even the blood. So what did he know?

She clamped her jaw shut, gripped the seat belt crossing her chest and didn't say a word.

JACK HELD BACK until Tuesday, then called Ric. As if they were good enough friends. "Just wanted to say I hope the reunion is going well." He made it casual. "I kept thinking about you and Gabby."

"It's…not going so well." Ric sounded strange. "I shouldn't have assumed she'd want to stay with me, but I did. I didn't take it well when she asked me to drop her at a hotel."

"You blew up at her?"

"Not that bad." Ric sighed. "We had a really awkward dinner at the restaurant in the hotel. I haven't talked to her today."

"Where's she staying?" He caught himself. "I mean, she's here in town, right?"

"Oh, sure. The Wilmont. I know I need to talk to her, but how are we supposed to get to be friends if all we do is have a few restaurant meals?"

That was a really good question. "You know snow is being forecast."

"Why didn't she come when the leaves were changing and the weather was dry and crisp?"

Another good question. "Did she have a winter break from a job?" Like her job teaching at a community college? The one he shouldn't know about?

Except, come to think of it, this was mid-November. Thanksgiving was next week, which made it too early for school breaks.

"Maybe." Ric's tone eased. "Yeah, that's probably it, but she didn't sound enthusiastic about what she's been doing. She didn't *say* she'd quit, but I wonder."

"Yeah? Where's she been living?"

"Oh, New Hampshire. Concord Community College. Actually, that's the second—no, third—college where she's taught since she finished grad school. Supposedly she's working on her dissertation, but she didn't seem all that interested in talking about it."

"She say how long she plans to stay here?"

"I was careful not to push it." Ric grunted. "It was

like a really bad first date. You know, when conversation never takes off. Except in our case, there's this history. I kept looking at her and thinking, she's my little sister. I used to pull her pigtail or steal this stuffed hippopotamus she wouldn't go to bed without. Only… I can't make the two pictures merge."

Part of Jack sympathized, and part of him was afraid Gabby Ortiz would decide to leave town before he had a chance to talk to her at all. This might be his only chance.

"There's a lot of years in between," he pointed out. "Me, I was picturing this little girl with plump cheeks who always wore pink scooting up and down the sidewalk on that plastic tricycle. Like she was waiting for you."

"I think she was."

"Listen, I was off today, just stayed home because the weather stinks. How about if I take the two of you out? Fancy, if you think she'd like that, but we could just go for pizza and beer. Maybe having someone else with you would lower the pressure."

"You'd do that?" Ric sounded surprised, and for good reason, considering they were more acquaintances these days than friends.

"Why not? I think what happened to your mother was one of the reasons I went into law enforcement. What Gabby saw back then—" He cleared his throat. "I wouldn't mind seeing her, all grown up."

"Man, if you mean that, it would be great. That is, if she's okay with it. I can't think of any of her friends who are still around here, but even the couple guys who were at my house the most often are long gone. Not that she probably remembers them anyway."

"Why don't you check with her?" Jack suggested, sounding a lot more casual than he felt.

"I'll do that and get back to you."

If she said no? Jack fully intended to find a plan B.

Chapter Two

"All right. What's this about?" Chief Keller asked brusquely.

Jack's sergeant had walked up to the office with him, having given his provisional approval for the request. But he decided they needed permission from above. As soon as Jack had firmed plans for dinner with Ric and Gabby this evening, he'd driven straight to the station.

Now, Sergeant Rutkowski stayed silent, leaving Jack to say, "I'd like permission to open a cold case."

Dean Keller had risen through the ranks and was respected within the department. Since Jack rarely had anything to do with the chief, he couldn't claim to know him, or guess how he'd react to an upstart detective thinking he could accomplish something his predecessors hadn't. Solving Colleen Ortiz's high-profile murder. Leclaire Police Department's failure to make an arrest had been a black mark in the eyes of the public.

Keller studied Jack keenly. "What's your interest?"

"I read about it when I first came on board," Jack said. He hesitated, then admitted, "My father was an initial suspect in Mrs. Ortiz's murder. He talked about it."

The chief's expression changed. "Cowan." Then, more slowly, "Brian Cowan. I remember the name. I was a patrol officer at the time. Does your father still live locally?"

"No, he's in Bend, Oregon."

"What would he think of this idea?"

Jack had no idea. Dad had long since resigned himself to his many losses in a way Jack wasn't willing to do. "I didn't discuss it with him. I have to believe he'd be glad if Mrs. Ortiz's murderer was arrested."

Keller's gaze shifted to Sergeant Rutkowski. "What do you think?"

"He's got a chance that may not come along again. Cowan has a hell of a closure rate. You know that. I'd have chosen him to take something like this on." He shrugged. "The timing is good. Major crime usually drops when people are stuck at home because of snow or ice."

"What's this 'chance'?" the chief asked sharply.

Jack answered, "You may recall that Mrs. Ortiz's daughter witnessed the killing."

"Good God, she was a toddler! From what I heard, her testimony—if you can even call it that—was worthless."

"She was four and a half. Actually, closer to five. Kids are pretty verbal by that age." They sure as hell knew their colors. Gabriella Ortiz had insisted the man had worn all blue. "They start learning to read. She was traumatized. I'm hoping that she remembers something she was afraid to say then, or as a young child didn't understand but now does."

"If so, why hasn't she come to us?"

"Again, the event was pretty traumatic. She may have been encouraged to block out what she did remember, especially if it was giving her nightmares."

"And this woman lives...where? Are you expecting the department to fund your travels?"

"No, sir." He knew how tight the budget was. "I happened to learn that Ms. Ortiz is here in Leclaire for a visit. Her brother still lives here."

"Huh." Chief Keller leaned back in his desk chair, rubbed a hand over his jaw and brooded for a minute. "Can you keep this reasonably quiet?"

"I can't control Gabrielle Ortiz or her brother, Ric, should they decide to go to the press. I think that's pretty unlikely, though." He decided not to mention that Ric had been hot to reopen the case for years. Since he wouldn't know Jack was reopening it, at least for the time being, Jack didn't see a problem. "Ric and I went to high school together, both played football and baseball. I happened to run into him a week or so ago, and that's when he told me about his sister's visit. I figure it's at least worth sitting down with her."

The sergeant didn't say anything. Jack stayed physically relaxed, despite the determination that simmered at a near boil. Had to appear intrigued but dispassionate. He was curious, that's all.

"Okay," Keller said. "We may have to cut you off if we get too busy or if it's obvious you aren't getting anywhere, but we'd all like to see this one closed. It's worth a try."

"Thank you, sir." Jack rose from the chair, nodded and walked out, waiting in the outer office for the sergeant, who'd paused to exchange a few words with the chief.

Both men nodded at Chief Keller's assistant and continued to the elevator together. Jack pushed the button. While they waited, Rutkowski said, "Didn't expect a problem. I really hope you get somewhere with her."

"I do, too," Jack said with complete sincerity—and no intention of admitting that he was making the initial approach to Gabby Ortiz as neighborhood kid grown up, a casual friend of her brother's, not as a homicide detective with his eye on her as a witness.

Testing the waters, that's all. Going with his instinct, which said that a woman who'd refused to come back to town for twenty-five years wouldn't immediately open up to an investigator who demanded she mine her most painful memories.

Even when he did tell her he was reopening the case, he could claim he'd just decided to do it. That he'd had an ulterior motive all along...well, why would she ever have to find that out?

RIC HAD SUGGESTED an Italian restaurant only six blocks from Gabby's hotel. Of course he offered to pick her up, but the Wilmont offered free Uber service within downtown, so she said she'd meet them there.

Them.

Having arrived before the two men and been seated in a booth, Gabby let herself wonder why Ric was bringing someone else. It didn't sound like this Jack Cowan was a really close friend, but she did remember the name. She even thought she could picture him, a tall boy with ruffled brown hair that must have had some curl. Later, though, Dad had sent her articles from the local newspaper about the successes of both Ric's high school baseball and football teams. Ric had pitched, Jack had been the first baseman. On the football field, Jack was the quarterback who'd led the team to a state championship, Ric his favorite wide receiver. Gabby had hungrily studied the couple photos of her brother, but only one photo of Jack Cowan lingered in her memory. They'd been seniors the year their football team went all the way, so she would have been...thirteen. No, probably fourteen. Definitely boy crazy. She'd thought Jack's broad, triumphant grin was sexy. She'd thought *he* was sexy. The idea was laughable now, given how skinny he'd undoubtedly been, how immature.

Still…having him here might ease the tension between her and Ric, who'd had more expectations of her than she could handle. Wow, if he had any idea she intended to try to do what he'd long demanded of her, he'd turn into a bulldozer and drive her nuts.

Sipping her glass of water, she was facing the door when Ric and another man walked in. A group of three women at a nearby table turned their heads in unison. Gabby didn't blame them. She felt appreciation for a fine sight.

Ric was really good-looking, his Latino heritage showing in near-black hair and dark eyes. The height came from Mom's side of the family. Jack Cowan had a craggier face, not as obviously handsome, but there was something elementally male in that big, broad-shouldered body and the saunter that seemed unconscious.

She lifted a hand, Ric spotted her and said something to his friend, who looked straight at her and changed his path between tables. She wasn't sure his eyes ever left hers until… He arrived at the booth, he stood looking down at her.

His medium brown hair, cut short, was still unruly, and his eyes were a bright blue.

Then he grinned. "I'd never have recognized you."

"You remember me?"

"Yeah, you had that pink tricycle you'd pedal up and down the sidewalk."

Gabby wrinkled her nose at him. She'd loved all things pink at that age, had even thrown a temper tantrum if Mom wanted her to wear any other color, except occasionally purple.

"No more pink," he added.

To her puzzlement, he kept standing there, his assessment unexpectedly...thorough. After a moment, he glanced toward the front of the restaurant, then the nearby hall leading to the restrooms and kitchen. Her brother raised his eyebrows, edged by him and sat beside her.

At last, Jack sat, too, but slid all the way across and relaxed against the wall, half-facing them and half-facing the room. "A pitcher?" he suggested, lifting a hand for an approaching waiter.

"Gabby?" her brother asked.

"That's fine." She didn't love beer, but wine and pizza would be ridiculous. And, really, she wasn't much of a drinker at all. Great-Aunt Isabel hadn't approved of "spirits."

Jack Cowan went back to studying her as Ric ordered the pitcher. "You look good," he said after a minute.

Something about the intensity in his gaze unsettled her—or maybe it was her reaction to him. "Did you expect terrible?"

He laughed. "I guess that was rude. I just expected..." He hesitated. "Chubby cheeks."

Oh, lord—she'd been plump back then, to put it kindly. Mom said she had chipmunk cheeks. In pictures where she was beaming, her eyes ended up squinty in that fat face. *She'd* expected to grow up with chubby cheeks, like the women on Dad's side of the family. Instead, she had apparently acquired her mother's fine bones and ivory skin. Not Mom's height, though, or warm brown hair; nope, Gabby's was black, thick and stubbornly straight.

One side of Jack's mouth turned up. "You and Ric look like brother and sister."

"Except for the foot difference in height." Her brother

just couldn't help rubbing it in. "Not to mention some actual muscles."

She lifted her chin. "I exercise. I just don't admire myself in mirrors while I sculpt unnecessary muscles."

Jack gave a crack of laughter, and even Ric grinned.

"Sharp-tongued little thing," he observed.

Amusement still lingering on his face, Jack said, "I like that in a woman."

She was terribly afraid her cheeks heated.

They settled down to choosing a pizza, a giant one. The men considered ordering two, but she reminded them that she, at least, wouldn't be taking any leftovers. Irritation crossed Ric's face. Jack's eyes flickered as he took that in. He was exceptionally observant, she couldn't help thinking.

Once the pitcher arrived and he'd poured glasses of beer for all three of them, he said, "Ric tells me you're a college professor."

"Well…halfway. I've been taking lecturer positions at two-year colleges while I work on my dissertation. My chances of getting on at a good four-year school are zilch until I have the PhD."

"History?"

"Yes. One of those majors that does not lead to sky-high salaries."

He laughed again. She really liked what that laugh did to his face. "We have that in common. I'm a cop."

She froze, the glass almost to her lips. A cop? Why hadn't Ric told her? Pulling herself together, she took a sip of beer to give herself a moment. Was he someone she could talk to, if she got to that point?

"Yeah? Did you get a degree in criminology?" She congratulated herself on sounding no more than pleasantly interested.

"I did. Went to Portland State. My dad moved to Oregon my senior year in high school. I stayed here with a friend's family until I graduated."

"And came back once you had your degree?"

His big shoulders moved. "It's home."

Her brother didn't seem to recognize any awkwardness. Sounding smug, he said, "I'll bet I outearn you both."

She stuck out her tongue.

Jack grimaced. "Safe to say."

A mechanical engineer, her brother worked for a company known for their specialty tools. He hadn't told Gabby how much he made, but it had to be plenty—certainly enough for him to have bought a different house.

But, no, Ric had gone to Washington State University here in Eastern Washington, and was now on his second job in Spokane, an easy commute from Leclaire. None of that was chance. Of course, Dad had kept *him*, and this was his home, as it was Jack Cowan's. And Ric and she had experienced Mom's murder and the aftermath in completely different ways.

Which reminded her... "Are you with Leclaire PD?" she asked Jack. Seeing his nod, she asked, "What do you do with the department?"

"Started out at the bottom, took the detective exam a few years back and I'm now assigned to major crimes. I wrapped up an ugly home invasion and rape case just recently, for example."

Ric hoisted his glass. "I read about that. I didn't realize you were the investigator."

"I was."

"That must be...hard," she murmured. "I mean, seeing what you do."

Seeing what she had. That had to be what she was thinking.

"Sometimes," he agreed, his gaze holding hers even as he braced himself. Lying on the job was often necessary, but lying to this woman...

I am on the job, he reminded himself, still not happy about looking into her eyes and saying, *Nope, I barely remember your mother's murder. And you? A witness? Wow, nobody told me.*

No, she wouldn't buy that.

"You know about our mother," she said flatly.

"Yeah, I do." He tried to make his tone gentle as he picked his way through the minefield. "Ric and I were friends, teammates. How could I not? In fact, I told Ric the other day, I think what happened to your mom and your family is part of what motivated me to consider law enforcement for a career. Becoming a detective was always my goal. People forget that a murder sends out ripples of pain. Family and friends becomes victims, too, in a sense. I can't claim to understand, but even as a kid I could see it happening to your family."

She swallowed and looked away. After a moment, she nodded. "Can we not talk about it?"

"Always your solution," her brother mumbled.

"This isn't exactly the time or place," she snapped.

Her green-gold eyes already held Jack's attention. Now a flare of pain or anger or both accentuated the gold.

Damn. He hadn't anticipated his attraction to this woman—the woman he intended to deceive and, eventually, press for every painful memory she'd buried.

And he couldn't kid himself. He wouldn't be doing it for her. He wanted to shame every person who'd ever looked with doubt at his father.

Because his own family had been broken by Colleen

Ortiz's murder, too. And if Gabby remembered anything, she owed all the other people who'd been hurt to lay it out in the light of day.

But she was right. This wasn't the moment for that. Instead, Jack set out to tamp down the tension between sister and brother.

"My fault the subject came up. Hey, I hope that's our pizza. I'm starved."

"Because you slaved all day?" Ric mocked him, apparently willing to go along.

"Yeah, that was me."

Once the pizza was in front of them and Ric was handing out plates, Jack continued, "Lounged on my couch in sweats and watched a Seahawks game I missed." True as far as it went.

The beautiful woman sitting on the other side of the booth looked askance at him. "But you must know how it came out."

"Well, sure." He let her take a slice, then dished up a bigger one for himself. "But I wanted to see more than the highlights."

She rolled her eyes. "I mean, I follow the NFL. But it's no fun once you know who has won or lost."

Jack narrowed his eyes. "Please don't tell me you're a fan of the—" He couldn't even say it.

"The Patriots? Of course I am. I live in New England."

Making a strangled sound, he fell back in pretended anguish.

Her brother laughed. "I should have warned you."

They moved on to talking and arguing about a dozen topics while devouring the pizza. Well, she stopped after two slices, but he and Ric took care of the rest. Nobody would be taking any home.

Ric insisted on handling the bill, smirking as he reminded them of their relative poverty. As they walked
out, he offered her a ride back to the hotel, but she shook
her head with a smile and held up her phone.

"I already sent for the Uber."

Ric zipped up his coat, pulled on gloves and started
down the sidewalk. Zipping up his own parka, Jack raised
his brows.

"You lied."

"I didn't… How do you know?" she demanded, her
indignation obvious.

"I was walking behind you."

"Hmph. Well, I'm going to do it right now."

"Why don't you let me drop you? My car is only half
a block away."

Her teeth closed on her lower lip as she hesitated, then
finally nodded. "Thanks. I'm at the Wilmont."

"Ric told me."

"He's mad."

"He told me that, too."

They set out down the sidewalk together, Jack shorten-
ing his steps. She probably wasn't more than five foot two
or three inches at the most. At least she'd come dressed
for the weather, probably not surprising for someone accustomed to Vermont winters. No, wait—currently New
Hampshire. Couldn't be much different.

With half a dozen restaurants and upscale bars in a
two-block span, there was quite a bit of pedestrian traffic, enough that he laid a hand on Gabby's back briefly
when a group spilling out of a door engulfed them.

He unlocked his Tahoe from a distance away, then
opened the passenger door and hovered behind her until
she'd climbed up to the seat before going around to his

side. As he started the engine and turned down the fan until the heat cranked up, he said, "It's early here for such crap weather."

"It's been cold in New Hampshire, too."

Interesting she hadn't said "back home" or the like. After pulling out into traffic, he asked how long she planned to stay.

"I...haven't decided. I guess it depends how things go with Ric."

"What about your job?" Her timing was definitely odd, whether her college was on a quarter or semester system.

She stole a sidelong look. "I haven't told Ric yet, but I quit after the fall quarter. They'd only offered me two classes for winter quarter. It depends on enrollment, you see. Being part-time means no benefits—"

"And no living wage."

"Right. So I figured this was a good time to make myself finish the damn dissertation."

He found himself smiling. "Don't you have to present it in person? I hope you summon a little more enthusiasm than that for the profs."

Gabby had a great laugh, a ripple of humor that felt like fingertips dancing over his chest. "I'll try."

The hotel was coming up. *Give it a shot.*

"Listen," he said, "I've enjoyed myself tonight. I don't know if you're reserving all your time for Ric, but if not... I'd like to take you out. Say, dinner tomorrow." Or the next day. Any day.

"Oh."

He glided to the curb and braked. A doorman appeared in the gilt-trimmed glass doors into the hotel. Time was running out.

"I'd like that." She sounded shy. "Tomorrow would be great."

His triumph was mixed with a hint of guilt—but he'd take what he could get anyway.

Chapter Three

"Someone tried to break into my house last night."

Phone to his ear, Jack straightened abruptly in his desk chair in the detective bullpen. "What the hell?"

Fellow detectives at neighboring desks were on the phone—probably on hold—hammering on their computer keyboards or huddled in conversation. None of them even turned their head at his exclamation.

Ric Ortiz said, "You heard me. I mean, sure, the neighborhood has an occasional break-in, the kind where the TV and iPod get stolen. But at night? When chances are good a resident is home?"

"Were you parked in the driveway?"

"Garage."

"What happened?"

"Pure luck," Ric said grimly. "A neighbor was coming home, saw the motion-activated floodlight was on in back. The guy probably heard the car engine and the sound of the garage door opening. Could be, it even sounded like it was at my house. Anyway, Chuck saw a dark figure running between my house and the one to the north and up the sidewalk. He called 9-1-1."

"So you did report it."

"Oh, yeah. For what good that did. Officer pretty much

shrugged and said it happens. He drove around a little bit, but of course the guy was long gone."

"It does happen," Jack said automatically, even though he was disturbed. For one thing, *he'd* grown up in that part of town, about a mile from the Ortiz home. But more than that…

"You told many people your sister's back in Leclaire?" he asked.

The silence suggested surprise…or that Ric had been thinking the same, however subliminally.

"Quite a few," he said after a minute. "No reason not to tell my friends and some of the neighbors who were here then. I ran into Mr. Corcoran, too—remember him?"

High school principal. Of course Jack remembered him. Corcoran was now the district superintendent.

"And I guess I've seen a few of Mom and Dad's friends," Ric added.

In other words, word would have spread like wildfire among those who remembered the brutal crime.

"Does anybody know she's not staying with you?"

This silence was different. It was followed by a curse. "No," Ric said. "You don't really think—"

"I actually don't." Truth. "It was probably a dumb teenager after some electronics or cash. Dark house, thought he could sneak in and out unseen. I'm just being paranoid. Occupational hazard."

"I can see how you'd get like that." Ric sounded relieved.

"All the same…" He hesitated. "If you haven't told anyone where she's staying, don't."

"I haven't wanted to admit she's not staying at the house." Gabby's brother sighed. "Yeah, okay. Should I tell her what happened?"

Jack mulled that over. "Ah…why don't you let me."

"You have her number?"

"I do." Whether this was a good idea or bad, he had no clue, but if he didn't tell her brother, Gabby would. "I'm actually having dinner with her tonight. I hope you don't mind."

Ric muttered something Jack didn't catch. Probably just as well. Then, "Gabby has made it pretty clear I don't have anything to say about her life."

"She's here in town. To see *you*. Don't knock it."

After a few more grumbly sounds, Ric said, "She *is* my sister. Watch it with her," and ended the call.

Jack set down his phone to brood for a minute before focusing again on his current investigation.

Not twenty minutes later, his sergeant stopped by his desk. "What are you working on?"

Jack tore his eyes off his computer monitor to focus on Rutkowski. "The large equipment stolen from the WKB construction site."

It was the dollar amount attached to the bulldozer, forklift and other equipment that had resulted in the theft being bumped up to his caseload.

The sergeant scowled. "Has to be an inside job. Or even an insurance scam."

"I agree." He nodded toward his computer. "I'm look-ing into the contractor's finances right now."

A short nod expressed approval. "Get any start on the Ortiz murder?"

Jack glanced around but saw no sign anyone had heard the name. And after Ric had told so many people about Gabby's return, keeping this investigation quiet probably wouldn't fly. Still, he'd rather try.

"Had a casual meeting yesterday. Because I was friends with her brother, I was able to get away with not telling her yet what I'm planning. Figured if she's comfortable with me, she'd be more likely to open up later."

"You going to be able to separate her from the brother?"

"I'm working on it."

"Keep me informed."

"There's no urgency, is there?"

Rutkowski shrugged. "Chief asked."

Watching the sergeant walk across the squad room to his office, Jack wasn't pleased to have caught Chief Keller's interest and attention. He'd hoped to keep this investigation low-key.

He *would* keep the investigation low-key, he vowed. This was his idea, he'd been given the go-ahead, and it was unlikely anyone in the command structure would second-guess him. If they did…he'd fight back.

Satisfied, he returned his attention to the credit report he'd been studying.

TWO BLOCKS AWAY from the house, Gabby realized how fast she was breathing. She didn't have the excuse of having run across town. Nope, she'd driven.

She braked at the corner, glad there was no other traffic. She'd decided this morning to rent a car rather than rely entirely on taxis or Ubers—or her brother. This gave her the freedom to drive around the town of which she had only hazy memories, and to start exploring her childhood without pressure from anyone else.

A department store downtown in a tall granite building accented with elaborately carved flat stones was definitely familiar. It had been a Macy's. Mom had loved to browse there more than actually make purchases. Target now occupied the building—not quite the same thing.

She recognized a burger place with a drive-through that wasn't part of a chain, too. Yes, they'd gone there once in a while as a big treat. Her family hadn't had a lot of money.

Otherwise, not much looked familiar. That was partly because the town had changed drastically in twenty-five years, and partly because she'd been so young when she left. A four-year-old didn't pay much attention to landmarks or stores. She pictured herself in the cart at a grocery store, begging for something she desperately wanted, but had no idea what that had been, whether Mom had bought it or what store it was then.

As she'd driven past the stores, no memories had upset her, so she'd felt confident about going by the house. She'd pictured it—but chances were good it had been painted half a dozen times at least, Dad or Ric might have built a new front porch, added a bay window or who knew what. She might not even recognize it.

Except, here she sat at a stop sign, on the verge of chickening out. She could do this another day, or wait and have Ric take her.

No, not that, because he'd want her to go inside, and she wasn't ready for that.

Okay, Jack. He'd probably be willing to drive by with her.

No, damn it. Gabby refused to depend on someone else—especially a man she hardly knew—to do something so…ordinary. She was stronger than that. She didn't even have to think about what happened to Mom, not yet. Just scope out the home where she'd spent hours at a time playing in the front yard or riding that plastic trike up and down the sidewalk until she knew every crack, every tree that overhung it.

She could do this.

She lifted her foot and let the car roll across the intersection. Yes, the neighborhood was familiar. Houses all dated to the same era, 1940s at a guess. Some were boxy, a few a classier bungalow-style with porches that went all the way across the front and square pillars supporting the roof and arched trimming. Several homes on this block had picket fences, as, she saw ahead, did ones in the next block.

Her block.

These were nice family homes. A few might be rented, but all were so well kept, she guessed they were mostly owner occupied. Lawns were brown, of course, the grass probably crisp from the well-below-freezing temperatures. Big old trees, maples and cherries and oaks, looked sculptural with no leaves.

This cross street had no stop sign. Lucky there wasn't any other traffic, or kids out riding bikes, because her gaze had locked on a house halfway down the block on the left.

The Ortiz home was one of the plain farmhouse-style ones. If Dad or Ric had done any remodeling, it didn't show from the outside. The picket fence almost had to have been replaced at some point, but it looked identical, painted white. The arbor over the gated walk from the sidewalk was draped with thick thorny stems of a climbing rose bush. The blooms, she knew, were a deep pink, and fragrant.

Her heart was pounding so hard, once she braked at the curb across the street from her childhood home, she pressed the heel of her hand hard against her chest.

A memory superimposed itself over the reality. Her pink plastic tricycle sat in the driveway near a bike that lay on its side, a helmet slung over the handlebars. Daddy got mad at both of them if he had to get out of his car to move bikes out of the way before he could drive into the garage. He *'specially* got annoyed at Ric, who was old enough to know better.

Why was she across the street looking at the house? Mommy said *never* to cross. *Never* to step into the street. Gabby was always supposed to stay in sight of the front windows, too. She was big enough to look for traffic before she started back across, but too late. Mommy burst out the front door.

Whimpering, Gabby sloughed off the memory and saw that the front door was painted red, just like it always had been even though the house had been white trimmed with black.

It still was.

The anger she felt at her brother swelled until she felt as if it would split her skin. Was Ric *nuts*? Did he think if he didn't change a single thing, time would magically replay itself? Well, even if it did, *he* hadn't been there to change a single thing.

Oh, dear God. If they'd replaced the kitchen floor, had they bought vinyl with the exact same pattern? She saw it, a black-and-white checkerboard, flowing with blood as shiny and red as the front door.

With a groan, she put the car back into gear and pulled away from the curb. Eyes glazed by tears, she drove a few blocks before she stopped again to mop her face and regain her composure.

How could Ric live there? And how could he *imagine* she'd be willing to walk in the door, far less stay there with him?

What had she been thinking to come back to Leclaire at all?

If she wasn't having dinner with Jack Cowan tonight, she'd have been hugely tempted to go straight back to the hotel, go online and buy an airline ticket out of there, even if it meant Ric never spoke to her again.

So much for the calm determination to find answers she'd started out with. Was it even possible to overcome trauma that occurred when a child was as young as she'd been?

She had no idea.

"What?" Jack's words ricocheted in her head. If she hadn't gone by the house today, she might not be so shocked. As it was…a chill crawled over her skin, as if she'd walked outside without her wool coat.

Jack was watching her with those too-discerning eyes. "Ric was really disturbed by the break-in. If the neighbor hadn't happened to come home at the right time…"

Her brother might have woken up to the sound of the floorboards creaking outside his bedroom…or even the squeak of his bedroom door opening.

"Why didn't he call me?" That was one of the questions tangling in her mind.

"I said I'd let you know." Now Jack looked wary. "I, uh, told him I was seeing you tonight."

Uh-oh. "What did he say?"

He smiled. "To watch myself."

Gabby made a face. "He hardly knows me. It's kind of ridiculous for him to go big brother on me."

"Maybe it's even more natural for him. He still thinks of you as a child, the one he was supposed to watch out for."

She tipped her head. "Do you have sisters or brothers? I don't remember Ric ever saying."

They were at a Thai restaurant tonight, only a couple of blocks from her hotel. Leclaire had a nice downtown, but it wasn't large.

He wiped any expression from his face. "A younger sister. After my parents divorced, she went with Mom, I stayed with Dad. I haven't seen her in years."

Gabby opened her mouth then closed it. If he wanted to tell her what had split his family so irrevocably, he would—but the very lack of expression said the subject was taboo.

"I drove by the house today," she blurted.

He dropped the mask again to let her see concern. "Did you remember it?"

"Too well." She told him that neither her father nor brother had changed anything about the house. Not the paint color, not the landscaping, not new windows. "It's creepy."

"Yeah," he said slowly. "I can see why you'd feel that way. Sometimes I wonder—"

He stopped so suddenly, she almost heard the squeal of brakes.

She'd respect some walls he threw up, but there was a limit. "What do you wonder?"

Lines on his forehead and even between his nose and mouth deepened, making him even less conventionally handsome, and yet… Gabby saw something that made her pulse accelerate.

He set down his fork and his eyes met hers. "Whether coming back to Leclaire was a healthy choice for me."

"Because you weren't happy here."

"Oh." His big shoulders shrugged and some of the careworn expression eased. "I was and I wasn't. School was good. I was a jock, and I liked being a star." This grin had to be genuine. "Home…that was harder."

She nodded. "I never let myself wonder why Ric stayed. I mean, he could have gotten a job anywhere. It's not like he had any family left here."

Jack stayed quiet, letting her pursue her thought. "If he'd sold the place, bought another one, or even remodeled the damn house, I'd think he just liked Leclaire. As it is…" She shook her head. "I guess he can't move on."

A nerve jerked in Jack's cheek, and she guessed he was thinking he hadn't been able to move on, either. Except she had no idea what his issue was. *His* mother hadn't been murdered in his childhood home.

"Maybe you should ask him about it," Jack suggested. "It might only be that he sees the house as a trust, like he has to preserve it in your mom's memory or because your dad asked him to. Or maybe he feels less lonely there."

Gabby couldn't decide if the idea was comforting or, once again, just plain creepy.

"Hey." He reached across the table and laid his hand over hers, gently squeezing. "You did come home to get to know him."

She scrunched up her nose. "I was thinking more, we're adults now, can we be friends? There is zero point in trying to time travel."

Her vehemence might explain the flare of something in his eyes, but it might not, too.

"Your mom's killer was never caught," he said.

"So Ric keeps pointing out." Hearing how acidly that had come out, she closed her eyes for a moment. "I'm sorry. I shouldn't take my annoyance with him out on you. Do you think we can talk about something else?"

"Sure." Jack smiled. "Please tell me you don't have a boyfriend back in New Hampshire."

"No, if I did I might not have quit my job and made this…pilgrimage." Heavens, was that what this trip was? "What about you?"

"Give me some credit. If I were seeing anyone, I wouldn't have asked you out for dinner tonight."

"Have you been married?"

"Never even come close." He shrugged. "There are women who like the idea of dating a cop. The reality always turns out to sour them. Nobody likes being stood up over and over again."

"You think that's the problem?"

He grinned wickedly. "What else could it be?"

She laughed at him. His ego wasn't suffering. "I wouldn't dare guess."

"So, what's your excuse?"

That was a better question than she wanted to admit. "Does a woman my age need to have an excuse for not getting married? Maybe I'm not ready." How could a woman who couldn't even commit to a long-term job *be* ready? "Maybe I like my independence."

He bent his head toward her. "Both good reasons. So tell me more about you. How was living with your great-aunt?"

"Hard when I was so young. She was…stern. I really grew to love her, though, and I miss her."

They switched to more usual topics for a first date: music, movies and TV shows, books, sports, what they liked to do in their spare time. Kind of pointless, she kept thinking, given that she had no intention of staying in Leclaire and was, in fact, half wishing she hadn't come at all.

Except, if she hadn't, she wouldn't have met Jack. And wasn't that an unnerving thought. She couldn't remember ever being so conscious of a man—every shift of expression, his big hands, his crooked smile and that undisciplined hair.

He'd handed over his credit card to the waiter when she heard herself say, "So, this guy who tried to break into Ric's house. What do you think that was about?"

Apparently, her subconscious had been dwelling on the near break-in.

Looking surprised, Jack said, "Probably the usual. Every place is plagued with that kind of crap. We have drugs, gangs and stupid teenagers here, too."

"You don't think—" Her throat seemed to close up.

"That it had anything to do with your mother? How could it?"

She stiffened at what sounded like condescension, but couldn't really blame him. "Never mind," she mumbled.

His forehead creased. "Or are you thinking someone is reacting to you coming home?"

"Of course not!"

"You saw it happen, didn't you?"

Had he just dredged that up out of his memory? Gabby wanted to think so. Either way, she didn't like his next question.

"There's no reason you'd be a threat to anyone, is there?"

SHE REACTED TO his question as if he'd just accused her of child abuse. Her eyes widened in either shock or outrage and she snapped, "Of course not! In case you don't know, I was a complete failure as a witness." Without looking at him again, she shoved back her chair and jumped to her feet.

The waiter who'd just brought Jack's card back and the slip for him to sign looked surprised.

Jack scribbled his autograph and pocketed his credit card without even pulling out his wallet. Gabby quivered as if she wanted to run away, but she waited for him to stand and walk her to the coat rack at the entrance.

Once they'd bundled up and left the restaurant, he said

quietly, "I'm sorry. I get used to asking nosy questions. I didn't mean to upset you."

"I'm not upset." She walked fast, keeping a distance between them on the sidewalk.

He'd had to park farther away tonight; he could just as well have walked her back to the hotel, but he was glad she hadn't turned that way. They'd have had no privacy at all. She sure as hell wasn't going to invite him up to her room.

Once at the hotel, he pulled into an Unload zone. "I really am sorry. I was having a good time."

"I was, too," she said softly.

"Okay." No sign of a valet or any pedestrians at the moment. He realized she was looking at him, her face a pale oval.

The temptation he'd felt since he set eyes on her overrode his common sense. Jack leaned forward and kissed her.

Chapter Four

Jack's warm mouth captured hers. This was no gentle good-night kiss. Oh, no. He ran his tongue down the seam of her lips until Gabby parted them. Then he nibbled at them, stroked her tongue, kneaded the nape of her neck with a big, strong hand. She succumbed with shocking speed, grabbing a fistful of his shirtfront to keep herself from sliding to the floorboards, and kissed him back.

When he lifted his head, they stared at each other. Passing headlights illuminated his face, highlighting every craggy feature, before darkness shadowed it. She'd never so much wanted to ask a man to share her bed even if it would be a one-night stand, but that wasn't something she ever did. And she couldn't forget the sting from his questions.

She opened her fingers to release his shirt, clenching her hands on her lap instead. "You think I'm a coward," she said in a voice huskier than her usual.

"Coward? What are you—" Comprehension brought him to a stop.

Gabby turned her head and gazed straight ahead at the rear of another SUV parked at the curb in front of them. "Ric accuses me often enough. Maybe he's even right. I'd have more respect for his opinion if he had any idea what it was like. It would be bad enough as an adult to see that kind of violence happen right in front of you, but I was a little girl. I remember men who interviewed me back then assuming that I saw it like a cartoon. You know, the anvil drops on Roadrunner, flattening him. But naturally, he squeaks out from under, shakes himself and, except for a lump on his head, all is well."

"Children do see enough cartoon violence to equate it to—"

She ignored him. "It was *nothing* like a cartoon. Nothing. I didn't for a second think she'd pop back up and start making sandwiches. Watching my mother die was horrible beyond belief. I'll bet even you've never seen anything like that."

"I see more than you'd think."

She shook her head. "The aftermath. And you didn't love the person whose body was lying right in front of you. She wasn't your mommy."

"No." Pure gravel, his voice shouldn't have been comforting, but was. "You're right."

"Do I want to remember every gory detail, even if I could after twenty-five years?" Wasn't that what she hoped to do? Still, she looked fiercely at him. "I would if I thought I could identify her killer. But I was so fixated on—" She pressed a hand to her mouth.

"Gabby." He reached over and gently took her hand, pulling it away from her mouth, holding on to it in a warm grip. "You'll give yourself nightmares."

Her laughter burned her chest. "Oh, I have nightmares, no matter what I do. They never go away." She wrenched her hand from his, undid the seat belt clasp and reached for the door handle. "Thank you for dinner—"

"Please," he said. "If I promise not to raise the subject, can we have dinner again tomorrow night?"

"I already promised Ric." She climbed out onto the

sidewalk. "I don't know if he'd be mad if you joined us...
But that's not what you had in mind."

"I'll take what I can get," he said with what sounded
like real honesty. "Lunch?"

Gabby hesitated. He knew she'd be leaving town
within a few days if not weeks. Why was he pursuing
her like this? He'd probably had a dozen girlfriends more
beautiful than she was.

Did he like the idea of an end date? Get her in bed
without having to worry about her getting clingy?

But something in his expression gave her pause. For
whatever reason, however brief their acquaintance, she
mattered to him. Even during dinner, she remembered
the way he'd never looked away from her face. She
wanted to dismiss the very idea, but couldn't quite, because from the minute she saw him walking toward her
through the Italian restaurant, she'd reacted to him in a
completely unfamiliar way. He might be as confounded
as she was.

That wasn't impossible, was it?

"Can you really get away for lunch?"

"Sure I can." There was the cocky guy she'd first met.
"*And* dinner."

Gabby had to laugh. "Ric and I are going back to that
same Italian restaurant," she said. "We've resolved to try
something besides pizza. Supposedly, the food is great.
Um. He said he'd made reservations for six thirty."

"It is great. That's why I picked it in the first place."
Jack's mouth curved. "Shall I surprise him?"

"How about if we have lunch, and then talk about it?"

"Deal." He suggested calling her in the morning to set
a time to pick her up.

Gabby agreed, shivered and realized how cold she
was, and slammed the car door. She could see enough

reflection in the double glass doors of the hotel to know Jack didn't pull away from the curb until she was safely inside.

JACK DROVE HOME in a crappy mood. Seeing the anguish Gabby had lived with for most of her life made him feel guilty as hell. She was right; as a cop, he'd seen countless gory, senseless scenes, picked up bodies off the pavement and pried them out of crushed metal in car accidents, studied multiple fatalities after someone had lost it or a family fractured into violence. But those were the bodies of strangers, not his loved ones, not even friends. He'd heard of cops called to a scene only to discover one of the fatalities was a daughter or wife. He'd have said he couldn't think of anything worse, but turns out there *was* a worse. Watching the most important person in your world killed right in front of you.

He'd been bitter for years because she'd chosen not to relive that memory. Now he found out she did, whether she liked it or not, in the form of nightmares.

That kiss had hit him hard. If he'd had any intention, it was a peck on the lips—a first date, sitting in front of the hotel with a bellhop watching. That kind of kiss. But no. Stupidly, he'd surrendered to his intense attraction to this woman he was betraying every minute they spent together.

She would hate his guts when she found out that what he really wanted was to pick through her brain for clues, no matter what the experience did to her.

Yeah, but he was starting to want something else altogether, and he didn't like it. Mixed emotions were a bitch. He was used to setting goals and going for what he wanted. From the beginning, he'd understood that there might be some collateral damage, but his goals were important enough to justify it. He considered himself a decent man, but he enforced the law. He hunted for pieces of scum and brought them in even if he left a wife and little kids sobbing in his wake.

God, please don't let Gabby cry.

Let her hate him instead.

Once home, he locked up behind himself, gulped some milk from the carton in the refrigerator and turned off lights on his way upstairs to the bedroom.

He thought of the start he'd already made today in reviewing the crime. He could quit right now. Tell his sergeant and Chief Keller that she didn't remember anything useful. She'd been too young to be any kind of witness. They'd buy it.

In the bathroom, Jack stared at himself in the mirror over the sink. He could do that—if he could let go of the goal that had driven half the choices he'd made in his life. If he could look his father in the eye the next time he saw him, knowing he'd thrown away the chance to clear Dad's name, once and for all, allowing him to straighten his shoulders when he faced the world…

And then there was the fact that he now knew Gabby still had nightmares about her mother's murder—and what were those nightmares but memories waiting to be brought out of the dark?

Jack tore his gaze from his own face, groaned and scraped a hand over the stubble on his jaw.

Yeah, it was self-serving to think that what he'd also be doing was stealing from Gabby the chance to make her own awful memories really mean something. They haunted her; she'd acknowledged as much. If he could help her remember her mother's killer, wouldn't that free Gabby, too? She might not see it that way right now, but she would eventually.

Even if she also ended up hating his guts.

He grimaced. Something told him he wouldn't be sleeping like a baby tonight.

WITH REGRET, JACK left Gabby in the lobby of her hotel in front of the elevators. Conversation had ranged widely while they ate lunch at a deli a few blocks down the street. As he'd promised, it never touched on her mother, brother or early years here in Leclaire. Jack discovered her viewpoints were liberal and well defended. She did concede that, given his job, he had reason to look at the world with a more jaundiced viewpoint. She made him laugh more often than he had in recent memory, even as his gut stayed tight from guilt.

He had kissed her lightly before they parted because he couldn't not. He wanted to join her and her brother for dinner, but had a bad feeling that his hunger to see her this evening, too, didn't have anything to do with his cold case investigation.

Walking out to his SUV, he was glad the hotel had had the parking lot plowed. Yeah, snow had fallen last night, and tiny flakes still floated down. Pretty, but a pain in the butt for patrol officers who'd be responsible for endless fender benders, getting pickup trucks pulled out of ditches, and nailing idiots who wouldn't slow down on icy roads.

He interviewed the contractor who had reported the theft of the construction equipment, not going so far as to make accusations, but persistent enough the guy was getting rattled by the time Jack thanked him for his time and left. Sure as hell, he'd sold the bulldozer, forklift and all the rest, and now expected to double his profit with an insurance payoff. Some digging had uncovered the fact that the contractor had never gotten out of debt after sell-ing the last houses he'd built. Now he was in real trouble. This little scheme would allow him to pay the bills for another month or so, maybe long enough to finish the current building and sell it. Harmless, he'd think...except the insurance company wouldn't agree.

Minor corruption might end the guy's career.

Back at the station, Jack made more phone calls and did more computer research about other cases. He had roughly fifteen active cases and a dozen or more he kept at the back of his mind. And now he'd added a cold case. There was plenty to keep him busy, and no excuse for him to resent not being able to concentrate 100 percent on that cold case—or to be letting his mind wander to Gabby Ortiz and the way his heart stumbled when she smiled at him.

Brooding about her evening plans, he wrestled with himself, finally concluding that she and her brother needed time together without him there as a diversion. He'd call her in the morning.

Damn, he hadn't grocery shopped in a week. He wasn't in the mood to cook anyway. Maybe he'd go through a drive-through...

Or maybe he should concentrate on doing his job.

GABBY COULDN'T BELIEVE she hadn't packed any extra elastics for her hair. Since breaking her only one, she'd had to leave her hair out of its normal braid. Fortunately, there was no wind today as she walked the three blocks to the pharmacy the concierge had suggested. She declined his offer to summon an Uber. A walk sounded good.

The bitter cold made her feel right at home, as did the crunching sound underfoot from either salt that had been spread on the sidewalk or refrozen slush thrown from car tires or left by the plow. A New Englander, she was used to seeing her own breath in white plumes, and just walking briskly was a pleasure. She'd spent too much of her brief stay in Leclaire in her hotel room, a restaurant or one car or another.

At the pharmacy, she grabbed a package of hair elastics in multicolors and several other toiletries, just in case. She stumbled on a surprisingly sizeable book and magazine section, too, and chose a couple of books. After paying, she stepped back out onto the sidewalk, deiced here by a generous application of salt.

The green walk signal at the corner flashed. Since walking in the bitter cold was one thing but standing around another, she hustled to make it. One glance told her no cars were waiting on the cross street at the intersection. An approaching SUV had plenty of time to stop. These must be the old-fashioned lights that changed at regular interludes no matter what traffic was doing.

Her mind started to wander. Even though she had good reason for wariness where Jack was concerned, she wished that they'd set another time to get together—and that his goodbye kiss had been more than a peck.

She was shocked back to the present by the huge SUV racing toward her at an unsafe speed. No sign the driver was braking for the light. Oh, damn, her walk signal had turned red while she'd been distracted. The driver must see her, surely, but Gabby broke into a jog anyway.

Her foot caught a bit of ice and she slipped, staggering to keep her feet. The SUV hadn't slowed at all, and suddenly assumed monstrous proportions. On a burst of adrenaline, Gabby dove forward toward the sanctuary of a parked car. One of her feet scraped against the black metal.

And then she hit the hard, icy pavement and skidded until her head bumped the curb.

Winded and shocked, it took her a minute to realize the speeding vehicle had gone through the intersection and continued on straight ahead, the driver apparently oblivious to the pedestrian he—or she—had just about taken out.

She heard running footsteps. Voices called out, blending together. "Are you all right?"

"Did you fall?"

Only one said, "Man, I wish I'd gotten the license plate."

Gabby struggled to sit. A couple of the people who'd reached her stepped forward to help her up. She winced when she put weight on her right foot, but she was sure it wasn't broken. Someone else retrieved her shopping bag, which had gone flying. Fortunately, it was intact.

The anxious, kind faces around her were the reassurance she needed to smile. "Thanks. To all of you. Um... did any of you see the license plate of that SUV? Or even notice what make or model it was?"

Most people had been half a block or more away and hadn't. A few hadn't noticed a vehicle at all. The two people who'd been closest agreed it was black, but argued about whether it had been a Chevy or a Dodge or...

She gave up, decided her ankle would support her, and hobbled the two more blocks she had to go.

Hotel staff rushed to her in alarm, but she assured them she'd taken a tumble but was fine. All she needed was a hot shower. Thanks to her heavy garments and gloves, the only place she'd even skinned a little was her jaw, and she had antibiotic ointment in her travel first aid kit.

A bellboy insisted on walking her up to her room and refused a tip.

Gabby sank onto her bed, a lot shakier than she'd let

any of the strangers see. She had come within inches of being badly injured or even killed.

Of course it was an accident. It had to be. Maybe the sun had been in the driver's eyes, or he'd been distracted by an incoming text. After all, who *hadn't* ever been distracted while behind the wheel?

It was just… She closed her eyes. One of the "incidents" that had preceded Great-Aunt Isabel taking her away had been another near miss. That time, she'd been on her training bike on the sidewalk. Just sitting there. She'd been outside only because Dad had insisted she do something besides watch TV or cling to him.

It was a sedan that time. She hadn't been paying attention at all, but Mr. Monroe next door saw it jump the curb. He'd come out for his mail, and snatched her out of the way barely in time. The car flattened her bike, swerved back onto the street and burned rubber as it ran the stop sign on the next corner and kept going.

The driver was probably a drunk or a reckless teenager who'd gotten the scare of his life, people kept saying. Even the police didn't take it all that seriously. Dad did. Only a week before, a bullet had hit the fender of his car in the grocery store parking lot, missing her by inches. Drive-by shootings had been a recent problem, the responding officer had told him gravely. But only days later, Dad found a plastic container of cookies on their doorstep with a note that said, "In sympathy." Neighbors always rang the doorbell, they didn't leave anonymous gifts. He was suspicious enough to take those cookies to the police, who determined they contained rat poison. While the cookies could have harmed Dad or Ric, too, she was the smallest and would have likely been killed.

Today was different, she promised herself. Even if

she'd been hit, she was more likely to have been injured than killed. Unless she'd been flung ahead of the SUV and the driver had just gone right over her and still fled. One of her most powerful flickers of childhood memory was seeing her beloved bike—pink, of course—crushed on the sidewalk. Could a human body look like that?

No. Ridiculous.

Gabby blew out a long breath and decided she should call Jack anyway.

SHE TALKED HIM out of racing to her side, but it was a close call. Jack knew he couldn't actually do anything, and had a suspicion she'd downplay any aftereffects of the near miss. She was seeing her brother tonight, though, and it would be hard to hide any injuries from him.

Jack had grilled her about every detail of what happened. He couldn't believe she hadn't gotten the names and phone numbers of any of the witnesses.

"But they didn't see anything!" she kept protesting.

Except for the two of them who agreed with her that the vehicle had been a full-size SUV, and black. And one, she admitted, had been sure the driver was a man. "Big," he said, and maybe wearing a baseball cap.

Jack made some calls to find out whether any nearby stores had security cameras, or whether that intersection had a traffic camera. The answer was no. The city of Leclaire was running behind on updating old traffic lights and adding camera surveillance that would reveal the license plates of vehicles that ran a red light. The first was just a money issue, while the cameras faced significant protest among residents rebelling at the idea of being watched.

What if Gabby had died today and they couldn't arrest the hit-and-run driver in part because of the lack of new technology? Jack ground his teeth.

"Cowan?"

He spun his desk chair to face Sergeant Rutkowski.

"There a problem?" the sergeant asked, no doubt registering his expression.

"Gabrielle Ortiz was damn close to being the victim of a hit-and-run accident this afternoon. She had to dive out of the way of a speeding vehicle."

The sergeant's homely face creased. "By her brother's house?"

"No, she was downtown doing some errands. She'd just left the Walgreens and was crossing a street. Unfortunately, there were no witnesses close enough to catch a license plate, and none of them even agreed on the make or model of the vehicle. I can't find a camera in the vicinity. It's a dead end."

Rutkowski frowned down at him. "You don't think this was a deliberate attack."

Jack took a few deep breaths before he answered. "It's unlikely. I can't rule it out, though, because there were several possible attempts on her life right after her mother's murder. One could have been malicious, although investigators couldn't figure out a motive. The other incidents could fall into the bad luck category, but all these things happened in a matter of weeks."

The echo of the speeding vehicle and a driver who didn't stop sent up a flare for him now that he couldn't ignore.

"Have you read up on the Ortiz murder?" he asked.

"I did when I first came on board with this unit," the sergeant said, "but it's been years."

Unsurprised, Jack said, "One of those three near misses was a car jumping the curb by her house. She'd be dead if a neighbor hadn't been close enough to snatch her out of the way. Car swerved back onto the street and booked it. Investigators didn't find anything."

"I don't blame you for being uneasy," Rutkowski said, "but unless a better witness comes forward…" He shrugged.

Jack's jaw ached as he watched the sergeant walk away. No, there wasn't a damn thing he could do, and he didn't like it.

He accomplished some more work, but still felt unsettled when he left the station earlier than usual. Maybe he'd go to the gym. Some hard exercise might reduce his tension. Between the weather and Gabby, he hadn't gotten in a workout in nearly a week.

He was still waiting for his car to warm up when his phone rang. He groaned. He should be down the list to have to take the next crime referred to the unit…but someone ahead of him could be sick, snowed in, who knew. Only then he got the phone out of his pocket. Ric again? Jack accepted the call and put it on speaker.

This couldn't be good news.

Chapter Five

Fifteen minutes later, Jack parked at the curb in front of Ric's house. Walking up the driveway, he scanned the facade. Gabby was right; he might have time traveled. Not one single thing about the exterior of this house had changed from the days when this had been a frequent stop on the carpool circuit.

A patrol officer walked out the front door and saw him. They met a few steps from the porch.

"Could just be teenagers," Officer Engman said, but not sounding as if he believed it. "Strange after the attempted break-in night before last, though."

Jack knew Engman, although not well. "Has there been an upsurge of this kind of thing in the neighborhood?"

"No." A few years younger than Jack but no rookie, Engman gazed at the house. "This area is one of the safest in town. Mostly homeowners—people know each other." He shrugged. "We patrol here, but not as often as we do around Hawthorn or west Leclaire."

Jack nodded his understanding. "Mr. Ortiz inside?"

"Yeah. Not happy."

Jack grunted. "You'll write a report?"

"Yes, and recommend we drive by more often, at least for a few days."

"Good. Thanks."

Engman left. Ric met Jack at the door.

"Had to be the same guy," he growled.

Jack hadn't liked the coincidence of the original attempted break-in coupled with rumors spreading about Gabby's return to Leclaire. That somebody would take the chance to come back to the same house, break a window and let himself in, this time in broad daylight? And, oh yeah, while leaving a trampled path in the snow around the side of the house? Of course it was the same guy, with the same goal.

"Anything stolen?" he asked.

"Yeah, smaller electronics. A brand-new iPad, a nice pair of wireless earphones and a portable keyboard. I'm out maybe a couple of thousand dollars."

"That could have been the point," Jack felt he had to say.

"You kidding me?"

"No, I don't believe it any more than you do." He nodded past Ric. "You going to let me in?"

"Yeah. Sorry."

"Did Gabby tell you what happened this afternoon?"

"Shit. Yeah. I got to tell you, I don't like any of this."

Jack didn't either, even if it was hard to imagine somebody had broken in here, searched the house, then happened to get lucky enough to not only spot her, but be in a position to take a run at her when she crossed a side street alone.

They started a walk-through, which didn't tell him much except that the kitchen looked exactly like it had in the twenty-five-year-old crime scene photos he'd pored over. Jack was with Gabby on this one; how had her father, and now Ric, been able to stay in this place?

The door to the garage, which had only one of those

useless push-button locks, had been unlocked when Ric got home. To get to it, they passed through the utility room. He hated seeing how close the long-ago killer had been to Gabby's hiding place when he'd walked out.

The garage was remarkably tidy, Jack saw, a home to tools, lawn mower and presumably Ric's car, but not much else. A few tubs sat on shelves, but they were all made of clear plastic, revealing obvious stuff like Christmas decorations.

"Don't you have boxes of old family pictures, record albums, stamp collections and, I don't know, your parents' stuff that you don't know what to do with?" he asked.

Ric looked surprised. "Uh, yeah. In a small storage unit. Dad started it and… I've just kept paying for it." He sounded chagrined. "I know that's dumb when there's so much room here, but… Dad wanted it out of the house."

Dad, Jack couldn't help thinking, had some major issues that included denial.

Ric's brow creased. "Maybe Gabby and I could go through it."

There was a concept. Not that Jack didn't suspect he'd find an accumulation of crap at his dad's current house, when the time came.

Back in the house, Jack asked, "Was everything that was stolen out in plain sight?"

"Yeah." They'd mounted the stairs, and Ric led the way into what was apparently his bedroom. "And everything taken was downstairs. Have a look at this," he said, pulling open the drawer in the bedside stand.

Jack looked down at the watch that lay atop some clutter. Stainless steel, but the name on it was Longines, which he had a feeling meant expensive.

"That's a two-thousand-dollar watch," Ric said flatly. "Perfect condition."

"So either this guy didn't bother opening drawers, or he didn't know the watch was worth anything." Which argued teenager or a druggie, but Jack didn't bother saying so. He thought a few pieces of electronics had been grabbed as a cover.

"Closet doors are open, but nothing's been touched. Same for the master bath. He did check out both of the spare bedrooms, which are obviously unoccupied." Ric stood aside to let Jack walk into the first room, where one side of the standard double-closet doors had been pushed open. Ditto in the second, across the hall. In both rooms, the closets were empty, no boxed-up miscellany there.

Both rooms seemed impersonal; if the downstairs had gone unchanged, that wasn't the case up here. Neither bedroom shouted "teenage boy," although the walls in one room were painted pink. Left that way in case Gabby ever came home? At some point, Ric had moved into the master bedroom, which either he or his father had thoroughly updated.

Jack looked into the hall bathroom and saw that the medicine cabinet door was open a crack and one drawer on the vanity had been dropped on the floor.

"He wanted to know whether you had a houseguest," Jack said slowly.

"That's my take." Ric looked grim. "Now he knows I don't."

The two men stared at each other.

"This is crazy thinking," Jack said after a minute. "She testified at the time. Why would she be a threat to him?"

"I don't know. He's afraid she saw his face?"

"So what if she did? She was four years old. If she'd

recognized the man, she'd have said so then. Now what can she say? He had brown eyes and he looked mad?"

Ric shoved his fingers through his hair. "Do I tell her?"

Crap. Jack thought fast. Did he have to admit that he'd already reopened the investigation into Colleen Ortiz's murder? Ric would be glad he had, in one way, but he'd also immediately understand how Jack had used him.

And then there was Gabby.

His instinct still said to put it off. Be a friend, not an investigator. Jack could see her clamming up right away. But...

Reluctant, he said, "I think we have to. She needs to be careful."

"What if she just decides to leave town?" Ric sounded frustrated and helpless, both feelings Jack shared.

He tried to be honest with himself. Would she be safer if she did go? Or now that she'd appeared and possibly scared the killer, would he figure it was worth the cost of a round-trip airline ticket to shut her up permanently?

"I'd rather she stay where we can keep an eye on her," he said at last. "But she may not see it that way."

Ric suddenly swore. "What time is it?"

"Ah..." Jack checked his phone. "Just after six."

"I'm supposed to meet her for dinner. I've got to go."

Jack swallowed what he really wanted to say. "Have you boarded over the broken window?"

"Why bother, when the horse is long gone?" Ric grimaced. "No, but I can do it quick. I have some lumber scraps in the garage."

Jack waited in the kitchen while Gabby's brother disappeared into the garage. The kitchen door had a glass pane, something that was all but an invitation to robbers, in Jack's opinion. The dead bolt lock would be useless.

Not that he could say much, given that he'd replaced the original French doors at his place with ones that still suited the age of the house but were double-paned. Security-wise, they weren't a good choice, though.

Once Ric had positioned a small piece of plywood over the broken window, Jack handed over nails for Ric to tap in.

"Might want to consider replacing this door," he suggested mildly. "Steel might be good, no glass."

"That has crossed my mind." Ric cleaned up and they went through the house to the front door. "Listen, I don't know if you have plans. If not, you're welcome to join us for dinner."

"If you're sure, I'd like that." He hoped his eagerness wasn't too apparent. "She told me you're going back to the same place."

"Yeah, I'm picking her up." Ric pulled out a key fob and unlocked his car. "See you there?"

"I'll be right behind you."

Ric was already backing out of the driveway when Jack got into his own vehicle. He started it up, but didn't touch the gearshift right away. Instead, he studied the house, trapped in a time warp. He agreed wholeheartedly with Gabby.

It was creepy.

And he had to wonder what Ric was thinking—and why it hadn't occurred to him how his little sister would feel about it. This being the little sister who'd actually *seen* her mother slaughtered, right there in the kitchen that appeared unchanged from that day to this one.

"But…it's ridiculous to think someone breaking into your house has anything to do with me!" Gabby exclaimed. She suppressed the flicker of fear but not that

anxiety that had flared when she heard how the house
had been searched.

She and the two men claimed the same booth at the
restaurant, except this time Jack had achieved what she
guessed was his preference for having his back to the
wall. He'd slid into that seat fast enough, and she'd seen
the way he scanned the restaurant before he grimly studied the abrasion on her jaw. Even now, his gaze kept flick-
ing from her eyes to that scrape.

"Did Jack put this into your head?" she demanded of
her brother, sitting beside her. "I can understand why
he'd be paranoid."

"Gee, thanks," Jack said, with a hint of amusement.

Ric glared at her. "Because I'm so easily influenced?"

"Well…you know what I mean."

"I do, and no. I'd have had to be an idiot not to realize
that whoever searched the house was more interested in
the guest bedrooms and bath than he was in my room or
downstairs. Yeah, he picked up a few small electronics
that can be sold, but he'd have found more if he'd looked.
What could he have imagined would be stowed in the
hall bathroom?"

"Prescription drugs?"

"In a bathroom I obviously don't use?" Her brother
shook his head. "I hate to say it, but I'm glad you didn't
agree to stay with me."

The anxiety was growing. Gabby nibbled on her lower
lip. "Who even knows I'm in town?"

Ric gave her a list that kept growing. "I thought people who remembered you would be glad to know you're
visiting."

He sounded defensive, she couldn't help noticing.

She turned her gaze to Jack, a solid presence she'd
have thought to be reassuring if it weren't for the way

he watched her. Assessing her reaction, she guessed. To see if she was faking it?

She'd already had a really crappy day and more aches and pains than she'd expected. She didn't need this.

Suddenly mad, she said, "Mom was killed twenty-five years ago. I was four. Four years old!"

"Almost five," Jack murmured.

"Do *you* remember much from the year before you started kindergarten?"

"A few things that made an impression."

"Like?"

His eyebrows rose at her challenge. "I saw big kids jumping from swings at the playground and decided to try it. Came down hard on my back. I vividly remember that moment, lying there, looking up at the sky, not able to breathe, pain just starting to roll over me."

Silenced, she didn't say anything.

"There was another time. Dad had taken us sledding. On the way back, a deer ran in front of the car. He had to slam on the brakes and we spun in a full circle before coming to a stop. It stunned me."

Gabby closed her eyes. He had made his point. Yes, she could summon the scene when her mother was stabbed, but—

"I think I closed my eyes some of the time," she mumbled. "I remember whimpering and then being so scared *he'd* hear me."

Jack reached his hand across the table, and she laid hers in that now-familiar, reassuring clasp, uncaring what Ric would think.

"It…none of it made sense to me. An adult might have been thinking, *I have to notice details so the police can catch him.* But I just tried not to move and hoped it would be over before I got so scared I had to run, because I knew he could catch me."

Jack gently loosened her hand and she saw that her fingernails had bitten into his flesh.

She also realized she'd hunched into herself as if she was a little girl again—squeezed into the corner, rounded her shoulders, pressed her knees together. She hadn't quite pulled her feet up to the seat so she could wrap herself into an even tinier ball, but it was close.

She hated that. It hadn't happened in a long time. Gabby swallowed and looked from Jack's face to her brother's and back again. She didn't like their expressions. She hadn't been asking for her brother's pity—or for Jack's unnerving, narrow-eyed interest.

It took some effort, but she loosened her body, lifted her chin and snatched her hand back from his grip. "You know, several police officers had me tell them what I saw. Enough that I started getting muddled." Now she glared at Ric, whose oft-expressed anger and contempt at her failure to point a finger at the killer had hurt her. Undermined her self-esteem, she had realized in recent years.

"Maybe I should take out an ad in the *Courier*? 'Child Witness No Help to Police.' How does that sound?"

Jack was either frowning or…bothered. "I half wish we could."

"Oh, for Pete's sake!" She looked down to see that she'd barely touched her salad, and a beaming waitress had arrived with their entrées. With a churning stomach, Gabby wasn't sure she could do any more justice to her bean ragout than she'd done to the salad.

Both men picked up their forks the minute the waitress walked away. *Their* appetites were apparently intact. Somehow, she wasn't surprised that Jack had ordered a more traditional entrée, lasagna alla Bolognese. Ric always had been an adventurer where food went. He'd ordered a pasta with mushrooms and white truffle oil.

With a sigh, she picked up her fork, too.

"Maybe we are being paranoid," Jack said suddenly. "I'll check out the hotel's security measures. We just want you to be careful. Be sure not to get caught alone. And be wary if someone you might or might not remember pops up, excited to see you again."

"What am I supposed to do? Sit in my room all day? Watch soaps?" Although at the moment she wasn't all that enthusiastic about going out on her own.

He flashed that infuriatingly sexy grin. "How about working on your dissertation?"

That *really* silenced her.

JACK PARTED RELUCTANTLY from Gabby and her brother out front of the restaurant. He trusted Ric to see her safely to her room, especially since he'd seized the opportunity when she went to the restroom to suggest Ric do a quick walk-through that included her bathroom.

He'd given a short laugh. "Peek behind the shower curtain, you mean? Bet she'll love that."

"Tell her you'll feel better."

"I will."

So would Jack, but he didn't say that. He hadn't kissed Gabby good-night, either, even lightly. Best not to introduce any more awkwardness between the three of them. Ric hadn't looked thrilled when Jack and Gabby had held hands. He wanted Ric to keep calling him with any worries or other strange events. And Gabby…he'd call her first thing tomorrow. Maybe from downstairs in the hotel he fully intended to assess for security weaknesses.

Noticing that the snow had stopped falling but wouldn't melt unless the temperature decided to rise tomorrow, Jack finally drove home. That was a word he used automatically, but despite the pleasure he'd taken in remodeling the house, he hadn't done much with furniture or decor. He still ate at the breakfast bar in the kitchen, leaving the dining area empty. Art was nonexistent. A few family pictures hung on the wall in the office. Those pictures motivated him. Every time he glanced at them, he could see what he'd have had if Colleen Ortiz hadn't been murdered—and if the police hadn't failed to identify and arrest the killer.

The sight of those happy family moments used to work better. As an adult, he'd become cynical enough to suspect that whatever love—for want of a better word—had cemented his parents hadn't been very strong. He hadn't understood then, and still didn't, why his mother hadn't believed in his father. Why she'd let whispers influence her to doubt his fidelity and, worse, come to believe he was capable of committing a crime so brutal.

All in the absence of any actual facts beyond him having been seen knocking on the door at the Ortiz house the day before the murder.

The police believed Dad's explanation. Mom didn't.

After everything went down, Jack's father had been closemouthed about his mother, however broken he was when she left him not long after. He wouldn't criticize her, which Jack respected.

In the past few years, his cynicism deepened. Had Dad cheated on Mom at some point in the past? Was that why her trust had been so shaky?

Jack had trouble seeing it, though, and the possibility still didn't shake his belief in his father. Anyway, why wouldn't Mom have told him, once he was an adult? But she wouldn't defend herself; she just got mulish and pouty when he tried to get her to talk to him.

It had been several years since he'd bothered calling her at all. He talked a little more often with his sister, and regretted not getting to know her kids. But once Humpty Dumpty fell off the wall, there was no putting the pieces back together again.

Prowling through the house, he thought back to the day. Had somebody tried to kill Gabby, or was it pure happenstance she'd been in the way of a drunken or foolish driver? And then there was the break-in at the Ortiz house.

What surprised him was to discover that exhilaration had him feeling wired.

Gabby was opening up, whether she knew it or not. Twice now, she'd revealed memories so vivid, she'd reverted physically in small ways to the child she'd been. Over time, people's memories tended to blur; sometimes they altered. Who wanted to remember being a victim? It was better to convince yourself you'd really been heroic, or at least smart. She *was* smart to hide—but he doubted she'd think of it that way. If he'd sat down with Gabby in an interview room and insisted she tell him what she remembered, the narrative she offered wouldn't have convinced him. When she was flung back to *being* that child, he could almost see through her eyes.

Her small flashback tonight fully justified his somewhat underhanded tactics. If he'd taken the straightforward route, he'd have gotten nowhere.

The entire reel, beginning to end, was in Gabby Ortiz's head. If he could coax her into playing it, he'd finally catch the son of a bitch who'd killed her mother. He had closed a lot of cases since he became a detective, but this one would mean the most.

It was personal.

Chapter Six

The hot tub had felt fabulous this afternoon, but, sad to say, the therapeutic effect had worn off. A dip in the pool would feel good now.

On the other hand, Ric and Jack had combined to awaken uneasiness that made Gabby decide to wait until Jack—how had he put it?—assessed hotel security. If there weren't cameras in the pool area, she could be really isolated in the evening once families with children returned to their rooms.

And what if she wasn't alone? A guy on his own might wander in. If he was young enough, she wouldn't have to worry, but what if he was in his forties, say? Fifties? She wouldn't recognize anyone her parents had once known.

She'd already had an eventful day and didn't need to add any more stress. Digging out the ibuprofen she carried in her handbag, she took two with water. She could brew a cup of coffee, but that seemed like too much effort. She grabbed the two books she'd bought today, determined to start one of them. Worry was clearly going to make it hard to concentrate, though.

Now that she'd gotten together with Ric a few times, maybe she should give up and go home. Except, the apartment in Concord she'd probably be giving up soon wasn't home, and she'd sold Aunt Isabel's house to pay off student loans as well as grad school tuition.

Face it—she didn't have anything approaching a true home. Which was probably the most deep-seated reason, she admitted ruefully to herself, she was here in Leclaire. It had called to her. It was once home, and Ric was her only family. He even lived in the family home.

Too bad she wished that it had burned down to the foundation at some point in the past twenty-five years.

Knowing she'd really lost it at dinner humiliated her. Would Jack bother to call again after seeing her childish display?

Sure he would, Gabby thought, depressed; he'd promised to do that security check, and he would. He'd feel obligated to report on it, too. To offer further advice, probably.

And if he didn't suggest dinner or lunch…well, she should be glad. No, Leclaire didn't feel like home, either, and she wouldn't be staying. Why start something with a guy she'd never see again once she left town?

Knock, knock.

She jerked. A quick glance toward the digital alarm clock on the bedside table told her it was 9:05. Who could possibly be here?

For some reason, she tiptoed to the door. Thank goodness she'd not only locked it, she'd put on that latch doohickey, too. "Who is it?" she called.

"Room service, ma'am." The voice was a man's.

"I didn't order anything."

She couldn't entirely make out what he said, but the word *complimentary* was in there. That wasn't impossible. This was a classy hotel. She actually reached for the knob before she thought better of it.

You need to be sure not to get caught alone.

There might be security cameras in the hallways, but there wouldn't be in the rooms. There'd better not be, anyway.

"Thank you, but I don't want anything," she called back. "I'll let room service know I refused you."

Then she listened hard.

The man didn't say anything. No *Very well, ma'am.*

She didn't hear footsteps, either, although with the plush carpet in the hall, she probably wouldn't. But if he'd knocked on any neighboring doors, she'd probably hear that, if only faintly. And if she was being offered some complimentary goodies, wouldn't you think other people staying here would be, too?

Nothing. The hush was so complete, it scared her even more.

She backed away from the door. Hurried to the slider that led out to a balcony and checked that lock, too.

Then, heart pounding, she sat back down. She was okay. The waiter was probably legit—but she'd tell Jack about him.

Galvanized, Jack turned back to the security office even before he ended the midmorning call to Gabby. He didn't fool himself that it could be this easy. He had too much experience watching endless security footage, only to find it too grainy to make out the needed detail, or to learn that the camera pointed the wrong way. His favorite was being told that a particular camera hadn't been operative for weeks or months. Business owners invariably thought that the existence of a visible camera was good enough.

The head of security answered the knock on the door, looking startled at Jack's quick reappearance. At least he'd taken Jack seriously, especially after being told that one of the hotel guests had come damn close yesterday to being killed on an icy street only two blocks away.

"You have another question?"

"I just spoke to the woman in question." He explained about the knock on her door after nine last night, and that the man knocking had claimed to be a waiter with something complimentary for her.

Art Lessiter shook his head immediately. "Truffles are placed in every room daily by cleaning staff. Occasionally we offer something like a free spa service to make up for an unsatisfactory experience here at the Wilmont, but we would never send food that hasn't been ordered." He sounded deadly serious. "And to expect a single woman guest to open her door to a male staff member, when she hadn't requested food or assistance? Aside from common sense, that could open us—and rightly so—to liability. I feel confident in saying that whoever knocked on her door is not employed by this hotel."

Nothing Lessiter said was a surprise to Jack. "Let's see the footage. She said the knock came at 9:05, although she was looking at the bedside clock, not her phone. Those wouldn't be as accurate."

"The maid is supposed to check the time on the clocks daily."

Jack waited tensely. He could see the current view of some hallways on screens. None of those were watched 24-7; whoever was on shift switched between cameras regularly.

It took Lessiter a minute, but once told the room number, he found what they were looking for. "I'm starting it at 8:55. We can go back further if we have to."

Both men stared at the monitor displaying a currently empty hallway in black-and-white—really an overall gray. One minute in, the elevator doors slid open and a couple emerged, turning toward the camera. They were smiling as they let themselves into a room.

A single man in a business suit came out of the elevator next, expression preoccupied, and walked away, passing Gabby's room and letting himself in to one several doors down and across the hall.

Then nothing.

At 9:04, the elevator opened and another man emerged. He was well dressed in a suit and overcoat, had on gloves that were probably leather, and wore a black fedora that hid his face. He started down the hall without once exposing his face to the camera.

Jack stored up his impressions. This guy was good-sized, bulky in a way that suggested a once-athletic man who had softened. He had a slightly rolling gait. And damn, he stopped outside Gabby's door and knocked.

He also kept his back turned to the camera. Presumably he spoke, because he waited for a minute. Then he strode away—in the other direction.

"Is there another elevator?"

"Yes, around the corner."

The security chief found that footage. The man reappeared on it, but only briefly to open a door that Lessiter said was to the staircase.

This footage was from a camera on the fourth floor looking down. Gabby's room was on the third floor, so they could see only the set of the shoulders and the top of the fedora.

He continued down to the garage and immediately let himself out a steel door that led to the alley at the back of the hotel.

And that was it.

But Lessiter went back to the camera footage taken in

the stairwell. Inched it forward, then froze it. "Tell me I'm imagining that."

Jack leaned forward and cursed. Something black filled the space between the collar of the wool overcoat and the hat. "A balaclava," he said.

"Most people would think ski mask." The security chief sat back in his chair, his expression incredulous. "If he'd happened to meet someone getting out of the elevator, say, he could have pulled it down a little and mumbled something about not being used to nights this cold. Even without the hat, we wouldn't have seen his face."

He could not believe this. Colleen Ortiz's killer—or so the odds suggested—had been captured by three different cameras, and not one had revealed his features or anything else meaningful.

Except, that wasn't true. Yeah, the overcoat hid his body build, but not entirely. He was a good-sized man, tall and broad. He carried himself with shoulders squared—and then there was a distinctive gait.

"He knew where our cameras are," Lessiter said suddenly.

"He's either stayed here before and paid attention, or he cased the hotel. I wonder, if we went back…"

"When I have time, I might do just that." This was a pissed security chief.

"Let me know." Jack stood and thanked Art Lessiter, who promised to send copies of the footage to Jack.

Then Jack took the elevator himself, needing to see with his own eyes that Gabby was safe and well.

WHEN SHE ANSWERED the door, it was to find Jack wearing a suit, white shirt and tie. He looked extraordinarily handsome, but she surveyed him all the way down to his shiny black dress shoes with her eyebrows raised.

"I have to appear in court this afternoon," he said gruffly. "Don't get used to this."

A sharp pang served as a warning. She *wanted* to get used to Jack Cowan in all his manifestations—but it wasn't happening, she told herself.

Once Gabby agreed to have lunch with him, Jack said, "I'll be back in a couple of hours. Otherwise, unless you're having dinner with Ric tonight…" He paused meaningfully.

"What, I'm supposed to just skip meals?"

"You're not taking this seriously," he told her, his tone stern.

Maybe she had sounded a little sarcastic. "I am. I'm just not used to taking orders." She could be diplomatic when necessary, especially where academic politics were concerned, but obeying without question? No.

She'd spent a lifetime trying to insure she never felt helpless again. If that occasionally made her prickly, so be it.

The timbre of Jack's voice changed, became intimate. "You're right. I'm sorry. I'm used to snapping out orders and assuming people will jump to obey them. I just want you to be extra careful, okay?"

Gabby sighed. "I won't leave the hotel. Like I said, I'll leave the room only if I hear multiple people in the hall. It's just—" She hesitated.

"You don't want to order room service. I get that. *I* don't want you answering the door for anyone but me or Ric."

Left alone, Gabby plunked her laptop on the worktable and stared at it for a long time. Jack was right, this was a great block of time she could use to polish her dissertation. But there was no way she could really concentrate.

Great excuse, a voice seemed to whisper.

She ignored it. She changed back to her pajamas and spent the morning alternately reading and streaming shows she'd always wanted to catch up on. She even napped.

The firm knock on the door came at precisely noon. "It's me," Jack said, loud enough for her to hear.

She let him in before noticing he carried a laptop case under his arm. "I thought we were going out."

His sharp blue eyes stayed on her face. "We are, but I want to show you that footage first. In case this guy looks familiar to you."

"How could he?"

He'd think she was determined to bury her head in the sand, but realistically, how could she relate camera images to a man she'd seen once, when she was four years old?

Unless, of course, she should have known him because he'd been at the house before, like Jack's father had, or even more often if he'd been one of Mom and Dad's friends.

No matter what, she resented both Ric's *and* Jack's automatic assumption that she was a coward. She couldn't have denied that she carried the trauma that had shaped her life as if it was an unhealed wound, painful, hot, somewhere inside her chest, or that she'd spent much of her life refusing to examine it too closely. But she was trying to change that, and neither of the men knew how hard it was to do that. They had no idea how many times Aunt Isabel had insisted she had to put it behind her.

Jack had been watching her, as if he guessed she was fuming, but all he said, mildly, was "You've been out on your own a few times since you got into town, right? It's possible this guy has followed you."

Cold fingers slipped up her spine.

She retreated to the bed. "I thought you said you couldn't make out anything about his appearance."

Jack sat beside her, his greater weight compressing the mattress. She raised her head to meet his gaze and saw the tenderness on his face.

"The way people are built and move can be individual enough that we recognize someone coming from a distance away. Not everyone, but you know what I mean."

She did—and had the sinking feeling that Jack was one of those people for her. His long, athletic stride, the set of his shoulders, the way he so often turned his head as he remained aware of everyone and everything around him... Oh, yes, she'd know him long before she could see his face.

She only nodded.

He removed a thin laptop, opened it and called up an app and then the camera footage. Then he handed the computer to her and tapped a key to set the still picture into motion.

Gabby wasn't sure she breathed as she watched the elevator open and a man step out with his head bent and angled away from the camera. He walked down the hall. If he glanced at room numbers, she couldn't tell. He stopped at her door, raised a gloved hand and knocked.

Her lips moved as she mouthed what he'd said, what she'd said, and remembered the silence. Without physically showing any frustration, he walked swiftly away from the camera until he disappeared around a corner in the hall.

"You're shaking," Jack said with quick concern. He wrapped his arm around her, took the laptop away and set it on the bed, then cuddled her close. "I'm sorry. I wish—"

"I needed to see it," she mumbled against his shoulder.

"Was anything about him familiar?"

She shook her head vehemently, even though…she didn't know.

"There's something," he said slowly.

"Yes…no." She swallowed. "I don't know. It's just that seeing him makes it real. A stranger wanted me to let him into my room last night. It wasn't some kind of mix-up by room service."

"No." His voice roughened. "I didn't tell you this guy was wearing a balaclava to hide his face. I doubt he intended even you to see it."

Her head bobbed. "If only I could tell him that I don't remember him."

After a discernible pause, Jack straightened, his arms dropping away from her. "Is that really what you want?"

"To not be wearing a target?" she shot back.

"Don't you think your mother deserves justice?"

Scooting away, Gabby would have sworn she'd find a thin slice oozing blood somewhere on her body. Maybe he hadn't sounded as cutting as she'd thought…but the alternative was contempt. She struggled plenty not to despise herself for sticking to Great-Aunt Isabel's advice. For protecting herself.

"You know…" She stood. "I think I'll skip dinner tonight."

"No." He bent his head and pinched the bridge of his nose between his thumb and forefinger. The regret he showed when he looked up couldn't possibly be fabricated. "I'm such an ass. I stumble over my job sometimes. My…biases. You don't know how frustrating it is when a witness won't talk. Half the time after domestic violence calls, the victim refuses to testify." This all came out raggedly. "We've wasted our time. We *know* he or she'll get hurt again, and we can't do anything."

Still hurt, she said, "*You're* refusing to accept that I don't know anything to tell you. I *want* to remember. I do. But it's not that easy, especially after I've spent a lot of years trying—"

"To forget."

Gabby closed her eyes, feeling the dampness in them. "Yes."

She felt the rush of air when he stood. She still hadn't opened her eyes when he enclosed her in his arms. "I'm sorry. I...don't want to lose the time with you."

She should stick to her guns, but...she didn't want to lose the limited time she'd have with him, either, so she nodded. "I probably overreacted. Ric has said things like that to me so often over the years. I agreed to this visit partly because I know he's right."

Jack lifted her chin gently with his hand. "He needs family, too, Gabby. You're not the only one scarred by what happened."

She tried to smile, if only to lessen the intensity of the moment. "I know that, too."

He bent his head and kissed her. Not with passion this time, but gently, telling her without words that he understood, that he cared.

She didn't know why, couldn't let herself wonder how much he could care, if only they had time. Right now, she'd take what she could get.

Once he looked down at her again, she found a better smile. "To tell you the truth, I'm really starved."

Jack laughed. "Me, too. Let's go."

Chapter Seven

That evening, Ric took her to dinner in the hotel restaurant—the same place she'd had lunch with Jack today. The very fact that Ric insisted on coming up to her room to get her was a clue that the two men had been talking.

The same host remained on shift and seated them. His eyebrows flickered a little to see her with a different man and she thought there was amusement in his eyes, but she could hardly exclaim loudly, "This one's my brother!"

Once she and Ric had ordered, he commented on her latest near miss. What if she hadn't thought twice about opening the door?

"It was scary," she admitted. In a different way, far more terrifying than having to jump out of the way of a speeding SUV. "Weird, too. I mean, how did he know where I'm staying? What room I'm in?"

"He could have followed you." More slowly, Ric said, "Or me. Probably not Jack."

No, she had a suspicion Jack would have noticed if anyone had tried to follow him.

When she voiced her thought, Ric said, "Yeah, Cowan makes me nervous even at the health club. It's the way he looks at people. He seems to have eyes in the back of his head. You know?"

Gabby wrinkled her nose. "I've noticed. He's hyper-aware. It's probably a cop thing."

"I'm sure." He studied her with those dark eyes that reminded her of her father's. "Have you been anywhere on your own that this guy might have picked you up?"

She felt sick enough to hope their meals didn't show up too soon. "I...drove by the house. Actually, I parked across the street from it for a few minutes." Upset, she wouldn't have noticed another car that had stuck with her all the way back to the hotel. "But...he couldn't possibly have been hanging around the house for hours or days waiting for me."

"He sure as hell was determined to get *in* the house," her brother snapped.

They stared at each other for a minute. Gabby wanted to say again how weird all this was, but...it was beginning to seem all too real.

If the killer had seen her at the house and followed her back to the hotel, he wouldn't have known whether she was staying there or just meeting someone for lunch, say. Was it logical that he'd have then broken into the house to find out for sure whether she was staying with her brother or not?

"How did you feel about it?" Ric asked suddenly. Seeing her confusion, he said, "I mean, the house."

Should she opt for honesty? Or pull her punches? No, what was the point in lying?

"I hated looking at it. As far as I could tell, neither you nor Dad has changed a single thing. You haven't painted the house a different color, not even the front door. The arbor is still there, probably with the same roses climbing over it. It was..." She had to look away. "I felt like I was having a flashback."

"That's harsh. The house is white. It's not like it's all that distinctive."

She made herself meet his eyes again, but didn't say a word.

He flushed. "I guess I never think about it. Dad didn't want to change anything, and... I was a kid. Boys don't think about things like remodeling. You know?"

"It's *your* house now. It has been for eight years. What, you still think you're twenty-one and lucky because you don't have to pay rent?"

He groaned and kneaded the back of his neck. "Maybe. Sort of. I did finally remodel the master bedroom and move into it. I put in a Jacuzzi tub. I stayed in my own bedroom longer than I should have. I couldn't bring a woman home with me and explain that, yeah, I slept in a full-size bed because that's all that would fit in the bedroom where I'd grown up."

Gabby was startled into a giggle. "No, that would lead to some awkward questions." She sobered quickly, though. "But...the rest of the house?"

"Dad wanted it to stay the same. The kitchen is really dated, but even though he could have afforded to redo it, he wouldn't hear of it. 'There isn't a damn thing wrong with it,' he'd say."

"Except for the fact that Mom was murdered in that kitchen."

His jaw tightened. "I think he wanted it kept the same as a memorial. Or maybe he deluded himself that she'd walk in the door someday. I don't know."

They were silent, brooding, when their entrées finally appeared. Gabby decided she was hungry enough to eat despite the subject of conversation. In fact, she had several bites before Ric said, "I guess I was trying to honor Dad's wishes."

She nodded. "I can see that. Except…doesn't it bother you?"

"No, my memories are mostly good ones, you know. Dad never let me into the house until it had been cleaned up."

Gabby remembered. She had a vague memory of staying in a hotel, something their family never did. Summer vacations were spent camping. She couldn't remember how long they'd been in the hotel, but she thought at least a week, on top of her hospital stay. Now she guessed the crime scene tape had stayed up for a few days, and afterward…she didn't remember Dad leaving her and Ric, so maybe he'd hired someone to eradicate any remaining evidence of his wife's gory death. Still, wouldn't you think he'd have been reluctant to go home?

She sure was. She'd had hysterics when they'd first returned home. The flash of memory startled her. She'd forgotten her terror.

"Where were you when Mom was killed?" she asked. "Were you in a sports camp or something?"

He flinched, then croaked, "No." He put down his fork. "That's…the worst part for me. I guess I never told you. Dad never knew."

"Told me what?"

Shame infused his voice. "I didn't want you to know."

Unnerved, she waited.

"I was supposed to be home. Do you remember Paul Olsen?"

Supposed to be home. Suddenly short of breath, Gabby couldn't help wondering. If Ric had been there, what would have changed? If the killer had known someone else was in the house, he might not have come in at all, or he might have left without hurting her mother.

Hurting. There was the king of euphemisms.

Or he might have killed Ric, too. Her noisy, nearly hyperactive brother would never have instinctively hidden, the way she did.

Ric reached for her hand. "Gabby?"

"I…" She shook her head. "I'm sorry. What did you say?"

He repeated himself.

"Paul was blond, right?" she asked him.

"Yeah, that was him. Still is, actually. I was at his house, but Mom had told me to be home for lunch. Only, we got this great idea and rode our bikes to the river with a couple of other guys who sneaked away, too."

Her eyes widened. Her eight-year-old brother hadn't been banned from crossing the street, like she was, but he'd had strict limits. The river was at least a mile from home, and to go there without adult supervision…

"You'd have been in so much trouble."

"Yeah." He rolled his shoulders. "We got back to Paul's, and his mother fed us lunch. She thought we'd been down the street at Jeff's. Mom hadn't even called. I thought she'd forgotten." His eyes closed. "She didn't call because she was dead."

And Gabby might still have been huddled in terror in the utility room. She had no idea how long she'd stayed there before she found the courage to slip out the back door and run to old Mrs. Soriano's house, knowing she was practically always home.

Also, Gabby hadn't had to cross the street to get there. Mrs. Soriano lived on the same side and the same block.

"I'm sorry." Ric's Adam's apple bobbed. His hand squeezed Gabby's hard. "I'm sorrier than I can ever say. If I'd been there, like I should have been—"

"You'd probably be dead, too," she said bluntly. "You feel guilty? Get real. You wouldn't have had the sense to hide, and you were old enough to be the kind of witness the police couldn't dismiss."

"You think they dismissed you?"

"I know they did."

"I…" He didn't move for a long moment. He might not even have breathed. "I guess I always thought—"

"It wouldn't have happened if you'd been there."

"Yeah, or I could have hit the guy with my baseball bat or—" He stopped. "I had a lot of fantasies. I always did *something*. Mom lived, and I could have been a hero, except I'd sneaked away to break all the rules."

"Oh, Ric." Tears prickled in her eyes. "You have no reason to feel guilty. You couldn't have stopped what happened. And think how much worse it would have been if Dad had lost you, too? If I'd had to watch—"

"Yeah." Her big brother cleared his throat. "I never thought about that. I was a kid. I guess… I never got past that."

"I don't think I ever did, either," she admitted, hating the way her voice broke. "A part of me got stuck in that moment."

His eyes were wet, too. "I've been, too, except for me it was a different moment. It was when Mrs. Olsen saw all the police cars and an ambulance with their lights on, and decided they were on our block. She didn't say it was my house—she probably couldn't tell from her front porch. She tried to stop me, but I tore away, jumped on my bike and rode as fast as I could, but when I got there, a police officer grabbed me and told me I couldn't go in. Dad must not have been there yet, or he was and I just didn't see the car, so the officer finally drove me back to the Olsens' house and made me promise to stay there."

"I was at Mrs. Soriano's." From his nod, she saw that he knew that. "By then, I was curled into a shaking ball.

I remember rocking and rocking and—" Gabby swallowed. "She tried so hard to reach me, but I think now I was somewhere else."

"You spent a couple of days in the hospital, you know," Ric said slowly. "It took that long before you could talk, tell the cops what you'd seen. Even after…" He frowned. "You didn't really talk much. Before that, you were kind of a motormouth."

"I was, wasn't I?"

"Were you again? I mean, after you went home with Great-Aunt Isabel?"

Gabby shook her head. "I think it was years before I relaxed enough to really talk. Aunt Isabel worried—" She shook her head.

"I've been a butt, haven't I?" His gaze was somber. "I wanted you to make it better, but arresting the killer wouldn't really have made anything better, would it?"

"In a way, it would have. I'll bet you were scared he'd come back, weren't you?"

Rapidly shifting emotions on his face didn't surprise her. Finally his mouth twisted. "Yeah. I never told anyone, but…yeah."

"Also," she said more practically, "I wouldn't have the problem I have now."

"You mean, having someone out to shut you up? Probably not."

That was almost funny…but not quite.

A SINGLE DRIP fell from the man's elbow. Her eyes followed it to the floor. Then came another, and another. *Drip, drip, drip, drip.* Was it raining in here? She turned her face up to the ceiling, then cringed.

Can't move, can't move. He'll see me.

His arm rose and fell. Liquid sprayed upward, a fountain, only the water was a vivid red color. That was why those drips were red. Why the rivulets were scarlet against the black-and-white checkerboard floor. It went on as far as she could see. Now it was threaded with red, as if she could see its veins. *Did floors have veins?* she wondered.

Then she quit wondering anything, because *he* was turning. His eyes met hers, and horror flared to life inside her—

GASPING, GABBY BOLTED AWAKE. Oh, God—that had been the most vivid nightmare she'd had in ages. The colors… Yet it was fading already, even as she tried to hold on to it.

The floor, veined like the human body. He saw her.

The vivid shade of red.

He hadn't really seen her. Gabby felt sure of that, or he'd have killed her, too. Dreams were most often nonsensical, combining bits and pieces of recent events or thoughts or fears, but a nightmare could also warp memories.

Dripping. What had been dripping in the dream? She was almost grateful the nightmare was slipping away. All these years, and they kept returning. Not always the same, but she knew, she *knew*, they were about Mom's murder.

Shuddering, she rolled onto her back. Her nightgown felt like a boa constrictor squeezing her. Her teeth actually chattered when she sat up to untangle the fabric. It felt chilly here in the room, probably because she was sweating and her nightgown was damp. Maybe she should just get dressed. She couldn't imagine falling asleep again.

Gabby looked at the glowing numbers on the clock. 4:37. She'd be exhausted later in the day if she didn't get some more sleep…except it wasn't like anything would stop her from going to bed early tonight.

Her eye fell on the black slab of her phone lying on the end table. She'd spent a lifetime suffering the nightmares and their aftereffects in silence. Even at five and six years old, after she'd gone to live with Aunt Isabel, Gabby had never cried out aloud, never slipped from her bed to sneak into her aunt's for comfort. She remembered telling Ric that it took years for her to be able to chatter at all normally. From the minute she'd told herself she had to be quiet in the utility room, she couldn't make a sound, she hadn't been able to relax and think, *It's okay now*. It wasn't okay.

Since coming back to Leclaire to get to know her brother and face her fears, she'd discovered nothing was okay. The killer was still here, not two steps away. His hands wouldn't still be bloody—they'd look like anyone else's—but she saw the dripping, as if out of the corner of her eye.

Blood. That's what had been dripping.

Her arms wrapped herself as tightly as she could manage while she resisted the pull to pick up the phone. For the first time in her life, she wanted to hear someone else's voice.

Jack's.

She wanted his arms around her, too. She wanted him murmuring reassurances even as rage underlaid every word. *He'd* keep her safe.

But she didn't reach for the phone. Couldn't. He'd talk to her, she knew; come to her, if that's what she wanted. But letting herself rely on someone else would only weaken her. In a few days or weeks, she'd leave town, and be alone again.

Once she was far away, these maddening nightmares

would recede again, become only occasional. This one had been so shockingly real only because, thanks to Ric and even Jack, she'd been remembering.

She should be celebrating. This was the biggest reason for her visit. Those memories were coming back to her, just as she wanted.

And they were every bit as horrifying as she'd feared.

BY SATURDAY, JACK had cleared enough of his other cases to focus solely on the Ortiz murder. Given the window of opportunity, he checked out every scrap of information available from Evidence, excepting the victim's slashed, blood-soaked garments. Those, he didn't need to see. If he found a viable suspect, that might change; DNA recovery and tracing had come a long way, and he couldn't imagine that the killer hadn't cut himself, too, given his frenzy. Chances were excellent that tiny spots of blood that weren't Colleen Ortiz's would be found. At the moment, that wouldn't be helpful. Sure, the DNA could be entered into online databases to search for a forensic hit or even offender match—but Jack didn't believe for a second that this killer would be found there. He hadn't been a wandering serial killer. Colleen had known him.

The murder weapon wasn't here, either, presumably because the killer had brought it with him and taken it away when he was done. No knife with the right kind of blade had been missing from the Ortiz kitchen.

Most of this, he'd already accessed on his computer, but it was past time to look for holes in the original investigation. He was determined to dig deeper, starting with anything that *hadn't* been included in reports. Tapes of interviews had been transcribed, but he'd listen to them anyway. There could be a scrap of paper with a forgotten bit of information from a phone conversation. He wanted to see who, besides his father, had been even briefly considered to be a suspect. Why hadn't there been other witnesses? Hadn't a single neighbor within earshot of what had to be terrible screams been home?

He plunged in, impervious to the comings and goings and voices of surrounding coworkers.

After the murder, of course, neighbors at least a block in every direction had been canvassed.

Nobody had seen the killer come or go. Except for a couple of seniors, people in the nearest houses had been at work, kids in summer camps or daycare. The old lady Gabby had run to didn't have good vision, and had been five houses away. The old guy next door—the same one who snatched Gabby from the path of the speeding car—had been napping. He'd heard what must have been the screams and was only annoyed, figuring they came from the teenagers at a house behind him who had been playing loud music, partying, yelling and generally making a nuisance of themselves that summer while their parents were at work.

The greatest mystery was how the killer had left the house without leaving a trail of blood and bloody footprints. He hadn't gone out through the garage, thank God, because if he had he'd have passed through the utility room and been inches from the little girl hiding under a sheet. Instead, he must have used the back door.

Speculation at the time—and Jack wouldn't argue—was that the killer had parked at the side of the house. Raul Ortiz owned a small utility trailer kept in the backyard, hidden behind gates in the fence. But a dirt lane from the street led to those gates. The killer's vehicle would have been a lot less visible there, unless the old man next door had looked out the window in his garage—which he hadn't.

But why hadn't the guy left bloody footprints on his way out? Some remnants of blood were found in the kitchen sink, but not in large quantities. There was no hint he'd gone upstairs or taken a shower.

Jack brooded over the problem for a few minutes. Something like coveralls was the obvious answer. A Tyvek suit, hood off when he entered, pulled over his head to protect himself from blood spatter as he stabbed the victim. Or even the kind of coveralls workers sometimes wore, paired with rubber boots, say. Strip it all off, bundle it into a plastic bag, and walk out.

But Gabby had said the man wore blue. Had both the coveralls and the clothes he wore beneath been blue?

Frowning, Jack continued.

A woman named Margaret Vaughn had lived across the street from the Ortiz home. She'd been shopping the afternoon of the murder, but she'd reported seeing a man in a blue uniform ringing the doorbell the day before the murder. He'd caught her eye mainly because he wasn't carrying a clipboard, a package or any equipment, and he'd knocked after there was no response to the doorbell. Even then, she didn't think anything about it; his van was parked in the driveway, and she'd been sure it had a business name emblazoned on the side. Cowan something, she thought.

If Margaret Vaughn hadn't witnessed Jack's father on the Ortiz doorstep, his life wouldn't have been ruined.

How could Jack blame her, though? That was exactly the kind of tidbit that led to arrests.

He perused notes from multiple interviews, mostly with other men who'd been at the house previously. The investigators had favored friends of Raul and Colleen. They'd spoken to an insurance agent who'd come out to give them a quote. One of the detectives commented that

Raul seemed to handle most repairs around the house. The furnace seemed to be an exception.

Finally, Jack plugged in the tape player he'd borrowed from the tech gurus and began listening to interviews. He jotted notes on what his father said in several interviews then. It had stayed consistent. How much of it would Dad remember now?

Only then, with deep reluctance, did he pop in the tape labeled Gabriella Ortiz #1.

Chapter Eight

Hearing the small, high, faltering voice made him feel as if he'd swallowed battery acid.

Jack couldn't help noticing that Gabby sounded even younger than she'd actually been, which shouldn't have come as a surprise. Reverting after trauma was a typical response in a child, one that investigators should have kept in mind.

The first interviewer, a detective named Scott Hudson who was long since retired, had tried to sound sympathetic, but Jack suspected he didn't have any children of his own, because he wasn't good at it.

"Mommy looked so scared," four-year-old Gabby whispered. "I didn't know why."

"Was the man already there when she looked scared?"

Silence. Jack's gaze dropped to the transcript, where someone had noted: (Nodded)

"Did your mommy let the man in through the front door?"

(Confusion)

"Did you *see* the man come into the house?" A hint of irritation was creeping into Detective Hudson's voice.

"Uh-uh. I heard Mommy yelling. Like when she's mad at Ric."

"Your brother."

"Uh-huh."

"Did you hear what she said?"

"I… I don't know." Gabby was whispering again.

"Can you try to remember?" Hudson asked more aggressively.

"She said 'What're you doing here?'"

"That's it?"

(Hunched. Teeth chattering)

Jack paused the tape, rolled his head, then his shoulders. He'd *seen* her hunch over like that. That time at the restaurant. Her teeth weren't chattering, but…damn. That wasn't hard to picture.

Hudson pressed her harder about what she'd heard and got nothing. Finally, he shifted to, "What did the man look like?"

The chattering teeth could be heard on the tape, unless Jack was imagining things, followed by a tiny whisper. "I don't know."

He finally extracted from her the information Jack already knew, that the man had blue pants and shirt.

By that time Gabby was crying. Hudson had to give up.

Bothered by something he couldn't put a finger on, Jack rewound the tape. In attempting to get a description, the detective said, "The man must have walked right by the doorway into the utility room. Close to you."

(Shaking)

"You could see what he was wearing."

(Nod)

"Can you tell me?"

Silence. No transcript notes.

In one of her more coherent answers, Gabby said, "That man had blue pants and a blue shirt. And black shoes."

Whoa. Jack rewound again, intently listening for the slight emphasis apparently no one else had noticed.

"*That* man had blue pants and a blue shirt."

Had she seen *two* men? Why the hell hadn't anyone asked? A single killer still seemed likeliest—multiple stabbings almost always meant anger and a personal motivation. If that was the case, had Gabby seen the man in something like a Tyvek suit and not realized he was the same man who walked out past her, almost close enough to touch?

Would it help to know what he'd worn during the murder? Maybe, maybe not. But, damn, Hudson's interview had been incompetent, to put it kindly.

In the ensuing days, two other investigators went at it, neither with any more skill. By the second interview, Gabby didn't remember anything her mom said. She remembered blood. That memory ended interview number two.

By number three, five days after the murder, Gabby said, "He kept hitting Mommy, and hitting her and hitting her! An' yelling at her!" Her voice rose with each repetition until it was almost a scream. "And I wanted to hit him, 'cept..."

She was a little girl, and terrified.

"What was he yelling?"

"She ruined something. But Mommy wouldn't."

Why hadn't those idiots found a woman to interview their young witness? Or at least a kindly father of little girls? Why hadn't they gently asked simple, specific questions, like, "What color hair did the man have? Was it brown like mine? Black like yours?"

No—to be fair, detective number two had asked that. He just waited until she was already sobbing after their discussion of the blood.

Why hadn't they sat her down with her father, and let *him* ask the questions?

All three investigators had concluded, and so noted, that "witness is too young to provide reliable information."

Had Raul Ortiz ever talked to Gabby about what she'd seen? If so, had she been so confused by then, he hadn't gotten anything useful? Or had he tried to tell one of the investigators what she saw and was blown off?

Frustrated and angry, Jack wouldn't be surprised if that was exactly what happened. But, damn it, wouldn't Raul have told someone else? Ric would have been too young then, but later?

The detectives had sought out the victim's friends, but all of them insisted she hadn't said anything about a man who made her uneasy.

The killer hadn't raped her. Hadn't stolen anything from the house that day so far as investigators could tell, unless it was inconsequential, a memento. Hadn't thought to look for Colleen's young daughter—or didn't know she had one until later.

Colleen hadn't just screamed, "Get out!" Hard not to conclude that she'd known her killer. But how? And was he someone she'd met recently?

Or someone she'd known from her past?

"Jack." His father sounded pleased to hear from him that evening. "It's been a while. Something new?"

"Yeah." He cleared his throat and kicked back in his recliner, gazing at the blank television. Bluntness came naturally to him. "I've gotten permission to open a cold case. Colleen Ortiz's murder."

The silence was deafening. When his father finally spoke, it was hoarsely. "You can't rewrite history."

"I can if I put a name to the killer. If I arrest him."

"If you're doing this for me, don't."

"I'm not." Jack sat up straight and put his feet on the floor. Where in hell had that come from? Of course his lifelong quest had to do with clearing his father's name once and for all.

But things had changed, he realized, when he got to know Gabby. Ric, too, to some extent. *They* needed closure, and deserved it.

A grunt told him Dad didn't believe him.

"How do you expect to learn anything the original investigators couldn't?" his father asked. "Neighbors have moved, died, forgotten whatever they once knew. I heard Raul Ortiz died a few years back. Who is left? The kids?"

"The youngest is thirty now. The son still lives in the house." He paused. "I reopened the case because the Ortiz girl just came back to Leclaire for a visit."

"They talked to her then. For God's sake, Jack, she was a little girl! What do you think she can tell you?"

"She's already told me some things," he said in a harder voice than he'd intended. "Among them, she admits she's spent her entire life haunted by what happened, and by what she witnessed. Turns out her brother, Ric, feels the same, even though he escaped seeing his mother killed or even the house before it was cleaned. For him, he went off to hang out with friends, and his whole world changed. Next thing he knew, his little sister was yanked away. Did you know he hasn't seen her in over twenty years?"

"You're angry."

"Yeah, I am. I always have been. I lost *my* family because you were unfairly looked at for that murder."

"No. Things are never that simple. You know that."

He did. If his parents' relationship had been tight, Mom would have supported Dad and nothing would have changed for him. As it was, there might well have been a divorce in the next few years, anyway, but that wouldn't have been the same. His parents would have traded kids for visits, Mom might have stayed in the area, and Kristine and he wouldn't have had to choose between Mom and Dad.

"The murder was a dividing line."

"It was that," his father admitted sadly.

Part of Jack wanted to push until Dad admitted what had been wrong, why the split had been so bitter. But he took a deep breath, closed his eyes and reminded himself he could do that anytime. Maybe over Christmas, which he usually spent with his father. Right now, his driving goal was to identify Colleen Ortiz's murderer. And one of the first steps was to interview again anyone who'd had knowledge pertaining to the crime.

That included Brian Cowan, the only serious suspect in her murder.

"I've been listening to the tapes of the interviews," Jack said. "I wanted to hear the subtleties that don't show up in a transcript. The investigators took most of the obvious steps, but the interviews with Gabby Ortiz were a joke. I have the impression they dismissed her as too young to be any use even before they talked to her. She was a traumatized child, and they didn't even try to ask questions in a way she'd understand. Instead, they pushed her into crying and gave up. I think Gabby saw plenty, and I think she can still pull those memories out of hiding."

He winced at how grimly determined he sounded. Was he any better than the jackasses who'd further traumatized her? What was he going to do, crack open her head and yank the memories out even if he left irreparable damage behind?

Jack squeezed the back of his neck. His muscles had knots on top of knots.

Damn it, that's not how it would be. He had to believe she'd be *glad* to get it all out in the open.

But he knew he might be kidding himself. Cops had to be ruthless. They couldn't tiptoe around the sensibilities of witnesses and suspects, or they'd never arrive at the truth. A few faces in particular flashed past his eyes. Right this minute, he didn't much like himself.

"I met her," his father said. "Gabriella."

Jack's hand dropped from his neck. "I didn't know that."

"I worked on the furnace pretty close to a week before the murder. She was a curious little girl. Her mother kept telling her to leave me alone to do my job, but I told her I didn't mind. She was smart. Her questions were sharp for a kid that age." There might be a smile in his father's voice. "Cute, too, with those pigtails and bright eyes. Hell, you must have known her."

"I remember seeing her around, but that's all."

He saw her now. Disconcertingly so.

"What I really called for is to ask you to tell me again what you overheard that bothered you enough to feel like you should go back to check on a woman you didn't really know."

His father surprised him once again. "I'd done maintenance on their furnace several times over the years. It was getting old, but they didn't feel like they could afford a new one. Anyway, I'd talked to Colleen and her husband both before."

Why didn't the notes from his father's interview mention that? Was it possible he'd made a move on Colleen? No, if he had, she or her husband would probably have called another furnace company. Unless Dad and Colleen had actually had consensual sex… But, again, Jack found himself shaking his head. There was nothing in Dad's tone to suggest anything like that. Gabby would have been around on previous visits, too.

"Nice lady," his father added, "which is partly why I worried. I should have stopped by or called sooner. I talked it over with your mother, but she thought I was making a mountain out of a molehill."

Until it turned out that Jack's mother was very wrong.

"I was just coming up the steps from the basement when I heard her say something like, 'You saw me.' She sounded…alarmed."

Had Colleen been doing something she shouldn't have? Or could she have seen the killer, someone who scared her, and hoped he hadn't seen her?

"I got to the top of the steps and could see that she was on the phone. She had her back to me, or she'd have probably moved out of earshot. Instead, she snapped, 'If you keep bothering me, you should know I kept evidence. I won't hesitate to take it to the police.' Her voice was shrill. That's when she turned and realized she wasn't alone. She said goodbye and hung up the phone. Even while she was writing a check for me and chatting, I could tell she was upset. I asked if she was okay, and she said of course. What could I do? But…it just stuck in my mind. You know? She had evidence of a crime? That's what it sounded like."

Dad was right. That *was* what it sounded like. And Jack thought her threat had been a bad idea.

And then he had another thought. What if the intruder in Ric's house hadn't been checking to find out whether Gabby was staying there? What if, now that she was in town, he'd gotten worried about that evidence? Assuming he hadn't found it twenty-five years ago—and there'd been no sign the house had been tossed—he might have figured nobody would recognize that evidence. But now Gabby was home. She might know something—or her brother might hand over some of their mother's things because he thought she'd want them. So he'd gone through the house and found nothing except Christmas ornaments stored there. He didn't know about the storage facility. And, damn, Jack had to be very sure nobody followed Ric and Gabby there when they got around to looking through the stuff. He also fully intended to go with them and stand guard.

He'd have to finesse any explanation of why he needed to accompany them, but he'd manage.

AT THE HEAD of the driveway, Gabby's feet refused to move. Easier to decide she was going to walk through the house with her brother than to actually do it.

"You just going to stand there forever?" Ric asked from the porch steps.

She glared at him.

His eyebrows arched. "You're the one who wanted to get it over with."

"Why do I have to do it at all?" Gosh, maybe because revisiting her childhood home in hopes it would spark memories was part of what she'd been determined to accomplish?

"You don't," her brother said reasonably. "But wouldn't seeing the indoors looking normal and lived-in help wipe out your bad memories?"

He was right, except—"Yeah, good plan, if you and Dad hadn't kept the house as a damn shrine."

Although, the fact that they had might be a good thing, it occurred to her. The house served as a visual aide in her memory recovery process.

Ric kept scanning the block. "Let's not stand out here. It's cold."

His eyes darted back and forth as if he expected— what? A gunshot? *She* hadn't even known what that ping of metal off metal had meant when she'd been a child, or why Dad had grabbed her and Ric and all but thrown them behind the car and covered them with his body. Tires had squealed, but he hadn't moved until a police car pulled up. Witnesses hadn't heard a shot, either, which meant the gunman had used a silencer—actually, as Gabby had since learned, a suppressor. Gang members sometimes did, the officer had said, looking suspiciously at her father. Even she hadn't liked the way that policeman had studied Daddy.

"You're right," she agreed now. She'd take the grand tour. Wasn't seeing her home part of why she'd come back to Leclaire at last?

By the time she reached the porch, Ric had unlocked and opened the front door. Despite her resolve, she felt as if she were wading waist deep in a river, the current pushing back as she tried to walk forward. The spirit was willing, but the flesh was weak. Or was it the other way around?

To her relief, seeing the living room was okay. The hardwood floor must have been refinished at some point because she remembered it more scuffed and scratched. She and Ric had been hard on it.

Fireplace—check. The big flat screen TV was a major step up from the crappy color TV they'd had then. The new one was accompanied by the usual cable box and high-tech equipment, including a tangle of wires. Ric had to be the one who'd added a serious stereo system and speakers, too.

She didn't remember the sofa, either, but had an uneasy feeling the recliner might be the same one, albeit re-upholstered. Her gaze slid right past the coffee table, too.

"You actually have fires in here," she said, nodding at the fireplace. When she was a little girl, they used it only when the power was out. But a pile of newspapers, a wrought-iron wood holder and fireplace tools on the hearth made her think that was no longer the case. There was even a handsome screen and a colorful hearth rug.

"Yeah, Mom didn't like smoke, and Dad—I don't know, he just never built one, but I like having a fire at this time of year."

She smiled at him. "I would, too, if I wasn't always living in an apartment."

"I could make dinner for you some night. We could roast s'mores."

Gabby laughed, feeling way more relaxed. "Maybe."

Maybe not, she thought when her brother led the way past the dining room and into the kitchen. Forget "maybe not." "Not even on a cold day in hell" was more accurate.

Setting eyes on that damn checkerboard vinyl, she actually recoiled. "Oh, God."

Ric turned. "Oh, God what?"

It was like stepping into her most recent nightmare, the details of which she'd have sworn she'd forgotten. The endless black-and-white checkerboard floor with rivulets of blood everywhere. No, veins, as if skin had been peeled back from human flesh.

She shuffled backward even as she stared incredulously at a kitchen essentially unchanged from that hideous day. Wood cabinets painted white, white porcelain sink, bar stools with natural wood seats and white-painted legs. White eyelet curtains.

Out of the corner of her eye, she saw the doorway into the utility room. That's where she'd hidden, crouched behind the laundry basket with a sheet pulled over herself except for the fold that allowed her to see.

Drip, drip, drip.

Chapter Nine

She couldn't seem to wrench her gaze away from where her mother had died. "This is far enough." She didn't need to open cupboard doors to find out if the cereal was on the same shelf.

"It's been twenty-five years!" her brother exclaimed. "We've replaced the floor. Dad had to buy new bar stools—"

Because at least one had been splintered into pieces, and the others almost had to have been splattered with their mother's blood.

Nausea rose to choke her. She whirled and ran for the small downstairs bathroom, bringing up her breakfast in the toilet. Then she stood shakily in front of the sink and rinsed her mouth with handfuls of water. The strength of her reaction appalled her.

Ric's long arm reached past her. He took a bottle of mouthwash from the medicine cabinet and handed it to her.

She rinsed, then stared at herself in the mirror. She was too pale, and her eyes looked curiously blank. A thousand-yard stare. She'd read that description before, and knew it fit.

Ric's hand on her shoulder pulled her back to herself.

"Why don't we go upstairs?" he suggested, tone subdued. "Master bedroom and bathroom have been been redone."

She nodded.

The staircase was familiar, of course, but had no bad associations. The first bedroom had been Ric's, and was now painted white instead of...green was what she remembered. It held a double bed, not the twin one he'd had the last time she saw it. Yeah, this room wouldn't impress any women he brought home, she thought with a welcome flicker of humor.

Her bedroom was still pink, but otherwise so bare, there wasn't anything to react to, not even a bed.

"I think your dresser might be in storage," he said awkwardly.

Gabby nodded.

Linen closet—he didn't open the door. When they played hide-and-seek, she'd sometimes used the closet, but he always found her right away.

Bathroom—not really changed, but it had always been plain. No wallpaper, not even a border. *She'd* wanted Mommy to paint it pink, too, but Ric got mad, so it stayed cream-colored with standard white fixtures.

Ric had obviously claimed Mom and Dad's bedroom, because she didn't recognize a thing except the placement of the closets, window and door to the second bathroom.

"King-size bed," she murmured.

His grin looked forced. "Of course."

"You have a TV in your bedroom. Remember when you said you wanted one? One of your friends got to have one, and a game console, too."

"Nintendo. Man, I wanted that," he said reminiscently. "Mom said I couldn't go to Tony's house anymore."

Hearing his smugness and guessing how much time he'd undoubtedly spent there, she laughed. Ric, at least, had been allowed to run wild within the neighborhood. She'd never had that chance. Maybe she never would have, even if she'd stayed with Dad and Ric. After Mom was murdered, their father would have locked them down.

Gabby would be grateful to Aunt Isabel for the rest of her life. How could she have stayed in this house?

She pulled her wandering thoughts back. How strange it was that she could see Mom glowering at Ric, her hands planted on her hips and her eyes narrowed, and feel no more than the warmth of a memory.

Gabby went to the window and lifted the blinds to look out at the backyard. Dad used to have a vegetable garden at one end, and he'd improvised a batting cage for Ric to practice hitting. She remembered the crab apple tree, beautiful in bloom but hard on Dad's attempts to keep a lawn growing beneath it.

"The fence needs replacing," she commented.

"Yeah, yeah."

"I guess you don't garden, huh?"

He grimaced. "I try to keep up the front yard. And I mow."

The flower bed in front was currently bare, frozen earth, of course, except for the sticks of what were probably a few roses. And the climbers tied to the arbor close to the sidewalk. That almost had to have been rebuilt, it occurred to her, although of course it was unchanged from her memories.

"I'm done," she declared. "I've seen all I want to see."

"I'm sorry." His regretful dark eyes met hers. "I guess thinking you'd stay here wasn't realistic, was it?"

"Maybe if the whole house had been drastically remodeled, but I'm not even sure about that," she admitted.

"Listen, I was hoping you'd take a few hours to go through the stuff in storage with me. I've been paying for the unit ever since Dad died, and I don't even know what's in it. We can probably get rid of most of it, and I can move the rest to the garage."

"Sure, I can do that. Do you want to go this afternoon?"

"Why don't I take tomorrow off instead? I think this qualifies as a personal day."

Once they were downstairs, she averted her eyes so she didn't have to see the kitchen again. Ric insisted on stepping outside first and taking a careful look around before letting her join him. Had Jack given him basic bodyguard instructions?

Once they were in his SUV and he'd fired it up, he said, "If I decide to stay in the house, I'm having the kitchen ripped down to the studs and remodeled." He added on a burst of anger, "To hell with Dad."

She laid a hand over Ric's, white-knuckled on the steering wheel. Neither said another word about the house.

JACK HAD HOPED to spend Monday with Gabby, but this wasn't quite what he'd had in mind. For one thing, he'd envisioned the two of them together, not the three of them.

Building trust was the idea. Today's outing to the storage facility instead had him in his Tahoe, trailing a block behind Ric's vehicle, keeping adequate distance to be sure no one else was following them. Once they got there and slid open the metal door into the unit, which faced the street, his role was to stand guard, obviously armed.

Damn, he wished this had been an internal unit in one of the more modern facilities, but according to Ric, his dad had rented this one not that long after his wife's death. Storage facilities were a lot more stripped down in those days. Someone passing on the street would be able to catch a glimpse into the unit, which he didn't like.

He was dismayed to see how much was crammed in here, although it became apparent that furniture provided the bulk.

Neither Ric nor Gabby wanted to keep any of the furniture.

A black pickup truck with a canopy slowed on the street and turned into the facility. The gate slid open, which meant the driver had a code. Jack watched as it headed for a different aisle. After waiting a minute, he strolled far enough to see that it had stopped in front of a unit, and a man and woman were already unloading some apparently heavy plastic tubs to add to whatever they'd already stashed.

He shook his head and went back to his position in front of the Ortiz unit. Ric and Gabby had come up with a system by now; everything to get rid of that was too big to go in the back of Ric's SUV was being moved to one side of the unit, potential keepers to the other side.

Since they had to work their way toward the back wall, the stuff spilled out onto the concrete in front of the unit and leaned against fenders. More of a screen, letting him relax a little.

When Ric passed him carrying a scratched end table, Jack said, "You can load the back of my Tahoe, too, if you want. Why don't you put the stuff for the dump in my vehicle? I don't mind taking it."

"Thanks. That would help. I can run by the thrift store."

Gabby approaching carrying a ratty artificial Christmas tree in a torn black plastic bag. After putting it in the bed of his truck, she grinned at him. "I'm sure I speak for Ric, too, when I say that if you see anything you really like, feel free to keep it." She bumped his hip with hers and went back the way she'd come, leaving him smiling.

Things slowed down when she and her brother started opening boxes and going through the contents.

Jack felt edgy, needing to keep an eye both on the street and anyone entering the facility, but also on what Ric and Gabby were handling. Would they recognize the "evidence" Colleen had used to threaten her killer? Or had she made it up, and there never was any such thing? If it was real…what could it be?

If she'd taken a photo showing something incriminating—say, two men together who shouldn't have been—her son and daughter would undoubtedly toss it. He assumed they'd keep family photos, but ones of strangers? That was the kind of crap people left for their children to throw out.

He wanted to look at all the photos. He might recognize someone Ric wouldn't. It would be really helpful if Gabby gasped and cried, "That's him! Oh, my God, that's him!"

Jack wished he knew whether she'd seen the killer's face or not.

They worked until almost two o'clock, anxious to finish. The "keep" pile was pathetically small after two-thirds of the things their father had thought should be saved for posterity had been packed in one or the other SUV, destined respectively for the dump or the thrift store.

Jack, of course, had every intention of taking the discarded stuff home with him. He'd at least look through the boxes of smaller stuff, paper and photos. What little the brother and sister wanted to keep was to remain in storage temporarily. Ric planned to come back for it and close out the locker. It should be safe enough. Jack could ask to go through it later.

When? a voice murmured in his head. *After Gabby's gone?*

He didn't want her going anywhere.

He rode Ric's bumper on the way to a nearby café, where they took a booth and ordered.

Jack's fingers and face started tingling as the warmth penetrated. Gabby gave an exaggerated shiver. "That was fun."

"You could have come in the summer," Ric pointed out.

Her expression closed. "This was…a good time for me to take a break."

Did Ric still not know she'd quit her last job and was completely at loose ends right now? Jack started speculating on whether there might be a suitable opening at a local college. Even if a major university wouldn't hire her without the PhD, there were plenty of community colleges, both here in the Spokane area and across the border in Idaho. What if he suggested she looked?

"You know, that was actually kind of depressing," she said suddenly. "I mean, did Dad really think he was saving treasures for us?"

Ric sighed and rubbed a hand over his jaw. "No, I think with Mom gone, he just wanted a lot of stuff out of sight. Probably out of mind."

Sounding doubtful, Gabby said, "There wasn't much there that was hers that seemed personal. You know?"

"No. Well, family pictures."

"That's true." She wrinkled her nose. "Well, if he was going for the 'out of mind' goal, he wouldn't have encased the house in amber."

Her brother looked disturbed. "Maybe Dad just hated a messy garage."

"There is the basement."

Ric shook his head. "Remember that time it flooded? What little was down there got ruined."

Jack hadn't noticed a door leading to a basement, and was annoyed with himself. "Isn't the furnace down there?" he asked, as if he didn't know.

"Yeah, but it was installed on a concrete pedestal, so it was okay. The basement is only a partial, anyway. It sits under maybe half the house."

"Well, you'll have room for what you're saving in the garage, but everything that was in storage would have taken up most of it."

"Yeah, Dad never did like clutter."

Jack saw a fleeting expression on Gabby's face that cramped his chest. Sadness. Grief. Not having to do with the stuff they'd gone through today, he guessed, but with the fact that there had to be a lot about her father she'd forgotten, or never known.

Ric showed no signs of noticing. Jack increasingly thought of him as a friend—but in holding on to his anger, Ric had been more than a little insensitive to his sister's feelings.

Jack grimaced. Like he was anyone to judge, given that he'd been using and manipulating both of them. Guilt pierced him again, but he was doing this for the right reasons.

He just wished he thought Gabby would see it that way.

"When did your parents get divorced?" Gabby asked, being nosy but figuring her question wasn't unreasonable considering how much Jack knew about her life. She licked her fingers. Barbeque was messy.

Ric had claimed to have a date tonight. She didn't know whether to believe him or not. Maybe he'd just had enough of her company today. Truthfully, the tour of the house yesterday and the hours today spent sifting through the detritus of their past had been pretty intense. She was kind of glad to have a break from her brother, so she didn't blame him if he felt the same.

Of course, that left Jack stuck with asking her out, but she'd have said no if she'd gotten any vibe that he didn't actually want to spend the evening with her. He did say he'd have made dinner for them at home, except he hadn't grocery shopped all week. Red had tinged the angular line of his cheekbones when he said that, which made her wonder.

It was just as well, though. Being alone with him in his place would have challenged her ability to resist temptation. She'd have ended up in bed with him, and her deepest instincts said that this was too soon even if she wanted to disregard her fear of feeling too much for him, given that a future together was really unlikely.

Jack's eyes darkened as he watched her trying not to drip sauce down her front. More than that, a glint in those eyes told her he was aroused. Um, maybe that had to do with her licking her fingers. She grabbed a wad of napkins.

He pulled his gaze away, looked down at his own plateful of ribs, and reached for one. "Ah, I don't know if I said this, but my parents split not that long after your mom died."

"Really? Did you expect it?"

He shook his head. "I was a kid. They weren't yelling at each other, so what'd I know?" He tore meat off the bone with strong white teeth and demolished the rib in no time. His cleanup was more efficient than hers. "You know my father was briefly looked at for your mother's murder," he said abruptly.

She stared at him. "No. Once I was twenty or so, I pulled up all the articles I could find on the investigation, but there was never anything about that. I thought they'd never identified any suspects."

"I'm surprised. It was common knowledge around here. You know how people talk."

Gabby nodded. Wow, was this weird, or what? "Dad wouldn't have told me anything like that when he called. If he was more open with Aunt Isabel, she wouldn't have passed on anything he said."

"That makes sense."

"It was mostly your mother who drove the carpool, wasn't it?"

"Yeah, the only job she had was doing the bookkeeping for Dad's business. You might remember him. He had a furnace repair business. He came out to your house something like a week before your mother was killed."

She frowned. "I don't know why I remember that, but I do. He was nice. Most people got tired of my questions really fast, but he didn't." She studied him. "You look a lot like him, don't you?"

He shifted in a way that suggested discomfort. "People say so. I never think about it." He eyed her. "You don't exactly look like either of your parents."

"Maybe not my face, but obviously I got the black hair from Dad, but my eyes and lighter skin from Mom. I can see Dad when I look at Ric except he got Mom's height and, wouldn't you know, I got the short genes from Dad's side of the family." She still felt aggrieved about that. "His mother wasn't even five feet tall."

Jack obviously wanted to smile, but didn't. "How tall are you?"

She scrunched up her nose. "I claim five foot three, but my doctor says five foot two and a half."

Something about the way she said that made him laugh.

When her heart skipped a few beats, she decided to get back to the original topic of conversation.

"So, why did the police even consider your father back then? Just because he'd been at the house so recently?"

"Partly." He seemed to be watching her closely. "You described the killer as wearing all blue, too. His uniform was navy blue."

"I remember saying that."

"You don't sound so sure."

Gabby refused to give away her discomfort with body language. All she said was, "It's hazy." Except something tickled at her. She just didn't know what.

His hand closed over hers. His warmth and strength anchored her. She just hoped her hand wasn't greasy.

"Hey. I'm sorry. I wasn't trying to go there."

Wasn't he? Yet somehow he kept circling back to her mother's murder. Maybe it was the cop in him, or maybe that was just natural, given that it reared so hugely in both their memories. And then a thought struck her.

"How could the police talking to your father have anything to do with your parents breaking up?"

"I don't know how much it did. I think my mom was embarrassed by the gossip. From things he's said, there were already fractures. He's never been willing to talk about it, and neither was she." His expression closed down. "I don't have much of a relationship with my mother."

"I'm sorry." Gabby squeezed his hand, hoping she returned some of the comfort he'd offered her. "It would almost be easier to have parents break up if they'd been fighting or…or if there was abuse. Then it might be a relief instead of a shock."

He grimaced. "Maybe."

They both ate in silence for a minute. When he spoke again, it was to ask more about her aunt taking her away, and whether Gabby had had any understanding of what was happening.

As she answered, Gabby thought about how different this was from her typical dates. It felt as if they were truly opening up with each other. Sharing the experiences that made them the people they were, instead of sticking with superficialities. Of course, they'd never been strangers to each other, even though she didn't remember him ever saying a word to her when they were children. Why would he? She was just a way younger sibling. Ric probably grumbled about her to his friends. Still, they had in common a time and place…and it sounded as if her mom's murder might have had an impact on his parents' divorce. Which bothered her on some level she didn't want to think about.

It was easy to segue from talking about her stern but loving aunt to that never-ending dissertation.

Of course, at the end of the evening Jack walked her up to her room, and insisted on "clearing it" before she could do more than hover in the doorway.

"Bathroom is secure," he reported with a lopsided grin as stepped past her and allowed her to back into the room.

Her "good to know" sounded a little breathless. His eyes were intense, heated, and she knew he'd retreated into the hall to give her more choice about what happened next.

"Gabby?"

His low, husky voice played a chord low in her belly. She quivered, stepped forward and flung her arms around his neck.

Jack growled something, she had no idea what, and kissed her. One of his hands wrapped her neck, the other covered her hip and buttock so he could lift her. His tongue was in her mouth, the ridge of his erection pressed against her stomach. Gabby wanted to climb him, wrap her legs around his waist. She wanted...

He swung her in a slow circle. Her shoulder collided with the door frame, but she didn't care. She ended up plastered against the short section of wall that formed an entry to her hotel room, Jack's long, hard body pinning her. His hands roved, and she held on for dear life.

Every so often, he lifted his head to let them both breathe, the blaze of his eyes making her shudder. But this time, his gaze flicked to the side, and Gabby knew: he was looking at the bed. And, even as longing cramped low in her belly, all her qualms ignited, too.

She pushed against him, and he fell back, something like shock on his face. Had he been that sure of her?

"Good night." Not feeling coherent, the one word was the best she could manage, and there might have been a tremor in her voice.

Jack gave his head a small shake and said hoarsely, "Yeah. I'll, uh, check in tomorrow."

After closing the door, leaving him out in the hall, she couldn't remember if she'd said another word.

Chapter Ten

Jack drove home in distinct discomfort. He'd let that kiss get out of hand, partly because they'd been standing in the open doorway of Gabby's hotel room. A corner of the bed was in sight. And, damn, he knew she wanted him, too. She had tried hard to meld her body to his while he kissed her until he couldn't think about anything but her taste and her generous breasts pressed to his chest and the feel of her nicely rounded hip enclosed in his hand.

Braking now at a red light, he bumped his head against the steering wheel a couple of times. Thank God she'd come to her senses, because he had a bad feeling he'd passed the point of reason. And even though he'd never been in this position before, he strongly suspected that, while a woman could forgive a man for a lot, sleeping with her before true confessions wouldn't go over well.

I'm not lying to her. Exactly.

Good try. Every time Gabby started to open up about her mother's murder or anything related to it, he was viciously torn between not hurting her and wanting to push until her memories broke free.

He wasn't so different from the original investigators, he admitted, not liking the comparison but unable to deny it. He hoped he was more competent. Compassionate, too. He hadn't blown this by making love to a woman whose testimony he needed, but he'd come close. And he couldn't forget that those cops had been straight with her—they were police detectives interviewing her because of what she'd seen. Even a kid understood that.

Him, he was a police detective who was pretending his profession was incidental to his relationship with her. Had to be habit that had him jumping on her every time something slipped out. How many times had he apologized now?

Driving on autopilot, not so smart for anyone in law enforcement, Jack knew himself to be in deep trouble. He was seriously in danger of falling in love with a courageous, vulnerable, damaged woman who trusted him and shouldn't. A woman he'd been lying to since day one.

No, he should be glad she'd suddenly panicked and retreated into her room without inviting him to join her. Too bad his body still ached.

GABBY SHOULD HAVE been tired after Jack left—it wasn't as if she'd been sleeping well—but she wasn't. There was bound to be something on TV that could hold her attention. If not, the hotel offered a long list of current and older movies she could select from.

Latching on to the idea, she picked up the remote and started clicking through channels. She could watch hockey, football, basketball—hey, that game might actually be live—or curling. Gabby stayed on that channel for a few minutes. Men whisking brooms around on the ice held a certain fascination. Since she didn't understand what was going on, she clicked the channel button again. She lingered here and there, catching scenes from familiar movies and other ones from shows that didn't quite entice her to stick with them.

Suddenly, *Ghostbusters* popped up. Dan Aykroyd,

Bill Murray and one of the other guys whose names she didn't remember were running out of a building, garbed in their ghost-hunting getups. Gabby's heart took a sickening thud. Her hand was shaking so much, it took several seconds for her to push another button. This one turned the TV off.

She stared at the dark screen as if it were a window behind which a monster had showed its face. Ridiculous, but she'd never been able to watch any of the *Ghostbusters* movies once she was old enough to appreciate them. Ric had had the original two on video and thought they were the best. He frequently had one or the other on when she wanted to watch something different, or was playing in the living room while he watched. She'd been way too young to appreciate the movies, but they were still embedded in her brain. She pictured her mother rolling her eyes and saying, "Not that again! For heaven's sake, turn it off!"

So why did the very idea of *Ghostbusters* disturb her so much? And why hadn't she ever asked herself that question? She'd just…shied away.

It wasn't the actors, she was confident about that, or even the story lines. The whole idea was clever. And ghosts…she didn't believe in those. As awful as visiting the house had been, Mom hadn't been lingering.

So, what?

Confronting her disquiet directly for the first time, Gabby knew the answer almost instantly. It was the marshmallow man. Pulse racing, she opened her laptop case and went online, querying *Ghostbusters*. There he was, the eerily friendly-looking white monster striding down the street, towering over the people.

Just as he'd towered over her.

Teeth clenched tight, she closed the laptop. The Stay

Puft Marshmallow Man had murdered her mother. No, of course not—but her childish mind had related the killer to the movie visual. Gabby closed her eyes. White, loose fabric, covering the head, too. Gloves, there must have been gloves, and foot coverings.

In her nightmare, blood had dripped from a white elbow.

Wow. It seemed clear as day suddenly. That made her wonder if she could be manufacturing a memory, but she knew she wasn't. And she finally understood why she'd immediately clicked away from any news coverage during the pandemic showing medical personnel and body recovery workers wearing protective suits. She'd been annoyed by her own squeamishness without questioning the reason for it.

Her nightmares had diminished as the years went on, and they had always varied. Sometimes, all she could recall was blood, or her mother's face or the smell of the dirty clothes forming the cocoon that saved her life. The memory of the puffy white getup had obviously lurked in her subconscious, but maybe it was the most recent nightmares that made it resurface.

Her first instinct was to call Jack. Gabby actually looked around for her phone before realizing how late it was. He might still be up…but, really, telling him could wait. It wasn't like she could describe the killer, or suddenly remembered her mother exclaiming, "John Smith, why are you here?" This memory was another piece to the picture, that was all.

It wasn't like Jack was investigating the crime, but she gathered he did work on homicides. He could surely make note of what she'd recalled, in case any other information ever surfaced. Although actually…in a way he *was* on the case, considering the possible attempts on her life.

He was certainly determined to keep her alive, and the best way to do that was to identify her mother's murderer.

Or for her to fly back East and never visit Leclaire again, she supposed, oddly depressed by the idea. Ric would come visit her, she felt sure. Their relationship had come at least that far. But Jack…what if she never saw him again?

Oh, even thinking that was ridiculous. It wasn't much over a week ago that they'd met. No surprise, he was still largely a mystery to her. He had a lot locked down tight, she suspected. Of course, he wasn't alone in that, but circumstances had forced her to reveal more of herself to him and to her brother than she ever had to anyone before.

And that probably explained why she was starting to remember the few horrific minutes that had changed her life forever.

"WELL, NEITHER OF my kids was the same age as Colleen," Annette Davis told Jack. A pleasant-looking, slim woman who appeared younger than her sixty-five years, she hadn't bothered dyeing her short dark hair, which was attractively streaked with silver.

He'd called ahead to ask if she had time to speak to him. While they were still on the porch, she pointed out the house where Colleen's parents had lived.

"They retired to Arizona." Leading the way into the living room of the nice rambler, she shook her head. "They were both killed in an awful head-on collision on the highway not that much later. Gabrielle would have been only two or three."

When she offered him a cup of coffee, he accepted. If he ever knew, he'd forgotten what had happened to Gabby's maternal grandparents. She hadn't mentioned them. Probably didn't remember them at all. Isabel, he seemed to recall Ric saying, was a sister to this grand-mother who'd died so unexpectedly.

Gabby's family had suffered too much tragedy.

When Annette returned, he got her talking about the family next-door and Colleen in particular. She was such a nice girl, of course, but he had the sense that Annette really meant it.

"A good Catholic girl," she added. "Our families be-longed to the same church. Dolly and I served on the altar guild together, and put together dozens of potlucks over the years. My Matthew was an altar boy. Colleen sang in the choir her last few years of high school. She had the loveliest voice! I know she was active with the youth group, too. That girl never ran wild. Why, Russ and I had far more trouble with our daughter, although thank the good Lord she's happily married now, with three youngsters of her own."

"Colleen was an only child?"

"Yes, her parents doted on her, but she never acted as if she'd been spoiled."

It took her some effort, but she came up with the names of a couple of girls she remembered Colleen run-ning around with. Both families had worshipped at St. Stephen's. Annette's still did.

"Of course Colleen brought her family there, too, and Raul continued to bring Ric." Sadness softened this nice woman's face. "Ric had his father buried in the church-yard, right next to his mother, but like so many young people, his attendance at services dropped off as time passed. I hope he makes his way back." Her expression brightened. "Has he married?"

"No." Jack didn't see how it would hurt to tell An-nette about Gabby so he did. She grew teary at the idea of little Gabby home again.

"Having something so appalling happen to Colleen shocked everyone. Some of us who knew her still talk about it."

Jack had a thought. "I don't suppose the priest Colleen would have known is still at St. Stephen's."

"Oh, heavens no! We've had several changes. Father Ambrose was transferred… Oh, let me think." She pondered. "Matthew was in college, so Colleen would have been seventeen or eighteen, I think. We all missed him so much. His place was taken by Father Paul, who was also gone by the time Colleen died. We had Father Michael after that. He only retired a few years ago." Suddenly she blushed and pressed her hands to her cheeks. "I'm sure that was far more than you wanted to know! Gracious, you should have stopped me."

"No, I'm interested," he said, honestly. "A priest she trusted might be someone Colleen would go to if something was troubling her."

"That's true, although she wouldn't confess unless she felt she'd done something wrong."

He thought, but didn't say, *Maybe she did.* Maybe she had an affair. Maybe she'd just flirted when a good Catholic girl—or woman—shouldn't have. Slipped out at night without her parents knowing.

Except her killer didn't rape her, making it unlikely his motivation was sexual.

Having considered the possibility that the relationship between the killer and Colleen had dated back to her teenage years, he asked whether Annette knew if Colleen had had any boyfriends in high school.

"No boyfriends, as far as I know. I think Dolly would have said. Colleen had this one stretch—I want to say her sophomore year—when she suddenly started wearing more makeup and, well, revealing clothes. You know. She and her mother had more than a few clashes, although I thought Dolly was overreacting." She shook her head. "It almost had to be a boy, don't you think? By that summer, she'd changed again. No more silliness. She seemed more mature after that. Quieter, more service oriented."

Or was she wary? Nervous around boys? Or had the desire to be of service to others been a way of atoning for what she'd viewed as a mistake? Could there have been a pregnancy and abortion? If she'd taken that route, she might well not have told her parents if she could have gotten away with it, but might have confessed to her priest.

Yet none of that explained the boy growing into a man who'd hated Colleen enough to murder her so brutally.

He could only hope what few school friends of Colleen's he'd been able to identify would be as helpful as this woman—and that Colleen had confided any problems she'd had then with boys. Or men, for that matter.

He'd been following other threads, but none that seemed very promising. Two men the original investigators had identified as friends or even just acquaintances of Raul and Colleen had caught Jack's attention. Both had the kind of job that required them to wear uniforms. One repaired washers and dryers for Sears. He'd serviced appliances twice at the Ortiz house in the year and a half before the murder. The other was then a security guard at a manufacturing plant in Leclaire.

The security guard especially interested him. The man had changed jobs several times in the years before the murder. The detectives who interviewed Royce Tilman had no way of knowing that he'd be accused of rape a couple of years after Colleen's death. He'd been arrested, but prosecutors didn't feel they had enough evidence to bring him to trial. Not surprisingly, he was fired from his job.

The only thing was, his wife had stuck by him, and they'd moved out of the area. They'd gone to Bellingham, in western Washington, and stayed there for ten years. Royce had been steadily employed for those years.

That's when Jack lost him. They had to have moved out of state. Monday he'd call the employer in Bellingham and find out if, when he was resigning, he'd told them where he was going.

Sitting in his vehicle, wishing the heat would crank up faster, Jack made another couple of phone calls in an attempt to locate Tilman. Both were futile.

Colleen's friends next, he decided, then a coworker from the year she'd worked as a nurse before her marriage.

CONVERSATION LAPSED BRIEFLY while Gabby and Jack dug into their entrées. Tonight was Thai again, starting with fried spring rolls, one of her favorite foods. So far, neither had said anything about that kiss.

After a few bites of her red curry, Gabby gathered her resolve and laid down her fork. "Something happened last night."

Jack's gaze acquired an intensity it hadn't had a second ago. "What?"

She told him about channel surfing, and how she'd happened on one of the *Ghostbusters* movies, then how it tied to her nightmare and ultimately to her memory.

"So that's why—" He shook his head.

"Why?"

"I've gathered you didn't see his face."

"I was looking at his back when he killed Mom." How calm she sounded. "The only thing is..." Oh, why say this?

He waited with his usual patience, until she finally

admitted, "Lately, a couple of times in nightmares he's suddenly looked at me. I'm not…really seeing a face, but…" She shook herself. "It's probably symbolic of my fear that he'd see me."

"Probably." Jack said that more thoughtfully than she liked, but he must have learned to be dispassionate on the job. Then he studied her face, the lines deepening on his. "Why don't we talk about something else until we're done eating. Then…will you tell me everything you do remember? Maybe we can put it together into something that makes sense."

Her heart tripped a few times. She told herself gathering her courage to tell him the one recollection wasn't the same as immersing herself in the real nightmare. Plus, she thought she was ready. She appreciated the kindness she heard in his voice and the efforts he'd made to protect her, and by good fortune, he was a detective.

Gabby nodded. "Okay."

He did shift the conversation, asking whether her aunt had been a churchgoer, saying his mom had dragged him and his sister to church—in their case, Presbyterian— every Sunday, but after the divorce, his attendance had lapsed along with his father's.

Aunt Isabel had been Catholic as well, but Gabby hadn't stayed faithful any more than he had.

"I suppose it's hard to believe, doing the job you do," she commented.

He grimaced. "It is. Not impossible, but when you see something really bad, you have to ask why. When you don't get an answer—" He lifted one shoulder.

"Yet our instinct when we're scared is to pray."

"Because we want to be bailed out. Is that real faith?"

They argued amicably about the unanswerable question, then talked about friends who'd made drastically different life choices than they had. Once again, Gabby thought how different her conversations with Jack were than what she was used to on dates.

After their plates had been removed and they were sipping coffee, he said, "Would you consider inviting me to your room to talk? Or coming back to my place?" His expression was grave, and she knew he wasn't thinking about sex.

She nodded. "The hotel is closer."

"Okay."

In fact, they'd walked the several blocks to the restaurant, Jack staying on the curbside, his gaze constantly roving. He'd been so obviously in bodyguard mode, she hadn't even tried to start a conversation.

It was the same as they walked back to the hotel. Plenty of people were still out and about, which meant he frequently put a hand on her back and edged her out of the way of other pedestrians. She remembered what Ric said about Jack having eyes in the back of his head, and that had never seemed more true than tonight. He knew when people approached or came out of open doorways, even behind them, and screened her with his body when cars passed.

The reminder that there was a good reason for him to be so cautious wasn't exactly soothing, even if she was grateful for it. Then there was her agreement to let him interview her in a way that hadn't happened since her traumatic experiences as a little girl. By the time they passed through the hotel lobby and got into an elevator, Gabby felt sure a doctor reading her blood pressure right now would insist on medication.

But during that silent ride up in the elevator, she stiffened her spine enough to add that extra half inch to her height, and determined that she was going through with this. The time was right, and this man was right.

Chapter Eleven

He couldn't believe this was actually happening. He had to caution himself that she might not remember anything significant.

Jack moved restlessly around her room, peered into the bathroom to ensure it was empty and closed the drapes while Gabby waited, stock-still, in the middle of the room. She still clutched her handbag. Only her head turned to allow her to watch him.

He'd expected her to be nervous, but scared to death wouldn't help.

"Hey." He took the bag from her hand and dropped it on a table. Then he summoned a wicked grin, not hard considering his exhilaration. "You need to get comfortable before we start our session. I'd suggest you change clothes, preferably into something less confining. Say, a lacy negligee. Then you can stretch out on my couch." He waggled his eyebrows as he nodded toward the queen-size bed.

That broke the spell. She shook her head, rolled her eyes and laughed, if huskily. "Forget the couch. I do think I'll change clothes, though, if you don't mind waiting."

"Not at all." He planted himself in one of the room's pair of easy chairs. Waiting five minutes was no problem; he'd already waited fifteen years or more for this opportunity. Longer than that, of course, if he were to include the years before he started college with a single goal: arresting the man he'd blamed for shattering his father's life.

Gabby grabbed a few things from her suitcase that lay open on a luggage rack in the closet, then disappeared into the bathroom.

His mood strange, Jack thought about the most recent call with his father. Had he blinded himself all these years to the truth, that his parents' divorce had little to do with the brief police interest in Dad? That while there were things his mother had always refused to tell him, his father was hiding plenty, too?

Gabby had become more of a priority than he'd expected, too, and he truly believed that she needed to know her mother's killer was behind bars, that she herself would be safe. She needed to let go of guilt, to be able to release those horrific memories so they were out in the open instead of taunting her from the shadows.

The toilet flushed behind the closed bathroom door, and a moment later water ran.

Damn. Should he tell her now that he was already deep into a cold case investigation of her mother's murder?

But enough of his exhilaration lingered to make him balk. No, that wasn't all of it—but in telling her, he'd be taking a significant risk that she'd refuse to talk to him. She'd be mad, he felt confident of that. If she decided not to trust him...

He swore under his breath.

If he went ahead with this, he was very possibly ruling out any chance that she'd ever trust him again. He could be throwing away any hope of getting this woman who'd made him feel so much, so fast, into bed. But he'd be a fool to let this chance go by, he told himself grimly. If she couldn't understand why he'd made the decisions he'd had, then what kind of relationship would it be, anyway?

The bathroom door opened and she appeared, expression tentative. His body clenched at the sight of her in pajamas, even if they were the furthest thing from sexy. Still, beneath those flannel pants and thin knit T-shirt, she had to be naked. The movement of her generous breasts beneath that top as she walked toward him had his fingers flexing.

Too quick, she was past him and on the bed. Sitting back against the pile of pillows at the headboard, legs crossed, she clutched a pillow from the other side of the bed to herself, hiding her magnificent breasts.

He had to order himself to breathe. It was just as well she'd assumed such an obviously defensive posture. She wasn't trying to be seductive. In fact, between the pretzel she'd formed with her entwined legs and the way she hugged that pillow to herself, he was unpleasantly reminded of the little girl whose timid voice he'd heard on those damn tapes.

He forced a grin. "You followed my advice."

"It…seemed to make sense."

After a brief hesitation, Jack crossed the room and gestured toward a spot at the foot of the bed. "Okay if I sit there?"

"What? Oh, sure."

The mattress shifted under his weight, but he was a safe distance from her. "How do you want to do this?" he asked her. "I'll ask questions if you want, or you can close your eyes and tell me what you remember in order. Or what your nightmares are suggesting you remember."

Her beautiful eyes met his. "I…that might be best."

He pressed the heel of his hand against his breastbone in hopes of easing the unexpected ache.

"Well," she said. "Um, here goes."

INSTEAD OF CLOSING her eyes, she lowered her gaze to be sure she wasn't sucked into Jack's force field. For the first time in a very long while, she dragged herself back to that morning.

"My mother let me run through the sprinkler," Gabby told him. "She said I had to turn off the water before I came in, so I did. Only, I didn't take a towel outside, so when I came in I was dripping."

Dripping. Oh, God.

She corrected herself hastily. "I left wet footprints. Mom said to go to the laundry room and strip. There'd be towels in the dirty clothes basket I could use to dry myself before I went upstairs to change."

Beginning before the intruder appeared seemed to be helping. It was as if, once the reel had started, it didn't stop running. "That's where I was, when I heard the back door open again. Mommy said, 'Ric? Is that you?' Then…then…" Gabby swallowed. "She said, 'What are *you* doing here?'"

When she froze up, Jack asked gently, "Could you see him?"

"Uh-uh. Only Mommy." Vaguely, she knew how childish she sounded, but that's who was telling this story: the little girl she'd been. "She looked scared, like the time I crossed the street when I wasn't supposed to, and for a minute she didn't see me in the yard." She frowned. "I think that's when I crouched down behind the laundry basket. Mommy being scared made me want to hide."

"Good call." Jack's soft murmur barely touched her.

"Mommy backed up until she bumped into the island in the kitchen." Now Gabby closed her eyes as she strained to *see*. "She sort of shuffled sideways, like she was trying to go around it."

"How are you seeing this?"

"I'm peeking over the top of the laundry basket. She's yelling at him. I don't know what she's saying." She squeezed her eyes shut even harder, trying to pull herself back from *being* the child again. Failing. "Then he's in the way. All I can see is his back, but he's like the scary monster in *Ghostbusters*. He's so big! And…and he has something in his hand. Mommy is yelling about how she won't tell, she promises, and he says, 'Now I know you won't.'"

Lord. She was shaking, her teeth chattering, just like they probably were then. He could so easily have heard. The mattress compressed a little, and somehow she knew Jack had moved even before he wrapped an arm around her.

That warmth helped settle her. *It's all over. I'm not that little girl anymore. I never will be again.*

"She kept screaming," Gabby said dully, "and he yelled, 'You ruined my life.' Over and over. He lifted his arm and brought it down, over and over. Blood sprayed. I didn't know that's what it was, I just saw red. Red ran all over the floor. In my dream, it looked like veins in the human body, except it was blood that *wasn't* in a human body anymore. I…got so scared I pulled a pile of dirty sheets over me." Green sheets, which meant they were from Ric's bed. How odd. If someone had asked, she wouldn't have been able to tell them. "But it got quiet, so I peeked. My mother was just lying there, but her face was *wrong*, like she smashed it in spaghetti sauce. I couldn't really see *him*, but I knew he was still there. I think he turned on the water in the kitchen sink. I don't know what he was doing." She sounded robotic now, not like child Gabby or adult Gabby. "Then…he walked toward me. He had a full plastic trash bag in his arms. I had this moment of wondering if he was taking the garbage out. That was supposed to be Ric's job."

Abruptly, she realized she was wheezing. The safe distance wasn't working anymore. She pressed her face into Jack's chest and felt him lay his cheek on her head. He was saying something that sounded urgent, but she couldn't make it out.

Horror held her in a terrible grip. "He looked right at me. I never moved, and…and he walked by. That's when he was dressed in blue."

"Jeans?"

She did hear that. "No. I think they were like uniform pants. Navy blue. His shoes were black and shiny. Dad used to let me help shine his. These were like that."

"Bigger than your dad's?"

After a minute, she said, "Yes. Lots bigger."

"Did he go out the back door?"

"I don't know," she had to say again. "I guess he must have. I just…made myself small, wrapped in sheets and thought, *He can't see me. He can't.*"

"All right." Jack sounded angry. "That's enough, Gabby. Do you hear me?" He pushed her away enough to lift her chin with one of his hands. "No more."

"He can't see me," she whispered. "He can't."

"No. Damn it, he didn't see you!"

If he had, she'd be dead. Gabby had always known that.

But I *must have seen him,* she understood in horror. And *that's* why he wanted her dead.

Panting, she stared at Jack. "What if I told the police that I saw him look right at me? If I did—"

"You didn't," he said sharply. "Anyway, how would he know what you told them?"

"But if I didn't, why did he try to kill me back then?" she begged. "And why does he still think he has to kill me?"

"Because there's a risk you did see him. He must have heard there was a child witness. Even if you didn't see his face," Jack's voice slowed, "there might have been something else about him that would point investigators his way."

"Like him wearing blue."

"Yes, but that wasn't as much help as it could have been, because blue uniforms are fairly common in the service industry, and he might have happened to wear blue chinos with a chambray shirt."

"No."

He tipped his head. "No?"

Gabby scrambled. *Why did I say that?* Because…she could picture that much. "Chambray is usually a lighter shade of blue. I think his pants and shirt matched exactly."

"So we're back to a uniform. You said navy blue."

She nodded cautiously. "Is that the color of your dad's uniform?"

His mouth compressed and he nodded.

"Did he wear shiny black shoes?"

Jack stared at her for a long moment. "No. Work boots. He had to protect his feet from dropping something heavy on them. Shiny sounds like…"

"Dress shoes," she supplied. "Only…" She tried really hard to arrow in on that one specific detail. "I don't know," she said finally. "I can't quite see it."

His expression became calculating in a way that bothered her, but what had she expected? He was a cop. What a coup it would be for him if he could actually arrest her mother's murderer.

"He looked right at you."

She bit her lip. "At the pile of dirty clothes in front of the washer."

"If you know that, you must have seen his face."

Inexplicable panic rose in her. "I didn't really. I don't remember."

"Okay, sweetheart." His hands swept up and down her nearly bare arms. Did she actually have goose bumps? "Let's try it another way. Did he have a beard?"

"No." *How do I know that, if I didn't see his face?* But she was sure. Nobody in the neighborhood had a beard. A few of father's friends had moustaches. She'd have noticed anything like that.

"Was he blond?"

"I don't know."

"Dark haired?"

She shook her head and kept shaking it.

"Isn't hair color one of the first identifiers we notice about people?"

She opened her mouth to say, *I don't know,* but shut it.

"Was his face blurry?"

"Blurry?" And then she got it. "Like in movies when a bank robber wears pantyhose over his head."

"Right."

"I don't think so. I just think his head sort of turned toward me but I couldn't see that much of his face."

"Because your peephole was so small?"

"No...yes." Then words came from her mouth before she could analyze them. "He had on a hat."

The triumph on Jack's face disturbed her as much as the way he kept rapping out questions. Fast, inexorable. "A fedora?"

"You mean, like the man on the hotel tape wore?"

"Yeah."

Gabby frowned. "I don't think so."

"But it had a brim to shadow his face."

She nodded, because it must have.

"Baseball cap?"

She didn't even know why she hesitated, but that didn't seem quite right. The trouble was, her four-year-old self thought only *hat*. At that age, she had no idea what a fedora was or how to describe it, never mind a newsboy cap or—

Her mind shut down. All she could see was the glint of eyes beneath a brim. When she shook her head, Jack studied her, then tucked her close to his body again.

"It'll come to you," he said softly.

"I wish I could remember everything *now*. Get it over with." Something an awful lot like grief seized her in sharp teeth. This was twenty-five years too late, but she'd just seen her mother murdered again, and this time she'd understood what she was seeing.

She grabbed a handful of the Jack's collar and pressed her face harder into that solid chest. *I won't cry, I won't cry.* But of course she did. Not long, but when her body quit shaking, she felt drained, empty.

She hadn't known Jack had shifted her over on the bed and now sat where she'd been, his back against the cushioned headboard, his legs stretched out. Both of her arms wrapped his torso, and now she had his sweater in back squeezed in a fist.

"Your sweater is cashmere, isn't it?" she mumbled after a minute.

"Ah—I don't know. It was a Christmas present from my mother a few years back. I don't wear it very often because it has to be dry-cleaned, but I wanted to impress you. Did it?"

She gurgled a laugh. "Yes, except now I've cried all over it. There's probably a little snot mixed in."

His chest shook with a husky laugh. "That's what dry cleaners are for."

She kept lying against him, feeling no urgency to move. In fact, she drifted, thinking about, oh, small, immediate things. Sensations and textures. The deep blue of the cashmere was perfect with Jack's eyes. His mother had good taste, she thought dreamily. It was incredibly soft beneath her cheek, too.

Blue—no, she didn't want to think about colors anymore, except Jack did have beautiful eyes. After a bit, she began to wish the layer of cashmere wasn't between her and his broad, powerful chest. She could see brown hair curling at the neck opening. She could lift herself a little bit and kiss him there, on that hollow at the base of his throat.

Somehow, Gabby wasn't nearly as relaxed as she'd been. She was tempted to squirm even closer than she already was. She could pretend she was just trying to get more comfortable…

He hadn't moved in a couple of minutes, she realized suddenly. She'd swear his heartbeat had picked up. Was he breathing at all? She stole a peek and that's when she saw a ridge beneath the zipper placket of his chinos.

This was why she'd resisted inviting him into her room.

DAMN, HE'D HOPED she wouldn't look down. This was the worst of times for him to get so obviously aroused. Gabby had just been through another traumatic experience, had cried on him and was pulling herself together. And him?

He couldn't stop thinking about the curvaceous body he held in his arms.

Then a small, husky voice said, "Will you make love with me?"

Jack froze. Did she mean that? He gritted his teeth as his need for her surged. His brain didn't seem to want to work. He was already kneading her hip, his other hand making circles on her belly, easing upward toward her breasts.

"You're sure?" His voice had gone guttural.

"Yes." Gabby tipped her face up. Her even white teeth nibbled on her full lower lip. "I don't want to be a coward anymore."

With a groan, he twisted so that he could kiss her. He had her flat on her back in seconds, his body half covering hers. Her breast overflowed his hand, just firm enough to make him think of ripe fruit. The taut bud pressed against his palm. He wanted to see her, all of her, which meant backing off and stripping her, but from the moment he had set eyes on her, he'd also wanted to free her glossy black hair from the braid. It wouldn't hurt if he could rip his own clothes off, too. At least he had a condom; he'd carried a couple around since meeting her.

She tried to tangle her fingers in his hair, but it was too short to cooperate. He didn't mind her pulling it.

Feeling her struggle beneath him, he dragged his mouth from hers, only to realize she was trying to tug his sweater off. He cooperated and yanked the T-shirt over her head while they were at it. Then, when he saw the ripe swell of her breasts and the taut nipples, he lost it.

What reason he'd retained went AWOL. Forget his shirt, he was already suckling one breast while he reached beneath the elastic waistband of her pajama pants and slid his fingers along the slick passage between her folds.

Whimpering, she arched upward, lifting her breast to his mouth, her fingernails biting into his shoulders.

He kissed and suckled her breasts, returning every few minutes to her mouth. There was so much he wanted to do to her, with her, but he became increasingly desperate.

When he yanked down her pants, she squeezed him through the fabric of his trousers. His hips responded eagerly even as he struggled to get her naked. Once she became determined enough to start unzipping his slacks, Jack took over. Boots first, socks, then pants. *No, don't toss them. Have to keep my wallet.* He pulled out the two packets and had no idea what became of his wallet after that. Getting the condom on while he kissed her was a challenge. Then he explored her slick flesh with his fingers, said, "I need you," and parted her thighs.

"Yes. Please. Please, please," she chanted as he found her entrance and forged his way inside, going deep.

For one moment, suspended above her, he drank in the sight of her gorgeous face, lips parted, dazed green-gold eyes focused on his. And then he pulled back, drove deep again, and kept doing it as she pushed to meet every thrust, kept saying his name, wrapped one leg over his hip while the other foot stayed planted on the bed to give her leverage. It was madness, it was pleasure, it was frighteningly new. When her convulsions started and she made a sound he'd never forget, Jack let himself go.

Chapter Twelve

Gabby felt drunk, but in a good way. It was like becoming weightless at the same time as she reveled in *his* weight on her. When he stirred, her arms tightened. She didn't want to let him go.

"I'm crushing you," he mumbled.

"Uh-uh."

Of course, superior muscle mass meant he had his way. She grumbled after he rolled off until he rearranged her to sprawl half-atop him. With her head on that wide, powerful shoulder, she could study the curly hair on his chest, brown to match the hair on his head. She turned her head enough to kiss his taut, salty skin before settling down dreamily. Either she was hearing her own heartbeat, or that was his. Or maybe they'd synced to beat in time. Could that happen?

She drifted, her entire body tingling. Her toes kept curling. Why had she bothered resisting Jack? But she knew the answer, she'd already told him. They hadn't known each other much more than a week. Physical risks didn't scare her as much as emotional ones. She'd lost too many people in her life already and had shaped her decisions to avoid any more losses on that scale.

Right now, she felt too good to stiffen even as darkness began to tinge her thoughts.

He lifted his head from the pillow, distracting her, and gave her the single, sexiest smile she'd ever seen. "Your hair."

"What?"

The hand that had been stroking her back lifted her braid. The next thing she knew, he'd peeled off the elastic and was concentrating on freeing her hair from the tight confinement. Once the annoyingly thick black mass fell loose over her back and face and shoulders, he told her how beautiful it was as he ran his fingers through the waves left from the braid. The intense concentration and happiness on his face made her glow inside.

But amazing as she felt physically, awareness of her internal bruises awakened. Had she really remembered everything for all these years?

Yes and no, she decided. More memories had been waiting for her to call them up than she'd guessed, but her recent nightmares and coming home to Leclaire, even seeing the house, had stirred the bits and pieces she'd been missing. On a guilty pang, she wondered if she'd been able to tell this much to detectives at the time, would they have been able to find her mother's murderer?

She'd been too young to think like that. It had been days before she'd managed more than a few hysterical words. She'd curled her body as tight as she could make it most of the time, usually in bed under her covers just as she had beneath those sheets. *He can't see me. He can't.* She'd secretly started sucking her thumb at night, when no one would see her. Her father had had to haul her out for meals and when he couldn't stand knowing that's all she was doing.

The police... She couldn't remember their exact questions, but a few stuck out. The detectives had jumped around, as if they were trying to trick her into answering instead of patiently coaxing a child's narrative. They'd scared her, all three of those men. They weren't dressed like the other people at the police station, but she could see their badges and guns and hear their impatience.

Truthfully, Gabby didn't remember what she *had* told them. Obviously, that the killer had worn what looked like a blue uniform when he walked out, or else Jack's father wouldn't have been a suspect. Otherwise, she suspected she'd been huddling inside herself even when she was in a conference room or sitting on a chair in the hotel room being interviewed.

Why hadn't she told anyone the killer had been puffy and white when he appeared? Was she afraid it sounded too silly to say, "He was the marshmallow man"?

Her happy glow diminished further when she thought about Jack's relentless string of questions. *Was he blond? Did he have a beard? Blurry? Baseball cap?* And the hardness in his voice when he said, *If you know that, you must have seen his face.*

He's a cop, she reminded herself. Jumping in to question a witness must be second nature to him. Which meant she had been a witness in his mind until they finished and he regained awareness of her as a woman. He was a far more skilled interviewer than the ones who'd terrified her as a child, able to soften his tone and encourage her when that was what she needed, ask that sharp question when he sensed the answer was surfacing in her head.

And he hadn't backed off when she became distressed. *If you know that, you must have seen his face.*

Something he'd said had jarred her at the time. Gabby fought to separate it from all the rest. It didn't help that she was still reveling in cuddling with him, bare skin to bare skin, or relishing the sensations as his hands continued to wander from one sensitive spot to another. She could easily become aroused again if she weren't also bugged by what had come before.

Then it slipped into place. She'd been near frantic when she said, *What if I told the police that I saw him look right at me? If I did—*

And he said, *You didn't.*

How did he know she hadn't? Did he know more than usual about the investigation just because it had involved his father? Or had he gone digging when he first joined the police force, or more recently when the odd things started happening after she arrived in Leclaire? If so, why hadn't he told her? Wouldn't it have made sense for him to say, "I went looking for some background, and here are some things I learned"?

Yes.

Earlier, there'd been another thing. She'd explained about the marshmallow man, and Jack had said, *So that's why—*, then broken off.

He claimed he was thinking that's why she hadn't seen the killer's face, but he already knew she had seen the man when he wasn't wearing what she now guessed was a Tyvek suit.

So what had he meant?

JACK WAS REELING from a combination of the best sex of his life and Gabby's extraordinarily detailed testimony about her mother's murder. If the then-detectives hadn't been such fools, they might have gotten somewhere. He'd known some of the answers were in her head, but he was still stunned at how she'd woven the child's view with details her nightmares had helped her unlock. No, she hadn't identified the killer, but he had a feeling there was more yet lurking in her head. Even if she couldn't describe the man's face, she'd seen it. If she met up with him now, would her subconscious know him?

And that hat. He bet her adult self was already thinking, *Hmm. A four-year-old wouldn't know what kind of hat he wore, but I do.*

Jack hoped like hell that would happen, because he had a bad feeling about the hat, the navy blue uniform, the shiny black shoes that weren't typical dress shoes. Say they were more substantial, had a thicker sole that allowed for action.

He'd worn a uniform like that for seven years before he'd been promoted. There were plenty of workers in other professions that used protective suits, but they'd be readily available to a law enforcement officer.

"You…seem really invested in finding out what I remembered," she said suddenly.

Oh, hell. He turned his head on the pillow, but couldn't see her face well enough to read it.

"I'm worried about you," he said after a minute.

"Are you?"

He jackknifed to a sitting position, which sent her tumbling off him and scrambling to sit up herself. Worse yet, she clutched the sheet and bedspread to cover herself. "What does that mean? You don't think I give a damn if a cold-blooded killer runs you down on an icy street or murders you in your hotel room?"

She laid a hand on his arm and squeezed. "That's not true. I know you do. You wouldn't be in law enforcement if you didn't care. That…has to be a big part of your personality."

"You're saying I don't care about you personally."

This, when he'd realized just tonight what had been happening to him since he'd gotten to know her. His priorities had done more than shift. They'd tumbled on end.

His father didn't need him to be able to proclaim to the world, *See? You were wrong to suspect him for a second!* Even if Colleen Ortiz's murder had impacted his parents' relationship, they'd both moved on. He alone had stayed fixated on a single goal: arresting her killer. He still wanted to accomplish that, but only for Gabby. To give her answers, to free her from her fears, to stop a murderous bastard from killing *her*.

What he cared most about now was Gabby.

"I've gotten a funny feeling about you a few times." She sounded unnervingly thoughtful, but he heard the underlying distress, too.

He could keep lying to her. Tell her he'd gone digging in the files because of what had been happening to her and at the house. She'd believe him. But what if they had a chance at a future together? What if she ever found out the truth?

And could he go on with this kind of lie between them?

No. He'd known all along that he couldn't, that it would come to this. What he had to do was make her understand that she'd been an abstraction before he met her, but that everything had changed since.

Jack let out a long breath. "I've told you my father was a suspect."

Wary eyes watched him.

"What I didn't say is that a lot of people kept suspecting he really had killed your mother. The police couldn't prove he'd done it...but he was the only suspect they'd come up with. If there's smoke, there has to be fire, right?"

Gabby still didn't say anything.

"Things changed then between my parents. I still don't know if Mom believed for a minute that Dad would do something like that, or if she was embarrassed because she knew what other people were thinking, or—"

Wandering from the point.

"I grew up thinking my family would have stayed together if the cops had arrested the killer, that I wouldn't have lost my mother and sister, that Dad wouldn't have finally had to move away, too. I became a cop so *I* could arrest that monster."

"That's why you stayed in Leclaire," she said slowly. "Why you became a detective."

"Yeah. The job…suits me," he admitted. "It's not like I've been hunting your mother's killer night and day since I joined the force."

Even more slowly, she said, "Just since I came back to town."

True confessions. Damn. He wished he'd gotten dressed before they started this. What would she think if he reached for his pants?

"When I made detective," he said, "I read about your mom's murder, what I could without having to get permission. The only solid tie I had to those days was Ric, but we'd mostly gone our own ways. I wanted to keep in touch, so I changed health clubs so I'd run into him now and again."

"He doesn't know that, I assume."

"No."

Jack had the unnerving feeling she was watching him the way she might a student taking a test whom she suspected of cheating.

"He told you about my visit."

"He did. We'd…talked about you now and again." He moved his shoulders uncomfortably. "Because we had a history. He…kept me up to date."

"That's why you came to dinner that first evening.

Ric and I had already quarreled and you didn't want me to get away."

"It was more complicated than that."

She let out a disbelieving laugh. "Sure it was. That's why you asked me out the next evening, and every time since then. If I hadn't asked you to make love to me— no, to have sex with me—we wouldn't be in this bed right now, would we? I suppose you have enough sense of honor to think it was wrong to go quite this far to wring an interview out of me." Her voice could have etched glass.

"You have to know I was attracted to you from the beginning." He sounded as desperate as he felt. "I knew I had to tell you the truth before I made love to you or talked about where we can take this relationship. Yes, I wanted your trust, but I'd never have—"

"And yet you did." The pain in her eyes ripped him open. "I suppose I should give you some credit. Your goal was estimable. But you could have done this entirely differently. The irony is that I hoped to recover my memories when I came home. Once I worked through my instinctive panic, I'd have been glad to talk to you. Instead, you've left me feeling dirty and ashamed that I was too stupid to realize how obvious you were. Of course I'm the most beautiful woman ever, and you can't stay away." Her laugh was razor sharp. "Congratulations. You're good at your job. I have nothing more to contribute, so I'm asking you to go now."

"Gabby, damn it, listen to me! I shouldn't have let it get this far, but the way I feel about you is tangled up with my…quest." There was that damn word again. "Ric kept saying you refused to even talk about it, and I told myself you needed your mother's murder to be solved, too, that it had to have haunted you—"

She shook her head hard. Once. "Get out. I'll call the front desk if you don't leave right now."

"I know this is too soon, but I've been falling in love with you."

This laugh was worse. He didn't know why he wasn't bleeding. Jack managed to say, "I'm sorry."

In shock, he located his clothes and wallet. He got dressed, shoved his feet in his boots and looked around for his coat. At last he turned to face her and had the horrifying realization that she was holding herself together the same way she probably had as a child.

And *he'd* done this to her.

"I'll call you tomorrow," he said hoarsely.

"I won't answer. I never want to see you again."

This was worse than he'd expected, yet he couldn't blame her. After a moment, Jack nodded and left.

GABBY DIDN'T CRY. This felt too huge, too devastating. She'd have to tell Ric, but not tonight.

Tonight… Oh, God, she didn't know how she could bear all of this slamming her at the same time. The spray of blood, the ruin of her mother's face, the certainty that *he* had turned his head and looked right at her. Discovering how much she did remember caused guilt that she'd never told, that as an adult she'd been so determined to block it all to save herself from crippling memories.

And now Jack. It had happened ridiculously fast, but she'd been drawn to him at first sight, and liked all the complexities of his personality that she'd since discovered. Jack had slipped through her defenses, letting her see the boy he'd been, shattered by his parents' inexplicable divorce. He'd talked about his relationship with his father. Even about his job, the satisfactions, the frustrations, the need to learn to harden himself, in a sense, from the never-ending tragedy.

And he'd been lying to her—no, not just to her, to her and Ric—about why he wanted to spend time with them. He'd been deftly working her to the point where she'd spill all. She was furious, thinking of the several times he'd apologized for upsetting her with a question, or when he seemed angry at Ric for being so clueless about how seeing the weirdly unchanged house would affect her.

All a pretense, or at least, all carefully planned. She hated knowing how credulous she'd been, turning to him, trusting him, even going so far as having the passing thought that she might explore the job market around Spokane.

A raw sound escaped her as she remembered seeing Jack and Ric walking toward her that first night, at the Italian restaurant. Jack locking on to her like a heat-seeking missile, never looking away, traversing the crowded room with confident strides.

Oh, by the way, he was a cop. He'd seemed almost abashed when telling her he thought his choice of career had been influenced by her mother's murder. In retrospect, that was funny.

Well, yeah, he was a detective working major crimes—read *murder*—and he had a way of directing conversation back to the subject of Mom's murder even when she wanted to shy away.

He hadn't even been subtle, she thought now, feeling like a fool.

She'd had boyfriends, even a few semiserious relationships when she was in her early twenties and still pretending to be normal, but none had left her as devastated as she was now. She was tempted to grab her laptop and book a flight out of here tomorrow morning, but knew she had to talk to Ric first. Maybe get together with him again, let him drive her to the airport for a last hug.

It suddenly occurred to her that the day after tomorrow was Thanksgiving. She and Ric hadn't even talked about celebrating together, probably because the only place they could have cooked was his kitchen.

Or Jack's.

I've been falling in love with you.

Too bad that was as believable as just about everything else Jack had said to her.

THIS WAS REALLY bad timing to be summoned to Sergeant Rutkowski's office and find the police chief there, too.

Keeping his expression neutral with an effort, Jack said, "Sergeant. Chief. Can I do something for you?"

Rutkowski waved him to a seat. Jack felt like a sulky teenager summoned to the principal's office, especially since Chief Keller half sat on one end of the sergeant's desk. He appeared relaxed while also keeping a height advantage.

Jack sat, his back to a window with closed blinds that blocked the view into the squad room. He wondered if they were seeing the same death's head he had in his bathroom mirror a couple of hours ago.

"The chief dropped by to talk about something else, but your investigation into the Ortiz murder came up. You haven't given me much in the way of updates to pass on," Rutkowski pointed out. A big, bulky man with the homely face of a former boxer—although Jack had never heard he really had been—the sergeant was currently scowling. Best way to annoy him was to fail to keep him current on an investigation.

Chief Keller's expression was more curious than irritated, but Jack didn't know him well enough to guess whether that meant anything or not. Like the sergeant, Keller was a brawny man, any softening in his muscles disguised by well-cut suits. Handsome instead of homely, Keller had silver at his temples and scattered in his dark hair that helped give him a seemingly natural air of authority.

Dodging the necessity of really laying out what he'd learned, Jack still hadn't figured out what to say, and what to keep to himself. The memories Gabby had shared yesterday left him even unhappier.

Sergeant Roger Rutkowski and Police Chief Dean Keller were close to the age Colleen Ortiz would have been if she were still alive. Rutkowski had graduated from high school here in Leclaire, Keller attending for a couple of years, too, until his parents moved him to a military-style, regimented boarding school back East somewhere. In those days, there'd been only the one high school in town, so Colleen had very likely known or at least recognized either or both of Jack's bosses. Rutkowski had been raised Catholic, too, although his family had attended Assumption Catholic Church rather than St. Stephen's. Both men had been patrol officers when Gabby's mother was killed.

Both would have worn navy blue uniforms and kept the regulation black shoes shiny. That uniform included a hat.

Gabby hadn't mentioned seeing a holstered weapon or a shield—but the bulging plastic bag containing the bloody protective suit, gloves and separate shoe coverings, if there'd been any, as well as the knife, could well have hidden a badge and name on the chest pocket, and a gun and other accoutrements worn on the standard, heavy-duty black belt.

The Leclaire Police Department wasn't huge. Other

men had also spent their entire careers with LPD. Jack hadn't yet had a chance to work his way through the entire police force, but the ones he'd taken a look at didn't jibe with the security camera footage of the man trying to get into Gabby's hotel room. Either of these two men might.

Of course, even if the killer was a police officer at the time, he might no longer be, or had moved on to a different law enforcement agency. Reason said he could have been a cop with another agency here in the Spokane area—but the navy blue uniform ruled out the City of Spokane PD and the county sheriff's department. State patrol officers wore blue, but not a shade Jack would call navy. And how likely was it that a state trooper assigned to this region at the time of the murder would have had any history with a local woman? He'd pursue that possibility only if he came up short on his current avenues of investigation.

Jack had begun tracking, with so-so success, a few men who'd been with LPD then but had left in the intervening years. In most cases, finding a photo was enough to rule them out. He wasn't wasting a lot of time on the ones who hadn't stayed in town, because one of the things bothering him from the beginning was the rapid reaction to Gabby's return to town. He still couldn't rule out the killer having been a neighbor, a school principal, an old family friend—any of the people Ric had told about her upcoming visit.

Both Rutkowski and Chief Keller had known about her from the moment Jack asked permission to reopen the case.

The sergeant's scowl was deepening, and even Chief Keller was starting to look annoyed at Jack's prolonged silence.

"I've had several meetings with Ms. Ortiz," he said.

"She's been reluctant to revisit those memories, as you can imagine. I didn't want to push too hard or too fast."

"Have you learned anything new?" Sergeant Rutkowski demanded.

"Yes. I know now that the killer initially wore what she described as a 'puffy' white one-piece coverall with a hood. Once he'd killed Colleen Ortiz, he stripped off the suit, used the kitchen sink briefly—you may recall that trace amounts of blood were found in it—then left carrying a plastic trash bag that presumably held the blood-soaked garments. That's when Gabrielle saw him wearing all blue."

Both men stared at him. It was the chief who said finally, "That's pretty specific. I assume you got more than that."

He said reluctantly, "Yeah, I did."

Chapter Thirteen

He'd just lied to his commanding officers, if mostly by omission.

Jack walked back to his desk, opened his laptop and pretended to become immersed in what he'd been working on before being summoned by the sergeant.

He had told them both that the killer had yelled, "You ruined my life!"

To which Chief Keller had nodded. "I vaguely recall her saying the murderer said his victim had ruined something. 'His life' doesn't necessarily enlarge on that. It still could imply Mrs. Ortiz had broken up his marriage, or..." He obviously groped for a second option.

"Had told his family something that meant they cut him off," suggested Rutkowski. "Or he lost a job because of her." He frowned. "Did she work out of the home?"

Jack shook his head. "She had an LPN certificate and was employed as a nurse for a year and a half before she got married. Stayed home after that. She might have intended to go back to work once the kids were both in school. I don't know."

"Working as a nurse, she could have learned something about him that he needed kept private," Keller pointed out. "Like the guy had syphilis, which meant he'd cheated on his wife—"

Jack was shaking his head before the chief could finish. "Colleen's job was in a nursing home."

They threw around more ideas. Once, the chief looked him in the eye and asked directly whether he had anything else new to add to the picture, and that's when he'd flat out lied. He not only said no, he didn't tell them everything Gabby had shared: that she'd also heard her mother saying she'd never tell, or the killer responding with, "Now you won't."

He left out the shiny black shoes, the hat and the disturbing fact that the killer had looked straight at Gabby on his way out.

That Keller had remembered this particular killer saying the victim had "ruined" something for him initially raised a warning flag for Jack. On reflection, it didn't seem so unreasonable, though. Murders were a lot less common back then, with Leclaire having been a smaller town. The entire Spokane area had grown in the intervening years. A gruesome crime like this would be especially memorable, as well as an investigation that turned out to be a genuine mystery. It had probably made a big impression on all LPD officers.

In their early thirties, Keller and Rutkowski had hardly been rookies, though. Jack turned his head to be sure no one could see his monitor, then looked to see when each had been hired. Roger Rutkowski had signed on only three years out of high school, so by the time Colleen was murdered, he'd have already had…eleven years with the Leclaire Police Department. Colleen was thirty-one at the time of her death, and Rutkowski would have been thirty-two. He hadn't been promoted to detective yet—there'd been fewer opportunities then—which meant he'd still been wearing the uniform.

Jack was a little surprised to see that the police chief

had actually been hired on quite a bit later than the sergeant. He was younger, too. In fact, he was the same age as Colleen, making them classmates. They just about had to have known each other. He hadn't been at the high school her last two years, though, and he hadn't come home for more than potentially summers for a lot of years. His college degree was from Arkansas State University.

It was possible the young Dean Keller had just wanted to get away if his home life hadn't been great. He might have family in Arkansas, or had applied there to follow a girlfriend. Who knew? According to his online bio, he'd started his career in law enforcement in a small town in Tennessee, then moved on to Little Rock, Arkansas's largest city. In fact, he hadn't come home to Leclaire until a couple of years before the murder. Supposedly, Keller had returned to support a parent in ill health, which made complete sense.

So he would have been relatively new on the job when Colleen was murdered. Whatever his rank and job in Little Rock, he'd hired on here as a patrol officer, according to the records. However, he'd become a detective only a year after the murder. It was likely that he'd taken a look at the case at some point thereafter, just as the sergeant admitted he had, and Jack had in turn.

Looking seriously at these two men was probably a giant waste of time, but Jack couldn't let it go. He had to eliminate them as suspects, if only for his peace of mind.

He muffled a groan. Cops hated to admit that one of their own could have gone bad, but it happened. In this case... He tried to imagine arresting his own police chief, and covered his face with his hand.

Okay, if he were to consider either of his commanding officers as suspects, he needed to figure out what could have occurred to make them believe a well-liked woman, a "good Catholic" according to her neighbor, had ruined their lives.

At the moment, that was hard to see, as both had apparently successful careers—unless one had teetered on the brink of getting fired early on—and Rutkowski, at least, had recently passed his thirtieth wedding anniversary. Jack seemed to remember Keller had a divorce in his past. He'd check that out. If the entire marriage and divorce had taken place in Arkansas, Colleen couldn't be blamed for what had gone wrong.

Brooding, Jack made himself think logically. He should be looking at the year or two before the murder—and at the high school years, when Colleen had rather suddenly become more mature, more service oriented. Something significant had happened to change her from the typical teenager to an adult.

Yeah, he'd dig deeper…but not today. It was only three o'clock, but he'd worked many more than forty hours these past few weeks. He was going home. He had hardly slept last night. He needed to pull himself together if he was going to give his best to the investigation.

And yeah, he owed that to Gabby. He'd blown it in every other way, but she might be able to find closure—cliché though that had become—if her own effort to recover memories actually helped Jack identify and arrest the killer.

He closed his laptop, stuck it in its sleeve and under his arm, made sure his desk was otherwise bare, and started for the hall door.

Behind him, Sergeant Rutkowski called, "Cowan, hold up!"

If Rutkowski was going to give him hell for cutting

out early, Jack would have a hard time swallowing it. But he turned around.

The sergeant said, "Let's go out in the hall."

It was empty at the moment.

"I had a thought," Rutkowski said. "Has Gabriella Ortiz ever tried hypnosis?"

Jack blinked. The idea had crossed his mind, but Ric had set him up to believe she was utterly resistant to re-membering. He'd become fully convinced that wasn't true only yesterday, when she'd given him such a com-pelling child's-eye view of the crime—after which she kicked him out of her life.

"I haven't suggested it yet," he said.

"With a cooperative witness, someone who wants to succeed, it can be very effective. There are issues with details recalled only under hypnosis when it comes to trial, but we don't have to worry about that yet." He held out a Post-it note. "Here's the name and number for a psy-chologist who also does hypnosis. We've only used Dr. Adams a couple of times, but had good luck."

Then he nodded, said, "Take Friday, too, if you want," and went back into the squad room. With tomorrow being Thanksgiving, the sergeant must be offering a four-day weekend. Go figure.

Jack looked down at the name. Would Gabby even take his call?

"Uh… I TALKED to Jack."

Gabby was on the phone with Ric for the second time today. The first time, this morning, she'd told him how his good buddy, Jack Cowan, had used both of them in pursuit of his great and noble "quest."

Ric had sounded annoyed that Jack hadn't been straight with him, but not as outraged as she was. That annoyed *her.* As set as her brother had always been on her admitting what she remembered, no matter the anguish she'd suffer, Gabby suspected he'd have hopped readily on board Jack's plan to lie to her, if only he'd asked nicely.

If she'd found out Ric had cooperated in the deception, too, that would have been the end of any hope of a relationship between them. She wondered if he realized that.

She, of course, had done nothing but hang around her room and stew so far today. What *could* she do? Go for a long walk to find out if someone really was willing to run her down or shoot her? An especially violent mugging would do the trick, too. Ric, of course, was at work. He'd offered to meet her for dinner, but given that they'd finally made plans to have Thanksgiving dinner at a restaurant tomorrow, she figured she could survive a day on her own.

He must be home by now. She'd just been thinking about ordering a room service meal when her phone rang for the third time this afternoon. The other two calls— and messages—were from Jack. Messages deleted unheard.

"I was just about to order dinner," she told her brother. When he expressed alarm, she said, "It occurred to me I could request a woman to bring the food to my room."

"Oh. Good thought."

Then he moved on to the purpose of his call. Unlike her, he'd been willing to talk to Jack.

"He had a suggestion I think might be a good one. Uh. I know I've been a jerk before, and if you don't want to do this, I promise I'll understand and support you. It's just…"

"Do what?"

He explained about how the police worked with a psychologist who did hypnosis, who might be able to take her back to the day of the murder. "If you can go through the same events you described to Jack but be separated from your emotional response to them—"

"Is that possible?"

"Uh… I don't actually know. I've read about how they can get you to freeze a single moment, though, so you can study what the guy is wearing, or…"

Or his face.

Reluctant as she was to admit it, this was a good idea. That's probably why Jack had been calling. She should have realized he hadn't been leaving messages because he was heartbroken and desperate for her to listen to his excuses. Nope, he still had the same goal.

Mad as she was at him, she couldn't 100 percent fault him, because she had the same goal.

"Would I have to see *him*?" she asked suspiciously.

Ric immediately knew she meant Jack. "Maybe?" Pause. "Probably. He'd almost have to be there to give the hypnotist the background and prompt her to ask particular questions."

Damn, damn, damn.

Tomorrow was Thanksgiving. Sure as shooting, no professional would go into the office until Monday, which meant Colleen would be stuck in Leclaire at least until then.

She sighed. "All right. I'll do it."

"Do you want me to call him?"

No more cowardice. "I'll do it."

"Okay." Ric sounded more cheerful. "I'll pick you up at one tomorrow."

Gabby wasn't eager to hear Jack's voice again. Part of her knew that she'd overreacted. It had been her decision to sleep with him. He might well have seen their relationship as very casual. She hated remembering the tenderness in his voice, the times he'd comforted her, sympathized. Those made her feel most gullible.

What really hurt was that he'd let her think all those hours of talking were a mutual exploration, important to him, too. And he'd kissed her as if he meant it.

So he probably was attracted to her. She guessed he must have been, or he couldn't have... Well.

Sighing, she went to recent calls and touched his name and number. Two rings later, he answered with an urgent, "Gabby?"

"Yes. Ric passed on your suggestion that I undergo hypnosis. I wanted to let you know that I'm willing. Please schedule it as soon as you can."

"I'll do that. Gabby..."

"Let me know." With one stab, she ended the call.

She'd been right—just hearing his deep voice hurt.

GABBY STARED AT the house from where she'd just parked her rental car in the driveway. She hadn't even argued when Ric called this morning and started with, "So, listen."

The gist was that after getting home from their Thanksgiving dinner and going up to his bedroom, he'd happened to glance at the square in the hall ceiling that allowed access to the partial attic. Since their father died, Ric had never had reason to go up there, or even think about it, but talking to her had awakened a memory.

"Dad made me help him put some boxes up there. He was on the ladder, and I handed them up to him."

Ric had fetched the ladder from the garage and climbed up there yesterday, finding half a dozen boxes. He'd brought them down, peeked in a few, and realized this was all Mom's stuff. "Even her clothes," he'd said, sounding squeamish.

He wanted her to go through them with him, and had carried them all downstairs this morning.

With a groan, she got out of the car, locked it and went up to the front door, which opened before she crossed the porch.

"Thanks for coming," Ric said. "Man, I'm glad I remembered about these before you left town. Just the idea of going through her clothes—" He didn't finish. Didn't have to.

Gabby felt a little bit the same, but also…excited. She'd been so young when Mom died, her memories became more insubstantial all the time. If somebody asked what her mother had been like, she couldn't have said. Maybe looking through and handling her possessions would answer some of her questions.

Following Ric inside, she saw that he'd brought the boxes into the living room, probably so that she wouldn't have to look at the kitchen. She was somewhat reassured to realize that the idea didn't horrify her the way it had. Maybe because she'd already done that, maybe because she'd brought into focus memories that had lurked in frightened corners of her mind.

Hiding hadn't helped. Facing her fears headlong had.

She plopped down. "How do you want to do this?"

"Why don't you open the boxes, take things out, and once we make a decision, I'll put them in a pile depending on what it is?"

"Why do *I* get to be the leader?"

He grinned at her. "Because you're a girl? Mom was a girl?" He pushed a cardboard box closer to her.

"Oh, fine."

She unfolded the flaps and found herself looking at a jumble of items. Mostly shoes. A shoebox in pristine shape. Empty hangers, a sweater that had just been shoved in with everything else—

Gabby reached for the sweater, red, saggy and pilling. Ric's expression told her he remembered it as vividly as she did. It had been Mom's favorite to wear around the house. It really was ratty. No thrift store shopper would want it, but...

"Oh, Mom," she whispered, and hugged it to herself. Tears burned in her eyes from the powerful rush of familiarity. "I don't know what to say."

"We'll keep it." Ric's voice rasped. "Our kids can wonder why we'd keep something like this, and throw it away for us."

Gabby nodded. He took it from her and carefully folded the sweater. She thought he held it close to his face for a moment and inhaled, as if searching for a lingering perfume of their mother.

The shoes were easy, mostly too worn to interest anyone. The shoebox held a pair of black heeled sandals that didn't look as if they'd ever been worn. They were several sizes bigger than Gabby wore, so she said, "Thrift store."

Cars passed occasionally on the street in front, but not many. A lot of neighbors were probably away for the long weekend visiting family. Gabby couldn't help thinking of Mrs. Soriano and Mr. Monroe, both of whom, in different ways, had saved her life. According to Ric, both had passed away years ago. She wished she could have seen them again, thanked them.

My fault for not coming home sooner.

They went through two boxes of Mom's clothing. Their father hadn't packed it carefully. It was as if, unable to bear looking too closely at anything, he'd grabbed everything out of the drawers and shoved it into boxes.

Gabby could imagine how he'd felt. It must have been inexpressibly painful.

No garment besides the sweater rang any bells for her. She set aside a jewelry box. There was unlikely to be anything but costume jewelry in there, but she'd go through it carefully once they were otherwise done. She'd love to have a piece of jewelry to wear that reminded her of her mother.

"Did Dad bury Mom wearing her wedding and engagement rings?" she asked.

Ric moaned. "I have no idea."

The next box held books and a pair of handsome wrought iron fleur-de-lis bookends. Dad had never been much of a reader, but Gabby vaguely recalled her mother was. Mom was mostly the one to read to her kids, too.

Picking up the book on the top, Gabby said, "Poetry. I had no idea—"

She turned her head sharply and listened. She didn't hear anything, but…a shadow had passed in front of the window.

Ric was staring in the same direction. "Gabby," he said quietly, "I think there's someone on the porch. Grab your phone and run for the back of the house. Now."

She responded to the intensity in that last word and reached down for her phone poking out of the front pocket of her handbag. Then she jumped onto the sofa to bypass the boxes and tore for the kitchen.

Behind her, glass shattered and she heard a muffled *pop, pop, pop,* followed by a thud.

From the refuge of the kitchen, she screamed, "Ric!"

No answer.

Chapter Fourteen

Normally, Jack would have had Thanksgiving with his father. He really hadn't been in the mood, though, either for the drive or for celebrating anything. Part of that was his pain at losing any chance with Gabby, but more important was a raging frustration that she was on her own with a killer hunting her.

He kept reasoning with himself. The near hit-and-run really might have been a close call because of a distracted driver. Any cop knew how often that kind of carelessness resulted in tragedy. The man who'd tried to persuade her to let him into her hotel room was another story, though.

Yesterday, he'd known she was spending part of the day with Ric. That wasn't perfect; Ric didn't carry a gun and had no bodyguard or combat training. Still. Gabby should be safe in her hotel room, if she just stayed put.

Yeah, but she had to eat.

Thanksgiving had sucked, as far as he was concerned. If he hadn't gone about this all wrong, he could have invited Ric and Gabby to his place for their Thanksgiving meal. Never having cooked a turkey before, he might have had to take a speed lesson, or begged her or Ric for help, but they'd have had fun.

Instead, he'd microwaved a couple of burritos.

Today, his skin crawled with anxiety. Surely she was

being careful—but what was she doing? If only the psychologist had been able to see Gabby today, but no, she and her husband had flown to Phoenix to celebrate with his parents. Monday morning was the soonest she could get Gabby in, and she was shuffling appointments to manage that.

By now, Jack couldn't settle down to anything. He should have gone into the station. He did finally receive a call letting him know that the security officer who'd been arrested but not charged with rape had lived in the Houston area for the last fifteen years, and was wheelchair bound after a stroke he'd had the previous year.

One more name Jack could cross off his list.

He started for the kitchen to pour himself a cup of coffee, but found himself pacing instead.

Would Gabby answer if he called? What about Ric?

He reached the front door and turned back just as his phone, left on the kitchen table, rang. It could be anyone, but— He moved fast, pouncing on it when he saw Gabby's name. What did a call from her mean?

"Gabby?"

"Ric's been shot." Her breath hitched with what he guessed was a sob. "I'm at his house. We were going through some more of Mom's things, and— Can you come?"

"You called 9-1-1?"

"Yes. I was lucky because a patrol officer was really close, but the ambulance isn't here yet, and I'm scared. I…don't know how badly Ric is injured."

"I'm on my way." Jack snatched up his wallet and keys and went out the door. "Stay on the line with me if you don't need to make any other calls. I should be there in ten to fifteen minutes." Or less, if he stepped on it.

"I'll be a distraction." Already she'd collected herself,

or else he was hearing a chill in her voice. "I'm okay. Drive safe." Call ended.

He swore pungently as he leaped into his SUV and backed out of the garage.

GABBY DROPPED THE phone on the coffee table and went back to Ric's side. He was breathing. Thank God he was alive, but the police officer was applying pressure to a bloody mess on his shoulder and chest. It looked as if he'd hit his head on a corner of the hearth as he went down. She could see a smear of blood on the brick.

Realizing she was rocking, she made herself stop. "What's taking so long?"

The extremely young officer's expression betrayed more stress than he'd like to know. "I think I hear a siren."

"I do, too." She squeezed Ric's slack hand. "Hold on, Ric. I'm here."

Through the broken front window, she saw an ambulance rocket to a stop, then back into the driveway beside her rental. Thank God she'd left room. Barely a minute later, a man and woman appeared on the porch.

Their dark blue uniforms disturbed her on a fundamental level, just as the young officer's had. She had to shake off her reaction. Seconds later, she scooted away on her butt to give them room to evaluate Ric. They asked a couple of quick questions, applied fresh dressings, and with barely disguised urgency prepared him for transport.

Her gaze glued to her wounded brother, Gabby heard a squeal of brakes but didn't look up until Jack appeared in the open doorway. He looked straight at her, but spoke briefly with the EMTs before stepping aside so they could wheel Ric out.

Then Jack came to her, crouching so that he didn't tower over her. "I think he'll be fine."

"I have to go to the hospital!" she said frantically, jumping to her feet.

Jack gripped her arms. "Nobody there will be able to talk to you for a little while. Ric will be rushed into surgery. You won't do him any good sitting in a waiting room. Take a minute, calm down and tell me what happened."

Her first impulse was to fight off his hands, but she closed her eyes, focused on the strength in those hands, the steadiness in his voice, and nodded. When he nudged her to sit at the opposite end of the sofa from where she'd been before, she plopped down, watching him take a seat on the coffee table in front of her.

"Won't there be crime scene investigators?" she asked. "Should we be here?"

"This is my scene, and this should be fine for a few minutes. I'm not about to drag you into the kitchen."

She bobbed her head, held on tightly to her phone and waited.

It didn't take long to answer his questions. He could see the pile of boxes, opened and unopened. The glistening blood pooled where Ric had sprawled on the oak floor.

At least it would wipe up easily, she thought, in that annoying way the mind worked at times like this. If Ric didn't survive, cleaning up the mess would become meaningless.

Jack's question reined in her thoughts. "Are these boxes from the storage unit?"

She shook her head and told him about Ric remembering that some boxes had been stowed up in the attic space. "Once he realized they all held Mom's possessions, he asked if I'd help go through them."

Jack shifted gears. "When he told you to run, did Ric intend to follow you?"

"I assumed so," she said uncertainly.

"That's likely, but you had quite a head start."

She told him how she'd used the sofa to leap over the top of the boxes. Sitting there, she saw that one box had been knocked askew. "He must have stumbled over it."

Jack wanted her to show him how far she'd gotten. When she led him toward the hall, where the staircase rose and doorways opened to the kitchen and the utility room as well as the back door, he stopped and swore.

"That one must have barely missed you."

"What?" Her gaze followed his to the bullet hole in the wallboard. Her eyes were level with it. Feeling sick, she said, "I didn't know."

"Okay, sweetheart, that's it. I'll take you to the hospital."

"I can drive."

He studied her, those blue eyes penetrating. "Do you feel steady enough?"

She took a deep breath, analyzed how she felt and nodded. "The angrier I get, the better I feel."

His smile was both gentle and approving. It might have made her knees a little wobbly, if they hadn't already been. She stiffened them and followed him out the front door.

She started to go back for her handbag, but Jack did it for her. He stopped to talk for a few minutes to the responding officer, who nodded several times.

Then she started her car, backed out into the street and fell in behind his Tahoe as he led the way to the hospital. She'd noticed signs pointing to it, but hadn't been sure where it was.

Once there, it turned out he'd been right that Ric had

been whisked immediately into surgery. Jack requested, and got, a private waiting room for her that was behind the swinging doors into the surgery unit.

He nodded his thanks to the nurse who'd brought them there. "This should be safe."

Sitting on one of four upholstered chairs surrounding a table, she said, "Safe?"

He took the chair right next to hers. "I don't want you sitting out there in plain sight."

"Oh." She pictured herself as a bottle set up on a fence rail for target practice. They could have been followed, or the killer might have logically assumed this was where she'd be. He must have seen Ric go down. "Hadn't you better go back?"

As Jack regarded her, Gabby noticed for the first time how strained he looked. He might have aged a decade, furrows appearing.

"Yeah. I do have to. Gabby…don't go anywhere, with anyone."

"I'm not that dumb."

"I know you aren't." He ran a hand over his face, but didn't look any better when he was done. "You scared the shit out of me. Again."

Old anger bubbled up. "Afraid you'd lose your witness?"

"You know better than that. I meant every word I said to you. Think about that." Shaking his head, he rose to his feet. "I'll be back later. Wait here for me."

The door opened, closed and he was gone.

Leaving her filled with dread, her thoughts spiraling between the brother with whom she'd just reconnected and Jack. A man whose devastation she couldn't deny.

LOADING THE BOXES into his SUV a couple of hours later, Jack reverted to brooding about Gabby. Yeah, he'd screwed up, but did she really believe he was cold-blooded enough to care only that she was a critical witness in a murder investigation? Hadn't she noticed that he'd crossed town in half the time it should have taken, desperate to see with his own eyes that she was okay?

His phone rang. Gabby, at last. Ric had still been in surgery an hour ago when Jack had last called her.

"He's in recovery," she said, before he could get in a *hello*. "Ric's chances are good, but there was a lot of damage. He was hit by two bullets. The surgeon kept thinking he could close, and they'd realize there was still bleeding somewhere." Words kept tumbling out. "The head injury might be the greatest threat. He hit that hearth hard enough to fracture his skull."

"He's tough, Gabby. In great physical condition, which will help in his recovery."

"There's some swelling around his brain." Now she sounded almost numb. "They might have to punch a hole in his skull to…to let fluid drain."

Crap. "I know you're scared. Have faith, sweetheart."

She gave a broken laugh. "Is this when I start praying?"

"Haven't you already?"

Silence, which was its own answer.

"I'll be there in just a few minutes." He shut the hatch door. "I arranged for someone to nail plywood over the window."

"Front and back now."

"Yeah." He almost said, *Somebody has it in for you big-time*, but knew she already had to be thinking the same—unless she was stuck on the fact that her brother had taken two bullets meant for her.

"I'll see you when you get here."

Making phone calls the whole way, Jack obeyed speed

limits this time. He parked right in front of the emergency room entrance at the hospital in a slot saved for law enforcement. He doubted the killer had hung around to see him load the boxes, but Jack still wanted his Tahoe highly visible from the ER.

Upstairs, he suffered a jolt when he found the private waiting room empty, but when he snagged the first passing nurse, she told him Gabby had been allowed into recovery to see Ric.

Ten minutes later, Gabby reappeared. The sight of her hit him hard. Her skin looked as if it had been stretched tight over her facial bones and her eyes were sunken, accented by dark half circles beneath them. Hair stuck out here and there from her usually smooth braid. Her lips lacked color.

Wordless, he held out his arms. His heart cramped painfully when she hesitated, but at last she walked right to him. As he pulled her close, she wrapped both her arms around him and laid her head on his chest.

Jack didn't ask any questions, just offered physical comfort. Embracing her gave him comfort, too. Maybe she'd forgive him. The feel of her curves, the citrus scent of the glossy, if disheveled, hair beneath his cheek, her trust, they all gave him hope.

Finally she sighed, and he had to relax his arms enough to let her step back. She looked up at him with shadowed eyes, and said, "He's still unconscious."

"He did just have surgery," he reminded her.

"Yes, but…he should have opened his eyes by now."

"It's not a surprise that he hasn't."

"That's what the surgeon said, but… I let myself think…"

"Hey." He tugged her over to the chairs, sat them down and shifted his chair so he faced her and could hold both her hands. "You have to give him time. Aren't the doctors you've talked to optimistic?"

"Yes, but I'm afraid they're lying to me." A couple of tears trembled on her lashes, and she swiped them away impatiently. "Did you find anything?"

"Nothing useful." The frustration he'd pushed down gained power again, like a flash flood. "We've got a couple of bullets, of course, but they're a common caliber. The surgeon saved the two he dug out of Ric, although they're not in great shape. The bullets are only useful when we have a gun to match them to. Otherwise…" Jack shook his head. "He fired through the glass from the front porch. Probably didn't touch anything. With him using a suppressor, the few neighbors who were home didn't hear a damn thing, except for a woman halfway down the block who went to her front window because she heard the roar of an engine accelerating to what had to be dangerous speed. They've had trouble with teenagers speeding, she says. She did get a glimpse of the vehicle, but of course not of the license plate."

"Let me guess. It was a giant black SUV?"

He grimaced. "She told me it looked kind of like mine."

"If only there'd been a traffic camera there or where he tried to run me down."

If only were two of the saddest words in the English language.

"I'd like you to come home with me," Jack said.

Gabby reared back. "Now?"

"No, I don't expect you to leave right this minute, but I don't want you at the hotel anymore. It's not safe for you to come and go."

She blinked. "Then…what?"

"My house."

Jack didn't much like the way she scrutinized him, but he withstood her inspection.

"I don't suppose I have a lot of choices, do I?"

"No."

After a moment, she nodded. "I don't suppose you're going to give me directions to your house and head home."

"No, but if you'll give me your room key, I'll go get your stuff from the hotel and check you out. I don't want you going near that place."

Her teeth closed on her lower lip, but she nodded. It took him a minute to realize she was trying to tug her hands free. When he let go, she dug in her bag and handed him the room card. "I'm in 328."

"I remember. I'll see you in about half an hour."

He hoped like hell her brother hurried to regain consciousness.

STILL SCARED, GABBY had finally agreed to go home with Jack. With Ric in Intensive Care, she was allowed to sit with him for only a few minutes an hour. Around ten o'clock, Jack put his foot down. Today had been enormously stressful. She was so tired, she wasn't steady on her feet, he declared.

Unfortunately, he was right. That didn't keep her from feeling she was abandoning Ric, but in all honesty, with him still unconscious, her presence wasn't doing him a speck of good. She wished he had a girlfriend who'd want to take shifts at the hospital, or that she knew who any of his best friends were.

This time, Jack wouldn't let her drive, although he promised to bring her back in the morning. Something in his expression made her wonder if she would see her rental car any time in the immediate future. He didn't have to hint again that she might as well paint a target on herself if she walked out of the hospital and cut through the parking lot to the car. The shooting had been on the local news, with a promised update at ten o'clock. If the killer had thought for a minute she was down, too, he knew better now. He also knew where he could find her for the immediate future: the hospital.

Maybe she should call the rental company and ask them to pick up the car.

Gabby was weary enough not to object when Jack put his hands around her waist and lifted her up onto the seat before closing the door and going around to the driver side. However briefly the overhead light had been on, she'd seen enough to have her twisting to look back at the cargo space. There was her suitcase, tote and laptop case, but also...

Jack saw what she was looking at. "Put on your seat belt. Yes, that's the stuff you and Ric were going through. I'm taking it home so you and I can finish finding out what's in those boxes."

Gabby pulled the seat belt over herself before saying, "You think there might be something in there that's important."

He backed out, then shot her a glance she could see because the area right in front of the ER was brightly lit. "I do think that."

Her mind might be moving slowly, but it trudged determinedly on. "That's why you went to the storage unit with us."

"Partly. I also wanted to be sure no one could get to you."

No wonder he'd parked the way he had, and paced out in the cold instead of joining them inside the unit.

"Did you go through the stuff you were supposed to take to the dump?"

"Some of it," he admitted. "I didn't unwrap the plastic around the artificial Christmas tree."

Despite the sheer awfulness of this day, the wry humor in his voice almost made her laugh. If only she didn't like Jack so much.

If only... But she didn't let herself complete that wish.

Chapter Fifteen

Saturday afternoon, Ric groaned, rolled his head on the thin pillow, and opened his eyes.

Gabby leaped to her feet from the hard plastic chair next to the hospital bed. "Ric!"

He squinted at her. Worked his mouth a few times, then said, "Gab?"

Had his mind shorted out halfway through her name, or did he remember the whole family calling her that because of her nonstop chatter?

On the verge of tears, she smiled. "I've been scared for you."

"Why—?" He took in the room. "Hospital?"

"Yes."

She saw the instant it came back to him.

"Shot."

"Yes." Gabby sniffed. "Because you got in the way of bullets intended for me."

"That's…what…brothers…are…for."

"Who knew?" she said, almost lightly. "Your mouth is dry, isn't it? I'd better let the nurse know you're back with us. And Jack. He's out in the waiting room. He hopes you saw something I didn't."

"Wish."

She rushed out of the cubicle, which promptly filled

with medical personnel. As soon as she emerged through the double doors, Jack closed his laptop and stood.

"He's awake?"

"How did you know?"

He grinned. "You're glowing."

"It's such a relief." It had become habit to walk into his arms and draw strength from him. "The doctor is with him right now."

"Is he coherent?"

"Yes." She gave a teary smile. "He called me *Gab*."

His chest vibrated with a laugh beneath her cheek. "I'd forgotten that. We'd be pulling up to the house, and there you'd be waiting. He'd mumble, 'Gab, Gab, Gab.'"

"I haven't heard that in so long."

"I'll give them a few minutes, then ask to talk to him."

At the returning somberness, she straightened. "I don't think he saw anything."

When she explained, Jack grimaced. "The guy was bound to have his face covered anyway."

Nearly fifteen minutes passed before a nurse came out to say that Detective Cowan could speak to Ric. Jack insisted on bringing Gabby, of course. He hadn't left her alone in any public areas of the hospital all day, even though he must have better things to do than sit there.

He and Ric clasped hands and held on. It turned out that Ric had seen more than she had, but only a large, black-clad figure and what he was sure was a gun.

"Weird long barrel."

"Suppressor."

Ric nodded and winced.

Jack updated him with what little they'd learned and told him that he and Gabby would go through the boxes in case their mother had left any clue to the reason for her murder.

Ric looked at her. "Bet you've been here all day."

"Of course I have!"

"You look like crap. Take a nap. My head is pounding. I'm going to take some of the good stuff—" he lifted the button that would send pain relief flooding through his body "—and sleep myself. Doctor said they wouldn't transfer me to a regular room until morning."

"Fine. I don't need to watch you sleep." Gabby leaned over and kissed her brother's stubbly cheek. "Thank you," she whispered.

He lifted the hand with the IV needle to her jaw. "Sister."

Jack steered her out, told the nurse they were leaving and made sure she had both their phone numbers, and escorted Gabby through the maze of corridors to the ER entrance. There, he stepped outside alone and studied the surroundings before waving her out to his SUV.

Once they were driving, he said, "Part of me wants to start work on those boxes, but Ric's right. You need a nap and a decent dinner."

"I can hold out."

He shook his head. "Not necessary. This evening or the morning will be soon enough."

Gabby didn't argue. Last night, after barely managing to brush her teeth, she'd gone to bed in Jack's guest room and plunged into a state more akin to unconsciousness than sleep. Unfortunately, she'd woken up four hours later and only drifted in and out of restless sleep the remainder of the night. Ric was right; when she'd looked in the mirror this morning, she'd made a face at herself. She did not look good.

When they neared his house, Jack had her unfasten her seat belt and crouch down on the floorboards, just as he had last evening and again when they left for the hospital this morning. Not until they were in the garage and the door had descended did he tell her she could get up. She had yet to see the outside of his house, although she knew from the interior that it probably dated to the same era as the neighborhood where she'd grown up. This morning when she came downstairs, she'd discovered blinds were drawn so no one could see in—and she couldn't look out at the porch or yard, either.

The house couldn't be more than half-furnished, but had beautifully refinished hardwood floors, fireplace mantel, moldings and some built-in bookcases and, in the dining room, an original built-in buffet. She couldn't understand why he hadn't done more to make it feel like home.

Now, though, she only trudged upstairs, visited the guest bathroom and flopped down on the bed.

Laying her head on the pillow felt blissful. She pulled the quilt over herself and let the weariness wash over her, along with the memories of the day. Ric smiled. He kissed her cheek. He was going to be fine. She was smiling when she fell over the edge.

JACK FELT A little ragged, too, but he could sleep tonight. He frequently missed a night's sleep in the urgent hours after a murder.

When the quiet upstairs told him Gabby had gone to sleep, he went back to his research. He hadn't lost his uneasiness where Sergeant Rutkowski and Chief Keller were concerned, but he'd backed off somewhat on his suspicion. Rutkowski's suggestion that Gabby try hypnosis wasn't something the killer would do.

Except, Jack reminded himself, that two days later, there was an open attempt on her life. Rutkowski had to have known the psychologist wouldn't be able to get

Gabby in over a holiday weekend, giving him time to go on the attack.

Would he have told Chief Keller what he'd suggested? Jack couldn't think of a good way to ask, and wouldn't have the chance until at least Monday anyway.

Right now, Jack was intent on finding out what he could about a series of rapes that had occurred in the region back when Colleen had been in high school. Those rapes had been spread over five police jurisdictions and, as was too often the case, those agencies hadn't communicated with each other. Not until near the end had anyone connected the crimes. None of those rapes had happened in Leclaire, four had been in the greater Spokane area, and one across the border in Idaho. Descriptions and MO suggested one man had committed all the crimes.

All had been young girls, the youngest fifteen, the oldest twenty. Because so many women didn't report rapes even now, Jack suspected the guy had raped more women. Unfortunately, none of the reported crimes had been date rapes, when the victim could have named her assailant. Instead, women alone at night had been grabbed from behind and dragged either into the bushes or the back of a van. The rapist had worn a face mask. All the victims said he was big. "Huge," the fifteen-year-old had declared.

Crime victims invariably described their assailants as larger than they actually were, so Jack took that with a grain of salt. Still, the description did jibe with his observation of the hotel security camera footage. There was no question the man who'd tried to get into Gabby's room had been big—as tall as Jack's six-foot-two, and possibly broader.

Jack hunted down every scrap of information he could find on the long-ago rapes. What if this creep had also committed date rape, but intimidated or blackmailed his victims into keeping their mouths closed?

About the time Colleen had become quieter and more mature, the rapes had either stopped or no more young women found the courage to report them. Plenty of rapes had still been investigated, of course, but none sounded as if they'd been committed by the same man.

His mind took a logical, if disquieting, jump to the man who had left Leclaire not long after the last rape. Would it turn out there'd been similar rapes in Little Rock, Arkansas, during the years when Dean Keller had lived there? Trouble was, the only way he'd get the kind of details he needed was to call a detective there and ask him to delve into records. Explaining why he wanted them, though, that got touchy. They'd want a reason—and a name—before they committed to that kind of time. It wasn't hard to imagine the request getting back to Keller.

Goodbye, job.

Deciding to think about it, Jack started dinner. He enjoyed cooking when he had the time, which was rare. Once the spicy vegetarian chili simmering on the stove started to smell good, he stuck corn bread in the oven.

When Gabby appeared in the living room, he saw with approval that some of the strain had left her face and she'd obviously brushed her hair and braided it anew. The exhaustion and fear for her brother that she couldn't hide had had the benefit of helping Jack rein in his physical response to her the last two days, but now he felt the familiar punch. He loved every one of her curves, that glorious hair, her pretty mouth and the sparkle of gold in otherwise green eyes. Yeah, and now he knew what she looked like naked. How she'd responded to his touch.

If his voice was a little rough, he couldn't help it. "You got some sleep?"

"Yes, thank you. Something smells good."

"Should be ready." In fact, by the time he'd set the table, the oven timer had gone off, and they sat down in the kitchen to eat.

Gabby was very willing to continue going through the boxes, although she did say, "I wish Ric was here, in case I come across something meaningful to him."

"We won't throw anything away immediately. Once he's out of the hospital, he can take a look himself."

Later, when they'd finished dinner, Gabby sank down at one end of the sofa. He brought the first box to her, then joined her on the sofa close enough to look over her shoulder.

"More clothes," she said in disappointment. She was careful to lift every garment out of the box, however, and neatly fold it, restoring the piles to the box when she was done.

The next carton held pieces of her and Ric's childhoods: ratty stuffed animals, artwork sent home from elementary school, homemade Mother's Day cards and report cards. Gabby laughed a few times, got teary, and finally closed it all back up. "I'll want to keep some of this, and I'm sure Ric will, too."

She decided to go through the boxes of books later and decide what to keep. She admired two different sets of bookends, but put them back in the boxes for now. "I'll keep those unless Ric wants them."

Jack had brought the jewelry chest Gabby had left sitting on the coffee table at Ric's house. She did flip through the contents now, in case her mother had an unknown stash of valuable jewels. The only item of interest was a sterling silver charm bracelet that held only two charms, a tiny football and a book that hung open but looked like it might close.

"Isn't that strange?" Gabby murmured. "It's so tarnished. Well, I guess it would be after twenty-five years."

Or forty years, Jack speculated. "Do you recognize it?" he asked.

Gabby shook her head. "I doubt she'd have worn it, since it was only a…a starter bracelet. I mean, if Dad gave it to her, he'd have kept giving her charms, wouldn't he?"

"Yeah. And the book charm was obviously meant for her—you said she liked to read—but your dad never played football, did he?"

He bet Roger Rutkowski and Dean Keller had.

Gabby shook her head. "Heavens, no! Dad was only five-foot-six, you know. Mom never wore heels, because she was already a bit taller than him."

Jack had prepared himself with evidence bags, and he had Gabby drop the bracelet into a small one. The tiny book was the only part with a smooth enough surface to conceivably hold even a partial fingerprint, but that could be enough to be helpful.

Gabby looked askance, but didn't ask why he wanted to keep it.

The very last box held the treasure trove Jack had hoped for. Photo albums, a couple of high school yearbooks, two chocolate boxes repurposed to hold letters, notes and some loose photos. While Gabby started scanning the letters, Jack took Colleen's freshman yearbook and flipped to a photo of the football team. Sure enough, there was a very young Rutkowski and—it took him a moment to recognize the other face—Dean Keller, too. Dean had been a freshman, big enough to play varsity instead of JV, Rutkowski a sophomore. Jack found Colleen's freshman photo and recognized her smile as one that hid braces. He'd worn them himself, and hated every minute of it.

Then he studied the two boys' photos. Rutkowski had been homely even as a boy. Dean Keller had apparently always been handsome with an air of assurance not many kids that age possessed. As good-looking as he was, would he have bothered with a freshman girl with a mouthful of metal? Jack doubted it.

A year later, though... He reached for the next yearbook, then realized it was from Colleen's senior year. Maybe the other two were at the bottom of the box.

"This is weird," Gabby announced.

"What?"

She handed him a letter still in an envelope. The return address was the rectory at St. Stephen's Catholic Church. Jack unfolded the letter and attempted to decipher the spidery handwriting. It was addressed to "Dear Colleen" and signed "Father Ambrose."

It wasn't only the handwriting that had Jack struggling to understand the body of the letter. Father Ambrose wrote in a way Colleen presumably would have understood, but wouldn't give away any secrets if one of her parents had read the letter.

He regretted that he'd had no chance to speak to Colleen privately. As she might know, he had been transferred and would be moving away. He hoped for assurance that she was doing well, and that the measures he'd taken had sufficed to allow her to live with confidence and peace of heart. He encouraged her to call if there was anything at all he could do for her, but he had complete faith in his successor, Father Paul, whom she had already met. He closed by saying, "Go with God, child."

Jack reread the letter. What "measures" had a Catholic priest taken to protect a teenage girl in his parish?

Gabby made an awful sound. Jack turned his head to see shock on her face. She thrust a manila envelope at him, the flap open.

Jack dropped the letter and took the envelope. There was no mistaking a pair of flower-print bikini panties of another era. This time, he took a moment to don a plastic glove before he gingerly lifted out the panties. The fabric in the crotch was starting to break down from whatever had stained it in addition to a nickel-sized rusty splotch that had to be old blood. Jack would have bet anything Colleen had gotten home, rushed to her room and torn these off. She might have shoved them out of sight for a while, or had had the presence of mind to decide immediately to preserve them. Even in shock and sickened, she'd have known about DNA tracing. This had to be semen, and the blood from her having lost her virginity.

What his father had overheard came to Jack, word for word.

If you keep bothering me, you should know I kept evidence. I won't hesitate to take it to the police.

The panties on their own wouldn't be conclusive; the sex act could have been consensual. But if she'd told anyone that she'd been raped... Oh, yeah, that could definitely ruin a guy's life.

His gaze turned back to the letter that lay on his lap. For whatever reason, she had told someone: her priest.

And he'd taken measures.

GABBY HAD HERSELF tied in knots by Monday morning. The idea of letting herself be hypnotized freaked her out. To lose control of her own mind...why had she agreed to this?

And then there were the appalling discoveries she had made in a box of her mother's mementos. If only Dad had looked through them instead of just packing up everything, he might have been able to help the police find Mom's murderer. It would have been a lot easier to track down Father Ambrose twenty-five years ago.

Dad couldn't possibly have known she'd been raped as a teenager, or he'd have told one of the detectives. Why, why, had Mom pretended it never happened? Kept proof that it had, but not reported the crime? Did she blame herself, as so many women did? Believed she'd given implicit permission just because she'd sneaked out to meet up with her rapist? Worn clothing her mother had called suggestive?

If she really had sneaked out, versus gone on an approved date, the lie to her parents might explain why she didn't dare tell them. Since Gabby hadn't known her grandparents, she had no way of knowing how strict they'd been, how they'd have reacted to their daughter's rape.

Gabby felt sick just thinking what her mother had gone through.

Ric, at least, was doing well. Gabby and Jack had spent several hours with him at the hospital yesterday. Well, really, she'd spent time with her brother while Jack had sat in a corner hunched over his laptop, fingers flying. Occasionally he'd made phone calls, speaking just quietly enough she couldn't hear what he was saying.

But she knew he was trying to track down Father Ambrose, the priest who'd been transferred to another parish something like forty years ago. From what Jack said, Father Ambrose would probably be in his late sixties or older by now. Would he be retired, or did priests typically continue holding worship and counseling their parishioners until they were physically unable?

Now, Jack said, "We're here." He turned into the parking lot beside a medical building.

She wanted to say, *I can't do this*, but knew she wouldn't. Besides visiting Ric, yesterday Gabby had spent hours poring over her mother's photo albums, yearbooks, letters from friends and even the diary she'd kept in middle school and into her freshman year in high school. Gabby had believed she'd lost all chance to really know her mother, but she'd been wrong. And by God, she'd do anything in the world now to see the man who'd raped her mother and then, years later, murdered her arrested and imprisoned. That fury would see her through with this.

Jack held her hand as they walked into the building and took the elevator to the second floor. Before the doors slid open, he looked at her. "Are you okay with this?"

Gabby gave a sharp nod, and he kissed her, briefly, gently, and then he walked her into the psychologist's office.

DR. JOSEPHINE ADAMS spoke first to Jack while Gabby waited in another room. He told the woman everything he knew Gabby had seen, and suggested details that might well be buried in her mind. Then she allowed him to join her once she had successfully hypnotized Gabby, but cautioned him to stay out of sight and not say a word unless it was absolutely essential.

Gabby lay comfortably on an upholstered chaise lounge. He'd seen fleeting instances before of her regressing to the child who'd been watching her mother be butchered, but she had immediately swung back to being the adult Gabby. The woman he loved. This time, even her expressions were childlike, her voice slightly too high.

The pivotal moment came when the killer had passed closest to where Gabby had been hiding in the utility room. In the telling Gabby rushed past it, just as she had when she'd told Jack what she'd seen. But this time, Dr. Adams said calmly, "You know how to pause a video tape, don't you, Gabby?"

"Uh-huh."

"Stop what you're seeing right here."

Gabby nodded obediently.

"Now let's rewind, just a little bit, until you first see him walking into sight. He's dressed in dark blue, carrying a garbage bag. What color is the bag?"

"It's black."

"And is it full?"

Gabby's forehead crinkled. "Not really *full*, but there's stuff in it."

"All right. He takes a step or two and turns his head to look your way. Let's pause there again."

"He sees me," she said in panic. "He has to see me. He's looking right at me!"

"He's looking at the pile of dirty clothes," Dr. Adams said calmly. "He doesn't know you're hiding there."

Gabby took a deep breath.

"You said he's wearing a hat."

"Uh-huh."

"What does the hat look like?"

"It's blue. The part that sticks out over his face is shiny."

Jack's jaw was so tight, he expected a molar to crack. Damn, damn.

"Who wears hats like that, Gabby?"

"Daddy was in the navy." Her tone suggested she wasn't quite sure what that was. "There's a picture on the mantel of him in his uniform. He wore a hat like that, 'cept it was white."

"Anyone else you can think of?"

"A police officer who came to talk to Ric's class did. Mommy and I took treats that day and got to hear him."

"Very good," Dr. Adams said warmly. "While the man is frozen in front of you, can you see his face?"

"Only the bottom part. A little bit of his nose and..." She lifted a hand to indicate her jaw.

"Even after men shave, you can usually see what color the stubble is."

"Uh-huh. Daddy's is practically *black*."

"What about this man?"

"It's hard to see. He must've shaved this morning." She frowned. "It's brown, not gold like Sarah's daddy's."

Jack let out a long breath. Dr. Adams gave him a warning look. She asked a few more questions, about the day the car jumped up on the sidewalk and almost ran Gabby down, but then she cycled back instead to the blood spraying each time the man thrust his hand down. After a minute, the psychologist said, "All right, Gabby. I'm going to count down, and you'll wake up. Five, four, three, two, one."

Gabby blinked a few times, and her expression changed, becoming wholly adult. "Are we done?"

Dr. Adams smiled. "We're done. You did splendidly, Gabby."

Gabby sat up and swung her feet to the floor. That's when she saw Jack. She'd never looked more vulnerable than she did when she said, "Can we go home?"

To his house. He had to clear his throat before he could say, "You bet."

He thanked the doctor, and he and Gabby held hands all the way out to the car, neither saying a word.

Chapter Sixteen

Jack's tension had to be infecting her. From the minute he left her at his house, she jumped at every sound from the street and inside the house. The furnace startled her every time it came on, which was frequent given the cold weather. Having the windows covered so that nobody could see inside should have been comforting, but if anything, it had the reverse effect. She desperately wanted to peek between the blinds or around the edge of a curtain, but what if *he* was outside and saw? The words *dead giveaway* popped into her mind, making her shiver.

Not a soul knew she was staying at Jack's house, which made the likelihood of an attack here next to nonexistent, but logic didn't help.

At least Jack had left her with something useful to do this afternoon.

After the hypnosis session, the two of them had stopped to see Ric at the hospital, then ate lunch at a Greek restaurant Jack liked. She could tell he hated to leave her alone, but he'd decided he really needed to go into the station.

"I haven't even begun the paperwork on the shooting at your brother's house," Jack grumbled. "And you never know, our crime scene people might have magically found something."

Gabby shooed him out the door. If she hadn't, well, she was deeply afraid they'd have ended up in bed together. It was still possible they would tonight, but at least she'd have a little while to weigh the pros and cons. Number one on the "con" list being the anger and sense of betrayal that still simmered somewhere deep inside.

She wrinkled her nose. She was afraid not even the anger would help once Jack kissed her. Because on the "plus" side, he had come running when she called, bared his deep fear for her and given her everything she needed since.

Walling off her tangle of emotions, she made herself focus. The task he'd left with her was to continue the hunt for the priest.

Jack had found Father Ambrose's second posting, at St. Florian's in Detroit, but after ten years he'd been moved again. Nobody currently there had known him. Given that yesterday was Sunday, he hadn't been in contact with the archdiocese till this morning. That person had trouble accessing the records, but determined Father Ambrose had gone to a church in Haverhill, Massachusetts.

Taking up where he'd left off, she worked her laptop and phone, making call after call. Father Ambrose, Gabby finally learned, had retired just a year ago from his fifth church, this one in Boston. The man who gave her the information believed Father Ambrose had inherited a house somewhere in New England from his parents, but he would have to do further research to get contact information. Gabby wondered if he had to obtain permission from above before handing out contact info. That would make sense. She didn't believe for a minute that the archdiocese would lose track of their priests the minute they retired.

She mulled over possibilities. The priest presumably

hadn't been named Ambrose at birth. Would he have returned to his birth name, or held on to Ambrose? She
couldn't quite imagine him having a Facebook page, and
doubted priests used LinkedIn to communicate with their
fellow priests. Still, she did a search for an Ambrose Ke-
arney in Massachusetts, then some neighboring states.

Nada.

She pulled up white pages, got nowhere. Maybe Jack
would have better resources.

Astonishingly, at four thirty her time, her phone rang.
Father Ambrose now lived in Pawtucket, Rhode Island,
and still filled in for services in the St. Mary's Parish.
Gabby had an address and phone number.

When Jack came in the door after six o'clock, looking
tired, she said triumphantly, "I have a phone number."

Some of the weariness on his face eased. "Seriously?
Did you talk to him?"

He followed her to the kitchen, where she put the left-
over chili on the stove to heat and popped the corn bread
in the microwave while explaining that she'd left a message with Father Ambrose. Jack disappeared to change
from slacks, dress shirt and tie to jeans and a faded Seattle Seahawks sweatshirt.

When they sat down to eat, she asked about his afternoon, and got a grimace. "Pretty worthless."

She buttered her corn bread. "What if he doesn't remember Mom? It's been an awful lot of years."

"I'd like to say that's the kind of thing that sticks in
your memory, but priests must constantly deal with troubled teenagers, the aftereffects of suicide, dysfunctional
families…" He sighed. "We can only hope. Did you leave
my name and number as well as yours?"

Gabby nodded.

Conversation lagged as they'd finished eating.

Jack's phone rang. "My father," he said briefly. "Leave the cleanup to me..."

"Don't be silly. It won't take five minutes."

"Thanks." He stood, kissed her cheek and answered the phone. "Dad?"

Although he wandered into the living room, she could still hear his side of the conversation.

"Gabby's father had boxed up all of Colleen's stuff and stuck it up in the attic," he said. "We found enough to believe she was raped in high school. I think it has to be connected. She knew and dreaded seeing the man who killed her."

Gabby missed some of what Jack said when she ran hot water to wash the pan and rinse off their bowls and plates before putting them in the dishwasher.

"There's no question she's being targeted." He sounded grim now. "Friday, this guy walked onto the porch at the house where Ric Ortiz still lives and shot through the front window. Missed Gabby by inches but badly injured her brother. He's going to be okay but had emergency surgery and was just moved out of the ICU yesterday."

A couple of grunts followed. Then, "What am I doing to protect her? What do you think? She's staying here with me, of course." After a moment, "No, of course that's not usual practice—"

Done in the kitchen, Gabby hovered just outside the living room, not wanting to interrupt but assuming he didn't care that she could hear what he was saying, or he'd have gone to his bedroom. Even though he had his back to her, Jack turned as if he sensed her presence. The way those blue eyes locked on to her got to her as much as it had in the restaurant that first night.

"You're right," he said into the phone. "It is sort of ironic, isn't it?" He listened to his father for another minute, then said, "Listen, I've got to go." Pause. "Yeah, you, too."

Seeing him shove the phone in his hip pocket, Gabby said, "I'm sorry. I wasn't trying to eavesdrop, but I could hear you from the kitchen anyway."

"We didn't say anything private." Jack gave a crooked smile. "Dad was just accusing me of getting involved with you. He pointed out that I've never brought anyone involved with one of my investigations home with me before."

"Were any of them being hunted the way I am?"

He shrugged. "Maybe a gang member or two."

Gabby moistened her lips. "Did you try to defend yourself?"

"From Dad? No, why would I? He was right. I'm falling for you." His mouth twisted. "Have fallen."

Her chest cramped. "I'm still mad at you."

"I know." His throat worked. "I don't blame you. I had...tunnel vision. It made me stupid."

She nodded acknowledgment, struggling with contradictory emotions. It was hard to overcome feeling betrayed, but...she'd fallen for him, too. Wouldn't *she* be the stupid one if she held on to her grudge and threw away any chance at a future with the only man she'd ever felt this way about?

Yes.

"You won't lie to me again?"

"No. *God, no.*"

Gabby didn't even see him move, yet suddenly she was in his arms, holding him as tightly as he held her.

"This has been hell. Trying to keep you safe and knowing—" Jack broke off, his jaw muscles knotted.

"Knowing?" Her own eyes burned.

"You'd leave and I'd never see you again."

"I do have to find a job," she mumbled into his chest.

"There are a lot of colleges in commuting distance."

"I know." New confidence allowed her to lift her head and meet his eyes. "I've done some research."

He didn't blink for a long time as he studied her face. Then he groaned, closed his eyes and bent forward to rest his forehead against hers. "Thank you."

"No, I'm the one who should be saying thank you, after you've come running to my rescue time after time."

He nuzzled her. "Let's call it good. No debts between us."

"No debts." She pushed up on tiptoe to press her mouth to his.

He took control of the kiss, which turned passionate and so urgent, Gabby wouldn't have minded if he'd laid her down on the hardwood floor and stripped her right now. But he didn't.

"Don't have any condoms with me," he growled, and steered her toward the staircase.

It was awfully hard to climb with his hands all over her, but from the sound of his breathing, the impact wasn't one-way.

Naturally, his bedroom was the last at the end of the hall, but they made it. They were barely beside his bed when Jack yanked back the covers and started stripping her even as she tried to pull up his sweatshirt and then unbuttoned and unzipped his jeans. He swore, clothes tangled with their limbs, and they finally made it into bed, naked.

They kissed until her head spun. Jack seemed to know exactly how and where to touch her. His fingers slid from one sensitive spot to another. She was already arching when he released her mouth and slid lower to suckle her breasts.

Gabby kneaded his chest and shoulders, frustrated at her inability to reach that iron bar pressed against her thigh. Why did she have to be so short?

When he finally reached across her for the drawer in his bedside table, Gabby wrapped her fingers around him, squeezed and stroked and let him feel her fingernails. His hands were shaking as he put on the condom, and the heat in his eyes could have incinerated the sheets if his focus hadn't been so intensely on *her*.

The pleasure of joining was so powerful, she came with shocking speed. Jack drove her through the implosion and up again. There was nothing gentle or careful about this mating. That was not what she wanted, or what he needed. When he thrust a last time, hard, she came apart again. He collapsed on her, and Gabby didn't care if she ever breathed again.

AFTER THE BEST night of his life, Jack had never felt so energized…and so maddened by his inability to make any progress at all toward solving Colleen Ortiz's murder. It wasn't even lunchtime, and he had already called Gabby, needing the reassurance of hearing her voice. The sense of urgency that drove him was like a deep-seated itch he couldn't scratch, a just-heard drumbeat of warning.

She should be safe, but his gut said she wasn't.

Ric called to say he would be released from the hospital tomorrow morning. Yeah, he still felt like crap, but he could hire a visiting health aide to help with anything he couldn't manage. A couple of friends had invited him to recuperate at their homes, too. He hadn't decided.

Jack almost suggested Ric come to his place. He'd be company for Gabby. But something stopped him. He could be followed after picking up Ric, leaving the hos-

pital and driving home. Ric was in no shape to get between his sister and another bullet, either.

"I think you should take one of them up on the offer,"
he said. "We're making progress—" He turned his head
to be sure no one could hear his end of the conversation.
"Gabby is helping me with some research. I don't like
the idea of you alone in that house for now."

"You think I could be pressured to give away her
whereabouts."

"We all have our breaking point."

A long pause. "I don't think I'd rest easy at home, anyway. Not after everything that's happened. Okay, I'll do
that. But you'll stay in touch, won't you?"

"Count on it."

Jack ended the call and raked his fingers through his
hair. Father Ambrose either didn't have a cell phone,
or the diocese had chosen not to hand out that number.
What if he was taking a two week vacation in the Carib-
bean? Filling in for an ill padre far enough from home he
couldn't commute? He probably didn't check his voice
mail as incessantly as people of a younger generation did.

Or didn't he want to talk about Colleen Ortiz?

Damn. Jack thought about calling the parish where
Father Ambrose now lived and occasionally served to
beg for someone to hunt him down.

He glanced at his phone. It wasn't even lunchtime yet.
Give the poor guy a chance. Maybe he'd had a full morning. Maybe he was talking to Gabby right that minute.

Nobody knew she was staying at his house, he reminded himself. Except Ric, of course. And Jack's father.
Hell. How many friends here in town had Dad stayed in
touch with? He'd have no reason to tell anyone what had
been happening with the cold case, would he?

Jack's one accomplishment this morning was eliminating Sergeant Rutkowski as a suspect. He'd been talking to another detective he sometimes paired with on big cases. Mary Springer mentioned having worked Friday and Saturday both. Jack asked who else had been here, and she told him their sergeant was.

She'd grinned impishly. "His wife's sister and her family were with them for the four days. He said a little of the sister goes a long way, so he was hiding out. Really, all four of us at the station probably were, for our own reasons. None of us stepped foot out of the office. We ordered out for a big lunch—*not* turkey—and enjoyed the peace and quiet."

Relief flooded Jack. He *liked* the sergeant and had hated suspecting him.

Pinning down Chief Keller's whereabouts was inevitably a bigger challenge. Several layers of command separated Jack from the police chief. Until he'd asked to open the cold case, he'd had very little personal interaction with the man. Occasionally Keller dropped by to talk to Rutkowski. Otherwise, Jack saw their police chief giving statements during news conferences on TV, just like everyone else.

If the chief wanted to slip out, he had the advantage that the current city hall and police station were connected. He met frequently with the mayor or city council members. After all, Keller was a politician as much as anything, and probably spent half his time in those meetings.

Jack was good at strategy, but he couldn't figure out how to pin down where the police chief had been during fixed periods of time without sounding as if he was butting his nose in places it didn't belong. About all Jack had learned through common gossip was that Keller had taken the full four-day weekend, which meant he could have been anywhere.

What if he was upfront with Sergeant Rutkowski, who might be able to get answers to those questions without drawing unwanted notice?

Even imagining what Rutkowski would say to one of his detectives suspecting the chief of police of being a rapist and murderer had Jack wincing. It might be different if he could present even a grain of real evidence. The fact that Keller had left Leclaire High School after his sophomore year even though his parents didn't move away was damn suggestive timing. Add to that the fact that he'd stayed away until his father died, after which he immediately returned to Leclaire and took a job with LPD. As a puzzle piece, it dropped into place, cut to fit. But sure as hell, Dean Keller had told his story until it was completely believable.

They *needed* Father Ambrose.

Jack had run out of other strings to pull. The killer could well be someone he'd never considered, would have no way to identify. But his gut told him he was right. He just didn't know what he could do next, short of sitting in the parking lot watching for Keller to leave and then following him—which wasn't feasible.

Thoughts spinning in circles, he walked down the block to the nearby deli to buy a sandwich he could eat at his desk. Unfortunately, neither the brief activity nor the icy air outside cleared his mind.

He was stopped twice on his way in, once about another investigation, once by the patrol officer who'd handled the break-in at the Ortiz house and had just heard about the shooting. Jack filled him in on the continuing saga before taking the stairs rather than the elevator.

He'd intended to have his third or fourth cup of coffee with the sandwich, but saw the pot in the bullpen was down to sludge and crossed the hall to use the pop machine in the break room. Cold can in hand, he heard voices in the hall. Chief Keller and Rutkowski, he realized. Not prepared to produce another even semiconvincing update, he lurked a few feet inside the break room where he could see Keller's back blocking the detective bullpen doorway. His wait wasn't long. The police chief abruptly turned away and headed down the hall toward the elevators.

Feeling like a kid slinking around so Dad couldn't assign him a new chore, Jack crossed the hall without wasting time. He could see the chief striding away, and made sure to duck back into the bullpen before Keller happened to glance back.

At his desk, he started to unwrap his sandwich, but something niggled at him. Frowning, he turned to look toward the doorway to the hall. Had he ever seen Keller walk more than a few feet before? He had a distinctive stride—

Jack's phone rang, and his adrenaline spiked when he recognized the number.

"Detective Cowan here," he said. "Is this Father Ambrose?"

"It is. Given the questions, I thought it best to call you rather than the young lady." The priest had a strong voice that hadn't lost anything to age.

"Thank you. I don't know how much Gabby told you in her message, but I'm hoping you remember her mother, Colleen Ortiz."

"I do because that was such a distressing and delicate situation. I've asked myself many times over the years whether I made the right decision. To find out that she was later murdered… If I'd had the least idea…"

"I'm assuming what you learned is that she'd been raped."

"I wouldn't be able to tell you what she said in the confessional if she were alive, but given what Colleen's daughter said, I think I must."

"Colleen surely didn't blame herself for the rape to the extent that she felt she had to confess."

"No, her guilt came from her lies to her parents about where she was going. She wasn't a girl who did that kind of thing, but I gather she was completely infatuated with the boy. In the midst of telling me, she fell apart and it all came out. As…shattered as she was, she was absolutely determined not to go to the police. She already knew she wasn't pregnant, and she couldn't bear for her parents to know she'd been assaulted. She said that everyone would look at her differently, which is, regrettably, true. I had grave reservations about her thinking she could just put it behind her, but I couldn't ignore her wishes." The priest paused. "What a terrible thing to happen. Such a shock." He sighed. "I didn't know him or the family, since they didn't worship at St. Stephen's, but I had no difficulty locating them. I felt I was doing the right thing to take this to them. I don't believe Colleen could have borne seeing the boy every day at school. My meeting with the parents wasn't pleasant, of course. The mother was in complete denial, but his father agreed to withdraw him from the public school and send him to a boy's school, a military academy. He promised not to allow him to return to Leclaire. I…had the feeling that he'd already had some suspicions about his son."

Jack knew. *He knew.* Handsome and charming classmate well able to tempt a good girl to lie to her parents to meet him illicitly.

That rolling gait, the big, powerful body with a little softening around the middle told him enough.

Jack pushed back his desk chair and surged to his feet. Harshly, he said, "Father Ambrose, who was the boy?"

Chapter Seventeen

Dean Keller.

Who'd just gotten into an elevator either to ride up a floor to his office...or down, to leave the building.

Jack didn't know what else he'd said to the priest. What if Keller had been leaving? Electrified by fear, he knew only that he had to go home. Be there to protect Gabby.

He snatched his parka from the back of his chair and went straight to Rutkowski's office, rapping on the glass and entering without waiting for an invitation.

"Was Chief Keller going back up to his office?" Jack could only imagine what the sergeant saw on his face.

That had to be why he barely hesitated. "I don't know. You'd better have a good reason for asking." He picked up his phone and pushed a couple of buttons to route his call to the chief's office. "This is Rutkowski. The chief was just here. Is he back in his office yet?" Rutkowski's dark eyes met Jack's. "Thanks." He dropped the receiver into the cradle. "He's gone for the day."

"I think he murdered Colleen Ortiz, and I'm damn sure he's trying to kill Gabby. I need to get home in case—"

"She's there?"

"Yeah." Jack's voice was hoarse with fear. "I've got to go."

"I'm going with you." The sergeant grabbed his holstered gun from a drawer, snapped it on his belt and swept up his coat on the way out of the office on Jack's heels.

Heads turned when the two men ran from the squad room and down the hall. Without discussion, they took the stairs two at a time. That saying about seeing your life pass before your eyes? Jack saw the life he wanted to have, complete with kids. The one he'd lose if he didn't stop the son of a bitch out to kill her.

Rutkowski leaped in on the passenger side of Jack's assigned police vehicle, buckling himself in as tires squealed and Jack accelerated toward the exit. He had his lights and siren on by the time he swerved onto the street.

"Explain."

Jack did, in a few short words. "I kept thinking I was crazy. He's my boss. He's a respected cop and has been chief for—"

"Seven years." The sergeant planted a hand on the dashboard as they rocketed through a yellow light.

"You're not arguing." How long had it been since Keller left the station? Could he be at Jack's house yet?

"I had a few thoughts that made me uncomfortable. Got the feeling you weren't telling us everything, either. Started wondering why that would be, and that brought back a memory of seeing Dean and Colleen together a few times in high school."

Jack fumbled his phone from his pocket and called Gabby.

Ring. Ring. Ring. Went on and on.

Rutkowski continued talking, but in his terror Jack had quit listening. A thought hit him and he called his father, putting his phone on speaker.

"Jack?"

"Did you tell anyone at all that Gabby is staying with me?"

"Nobody you need to worry about," his dad said, sounding surprised. "Your boss called me out of the blue last night, said you'd told him recently where I'd relocated to, and he was curious enough to decide to touch base. Hadn't heard from him in twenty years or more, but I must have mentioned him before."

"No," Jack said tersely. "I had no idea you knew him."

"After I was brought in for questioning about the Ortiz woman's death, he was friendly. Went out of his way to talk me through what was happening and reassure me that the interest in me was routine. Nothing to worry about. Like I said, we talked four or five times over the next few years, but we didn't have much in common."

"Did he ask where Gabby was staying?"

"Why would he when he knew? He said something like, 'Have to admire your boy for taking a witness home with him.' Said he was pleased you'd reopened that investigation, mentioned that you were keeping him in the loop." There was a silence Jack read as appalled. "You're not suggesting—"

Jack said a word he rarely used and cut his father off so he could redial Gabby.

Still no answer.

You're too late, said a voice in his head.

He wouldn't accept it.

FEELING CHILLED, GABBY went upstairs to put on a sweater. While she was there, she used the bathroom. Washing her hands, she leaned closer to the mirror to study herself. Wow. Apparently, extreme stress had more impact on her appearance than all the happiness in the world could.

Where was the glow Jack had claimed to see when she was able to tell him that Ric had regained consciousness and was going to be fine? Shouldn't a night of astonishing sex with a man who hadn't quite told her that he loved her, but had come really, really close be giving her a glow?

Instead, her eyes were sunken and bruised-looking and her skin pasty. Maybe she should think about applying some makeup before Jack got home.

As if he hadn't already seen her this morning.

She made a face at herself, dried her hands and reached for her phone…only to realize she must have left it downstairs. *Dumb*. What if she'd missed Father Ambrose's call? Or Ric had taken a downturn?

She hurried toward the staircase and started down. The last place she'd been was the kitchen, where she'd rinsed out her coffee mug after who-knew-how-many refills. She could have set the phone down on the counter…

The familiar ringtone came to her. She probably couldn't reach it in time to catch the call, but—

At the sound of glass breaking, she froze with one foot hovering in midair.

That had to be at the back of the house, she thought, with a calm clarity that had separated itself from her panic. If she could get to her phone… But what if he was coming in the kitchen window?

A strange rattling made her hesitate. Blinds. She could all but see a hand reaching in through a broken pane on the French doors that led from the dining room out to a deck. Jack had left the blinds closed, as he had on all the other windows.

What if she ran for the kitchen, waited until she heard the intruder enter, and ran *out* the kitchen door? She might have a few seconds until the intruder realized that Jack had installed a sliding lock at the top of the French doors.

Splintering wood gave her all the answer she needed. He'd kicked his way inside, and if she went that direction, she'd pass within sight of him.

Upstairs. She felt her way backward with one foot before she overcame that instinctive need to mindlessly flee.

A voice whispered, *Wrong way.*

Already tiptoeing down the last few steps and rushing around the wall that framed the staircase and formed an alcove in the living room, she knew the voice was right. Upstairs, she'd be trapped. Worse yet, there was nowhere to hide. Jack was either a neat freak or just hadn't collected much yet. Under the bed might work playing hide-and-seek with kids, but not for hiding from a killer.

She could run for the front door, but unlocking the dead bolt would make noise. By the time she fled out onto the porch—if she got that far—he'd be on her. He could pump a couple of bullets into her back, go out the way he'd come and be long gone before anyone in a passing car noticed the woman's body half-fallen down the front porch steps.

The space under the stairs. Not really a closet, but unlike the rest of the house, it *was* cluttered, partly with the boxes holding her mother's stuff. The two that were definitely thrift store bound sat beside the front door, but Jack had shoved the others in there as well.

Rather than a door, it had a sliding panel someone might miss noticing. It allowed an opening just wide enough for a person to crawl in. She couldn't remember how much noise the panel made when it was moved.

Didn't matter. She was out of choices.

"GET A UNIT to the house," Rutkowski snapped into the radio. "Sirens, lights. Backup preferable. Do you hear me?" The obscenities he uttered told Jack all he needed to know. Dispatch didn't think they could get a patrol car to his house any faster than he and Rutkowski would reach it.

"Might be better," the sergeant muttered. "We have some rookies that barely shave. Would some kid, confronted by the chief, be able to shoot him?"

Jack hit redial, saw the light turning red ahead of him and barely slowed enough to be sure cross traffic had seen the emergency lights. Then he accelerated again.

"Try calling Keller," he suggested. If he hadn't thought to turn off his phone, the ringing could warn Gabby.

Rutkowski did. "Straight to voice mail. Unbelievable."

Jack was driving at unsafe speeds for the residential streets they'd reached, but he didn't care. No kid would be out riding his bike when the temperature was still below freezing.

"How far?" his companion asked.

"Two minutes," he said grimly. Too far.

THE INTRUDER HADN'T made a sound since he'd stepped into the dining room. If only the wood floors in this old house weren't so solid, she thought in despair as she eased open the panel. She could hear it scraping, but the sound was faint.

That was wide enough. She bent to whisk inside, had to stretch to step over one of the boxes and then reach back to flatten her hand on the panel. *Push it back, slow, slow.* He might be in the living room.

It was pitch black now in this cubby. To move without knocking something over or even tripping and falling, she had to depend on her memory from looking over Jack's shoulder as he put the boxes in here and from the brief moment when she entered.

The space was the same depth as the width of the

staircase, but extended at least eight feet in length, the far wall butting up to the utility room.

The one oddity in here was an indoor hammock Jack must have found he wasn't using. The two-piece frame leaned against the wall, the net heaped beside it. She could pull it over herself, huddle beneath just as she had hidden beneath the sheets in the laundry room when she was a little girl.

In plain sight.

Her teeth wanted to chatter, but she clenched her jaw.

Yes, she'd try hiding under the hammock, but she needed a weapon. She couldn't just crouch there with no way to fight back. Jack had plenty of sports equipment—a wooden baseball bat would have been ideal—but he kept all that out in the garage. If she could have gotten out there…

Not a chance.

Built of solid wood, the frame for the hammock was too unwieldy.

A *squeak* came to her ears. On a step right above her… but was he going up, or down?

Her mind jumped around. How had he found out she was staying here? Then an awful chill struck her. The only person Jack had told, to her knowledge, was his father. What if he'd murdered Colleen after all? He'd have had time to drive from Oregon if he'd set out right away after talking to his son.

Or he could have been here all along. With a cell phone, you couldn't tell.

If Jack had to arrest his own father… She shuddered. *Think.* If only she had her phone. *Well, I don't.*

Wait. What about the bookends packed in with the books? Both pairs were heavyweight. The painted, cast-iron fleur-de-lis had jagged edges as well as enough weight to hurt someone, but the other set, leaping cats carved out of marble, might be even better.

But where were the books? Which box held which set of bookends?

She gathered up the hammock and draped it over herself so that she could sink down beneath it at any moment, and carefully opened the flaps of a box she thought held books.

Yes!

The next *creak* came close enough to cause her to hold her breath. Where was that? Like most old houses, this one didn't have a coat closet. The nearest interior door was at the entrance to the kitchen, and it had been standing open.

She strained to hear even a whisper of sound.

The panel not two feet from her vibrated.

JACK HAD CUT the siren a couple of minutes ago. He and Rutkowski had debated coming in with siren wailing versus sneaking up to the house—and had gone with sneaking. It was too late to scare Keller away before he got into the house. Now, chances were too good he'd already popped a lock or broken a window.

First, though, Jack did one sweep around the back side of his block.

The black Cadillac Escalade registered to his name was parked in a driveway on the next block, in front of a house with a For Sale sign in the yard.

Jack had wanted to be wrong. Now he knew he wasn't.

"You ready?" he asked.

"Damn straight."

Three doors from his house, he jerked to a stop. By the time he put the gearshift in Park and yanked out the key, Rutkowski had sprung out, pushed the door not quite shut to avoid a slamming sound, and was running full out for the open space between Jack's house and his next-door neighbor's. The plan was for him to slip in the gate and enter the house from the back. Jack had responsibility for the front—and, he hoped, drawing Keller's attention and fire.

He sprinted for the near end of the porch, leaped to catch the edge of the broad flat top of the railing and hauled himself up and over. He tried to land lightly, but heard an inevitable thud and went still.

His phone vibrated.

entry french doors going in

He typed 15 secs.

The glass in both windows was intact. He sidled toward the nearest one, cursed himself for having left all the blinds closed, and moved fast until he was past it to the front door. No reason Keller would linger in Jack's home office.

He'd give a lot to be able to see in. To have even a hint of what was happening inside. The house was completely silent.

Nudging at him was the fear that Gabby hadn't answered her phone because she was already dead—but if that was so, why hadn't Keller already slipped out the back and driven away? No, Jack had to believe she'd had a chance to hide. But where? The old-fashioned kitchen pantry had some decent cupboards, but he guessed Keller had entered through the back, which would likely have cut off the kitchen. And, unfortunately, the garage, where there were more options for hiding—and some potential weapons.

He slid the key into the lock and turned it. Tiny click. Grabbed the doorknob and took a deep breath.

Go.

THE PANEL ABRUPTLY slid as far open as it went, letting light in. Gabby hunched beneath the rough striped fabric of the hammock. She could just see out around the edge, to an ominous dark shape blocking the light from the living room. He crouched to peer in. For a terrifying moment, she was four again. *Mommy screaming, blood splashing, grunts from the man stabbing, stabbing, stabbing. Mommy silent.*

Can't look, can't look. Have to.

He's *looking at me.*

Her head swam. She inhaled soundlessly and clutched the marble bookend. She wanted to smash his head. She wanted *him* to suffer.

"I know you're in here," he said. "Let's see. What about—"

Pop. Pop. A box jumped.

"No?"

The front door slammed open and, still at a crouch, he spun to face the threat.

Gabby pushed off the hammock, jumped over the box and ducked to avoid hitting her head. Then she swung the marble cat as hard as she could for the monster's head. It was like striking a jack-o'-lantern on Halloween. No, a pumpkin with innards intact. Brains. *Smash, squish.*

The sensations mixed with gunfire, men yelling, glass breaking—and something knocking her backward. *He* was down. Puzzled, Gabby raised her gaze to Jack, bending over the man—and then she dropped to her knees, to her butt, and everything went black.

GABBY KNEW FROM the smell alone that she was in the hospital. Lying still, she did a brief evaluation. Toes wriggled. Fingers, too. But her shoulder hurt. That stirred memories of waking up to a strange woman's face hovering over her, the woman assuring her that she was fine, the surgery had been successful, she could just rest now. She'd seen Jack a couple of times, too, hadn't she?

Gabby opened her eyes and blinked a few times. She felt truly awake this time.

"Back with us?"

She knew Jack's voice, and turned her head. He stood beside the bed looking down at her, every line in his face carved deep.

"How do you feel?"

"I…" She worked her mouth, trying to come up with some saliva. "Okay."

"Here." He sat next to her and helped her take a few sips from a cup of water.

Then they looked at each other.

"You're not supposed to leap up when guns are being fired," he observed, almost mildly.

She wasn't fooled. "He was going to shoot you."

"He did shoot me."

"What?" She struggled to sit up.

He gently pressed her back. "Hey. Stay put. I was wearing a vest."

"Oh." Gabby absorbed that. "Did you shoot me?"

"I'm afraid so."

Well, he was right. She'd sort of asked for it. Anyway, that's not what was most important right now. "He wasn't your father, was he?"

It was Jack's turn to say, "What?" Then he shook his head. "No. Why would you think…" He made the connection. "Because I told him you were staying with me.

No, of course it wasn't him, but he told the wrong person." If anything, the grooves in his forehead were even deeper. "Dean Keller killed your mother. He's the police chief. *Was* the police chief. My boss."

Her mind still wasn't sharp enough to consider the ramifications of that. "You shot him."

"I did." His blue eyes were momentarily cold. "Killed him, too—if your blow to his head hadn't already done the job."

"I hope it did. As I crouched there, one of the last things I thought was that I wanted to *hurt* him."

Jack took her hand. The warm strength felt so good.

"I can't even imagine how you handled that, having to hide from him a second time," he said, voice deep. "You're amazing."

"I…had a flashback or two," she admitted. "But… I was determined not to be so helpless again. It would have been nice if you'd kept a baseball bat or, I don't know, a great big knife in the closet, but no."

His hand tightened until the grip was almost painful, but he also managed a crooked smile. "Weapon in every closet from now on. Although you did find one. I didn't pay attention to those bookends, but that was a heavy sucker."

"Marble," she said with satisfaction.

"Damn, Gabby." He bent forward and nuzzled her, then gave her a feather-soft kiss. "I've never been so scared in my life."

She gave a tiny nod. She couldn't say the same, and he knew why.

"This is too soon to push you, but…" His chest rose and fell with a long, pained breath. "If you'll give me a chance, I'm willing to go wherever you want to live.

Staying in Leclaire can't have a lot of appeal. I can get a job anywhere."

Now that he'd straightened, she searched his face and found only desperate sincerity. He meant it. He'd really uproot himself for her.

Gabby tried to smile, knew her lips trembled. "Ric's here. And...if you're not in trouble—"

"For shooting and killing the police chief, you mean?" He grimaced. "I'm on administrative leave, which is normal after a shooting. My direct boss, Sergeant Rutkowski, was with me, which helps. No matter what, no one investigating can deny the son of a bitch was trying to kill you. If we had to try him for your mom's murder—" He stopped himself. "Guess that's not happening."

It wasn't. Because the man was dead.

Later she might have to grapple with the knowledge that she might have killed someone, but now—

She had to dampen her lips. "If...if you mean what I think you're saying, I wouldn't mind trying to stay in Leclaire. If I can't get a job, well—"

"Anywhere," Jack said huskily. "Anywhere at all. Anytime." His lips met hers.

This kiss expressed so much: passion, tenderness, commitment. And it was also brief, because Jack was determined not to hurt her.

They held hands and talked quietly, sharing plans and promises until she drifted back to sleep.

* * * * *

GUARDING COLTON'S CHILD

LARA LACOMBE

For Opa, who has the best stories.

Chapter One

Where had all these people come from?

Desiree Colton frowned as she watched a seemingly endless stream of people file into the ballroom. They came from every direction, a calm procession of smiling faces stopping here and there to mill about in groups. The noise level in the room rose considerably as the buzz of conversation hit a dull roar. She scanned these new arrivals, hoping to recognize someone, but they were all strangers.

Desiree turned to her cousin, hoping Melissa would know what was going on. As chief of police in Grave Gulch, Melissa usually had her finger on the pulse of the community. But all Desiree saw was the back of her cousin's head as she walked away.

Strange.

A loud, grating laugh pierced the air, making the hairs on the back of Desiree's neck stand at attention. She froze, unease melting into a growing sense of panic as she scanned the room.

Where was Danny?

"Danny?" She called out for her son as she began to

walk through the room, sidestepping people who leaned into her path. No one touched her, but moving through the crowd was claustrophobic and her chest felt tight.

"Danny!" *Desiree heard the panic in her own voice, but she didn't care. She had to find her son.*

The crowd parted and she saw the broad shoulders and strong back of her brother, Troy. Relief washed over her; Troy and Danny were great pals. He probably had the little boy in his arms and was beaming with his usual avuncular pride as he showed him off to anyone who looked their way.

Desiree walked over to her brother and touched his arm. "Troy, I'm so glad to see you."

He turned and gave her a smile. "Hey, Dez. What a party, huh?" *He gestured to the crowd with his beer bottle.*

But Desiree didn't follow his gaze. Her muscles locked up, panic rendering her unable to move.

"Where's Danny?" *He was supposed to be with Troy, but her brother's arms were terrifyingly empty.*

Troy shrugged. "I'm sure he's around. I passed him off to Palmer. He said something about showing Danny the horses."

Desiree shook her head. "What horses? There are no horses here!"

But Troy didn't respond. He turned away, melting into the crowd the same way Melissa had.

Desiree screamed her son's name, her voice rising above the din of music and conversation. She knelt down, hoping to find her boy hiding under one of the long tablecloths that draped over the edges of the tables. But he was nowhere to be seen.

Desiree's skin flushed as adrenaline pumped through her body. She had to find her baby. But how?

The crowd moved as one, everyone turning to face her. She tried to move, but was surrounded by a wall of bodies. Desperate, she flailed against them, slapping and kicking in a bid to break through. But her blows proved ineffective, and the people closest to her showed no response to her struggle.

"Danny!" she screamed.

Melissa suddenly appeared in front of her, a stiff smile frozen on her face.

"Danny's gone," Desiree said. But even as she spoke the words, she knew her cousin wasn't listening.

Desiree turned away from Melissa, frantically scanning the crowd for any signs of her boy.

"Danny!"

DESIREE SHOT UP in bed, arms outstretched as she reached for her son. She blinked in the darkness, confusion slowly giving way to awareness as she recognized the familiar shadows of her bedroom.

Her panicked heaving gradually slowed to calmer breaths, her body no longer feeling starved for oxygen. She sank back onto her pillow and raised a hand to her forehead. "It was a dream," she whispered into the still room. "Only a dream."

Danny was here, safe in his bedroom. They were together, as they should be. Everything was fine.

Desiree knew it was the truth, but the ever-present

knot of tension in her stomach remained. Her world had flipped upside down four months ago, when Danny had been kidnapped. And even though her son had quickly been found safe and sound, she hadn't gotten over the experience. Would she ever? Was it possible for a mother to truly let go of the bone-deep terror that came from missing her child?

Something inside her had undergone a fundamental shift, and Desiree recognized she was never going to be the same again. Some days, she missed the carefree ignorance she'd once enjoyed, that lack of suspicion that now clouded her every encounter with a stranger. Every smile directed at Danny, every comment like "Oh, he's so cute," which she'd once taken at face value, was now a potential threat. It was exhausting, living in this hypervigilant state. But Desiree couldn't seem to stop.

Logically, she knew that the odds of Danny being kidnapped again were infinitesimally small. Really, the only reason he'd been taken in the first place was because Hannah McPherson had been desperate to prove that her granddaughter, Everleigh Emerson, was innocent of murder. The old woman had picked up Danny during a wedding reception at the Grave Gulch Hotel and simply walked out. She hadn't hurt him in any way; quite the opposite, in fact. She'd taken him home, fed him a snack and rocked him while he watched cartoons until he'd fallen asleep in her arms.

Still, the event haunted Desiree. And, worse, it seemed to be happening again.

Just last week, another woman had tried to walk off with Danny when they were at the playground. Desiree had been talking to Dominique de la Vega, a reporter for the *Grave Gulch Gazette*. Dominique was working on a story that involved looking in to Randall Bowe, the forensic scientist who'd abused his role to corrupt evidence and frame several people. Danny's kidnapping back in January and the subsequent reevaluation of Everleigh's case had revealed Bowe's misconduct, and Dominique had been pressing to talk to Desiree about the whole thing. She'd finally relented, agreeing to meet at the park where she'd just spotted Randall Bowe skulking about.

It had been a beautiful day, bright and sunny, the temperature perfect. She and Dominique had sat on one of the benches near the playground, so Desiree could keep an eye on Danny while he ran around.

That was when it had happened.

Danny had moved to the other side of the slide, in pursuit of a bug. Desiree could still see him, but her phone had starting buzzing. She'd reached into her cavernous bag, searching for the device.

At that moment, Danny screamed. Desiree looked up to see him tucked under the arm of a woman in a straw hat.

Desiree had jumped to her feet and yelled for Danny. She'd started running to get to her son, dodging other kids and play equipment along the way. Before she got too close, the woman glanced over her shoulder and dropped Danny, then took off running. Desiree had wanted to follow as the woman disappeared into the trees at the end of the park, but no way was she going to risk leaving her son behind to do it. Instead, she'd scooped him up into her shaking arms and taken him back to the bench while she called the police.

Who was that woman? And why had she tried to walk away with Danny?

Desiree was certain she'd seen her once more since the playground, lurking at the grocery store. No hat, but same sunglasses. Once again, she'd disappeared before Desiree could confront her.

Was she being followed? Or was Danny the target?

GGPD were aware of the near miss at the playground. But, really, the officers couldn't spend all their time looking for a woman who hadn't succeeded in committing a crime.

Yet.

Guilt and worry plagued Desiree, night and day. Bad enough Danny had been snatched once. But a second time? How could she have let that happen? What kind of mother took her eyes off her child, gave a stranger the opportunity to walk away with them?

"A human one," Melissa had said, on more than one occasion. "You're only human, Dez. It's okay to make mistakes."

But Desiree couldn't bring herself to agree. A mistake was forgetting to take the garbage to the curb on trash day. What she'd done had put her son's life in danger. It was only thanks to the fast-acting work of the Grave Gulch police and Hannah's gentle nature that Danny was still okay. And, fortunately, this stranger—whoever she was—hadn't escalated her behavior.

In the end, maybe that was all that mattered. Danny was fine. At twenty-three months old, he was far too young to really remember the events of four months ago, much less be permanently affected by them. That was a gift. Desiree would be dealing with this near miss for the rest of her life, but it was a small price to pay, given how much worse things could have been.

She closed her eyes, wondering if she'd be able to get back to sleep tonight. Sometimes, the nightmares left her awake until sunrise. Other nights, she could grab a few more hours of rest before the day started. Hopefully this was one of those times...

"Mama."

It wasn't a loud cry, but the sound of her son's voice propelled Desiree from the bed. She could tell by his tone that something was wrong. This wasn't a normal, middle-of-the-night wake-up. He needed her for more than a pat on the back and a lullaby.

She forced herself to slow down before she entered Danny's bedroom. If she flew in at top speed, it would only scare him. So she gently opened the door and stepped inside, greeting him softly in the glow of his night-light.

"Hey, baby. Mama's here."

Danny was sitting up in his crib, rubbing his eyes with small fists. At the sound of her voice, he looked up and started to wail.

"Oh, sweetie, it's okay. I've got you." Desiree reached down and picked him up.

As soon as she felt his body against her chest, she knew he had a fever. And not a mild one, either—the boy was burning up.

Alarm spiked in her belly as she carried him into

the kitchen. Keeping the lights off, she retrieved the digital thermometer and pressed it to his forehead. The green light of the display switched to an angry red, and a warning beep sounded.

104.3 degrees.

"Not good," she muttered, patting Danny's back gently. He was crying in earnest now, and his voice sounded hoarse. Desiree quickly filled a sippy cup with cold water and handed it to him, hoping he would drink. He took one sip and started screaming.

Her heart pounded hard as she carried him back to the bedroom and grabbed her cell phone. She called his pediatrician's office, and while waiting for the night nurse to answer, she took him to the bathroom and ran a washcloth under the tap. He squirmed when she pressed it to the back of his neck, but she held it in place.

After what seemed like an eternity, the night nurse came on the line. Desiree told her what was going on as she walked back to her bedroom.

"Take him to the ER," the woman told her. "You need to get that fever down as soon as possible."

"Should I try to give him medicine first?"

"If he won't take water, he won't take medicine," the nurse replied. "Don't waste time. Just go in now and they can give him medication when you arrive."

Desiree ended the call and placed Danny on her bed. His screaming intensified, but she needed her hands free.

"I'm sorry, honey. Mama just has to get dressed."

She grabbed a pair of pants and a shirt off the floor—both were wrinkled and needed a wash, but she couldn't pretend to care. After throwing her hair back into a ponytail, she picked up her son again, threw her phone into her purse and snagged her keys.

"Here we go, Danny," she said, trying to keep her tone light as she carried him out to the car. "We're going on an adventure."

He clung to her shirt, face buried against her chest as he continued to cry. The sound broke her heart and added to her worry. He was so hot—she'd never felt a body that warm before. It was unnatural and thoroughly terrifying.

She loaded him into his car seat and draped the wet washcloth around the back of his neck. Tears streamed down his cheeks and dripped off his chin, and for a split second, Desiree considered holding him in her lap while she drove to the hospital. But, no, that wouldn't be safe.

Not for the first time, she wished things had worked out differently between her and Danny's father. It was a time like this she could have really used a second pair of hands to help. But that was not the reality of her life and wishing was a waste of time.

She took a second to gently wipe Danny's cheeks, then kissed his forehead. Her lips burned from the contact, adding fuel to her fear.

Go, go, go!

The panicked voice in her head urged her to move, and she closed the door and slipped into the driver's seat.

"It's okay, baby," she crooned, keeping her eyes on the image of her son in the rearview mirror as she pulled out of the driveway and set off down the street. "You're going to be fine."

He has to be, she thought to herself as she raced along the empty roads, coasting through stop signs and running the lights at deserted intersections.

The alternative was too unbearable to consider.

"DR. MAKRIS, YOU'VE got a new patient in room five."

Stavros Makris looked up from the computer screen, where he'd been working on charts. "What's up?"

The nurse glanced down at her notes. "Patient is a twenty-three-month-old male, temperature of one hundred and four degrees, pulse rate…"

Stavros listened with half an ear, his heart stuck on the boy's age.

Twenty-three months.

The same age as his daughter, Sammy, the last time he'd held her.

For a brief second, he flashed back to that horrible night when his world had shattered and his life had irrevocably changed.

Bright lights. Urgent voices. And his baby girl, lying motionless on the gurney.

Stavros forced himself to breathe and focused on the nurse's words, using all his willpower to snap out of his memories and tune back in. This boy wasn't his child. He could still help.

He listened as she finished her report. Thankfully, he hadn't missed anything. Years of studying and experience practicing medicine meant that his mind was cataloging the pertinent details even while his heart was shaking off the past.

"Okay, thanks," he said. "I'll head there now. Can you check room three? See if the pain meds have kicked in yet?"

"Sure thing, Doctor."

Stavros got to his feet and started down the hall toward his new patient. He moved calmly but quickly, anxiety pricking the edges of his thoughts and making his skin feel a little tight. Kids were always tough calls, and after losing his daughter… He shied away from the thought as soon as it popped into his head.

He'd spent the last five years learning how to cope with the loss of his baby girl. One thousand, nine hundred and eighty-two days of living with a shattered heart. He reflexively glanced at his watch; in ten minutes, it would be one thousand, nine hundred and eighty-three days since he'd last held her.

Stavros didn't know why he kept a mental tally of the days. It wasn't like he was going to hit a magical milestone and suddenly be relieved of his grief. If anything, he'd learned that he would always mourn his little girl. Not only for who she had been, but also for the person she never got to become. The future she'd never have.

He paused at the door to room five and took a deep breath, clearing his mind so he could fully focus on the child inside. This boy was his patient, and he owed it to the kid to provide the best medical care he was capable of giving.

Stavros tapped his knuckles lightly on the door in announcement and entered the room. He was greeted by the sight of a woman sitting on the gurney, rock-ing back and forth as she held a boy in her arms. She looked up as he entered the room, and when their eyes met, Stavros felt a little shock jolt through his body.

He knew this woman. But how?

Feeling flustered, he frowned slightly as he studied her face, wishing he'd taken a look at the chart first. "Hi, I'm Dr. Makris. What's going on tonight?" Even though the nurse had given him a report of the perti-nent information, he always liked to have his patients, or their parents, tell their story again, so he could hear the tone of their voice and see their expressions. Some-times, the way someone moved or what they didn't say was just as important as their symptoms.

"Danny woke up about an hour ago with a high fever," the mother said. "I tried to get him to drink water, but he refused. The night nurse at his doctor's office said to bring him straight here."

Stavros heard the fear in the woman's voice; it was clear she was scared for her baby. Empathy swelled in his chest. He remembered all too well what it had felt like to hold a feverish child, to fret and worry over every little cough or sniffle. He'd thought his medical training would give him some much-needed perspec-tive when it came to his daughter's health, but if any-thing, the opposite had happened. He'd been so aware of the worst-case scenario, of all the things that could go wrong. He'd been the one to call the pediatrician for every little thing, his wife standing in the background trying to calm him down.

"Tell me about Danny," Stavros said. He kept his

voice level and calm, and walked Danny's mother through the questions that would help him make his diagnosis.

She didn't hesitate to answer him, and based on her detailed responses, Stavros could tell she was an attentive mother.

"All right," he said. "Let's see if your little guy will let me examine him." Stavros already had a presumptive diagnosis in mind, but he always performed a physical exam to confirm his suspicions.

The toddler's mother gently turned her son, and Stavros got his first good look at the boy's face. "I know you!" The words flew from his mouth before he realized he was speaking.

Her expression turned guarded. "Oh?"

Stavros realized he'd put his foot in it, but there was nothing to be done for that now. He nodded. "I...uh... I helped look for your son a few months ago, after he was taken from the hotel."

"You did?" Stavros heard the relief in her voice, noticed the way her body relaxed now that he'd explained his reaction.

"Yeah. I joined a search party after my shift that night."

"Oh, wow," she replied. "That was very kind of you. I'm sorry I didn't recognize you. I didn't get a chance to thank all the people who helped look for Danny."

Stavros waved away her gratitude. He didn't want to tell her that he'd had to do it—he'd been driven by the memories of his own daughter's kidnapping. As soon as he'd heard another child was in the same kind of jeopardy, he hadn't hesitated. He'd jumped in his car at the end of his shift and headed to the hotel, needing to help in some way. Logically, he knew he'd been trying to save this boy the way he hadn't been able to save his daughter. But at the time, he'd been ruled by emotions and the desperate desire to make a difference. Finding Danny wouldn't bring Sammy back—he'd known that. But he wouldn't have been able to live with himself if he hadn't at least tried.

"I'm just glad he was found so quickly," Stavros said, swallowing down the memories of his own tragedy.

"Me, too." The woman extended her hand. "I'm Desiree. And in a strange way, I'm glad to meet you tonight so I can thank you now."

Stavros reflexively reached for her hand. Her skin was soft, her palm smooth against his own. A tingle danced up his arm at the contact, and his body's unexpected reaction nearly made him jump back. He was used to touching people—as a doctor, he touched his patients all the time while conducting an exam. But something about this brush of skin was different. It felt personal, almost intimate, in a way he couldn't articulate and didn't want to think about.

He cleared his throat and dropped her hand. "Stavros," he replied, then immediately started second-guessing himself. *I'm at work, not a party.* He wasn't one of those jerks who insisted on being called "Doctor" all the time, but while he was on shift in the hospital, he preferred to maintain some degree of emotional separation from his patients. It was a little thing, but absolutely vital to his mental health. If he didn't draw that line, he'd burn out in a heartbeat in the face of the things he dealt with on a daily basis.

Stavros mentally shook himself. Time to focus on Danny and the reason he was here. "Hey, buddy," he said softly.

Danny eyed him suspiciously, his eyes glassy with fever and fatigue. Stavros pulled a chair over to the gurney and sat so he was closer to the toddler's level. He grabbed one end of the stethoscope he had looped around his neck and presented the flat disc to Danny. "Have you seen one of these before?"

The boy extended a cautious finger and touched the stethoscope. Stavros smiled encouragingly. "It's a little cold, right?" He put the earpieces in place and gently moved the bell to Danny's chest. A reassuring *thump-thump-thump* met his ears, the beat steady and strong.

"What a good heart you have!" He moved the disc to the side of the boy's chest to listen to the toddler's breathing. "Sounds good, big guy. I'm just going to check your back now." He slid his hand around the boy, acutely aware of how close he was to brushing against Desiree's stomach as she held her son in her lap.

After a few seconds, he leaned back and looped the stethoscope around his neck once more. "Heart and lungs are good, Mom," he said, glancing at Desiree before moving to the next part of his exam. "Think he'll lie down for us?"

She lifted a shoulder. "We can try." She shifted Danny, easing him onto his back. The boy began to cry and grabbed his mother's arm.

"It's okay, Danny," Stavros said. "I'm just going to

check your tummy." He moved quickly, pressing here and there to make sure everything was as it should be. When he was finished, he nodded at Desiree and she helped Danny sit up again.

"You're doing a great job, kiddo," he told the boy. Danny sniffed, but didn't reply. Stavros reached into his pocket and withdrew his otoscope and a disposable speculum. After screwing the black plastic funnel in place, he extended his left index finger and shone the light on the tip.

"Did you see that?" he asked. He did it again, clicking the light on and off. Danny leaned forward a bit, his curiosity growing. "Can you show me your finger?"

Danny slowly reached out. Stavros flashed the light onto the boy's skin and clicked it off again. "Wow!" he exclaimed. "You're glowing, too!"

The corners of Danny's mouth lifted in a small smile. Stavros smiled back, his heart warming. Making a child grin was something that never got old.

"What's your favorite animal, Danny?"

The boy didn't answer, which wasn't unusual. He didn't feel good, he was in a strange place and a stranger was touching him. It was a miracle that Stavros had gotten a smile out of him to begin with.

"He likes dogs," Desiree said.

"Me, too!" Stavros leaned forward. "I'm going to shine this light in your ear and see if I can find any puppies in there."

Danny's eyes grew wide, but he didn't protest when Stavros checked his ears. A quick look up his nose revealed no surprises. Stavros set down the scope and moved his hands to the little boy's neck, gently feeling along the sides. He felt the bumps of enlarged lymph nodes on both sides, just as he'd known he would.

"All right, now I just need to look at your throat." He'd saved this part for last because experience had taught him it nearly always ended in tears.

"Can you open your mouth for me, nice and wide?" Stavros demonstrated, but Danny merely regarded him with a level stare.

"Come on, baby. Open up," Desiree coaxed.

"It's okay," Stavros told her. "This is about the time kids decide they've had enough of me and they're done playing nice." He grabbed two tongue depressors from his pocket and unwrapped them both. He passed one to Danny and held on to the other.

"I'm gonna need you to hold him," Stavros told Desiree. "Put your hand on his forehead and keep the back of his head pressed against your chest. He won't like this part, but I promise I'll be fast."

"All right," she said. As soon as she pulled Danny's head back, the toddler started to squirm and opened his mouth to yell. Stavros took full advantage of the opportunity. He put the tongue depressor in the boy's mouth and leaned in to look at his throat.

"Thought so," he muttered to himself. As promised, he removed the tongue depressor quickly. Danny started to cough, and in the next instant, Stavros felt a gush of warmth on his chest.

"Oh, my gosh!" Desiree cried. "I'm so sorry."

Stavros leaned back and surveyed the damage while Danny wailed in his mother's arms. "It's okay. Really," he told her, seeing the doubt on her face. "This is not the first time I've been puked on, and I know it won't be the last."

As he spoke, he got to his feet and walked to the small sink in the room. He ran water over some paper towels and passed them to her so she could wipe her son's face.

"It's strep throat," he said, raising his voice a little so she could hear him over the sound of Danny's crying. "We'll have to run a rapid test to confirm it, but I'm sure that's what he has. I'll send the nurse in with some Tylenol to bring his fever down, and we'll get that test done right away so we can get his antibiotics and send you home."

"Thank you." Desiree's eyes dropped to his chest, and her cheeks went pink. "I'm so sorry about your shirt. Can I pay to have it cleaned?"

Stavros laughed. "No need. It's just a scrub top. I'm going to change now and I'll check on you guys in a bit."

"Okay." She turned back to her son and began gently wiping his face. It was a mundane gesture, the kind of thing parents did a million times every single day. So why were his eyes suddenly stinging?

Stavros slipped out of the room before he made a fool of himself. He leaned against the wall and ran a hand down his face, trying to regain his equilibrium.

What was it about this kid that rocked him? He was no stranger to treating children; it was an unfortunately regular part of his job. Why, then, had this particular boy thrown him for a loop?

Because Sammy was kidnapped, too.

Her face flashed in his mind and his breath stalled in his throat. He knew all too well the terror Desiree must have felt when her son had been taken from her. He'd lived through that nightmare himself, after his ex-wife had taken their daughter and disappeared into the night in the middle of a snowstorm.

At least Desiree had gotten her child back.

He hadn't been so lucky.

The stench of bile and stomach acid burned his nose and pulled him out of his thoughts. Stavros pushed away from the wall. Time to get his head back in the game; he had to change clothes, and there were other patients who needed him.

He stopped by the nurses' station on the way to the break room. "Room five needs Tylenol and a rapid strep test," he said.

"Roger that," the charge nurse said, her eyes still on the chart in front of her.

He started to walk away, then stopped and turned around. "Watch out," he cautioned. "The kid's got a hell of a gag reflex."

The woman glanced up and caught a glimpse of his top. She bit her bottom lip, clearly trying to hide a smile. "Looks like you need to work on your own reflexes."

"Can't win 'em all," he replied. She snickered as he turned back and headed for the break room and the scrubs vending machine it contained.

"Almost done," he muttered to himself as he carefully removed his soiled shirt and put it in the machine to exchange for a clean one. Just a few more hours until he could go home and be alone with his memories.

The funny thing was, he didn't want to be alone. A part of him wanted to march back into room five and talk to Desiree, to spill his guts and tell her every detail of his sad story. Of all the people in this hospital, she was probably the only one who had any sort of idea what he'd gone through five years ago. But more than that, he simply wanted to be in her presence. She seemed to give off a gentle energy that he found immensely appealing. And, yes, she also happened to be a beautiful woman. Her dark brown eyes and curly hair perfectly complemented the warm bronze color of her smooth skin, and her full lips seemed to have their own gravitational field. Under any other circumstances, Stavros would have gladly let himself get pulled into her orbit.

Too bad it wasn't an option.

It had been far too long since Stavros had felt an immediate connection to anyone, much less a woman. After his ex-wife had kidnapped their child, he'd had trouble trusting his own judgment when it came to relationships. He'd never once thought Ellory was capable of doing what she'd done. But something had snapped in her after their divorce, leading her to abduct their daughter in the middle of the night and drive into a raging snowstorm. The accident that had claimed his daughter had killed Ellory, too, so in many ways, Stavros was still searching for closure. At least Desiree had the option to face her son's kidnapper in court, to see the woman punished for what she'd done. He'd never had that chance, and in some of his darker moments, Stavros felt that death was too kind of an outcome for Ellory.

The machine whirred and released a new shirt into

the bin. Stavros fished it out and slipped it over his head, then half-heartedly ran his palms over the fold lines in an unsuccessful attempt to make the fabric look less wrinkled.

"Oh, well." There were worse things than looking like he'd plucked his clothes from a pile off the floor. Hopefully his patients wouldn't hold his appearance against him.

The pager at his hip beeped, another reminder that he couldn't think about the past for too long. He owed it to himself, and to his daughter's memory, to keep moving forward.

One step at a time.

Chapter Two

Desiree held Danny against her chest, humming lullabies as she gently rubbed small circles on his back. It had taken several minutes to get him to calm down after the strep test and administration of medication. Not that she blamed him for being upset—he was sick and exhausted, and very likely scared to boot. Her heart ached for him, and she wished for probably the millionth time that night that she could explain what was going on in a way he could understand.

Too bad the doctor couldn't have been the one to do the test. He'd been wonderful with Danny, so patient and caring. It was clear he was a man who liked kids. He probably had several of his own running around at home. No way was a guy like him single. He was obviously smart, he seemed friendly and he was very easy on the eyes.

Part of her felt bad for even noticing something like that when her son was sick, but it was impossible to miss. His tall form and broad shoulders had seemed to fill the room, and the unconscious grace with which he moved had made even his shapeless green scrubs look appealing. She'd watched his hands as he'd examined Danny, and been captivated by his long fingers and the dusting of dark hair that extended partway from his wrists.

But what had really made her sit up and take notice had nothing to do with his physical features. It was the kindness she'd seen in his brown eyes, and the way he'd done everything he could to make Danny feel more comfortable with him. The exam could have been tear-filled and miserable for her son, but Stavros had connected with Danny and had even managed to make him smile. That was no small feat, considering how tired her baby was and how much his throat had to hurt.

No, not Stavros, she told herself. *Dr. Makris.*

Using his first name, even if only in her head, felt too familiar. Too personal. He was her son's doctor, not a man she'd met in a social setting.

Still, it was hard to think of him as just a doctor. Part of her was still reeling from his announcement that he'd joined a search party to look for Danny after her boy had been kidnapped months ago. The fact that this man, a complete stranger, had volunteered to help look for her son after completing what she imagined was a long day at work sounded almost unbelievable. And yet she knew in her bones that Stavros was not the type of person to lie about something like that. He hadn't told her because he was seeking her gratitude or praise; he'd seemed almost reluctant to reveal what he'd done.

In fact, Desiree was willing to bet Stavros never imagined she would find out he had helped search for Danny. And didn't that say a lot about his character?

The door opened and a nurse walked in. Desiree frowned as she watched her approach. This woman was wearing a mask, whereas the other nurse had been bare-faced, even while performing the strep test. Why the difference? Had the exam revealed something besides a simple case of strep throat?

Desiree's heart started to pound as worry coursed through her. Was something else wrong with Danny? If so, where was Stavros? She wanted him to explain it to her, not some new nurse hiding behind a mask.

The woman stopped at the edge of the bed and reached for Danny. "I'll take him now."

Desiree didn't let go of her son. "What do you mean, you'll take him? Where does he need to go? What's happening here?"

"We just need to check a few more things," she replied.

Alarm bells started ringing in Desiree's head. This seemed *wrong* somehow. Dr. Makris hadn't said anything about additional tests, and neither had the nurse who had come in earlier. If Danny had to go somewhere, Desiree was going to go with him.

"I'm coming, too," she said, swinging her legs off the bed to stand.

"No, that won't be necessary," the woman replied.

Desiree tightened her grip on Danny, causing him to yelp in protest. "I'm not letting my son go with anyone but Dr. Makris."

The other woman nodded and slipped one hand into her pocket. Before Desiree knew what was happening, she felt a sharp pinch in her upper arm.

"What the hell?" She pulled back and saw the woman holding a syringe.

"Just relax," the stranger said. "You're clearly on edge."

Panic propelled Desiree up, and she tried to take a step forward toward the door. She still wasn't sure what was going on here, but one thing was terrifyingly clear: Danny was in danger.

Her legs buckled and she landed hard on her knees. Realizing she couldn't move, Desiree opened her mouth to scream.

But the sound remained trapped in her throat.

Helpless, she could do nothing but watch as the other woman took Danny from her arms. Desiree summoned all her energy and managed to lift one arm, but it was too late. The woman walked out the door with Danny, and there was nothing Desiree could do to stop her.

Her arm dropped to her side, the momentum causing her to fall forward. Her cheek hit the floor, and for a second, Desiree was aware of the cold press of linoleum against her face. She tried to scream again, her heart calling out for her son. Then the walls closed in, and the blackness took over.

"HAS THE ANTIBIOTIC for room five arrived from the pharmacy yet?"

Stacey, the nurse who was taking care of Danny, held up a small glass vial of medication. "Just got it."

Stavros nodded. "I'll administer it."

Stacey's eyes widened. "Really?" The surprise was evident in her voice. "I've never seen a doctor volunteer to give a kid a shot. You all usually make us nurses be the bad guys."

Stavros shrugged, not wanting to admit that his offer had more to do with wanting to see Desiree again than the desire to give a toddler an injection. "I need to update the mother, anyway," he said, trying to keep his tone casual. "Might as well kill two birds with one stone."

Stacey seemed to accept this explanation. "Can I ask you a question, though?" she said as she handed him the vial of medication. "Why the injection? Don't strep patients usually get a prescription for antibiotics and sent home?"

"They do," he said, appreciating her curiosity. "But it can be difficult to get a small child to take medication. In this case, I'm trying to spare his mother the struggle of dosing him for the next ten days. Besides, one shot will have him feeling better much faster."

Stacey nodded, and Stavros could tell by the look on her face she was filing the information away for later use. She was a young nurse, but smart and quick to learn and adapt. She was also good with patients, which was why he'd made sure she was the one taking care of Danny.

Stavros paused at the supply cart to grab a sterile syringe and some alcohol wipes, then headed for room five. He wasn't looking forward to giving Danny a shot—kids never enjoyed the experience. But he did want to see Desiree again.

A funny fluttering sensation in his stomach made him feel like he'd just chugged a bottle of soda. He wanted—no, *needed*—to talk to Desiree. Not just about her son's test results, but about his own past. On the advice of his therapist, Stavros had joined an online support group for other bereaved parents in the wake of Sammy's death. It hadn't helped—the members were welcoming and kind, but he found it hard to connect with people through a computer.

Desiree was here, though, in front of him. Maybe they could talk to each other, help each other process what had happened to each of them.

Except...did she even need help?

The thought made him pause, and his steps slowed. What if Desiree didn't need to talk about Danny's kidnapping because she'd moved on? After all, she'd gotten her child back. She didn't have a gaping hole in her life where her son used to be. In fact, talking about the kidnapping might make things harder for her, might make her feel stuck in the past when she was trying to live in the present.

Doubts piled up in his mind, fast and thick. What right did he have to ask her to help him with his own personal trauma? They both knew what it was like to have a child get kidnapped, but that didn't mean she would automatically want to hear his sob story. He shouldn't just assume that she had the emotional bandwidth or desire to listen to him; they'd only met tonight, for starters. For all intents and purposes, they were strangers.

A faint sense of disappointment tinged his thoughts, along with an inexplicable sense of sadness. For some strange reason, Stavros felt like an opportunity was slipping through his fingers. But it wasn't fair for him to impose on Desiree. Better that he realized that now, before he made an awkward personal overture that likely would have been misconstrued. He shook himself mentally, imagining how she could have responded to his offer of coffee after Danny was feeling better. She might have easily been offended, thinking he was trying to make a romantic connection. She might even have gone so far as to report him, and that would have left a mark on his career, affecting him professionally.

No, better to keep everything on an impersonal level. Perhaps he'd run into her someday in town and they could strike up a conversation. But while she and Danny were in his hospital, he needed to keep his emotional distance.

Stavros rounded the corner and immediately jumped back to avoid running into someone. The woman let out a small yelp of surprise and dodged, but their shoulders brushed. Stavros caught a glimpse of her face as she pushed past him and frowned. Why was she wearing a surgical mask? And just who was she?

He turned to watch her as she walked away and noticed she was carrying something. *No, not something*, he realized. Some*one*.

Before he knew what he was doing, he started walking after her. Something wasn't right here.

A tuft of dark hair was visible over her shoulder, and he saw the fingers of a small hand curled around the woman's upper arm.

An electric shock zinged through him. *That's Danny*.

"Stop!" His voice boomed through the hall and he

started to run. He saw the stranger hunch her shoulders. But the woman didn't bother to look back—she broke into a run, headed for the door to the stairwell.

She had a head start on him, but Stavros was taller. His long legs quickly ate up the distance between them. Apparently, she could tell he was close. She turned to face him, her eyes shooting daggers. In a blur of motion, she threw Danny and then pivoted and pushed through the door and into the stairwell.

Stavros reacted on instinct. He caught Danny before the boy could hit the ground, drawing his little body tight against his chest. The child began to sob, clearly terrified by his sudden flight. Stavros stared at the door to the stairwell, feeling torn. He had to get Danny back to Desiree, but he wanted to find that woman. Who was she? And why had she tried to take Danny?

"Dr. Makris? What's happening?"

A few nurses were starting to gather around, drawn by his shout. He could leave Danny with one of them, chase after the woman…

In the end, though, the choice was clear. He couldn't let go of the boy, not until he'd given him back to his mother. "Code pink," he said shortly. "Page Security." Stavros carried Danny to the nursing station and used the phone to dial 911. Maybe they would get lucky and find the woman in the parking lot, though he doubted she would stick around for long.

He caught Stacey coming out of a patient's room. "Come with me," he said.

She blinked at his tone. "What's going on?"

"Someone just tried to kidnap this boy," he told her.

"I need you to help me while I check on his mother."
His gut twisted as they approached room five. Desiree
would never have willingly given up her son. Hopefully
she'd simply been tricked into thinking that woman was
part of the hospital staff. But he had a feeling she was
too smart to fall for such an obvious lie. Which meant
the woman had incapacitated her somehow...

His heart thudded hard in his chest as he pushed
open the door to the room. *Please, let her just be tied
up and gagged.*

No such luck. He saw her limp body sprawled on
the floor, one arm outstretched. His heart cracked as
he realized that even as she'd fallen, she was trying to
reach her son.

Behind him, Stacey sucked in a breath. "Oh, my
God."

"Here." Without taking his eyes off Desiree, he
passed Danny to Stacey. "Hold him and stay here while
I help her." He trusted Stacey, but he still wasn't about
to let Danny out of his sight until the police arrived.

Moving quickly, he knelt by Desiree and placed his
fingers on her neck. Relief flooded him when he felt
her pulse, steady and strong. He scanned her body and
ran his hands over her, searching for signs of an obvious injury. Finding nothing, he carefully rolled her
onto her back.

Desiree's cheek was already starting to bruise, but
he saw no other physical signs of trauma. He lifted her
shirt, scanning her torso, and felt along her legs. Desiree didn't respond to his touch at all, which worried

him. Whatever had happened here, she was well and truly out.

He spotted a droplet of blood on her upper arm, the kind of mark left behind by a rough injection. Someone had given her a shot of something. But what?

Another nurse appeared in the doorway. "Police and hospital security are on the way," she said. She spied Desiree on the floor and stepped in. "What's going on here?"

"I'm not sure yet," Stavros answered absently. His mind was churning through possibilities. "Grab a cervical collar and a bedsheet." He didn't want to move Desiree to the bed until her head and neck were supported. He didn't think she had a spinal injury, but he wasn't willing to take any chances.

The nurse returned quickly and Stavros carefully wrapped the foam collar around Desiree's neck. He placed the folded sheet on the floor next to Desiree, and, working together, he and the nurse rolled her onto the fabric.

"On three," he instructed. At his count, they lifted the bedsheet and put Desiree onto the gurney.

"I want a CBC, rapid tox screen and blood gas," he ordered.

"Dr. Makris," Stacey called out.

He shot her an annoyed look. "What?"

"Let me help."

He blinked at her, realizing what she was asking. "Oh. Oh, of course. Sorry." He took Danny from her, and she darted to Desiree's side and began helping the other nurse attach monitors and leads to Desiree.

Stavros took a step back and began swaying as he held Danny, who was now sniffling.

"Blood pressure, one-fifteen over eighty," Stacey called out. "Pulse ox, ninety-seven."

"Good," he replied. "Let's keep it that way."

The room became a blur of activity as hospital security appeared, followed by additional nurses and staff. To an outsider, the scene might look chaotic. But Stavros recognized the well-choreographed dance of emergency medicine. Granted, he'd never cared for a patient while holding a toddler before, but there was a first time for everything.

New faces appeared at the door. Stavros spared them a glance—the police had arrived.

"Dr. Makris?"

"That's me," he answered, keeping his eyes on Desiree.

"Can we talk to you?"

Stavros nodded. Desiree was stable, and it would take time to get the results of her blood work. "I have a few minutes," he said.

He walked over to the doorway. "Stacey, please call me if anything changes."

"Will do," she replied.

Stavros stepped into the hallway and the two officers followed. One was a young woman with delicate features and green eyes. Her blond hair was pulled back in a tight bun, making her look like a girl in ballet class.

She was staring at Danny with wide eyes, and Stavros got the impression she wanted to hold the toddler. Danny spied her and immediately reached for the woman. She gathered him into her arms and pressed a kiss to the boy's head. "It's okay, baby," she said soothingly. "Gracie's got you."

Stavros glanced at her nameplate: G. Colton. "I take it you're family?" he asked.

The officer nodded. "I'm his aunt Grace." She glanced into the room, her expression worried. "Is Dez going to be okay?"

"She's stable right now," he replied. "I'm not sure exactly what happened, but I think she was injected with a sedative. We'll know more after her blood work comes back."

Grace nodded. Her partner, a tall, dark-haired man with kind eyes, spoke next. "Can you tell us what happened here?"

Stavros launched into the story, describing his encounter with the woman in the hall and how he'd chased after her. "She threw Danny at me when she realized she couldn't get away," he said, shaking his head. "I'm glad I caught him." If he hadn't, Danny would likely be suffering from more than just a case of strep throat.

Stacey poked her head out of the room. Stavros's adrenaline spiked when he saw her face. "What happened?" He took a step toward the door, but Stacey held up her hand.

"The patient is fine," she said quickly, apparently sensing his worry. "But I remembered you were coming to treat the boy when all this happened. Did he get his injection yet?"

Realization dawned on Stavros. In all the activity,

he hadn't yet given Danny his medication. "No, I got a little distracted."

Stacey smiled. "I bet. Do you still have the antibiotic? I can treat him now."

Stavros fished the supplies out of his pocket and passed them to her. "Thanks. I appreciate it."

"No problem." A glint of humor entered her eyes. "Maybe next time, you can just tell me you've changed your mind about giving the injection? No need to go through all this." She gestured to the room and the officers.

"Very funny," Stavros replied.

Stacey beckoned to Grace. "Want to bring him for me? We'll go next door so he doesn't see his mama and get upset."

Grace took Danny and followed Stacey into the empty room. After a few seconds, Stavros heard a dull wail and knew the boy had received his shot.

"What happens to him now?" he asked the other officer.

"I take him home." Stavros turned at the sound of the new voice and saw a tall, redheaded woman with piercing blue eyes approach. She held out her hand. "Melissa Colton. Chief of police."

Stavros shook her hand. "Dr. Stavros Makris."

Melissa nodded, and acknowledged the other officer before turning back to Stavros. "Is Desiree going to be all right?" She craned her neck to see into the room, her brow furrowing as she spied Desiree lying unconscious on the bed.

"I believe so," Stavros replied. "We'll know more

once some of her test results come back, but for now, she's okay."

"Good," she said.

Everyone turned as the door to exam room six opened and Grace stepped out with Danny. The boy's face lit up when he saw the new arrival.

"Issy!" He lifted his arms, reaching for her.

Grace smiled as she brought him closer. "Am I on the bad list since I held you for the shot?" She transferred the boy to Melissa, who kissed him on the cheek.

"Hey, buddy," Melissa said. "You've had quite the adventure tonight." She glanced at Stavros. "Can I take him now, or do we need to wait for paperwork?"

Stavros shook his head. "You guys can go. He's been through enough already—I'm not going to make you stick around for the forms."

"Thanks." She hitched Danny a little higher on her hip. "When Desiree wakes up, please tell her I've got Danny and he's not leaving my sight until she's ready to take him again." She reached into her pocket and withdrew a business card, which Stavros accepted. "Please keep me posted on her condition."

"I will," he said, tucking the card into his own pocket.

"Officers, I'll look for your report soon."

"Yes, ma'am," Grace and her partner said in unison.

Melissa nodded and began to walk away. Then she stopped, spun on her heel and marched back over to Stavros.

"One more thing," she said, looking up at him.

"Yes?"

"Thank you." Her voice, heavy with emotion, dropped. The overhead light glinted off a thin film of tears building in her eyes, and Stavros realized that underneath her professional calm, she was truly upset about these events. "You saved Danny tonight."

A lump formed in Stavros's throat, and he swallowed hard. "I did what anyone else would have done."

Melissa shook her head. "No. Trust me—not everyone tries to help when they see something bad happening."

He ran a hand through his hair. "I just wish I could have kept Desiree safe, too." If he'd gotten to the room a few minutes earlier, he could have prevented the attack completely. Maybe he might have scared the woman away for good…

Melissa glanced into the hospital room and smiled faintly. "Dez is tough. She'll be okay. But Danny?" She swung her gaze to the little boy, who had rested his head on her shoulder. "Who knows what would have happened to him if you hadn't been there?"

"I'm just glad you don't have to find out."

"Me, too." Melissa smiled and blinked away her tears. "You're the hero of the day, Doc. I won't forget this."

Stavros shook his head, feeling suddenly embarrassed. "I don't need any attention." The last thing he wanted was for people to know what had happened here tonight. If the press caught wind of this story, they'd bring up his past again. He didn't want to relive his daughter's kidnapping and death in the public domain…

"Don't worry—I won't make a thing of it if you don't

want me to. But don't be surprised if the word gets out. Kidnappings, even just attempted ones, are newsworthy. And since Danny was taken a few months ago, it'll be even more notable."

"I know." He frowned, remembering the press coverage of his own tragedy. For a while, Stavros couldn't go anywhere without hearing whispers and seeing the sympathetic glances of people who recognized him. Every minute of every day, he'd been surrounded by reminders of the event. Not that he was in danger of forgetting what had happened—walking into an ER room to find your daughter dying on the gurney was definitely one for the memory books. But the coverage had been so unrelenting, so suffocating, that he'd very nearly applied for a transfer after his intern year.

Melissa studied his face, her eyes assessing. "Like I said, I'll do my best to keep your name out of it."

Stavros could tell by her tone that she hadn't missed his reaction. He thought he saw a flicker of sympathy in her eye and knew she must be thinking about his past, as well.

"Do you have a car seat for him?" he asked, changing the subject. It was a question he should have asked earlier, but he trusted the chief of police was familiar with the laws regarding children in vehicles.

She nodded. "I do. And now I'm really going to take him home."

"He might need more medication, if the fever comes back." Stavros took out his prescription pad and wrote some notes for her. "This is the brand name, and here's the generic. You can find it at any store. That's his dose.

He can have it every four to six hours, as needed. If he gets worse, bring him back in right away."

Melissa took the paper and nodded. "I'll send my fiancé to the store. Thanks."

"'Bye, Danny," Stavros said, waving at the little boy. Danny blinked sleepily at him, then laid his head back on Melissa's shoulder. Unsurprisingly, the trauma of the antibiotic shot had been short-lived. Unless Stavros missed his guess, the toddler would be asleep before they left the parking lot.

He turned to find Grace Colton and her partner standing a few feet away. He hadn't noticed them move, but they'd apparently taken a few steps back when Melissa had returned to speak to him again. Now they looked at him expectantly.

"Is there someplace we can go to talk?" Grace asked.

"There's a break room down the hall," Stavros suggested. "Will that work?"

"Sounds good," replied Grace's partner.

Grace hesitated, and Stavros could guess why. He didn't exactly like the thought of leaving Desiree alone, either. The chances of that woman coming back were slim, but he didn't want to risk it.

He spied a security guard headed for the elevator. With a wave of his hand, Stavros flagged him down. "Can you please stay outside this room until I get back? I have to talk to these officers about what happened tonight."

"No problem, sir," the man said.

Stavros leaned into the room. "Stacey, I'll be in the

break room. Page me right away when you have results or if her status changes."

"Will do, boss."

Stavros turned back to the officers and caught Grace's look of relief. Feeling better about the situation himself, Stavros lifted his arm and directed the officers down the hall. "I didn't see the woman's face, but I hope I can still help you."

"You can," Grace assured him. "Every piece of information you can tell us is useful."

Stavros had his doubts about that, but he hoped she was right.

Chapter Three

The room was spinning.

Desiree gripped the sheets tightly, her palms wet against the fabric. Why was everything moving? Was she on some kind of ride?

Her eyelids were so heavy, but she managed to open them a crack. Light speared into her brain, and her stomach immediately protested this new development. Nausea rolled over her in a wave, making her whimper.

"Hey, you're awake."

She turned to the voice, grimacing. After a deep breath, she managed to open her eyes again.

A tall man stood next to her, looking down from above. She caught a glimpse of dark hair, dark eyes and stubbled cheeks. Then his face changed, his features swirling around like some kind of strange painting.

The movement made her stomach lurch, and she recoiled from the disturbing sight. She tried to turn away, alarm building when her muscles ignored her brain's commands. Her heart thumped hard in her chest and she closed her eyes, needing to block the vision before her.

Is this real?

She peeked up at him. He looked normal now, but for how long? She stared hard at his face, looking for any signs of movement. Something was very wrong here; she just knew it.

The man leaned forward, bringing his face closer to hers.

"You're okay," he said. Desiree felt her muscles relax as he spoke. She felt a stirring of recognition deep in her brain, but it floated just out of her grasp. *I know him...*

"You were injected with a sedative," he continued, his voice low and soothing. "Ketamine, I think. It's normal to be confused. We're doing our best to get it out of your system."

"Stavros." She latched on to the name like a life raft.

He smiled, his eyes growing warm. "Yes. That's me."

Some of the pieces began to click into place. The hospital. Danny's fever. That woman...

A jolt of panic propelled her up. "Danny! Where's my son?"

She careened forward and would have fallen to the floor if Stavros hadn't caught her. "Whoa, easy there," he said. His large hands gently guided her back down until she was reclining once more. "Danny is fine," he said. "Your cousin Melissa came to the hospital and took him to her home. She wanted me to tell you she's given him his medicine and she won't let him out of her sight until you're ready to get him."

The fear drained from her body, leaving her feeling boneless. Melissa would never let anything happen to Danny, and since she was the chief of police, no one would dare try to take him from her. He was as safe as possible for the moment, and that knowledge dulled the constant buzz of worry Desiree heard in her head.

"Was he hurt? Was anyone else hurt?" The memory of the woman's eyes flashed in her mind and she shivered. Whoever she was, she'd been determined to take Danny. Desiree doubted she would have given him up without a fight.

Stavros shook his head. "Danny wasn't harmed. Just a little scared, but he got over it quickly once his aunt Grace and Melissa arrived."

She smiled faintly. "He loves his family."

"He's got quite a few, from what I could tell," Stavros replied. "After the police left, you had three other visitors—Troy, Palmer and Annalise."

"Really?" Her smile widened at that news. She and Troy had a special bond, but she was close to all her half siblings. The knowledge that each one of them— even Palmer, who lived on his ranch on the outskirts of town—had come to the hospital to check on her made her feel loved.

Stavros nodded. "Yeah, it was pretty busy here for a while. The only way I could convince them to leave was by promising to let them know when you woke up." He held up his cell phone with a half smile. "Looks like I'm going to be calling Coltons for the rest of my shift."

"I can do that." Desiree leaned forward, scanning the room for her bag. Her head began to spin and the edges of the bed grew fuzzy, but she was determined not to be a burden to Stavros. *No—Dr. Makris*, she reminded herself again. "My phone is somewhere. And I'm sure you have better things to do."

"Nice try." His warm hand covered her own and she stilled at his touch. She looked up to find him regarding her with an expression that could only be described as amused. "You need to rest. Whatever drug that woman gave you isn't fully out of your system yet. Besides, I hardly ever get to make calls to relatives to deliver good news. You're doing me a favor."

"Uh-huh." She didn't believe him, but it was hard to argue when he smiled at her like that. Maybe it was the lingering effects of the drugs she'd been given, but in this moment, Desiree swore he was the most attractive man she'd ever seen. His dark brown gaze was hypnotic—she could literally feel the pull on her body. Her gaze dropped to his wide, solid chest. How would it feel to be pressed against him, to have his arms wrapped around her? Was he as warm as he looked? He probably smelled amazing…

"Are you okay?" She snapped back to attention to find him watching her, his eyebrows drawn together. "You look a little flushed."

"I'm fine," Desiree replied, embarrassment creeping in at having been caught daydreaming about Stavros while he was standing right in front of her. A horrifying thought popped into her brain: Had her fantasies stayed safely in her head, or had she said something out loud to tip him off?

She leaned back against the gurney, wishing she could press through the mattress and disappear. Of course, there was no chance of anything romantic happening between her and Dr. Makris, but that didn't mean she wanted him to know about her attraction. Drugged or no, she still had some pride.

He nodded, apparently accepting her statement at face value. Either he truly believed her, or he was trying to spare her further mortification. Whichever it was, she was grateful.

"Oh, before I forget…" He ran his hand through his hair. Desiree tracked the movement, tuning out his words. *I want his hands in my hair.* For a second, she imagined him wrapping her curls around his hand, then pulling her close and tugging her head back so he could lean over and…

"They're using your sketch to search for her."

"What?" She blinked, wishing she could control her thoughts and focus. Her son had very nearly been kidnapped again tonight, but she was so fuzzy-headed she couldn't think straight. Imagining impossible encounters with Stavros was nice, but this wasn't the time for fantasies. She owed it to Danny to protect him, but right now she felt like her body and mind were betraying her.

"The police told me a woman tried to take Danny from the playground a few days ago?" Desiree nodded; it seemed to be the only thing she was capable of doing at the moment.

Stavros continued, "They said you made a sketch of her for them. They told me to tell you they're using the image to search for her."

"I think it was the same woman, but I'm not sure." Desiree bit her lip, trying to recall the face. The woman at the playground had been wearing large sunglasses, and the woman who had taken Danny tonight had been wearing a mask. Desiree hadn't been able to get a good look at either one of them, but the odds that two different women had recently tried to take her son seemed remote.

"Do you have a copy of your sketch?" Stavros asked. "I caught a glimpse of the woman's face tonight. She had on a mask, but maybe I can tell you if it's the same person from the playground."

"I have a picture on my phone," Desiree said. "But I don't know where my bag is." She glanced around the room but didn't see it anywhere.

"It's back here." Stavros bent at the waist and stretched to the floor behind the gurney. When he straightened up, he held her bag. "I think it got kicked to the side in all the activity," he said. "Sorry about that."

"I'm just glad you found it," Desiree said. "Otherwise, I wouldn't be able to get into my home." She fished her phone out of the bag and squinted at the display. The letters were slightly blurry and seemed to be moving a little, but she called up her photos and clicked on her latest sketch. "Here she is," she said, passing the phone to Stavros.

He took it from her, his eyes widening as he looked at the drawing. "Oh, wow, this is good." He glanced at her over the top of the phone, a gleam of respect in his eyes. "You're really talented."

"Thank you," she said softly. The compliment made her feel warm and tingly inside, likely another effect of the drug she'd been given. As a part-time sketch artist for the Grave Gulch Police Department, Desiree knew she was a skilled artist. But having Stavros acknowledge it made her feel special, even though she knew he hadn't meant anything else by it.

"I can't be certain," he said after a few seconds. "The way you've drawn her with the sunglasses is making it hard for me to tell, but I think it's probably the same woman who tried to take Danny tonight."

A chill skittered down Desiree's spine. Hearing Stavros confirm her suspicions made the situation worse somehow. In the back of her mind, Desiree had been hoping this was all a strange nightmare. But now she had to accept that it wasn't; she really had almost lost her son a second time. Something told Desiree that if this woman was successful in getting her hands on Danny, Desiree would never see her boy again.

She shivered involuntarily, unable to dwell on the thought for very long. It hurt too much to even consider for more than a second.

Misinterpreting her reaction, Stavros grabbed the edge of the blanket on the gurney. "Are you cold?" He pulled it over her body and placed her phone by her hand. "Would you like another from the warmer?"

"No, thanks," she said. "This is fine."

He frowned slightly, seeming to doubt her. "I have to go for now," he said. "But I'll check on you when I can. There's a guard posted outside your room, so I want you to try to relax. Danny is safe, and I won't let anyone hurt you again."

In truth, Desiree hadn't been worried for her own safety. But she was touched by his reassurance nonetheless. It made her feel special, almost treasured.

"Thank you," she said. "For everything."

He smiled. For a second, it looked like he was going to say something, but in the end, he merely nodded. "Press the call button if you need anything," he said, walking toward the door. "Otherwise, try to sleep if you can."

The door clicked softly behind him, leaving her alone in the room. Between one breath and the next, Desiree was struck by an intense longing for his return. It was unsettling, to say the least. She didn't know this man, not really, but he made her feel safe. There was something about him—the tone of his voice? the warmth in his eyes?—that comforted her, made her feel like she could rest. She'd been on edge and anxious for months, but when Stavros was around, she felt like she had backup. Like she could relax, because he was there to hold things together, to protect Danny and take care of her, as well.

She shook her head, trying to dismiss the feeling. The man was a doctor—he took care of people for a living. It was no wonder she thought him capable and caring. But that didn't mean he had any interest in helping her on a personal level. Besides, he very likely had his own family waiting for him at home.

If only she could say the same. It would be so nice to have a partner, to be with someone she could rely on. Once upon a time, she'd thought Danny's father was that person. But Jeremy had shown his true colors when she'd gotten pregnant. He'd made it very clear he had no interest in being a parent, and Desiree wasn't going to fight him on it. Her baby deserved a father who wanted to be there, who embraced the role and wanted nothing more than to shower love and attention on their child. But Jeremy had been more interested in his career, so she'd cut him loose. She'd been angry with him at first, and in some moments, she still was. Now, though, she could see he wasn't a *bad* man. He paid child support every month, made sure Danny was financially taken care of. He simply had no interest in seeing the boy or interacting with him in any way. That was his choice, and Desiree wasn't going to try to change his mind. Better for Danny to have an absentee father than a disinterested one.

Fortunately, Danny was still too young to wonder why he didn't have a father in his life. The day would come, she knew, when he would notice and ask. For now, though, Desiree was grateful to her brothers and the rest of her extended family for loving her son and spending time with him. He had a host of strong, caring men in his life, men who could patch over the hole left by his biological dad.

Still, she hoped that one day she would find someone to share her life with, someone who wanted to be a father to Danny just as much as they wanted to be her partner.

Desiree closed her eyes with a sigh, ready for her life to go back to normal. Back to when Danny was safe, and she didn't have to spend every moment of the day worried about someone taking her son. Would she ever find that peace again?

A rap at the door made her open her eyes, and she sat up in the bed, tendrils of anticipation shooting through her limbs. Was Stavros coming back?

The door opened, and Troy peeked into the room. A mild disappointment flickered to life, but Desiree quickly squashed it. "Hey," she greeted her brother.

"Hey yourself." He opened the door farther and pushed in a stroller.

Desiree's heart leaped as she saw her son, his small head lolling to the side as he slept peacefully. "Danny," she whispered, tears filling her eyes.

She drank in the sight of him, wanting so badly to touch him, to smell him. To reassure herself that he was truly fine and that his kidnapper hadn't harmed him in any way.

Her thoughts must have shown on her face, because Troy spoke quickly. "He's okay, sis. Everyone has checked him out, and there are no signs of any injuries. From what I gather, she didn't have him long enough to do anything to him. His fever is gone, too."

His words made her relax a bit, but she kept her eyes on her boy, unable to look away. "I can't believe it happened again," she said softly.

Troy wheeled the stroller to the gurney and sat in the chair by the bed. "Want me to take him out?"

Desiree shook her head. "He needs to sleep."

She heard her brother's soft huff of a laugh. "Yeah. Apparently, he slept in the car on the way to Melissa's. After she got him home, he wouldn't go down again. I offered to take him so she could get some rest. I'm off today and can always take a nap later."

"Looks like you have the magic touch."

Desiree glanced up to see Troy shake his head. "Hardly," he said dryly. "But I figured if the car ride worked for Melissa, it might work for me, too. I loaded him up and we've been driving around. He's been out for almost forty minutes, so I decided to risk putting him in the stroller and bringing him here. Thought you might want to see him now that you're awake."

"Thank you," Desiree said. Troy would risk his life to keep her son safe. But it helped to see him for herself, to know he was truly fine.

"Wanna tell me what happened here?" Troy used his foot to slowly push the stroller back and forth, keeping Danny in motion so he'd stay asleep. "I heard the report from Grace and her partner, but I'd like you to tell me what you remember, if you feel up to it."

Desiree felt the corner of her mouth turn up in a half smile. Troy was her brother, but he was also a police detective. She recognized his interrogation tone, even if he thought he was being casual.

She told him what she remembered, starting at the beginning. It didn't take long to fill him in on the details.

"I didn't get a good look at her face," she said ruefully. "The surgical mask covered her nose and mouth and chin. All I could see was her eyes." Desiree shivered as she recalled the intense light in the woman's eyes, the single-minded gleam of determination glowing like an unnatural fire.

"I'm just glad Stavros stopped her before she could get away," she continued.

"Who's Stavros?" Troy asked.

"Oh," Desiree replied, realizing she'd once again slipped and used his first name. "I mean Dr. Makris.

He was treating Danny and ran into the woman as she was running off."

"Dr. Makris," Troy repeated thoughtfully. He looked down at his lap, muttering softly to himself. "I know him…" After a second, he nodded and lifted his head to meet Desiree's gaze. "Yeah, I remember him now."

"How's that?" Desiree shifted on the bed, her curiosity growing. How did her brother know Stavros? Had he treated one of the people Troy had arrested before? Or had he been in some kind of trouble himself?

Troy shook his head, his expression turning sympathetic. "About five years ago, I got a call from Dispatch. A babysitter had phoned in, hysterical because the mother of the child she was watching had forced her way into the house and kidnapped the baby. She'd taken off in the middle of a snowstorm with the kid in the back seat. We had a BOLO for the car, and I was on duty that night, searching."

"The mother forced her way in?" Desiree asked. "So they were separated?"

Troy nodded. "Yeah. Father had full custody of the child. He was at work when this happened."

A sense of foreboding built in Desiree's chest. "Did you find the mother and baby?"

"We did," Troy replied. But she knew from his tone this story didn't have a happy ending. "We came across the car—it had flipped and smashed into a tree. Mother was dead at the scene. We managed to get the kid out." He swallowed hard and drew his hand down his face. "Ambulance took her here."

"What happened?" Desiree whispered.

"She died a few minutes after arrival," he said somberly. "It was horrible. We felt that call for months." He shook his head. "Kids are always hard."

Desiree was quiet for a moment, digesting this story. Danny's kidnapping had been terrible, but at least her son had come home safely. Things could have been so much worse.

"How is Stavros connected?" She had a guess, but she was hoping Troy's response would prove her wrong.

Troy sighed heavily. "He was the kid's father. I found out later he was paged to treat the girl, before they realized the doctor on duty that night was her father. She died in his arms."

Desiree's heart ached at her brother's words. She stared at her sleeping son and blinked back tears. How had Stavros survived that loss? If Danny died, she didn't think she'd be able to go on…

"Anyway," Troy said, shaking his head, "I'm sure all this brought those memories back for him tonight."

"It must have," Desiree whispered. Given his own history with kidnapping, Stavros had to be feeling especially raw. *No wonder he helped look for Danny*, she thought, recalling his comment about joining a search party back in January. It had to have been so hard for him to try to find a missing child, knowing his own would never return.

She looked at her son, watched the gentle rise and fall of his chest as he slept. Just the thought of losing him forever was enough to drive a spike of pain through her heart. Poor Stavros! Desiree was overcome by the desire to hug him, to pull him close and hold him in a bid to take away some of his pain. But even as she had the thought, she knew he didn't need her for that. He was a strong man—the fact that he was still working at this hospital was proof of that. And while she had no doubt he still carried the pain of his loss, she wasn't sure he had any interest in sharing his thoughts with her. After all, they were practically strangers. Last night's events had given her a false sense of closeness to him, made her feel like they had a connection. But that was just the adrenaline and emotion of almost losing Danny again. The fact that she'd heard this story from Troy and not Stavros himself only underlined the distance between them.

There was a short rap on the door—Desiree and Troy both turned. Stavros walked in holding some papers and wearing a smile.

He stopped after a few steps, his smile fading as he glanced from Desiree to Troy. "Everything okay?" He looked at Desiree again, concern in his eyes. "Did something happen?"

Desiree shook her head and blinked. "I'm fine," she said. "Just feeling a little emotional after everything."

Stavros nodded. "That's understandable. Are you still feeling dizzy?"

"A little," she replied. "But not too much." The conversation with Troy had distracted her from the lingering effects of the drug in her system.

"Good. You should feel back to normal in a few hours." He held up the papers he was holding. "And here's more good news—you can go home."

"Really?" Desiree sat up a bit.

"Already?" Troy frowned.

Stavros glanced at her brother. "Yes. There's no medical need to keep her here any longer."

"I'm ready to leave," Desiree said, interjecting herself back into the conversation.

Troy pressed his lips together but didn't respond. A soft buzz sounded in the room; he pulled his phone from his pocket and stepped away. Stavros gave Desiree a questioning look, and she shrugged.

"He worries about me," she said softly. "Even though he's my little brother, he's very protective."

Stavros nodded, then started to go over the discharge instructions with her. After a moment, Troy stepped closer. Desiree could tell by the look on his face that something was wrong.

"What happened?" A kernel of fear formed in her stomach. Hadn't they been through enough already?

"We've got another victim," Troy said grimly. "Looks like Len Davison has struck again."

"He left more evidence?" Desiree asked. She knew from her cop relatives that Davison had killed two men in Grave Gulch. He'd left DNA evidence behind at both crimes, but Randall Bowe had destroyed the evidence from the first one. Only after the killer had struck a second time were the police able to safeguard the evidence and definitively identify Davison. They'd been on the hunt for him ever since, but so far, he'd managed to evade capture.

Troy nodded. "Looks like it. Officers found blood at the scene that didn't come from the victim. This guy seems to have fought back." He turned to look at Stavros. "We'll be reaching out to area hospitals and clinics—it would help if you guys were on the lookout for a man coming in with injuries. I'll have more info for you soon."

"We'll help however we can," Stavros said.

"Appreciate it," Troy said. "There's something else you can do, as well."

"What's that?" Stavros asked.

Troy looked at Desiree. "Think you two can put together a sketch of the woman from last night for me? It would make our search a lot easier."

"Absolutely," Stavros said.

"Yes." Desiree nodded. "I can do it right now, if you have time."

"Whoa," Troy said. "Tomorrow is soon enough. We're going to be dealing with the murder for the next few hours. Besides," he said, glancing at his watch, "it's almost seven in the morning. I'm sure you both need to rest."

"That's true," Desiree said. While she wasn't exactly tired, she knew she would be soon. And since Stavros had been working all night, he was likely ready for bed.

"I'll send a couple of officers to watch your place tonight and tomorrow," Troy said. "So you can rest easy."

"Are you sure you can spare the manpower?" Desiree asked. Having officers outside her door would make her feel better, but now that Davison had struck again, she knew Troy and the rest of the force would be on high alert searching for the killer.

"You could stay with me, if you want," Stavros said.

Desiree turned to look at him, certain she had misunderstood his offer. "I…uh… I have a guest room," he said, glancing from her to Troy and back again. "And my building requires a security code to access. Plus, there's a doorman on duty twenty-four-seven, so even if someone were to get inside, Jim would immediately know they're not a resident."

"That does sound like a good setup…" Troy's words trailed off and he looked at Desiree for her reaction. "Would Danny be okay sleeping in a new place?"

Desiree considered it. "I think so," she said. "He's never had any trouble staying with you, and he's pretty good about napping on the go. As long as I'm with him, I think he'll be fine."

She turned, searching Stavros's face for any signs of hesitation. Part of her was excited by the prospect of spending more time with this man, but she didn't want to cross any boundaries. "If you're sure?"

Stavros nodded. "I'm sure. It's no trouble at all. Plus, we can work on the sketch later today, or whenever you feel like it. I'm off for the next twenty-four hours."

"Then it's settled." Troy clasped his hands together, looking pleased. "Dez, you can drop off the sketch to the police station whenever you're done. Like I said, we're going to be occupied for the next few hours, so try to get some rest first." He offered his right hand to Stavros, and the two men shook. "Thanks so much for your help, and for offering your guest room. I can't speak for my sister, but I feel better knowing she's not going to be alone after what happened here."

"It's really not a bother," Stavros said quietly. Desiree could tell he was uncomfortable with her brother's praise.

Troy leaned in and kissed her cheek. "Call me if you need anything," he said, his tone serious. "I mean it, sis—don't hesitate to pick up the phone and dial if so much as a breeze blows at you the wrong way."

Desiree laughed softly. "Yeah, yeah," she said. "Get out of here. Thanks for taking care of Danny."

Troy's eyes softened as he looked down at the still-sleeping boy. "You know I love him."

"I do. Be safe out there today."

Troy gave her a mock salute. "Always am." With a final nod at Stavros, her brother left the room.

Desiree turned to find Stavros looking at her. There was a glint of emotion in his brown eyes—was it longing? Hard to say; she blinked, and it was gone.

"Give me five minutes," he said, walking backward toward the door. "I just have to finish signing off to the day crew. I'll grab some extra scrubs for you to wear and some stuff for Danny. Then I'll be back and we can stop by your place for your things before we head home."

"Okay." She nodded, a bit surprised by his words.

We can go home.

She hadn't been part of a *we* in a long time. *And you're not now*, she told herself firmly. Stavros was doing her a favor, nothing more. So no matter what he said about going home together, she had no business getting any hopes up.

The last thing she needed right now was another disappointment.

STAVROS WAS BEGINNING to think this might not have been such a good idea after all.

Never in his professional life had Stavros brought a patient home with him. And not because there weren't people who needed the help—he'd lost count of the number of patients who didn't have a safe place to stay, a warm bed or food in their pantry. But he'd always recognized the limitations of what he could do, personally and professionally. He couldn't be all things to all people; he simply patched them up, tried to put them in contact with resources and sent them on their way. It was what he should have done with Desiree.

Why, then, had he offered up his place for her and her son? She had support from her family. Her brother had been willing to dispatch police officers to keep an eye on her home for the next several days. She wasn't walking out of the ER back to a life of instability and need.

And yet he hadn't wanted her to leave. For some reason, Stavros wasn't ready to say goodbye yet.

Before he'd had a chance to think, Stavros had blurted out his invitation. The offer had felt instinctive, almost like a reflexive response he was powerless to control. His words had seemed to hang in the air, and he'd seen the flash of surprise on Desiree's face.

In that moment, Stavros had wanted to disappear. Embarrassment had surged in his chest, and he'd braced himself for her rejection.

But, to his great surprise, she'd said yes.

It hadn't taken him long to get the guest bedroom ready for her and Danny. After a quick bite to eat, they'd all gone to their separate rooms to rest after the long night. On days like this, when Stavros knew he'd have a day shift in twenty-four hours after covering the previous night, he usually slept for a couple of hours and then woke so he'd be able to rest again later at night.

It was strange, having a woman in his apartment. He hadn't been in a long-term relationship in a while. In the aftermath of Ellory's actions, he hadn't trusted his judgment. A few years after the crash, he'd started to dip his toe back in the dating pool. He'd gone out with a few women, all of them nice. But no one he felt connected to, no one he found himself missing while he was at work. So he'd hit the brakes, deciding it was better to be alone than lonely while in a relationship.

Maybe he just wasn't ready to date again. Maybe he never would be. He'd said as much to his therapist after breaking it off with the last woman.

"You could be right," the man had replied. "It's possible you won't ever want a girlfriend again. But, Stavros, tell me something. If you were treating an athlete who needed a hip replacement, what would you say to them when they worried about ever playing again?"

Stavros had frowned at the change of subject. "I'd tell them it takes time to heal and to take it easy for a while. That they could come back, but it would take a lot of hard work and physical therapy."

Dr. Miller had smiled and leaned back in his chair. "That's what I'm telling you. Your heart has gone through one of the most painful experiences a human might possibly have. You need to give yourself time to heal. If finding someone is truly your goal, you can do that. But it will take a lot of work and patience on your part as you put yourself and your life back together."

Stavros stared up at the ceiling of his bedroom, Dr. Miller's words ringing in his memory. In some ways, could perhaps inviting Desiree and Danny to stay with him help mend his heart?

The faint wail of a toddler's cry made him jump. It had been years since he'd heard the sounds of a child in his home. After Sammy's death, he hadn't been able to stay in his previous place. There were too many memories of her there, the rooms heavy with the ghost of her laughter. He'd sold the house and bought this condo, needing to live somewhere completely different.

Danny made another sound, and Stavros braced himself for the sadness and grief that were sure to wash over him. But, to his surprise, they didn't come. He felt a twinge in his chest, the residual ache of his trauma that he knew now would never fully leave him. But having Danny in his home wasn't as emotionally difficult as he'd expected.

Danny calmed quickly. Desiree's muffled voice traveled through the wall, and even though Stavros couldn't make out exactly what she was saying, based on her cadence and tone, he could tell she was singing to her son.

He pictured it easily—Danny snuggled in her lap, his head resting on her shoulder as she rocked him and softly sang lullabies in his ear. He'd done the same for his own daughter. Putting Sammy to bed had been one of his favorite activities. It'd been the only time in his busy day he'd been able to stop the world and connect with his daughter. Rocking her, reading to her, singing her to sleep—he'd loved every minute of it. The occasions when he'd had to work the night shift had been tough, since it had meant he wouldn't get to tuck his little girl into bed. He knew Ellory hadn't enjoyed the evening ritual in the same way. Looking back now with the benefit of hindsight, Stavros wondered if her disinterest was a sign he should have picked up on sooner. Could he have saved his daughter's life if he'd done something differently?

With a groan, Stavros rolled out of bed. He knew from experience that those questions could never be answered and that the what-ifs would only serve to torture him. Today wasn't a day to get stuck in the past; his guests were awake, and he needed to check on them.

After a quick stop in the bathroom, Stavros walked into the kitchen. The growls coming from his stomach confirmed that it was lunchtime. Wagering he wasn't the only one who was hungry, he assembled the ingredients for sandwiches and got to work putting them together. He made enough noise to let Desiree know he was awake, but not so much that he might disturb Danny if she was trying to get the boy back to sleep.

He heard the rush of water through the pipes, and a moment later, she and Danny emerged from the guest bedroom suite. Stavros felt his heart do a funny little flip at the sight of her, but he tamped down his reaction. *It's just the newness of having company here*, he told himself.

She smiled shyly as she carried Danny into the kitchen. "Hello," she said softly.

"Afternoon," he replied. He winked at Danny, who

was staring at him with wide eyes. "Hey, buddy. Feeling better after that nap?"

"I think so," Desiree replied. She smoothed a hand over Danny's head in a gentle, unconscious gesture of affection. "His fever is gone and his mood has improved."

Stavros nodded. "Good. Sounds like the antibiotics are doing their job." He ran his gaze over her face, noting her tired eyes and slightly mussed hair. "And how are you?"

Desiree lifted one shoulder in a shrug. "Better, I think. My head isn't quite so fuzzy now. But I still feel like I could sleep for a month." She let out a short, humorless laugh. "I guess that's just motherhood, though, right?"

Stavros didn't reply. He remembered that exhaustion, the bone-deep fatigue that seemed endless. He'd thought the punishing schedule of med school and intern year had prepared him for the rigors of parenthood. But becoming a father had worn him out in ways he'd never imagined possible.

Desiree made a small choked sound and he glanced up to find her watching him, a distressed look on her face. "I'm s-sorry," she stammered. "I shouldn't have…"

"It's okay." Stavros smiled to ease the moment. So she knew about Sammy, about his past. Maybe that was for the best. They wouldn't have to dance around the subject. Still, he wondered when she'd realized who he was. She hadn't shown any recognition in the hospital when he'd introduced himself. Had she searched his name on her phone after he'd completed his exam of Danny?

"When did you figure it out?" He kept his gaze on the sandwiches, unable to look at her. The question was awkward enough—he didn't want to make her feel worse by watching her while he asked.

"Troy told me," she said softly. "He was on duty that night when the call came in. He recognized your name."

"Ah." That made sense. Stavros didn't remember seeing Troy that awful night, but to be honest, many of his memories remained a blur.

Desiree was quiet for a moment. He could feel her eyes on his hands as he finished assembling their lunch. "Stavros…" She sounded tentative, uncertain. He glanced up at her—she was biting her bottom lip, clearly nervous.

"I can't tell you how sorry I am for your loss. When Danny was taken…" She trailed off, shuddered. "I got a small taste of what you went through. If you ever want to talk about it, I'm here."

He could tell by the tone of her voice that the offer was genuine. Part of him desperately wanted to take her up on it—after all, just hours ago he'd been wishing for this very moment, an opportunity to share his emotions and grief with someone who might understand. Now that he had the chance, though, he wasn't so sure. Opening up to Desiree sounded nice, but Stavros wasn't quite ready to expose himself like that. He still felt raw from confronting Danny's would-be kidnapper and didn't trust that he could keep his emotions in check while sharing his past experiences with Desiree.

And could he even get the words out in front of Danny? Seeing that little boy in his mother's arms, his small hand resting on her shoulder, his head tucked under her chin… It was clear Desiree was Danny's safe place. As she should be. As he had been for Sammy.

Except for that awful night.

Danny was a sweet boy. He was also a living, breathing reminder of the daughter Stavros had failed to protect.

So, no, he couldn't talk about his loss in front of the toddler. It was simply too painful.

Desiree was watching him, clearly expecting some kind of response. Stavros cleared his throat and smiled tightly. "Thanks," he said. "I appreciate that." He moved aside the sandwich plates and reached out to tickle Danny's foot. "Now," he said, needing to change the subject, "what can I make for you, little man?"

"Do you have any apples?" Desiree asked. "He loves apple slices with peanut butter."

"That's easy enough," Stavros replied.

"I can fix it," Desiree said. "You've already done so much for us—you don't need to wait on us, too."

"It's not a problem," Stavros said. He noticed her cheeks had gone pink and knew she was feeling uncomfortable. "Just keep me company?"

She smiled. "Of course."

It didn't take long for Stavros to put together a plate for Danny. The three of them moved to the dining area, and he set the food down on the large live-edge table at the side of the room. Desiree and Danny slid onto the long bench against the wall, while Stavros took a chair opposite her.

"Wow." Her eyes grew large as she surveyed the table. It was a plank from a tree trunk, sanded smooth and epoxied to a glowing shine. Stavros loved the piece and had spent a lot of time studying the wood, taking in the rings of the trunk and natural inclusions and flaws. Just sitting here made him feel grounded, as if by putting his hands on the wood he was somehow connected to something bigger than himself. It was a nice way to decompress after a tough shift.

"This is amazing," Desiree continued. She ran her finger along the surface, tracing the irregular edge of the piece. "I've never seen anything like it."

Stavros smiled, a part of him pleased to see her response. "A few years ago, I treated a guy who'd been in a logging accident. His injuries were pretty gnarly, but we were able to get him patched up and he pulled through. A few months later, he comes limping back into the ER and asks to see me. I thought he might have hurt himself again, but he wanted to give me his card. Turns out, he makes these tables and he wanted me to have one."

"What a nice gesture!"

Stavros nodded. "I thought so, too. I went to his workshop and noticed this one. He saw me looking, offered to give it to me. I told him I had to pay, but he refused. So I said thanks but no thanks."

Desiree managed to detach Danny and helped him sit on the bench beside her. She offered him a blueberry, which he ate with gusto. "So then what happened?"

"Well, about a week later, I was here, doing laundry. I got a call from a man who said he had a delivery for me. I told him I hadn't ordered anything, but he insisted. I went downstairs to straighten things out, and he's got this table in his truck. He and his partner brought it upstairs and unwrapped it and placed it here for me."

"That must have been quite a shock." Desiree leaned forward slightly, and a little thrill zinged through Stavros as he realized that she was genuinely interested in his story. It had been so long since he'd had a non-work-related conversation with someone, much less a beautiful woman. It was nice, to say the least.

"It definitely was," he said, smiling as Danny grabbed an apple slice and started gnawing on it. "I immediately called him and told him I wanted to pay, but he wouldn't hear it."

"So what did you do?" Desiree took a bite of her sandwich and made a soft humming sound of appreciation that made his skin tingle. What else could he do to trigger that reaction? Would she hum like that if he kissed her? Laid her back on this table and cupped her breast with his hand while he…?

"Aba, aba, aba." Danny's voice cut through Stavros's burgeoning fantasy, and not a second too soon. He tuned in to see the toddler smacking his peanut-butter-coated hand on the table, grinning happily.

"No, Danny, don't do that!" Desiree grabbed his hand and began to wipe it off, shooting Stavros an apologetic look. "I'm sorry. I'll clean this up."

He laughed. "Don't worry about it. I promise, it's

really okay. He's just being a toddler. I'm not worried, and you shouldn't be, either."

She relaxed a bit, but still tried to clean the peanut butter off the table. "I'll get it," Stavros assured her.

"I bet you have to use some kind of special cleaner for something like this."

He shook his head. "Nope. Just a little soap and water. At least, that's what the maker told me."

"So you accepted his gift?" Desiree gestured at the table. She handed Danny another apple slice. "I mean, you must have, since it's still here."

"In a way," Stavros said. "I figured out this was a point of pride for him. He wanted to repay me for helping him, and it was important to him that I accept this piece. But it was also important to me from an ethical standpoint that I pay for the table. As a doctor, I'm not allowed to accept gifts from patients, especially on a scale like this."

"Sounds like you guys were at an impasse."

"Yeah. But then I did a little digging and found a fundraising page on the internet that a relative had set up to help pay for his medical expenses. After I verified it was legit, I made an anonymous donation that more than covered the cost of the table and delivery fee."

Desiree smiled, her eyes warm as she looked at him. "Did he figure out it was you?"

"He did. I got a call a few weeks later. He wanted to pay me back, but I told him I had to do it—that it wouldn't sit right for me to accept his gift without compensating him in some way. He seemed to get it. I also may have lied a little bit and told him the donation was nonrefundable."

Desiree laughed. "Do no harm?"

"Something like that."

"Well, I'm glad you figured out a way for you to both get what you wanted."

They ate in silence for a moment. Then she spoke again.

"I can see why you picked this one." She glanced around the room, looking at the large open space that comprised his kitchen, eating area and part of the living room. "It looks like it was made especially for this place."

Stavros followed her eyes, trying to imagine what she thought as she looked at his home. The wall of windows on one side of the condo afforded him a nice view of Grave Gulch and the forest beyond, and ensured the place was bright and airy. His furniture was solid, and he favored wood over metal. He'd tried to keep the colors neutral, opting for brown and oatmeal in terms of stains and fabric choices. Overall, Stavros considered his home a haven, a peaceful place to retreat to and recharge after a long shift. If it seemed a bit sterile, a bit empty, well…that was more a reflection of the amount of time he spent at work rather than a lack of interest on his part.

Still, he had to admit it was nice to have company. More than nice—it felt right somehow. Stavros hadn't been feeling particularly lonely, but having Desiree and Danny here made him aware of how quiet his life was when he wasn't working.

He glanced back at the pair of them, watching as she gently wiped Danny's face. They looked like they belonged here. With him.

A wave of longing washed over him, and for a second, he forgot how to breathe. He wanted this: a woman in his life, a child of his own. A family. The desire had been building for the last few years, and being close to Desiree and Danny, having them in his personal space, made Stavros realize how much he wanted to be part of a family again.

There had to be someone out there who felt the same way, who wanted the same things. Someone who would understand his past and help him work toward creating a new future.

Desiree glanced up and smiled at him, setting off small flutters in his stomach. He was definitely attracted to her. But it would be inappropriate to try anything; she was a guest in his home. The last thing he wanted was to make her feel uncomfortable, or to imply that she owed him for bringing them here.

No, best to keep his distance. When this was over and things were back to normal, he could resurrect his comatose love life. Until then, he'd treat Desiree like a coworker. Friendly, but distant.

It was the right thing to do.

Chapter Four

Desiree quietly shut the door to the guest bedroom and headed for the living room. Danny had just gone down for a nap, which meant she and Stavros could work on the sketch of her son's would-be kidnapper.

It was shaping up to be a strange day. Never in a million years had she thought a midnight run to the emergency room would turn into a stay at a handsome doctor's home. But Danny was taking it all in stride. After lunch, he'd happily explored Stavros's home and played in the living room. For his part, Stavros had been amazing. Desiree had been on edge, worried that Danny was going to accidentally break something. It was clear Stavros had not childproofed his condo, and why would he have? It wasn't like he had a little one running around all the time. But Stavros hadn't seemed the least bit bothered by her son's curiosity. He'd lifted Danny up to explore the bookshelves, taken him over to the windows so he could look out over the city and crouched down on the floor to play with him. He was a natural with kids, and Desiree's heart had ached at the knowledge of his loss.

She stopped in front of a painting hanging on the wall outside Stavros's bedroom. It had caught her eye earlier, but she hadn't had a chance to really look at it until now.

The piece was beautiful, dreamlike. A blue cityscape dominated the scene, and in the bottom left corner was a bed, an embracing couple perched on the edge of the mattress. Floating above it all was a blue angel, captured in midflight. Desiree studied the piece, entranced by the play of colors and lines, the textures of the paint on the canvas. Then she spied the artist's signature and gasped.

Is that...? It is!

She took a half step back, shock zinging through her. This was no reproduction. Unless she missed her guess, this was the real thing. And she'd been standing mere inches from the canvas, breathing all over this work of art.

She walked into the living room, feeling a little wobbly. What other treasures did Stavros have in his home? If Danny broke something, she'd never be able to replace it.

Stavros looked up as she entered the room. "Hey, are you okay?" He jumped up and walked over to her, putting his hands on her arms to steady her. "Are you feeling dizzy?" He led her to the sofa and helped her sit.

Desiree was touched by his concern, but she had to know. "Stavros, is that an original Marc Chagall painting in the hall?"

He blinked, apparently taken aback by her question. "Uh, yeah. You know his work?"

She nodded. "And the one in the guest bedroom—a

real Picasso?" She'd noticed it right away, but had assumed it was a copy. Now she wasn't so sure.

"Yes," he confirmed. "But what's going on with you?
You seem upset."

She shook her head, still trying to process the fact
that he seemed to live in an art museum. "Stavros, we
can't stay here."

He frowned. "Why not? Is something wrong?"

Desiree let out a sharp laugh. "No, it's just…" She
trailed off, gesturing to the room at large. "I have a toddler. He gets into everything. If he damages or breaks
something, there is no way I'd ever be able to replace
it. I mean, the paintings alone are masterpieces. I can
only imagine your furniture and the small sculptures
and decorations are priceless, as well." The memory
of Stavros handing Danny a hand-carved wooden bear
made her shudder. Danny had carried it around for most
of the afternoon and had even given the ears an exper-
imental chewing. What kind of treasure had he been
playing with?

Her eyes landed on a bronze in the corner. "Oh,
God," she groaned. "That's a Remington, isn't it?"
Danny had bumped into the pedestal several times
already—it was only a matter of time before her son
knocked it over and sent the statue crashing to the floor.

"Yeah, but—"

Desiree shook her head. "We can't stay here," she
repeated. "I appreciate you bringing us to your home,
but as soon as Danny wakes up, we're leaving."

"Don't you think you're overreacting?" Stavros

asked. "I mean, if I'm not worried about having you both here, shouldn't you relax?"

Desiree stared at him, considering and rejecting a dozen different responses as her blood began to boil. "No, that's not how it works," she said coolly. "If you want to play fast and loose with your stuff, that's your choice. But I'm not comfortable with the thought of my child accidentally damaging a priceless work of art."

"But it's just stuff!" She could tell by the look on his face that Stavros was genuinely confused by her reaction. "Yeah, they're valuable, but at the end of the day, they're only things. That's not what really matters in life."

A note of despair had crept into his voice. Desiree sat back, trying to see things from his perspective. He'd lost a daughter under horrible circumstances. After that kind of tragedy, was it any wonder his artwork wasn't a priority?

Still, she couldn't be so cavalier. Desiree loved art; she'd majored in art history in college, despite warnings from her parents that her degree wasn't going to pay the bills. These works had value that went beyond monetary—they were pieces of culture, representations of what humanity was capable of achieving. It would break her heart if something happened to them, especially if she or her child were to blame.

"Stavros…" she said quietly. "I get what you're saying. I really do. But it makes me sick to my stomach to think of what could happen. I could never afford to have even one of these pieces, much less the collection you've got."

"Money isn't everything," he said darkly. "Most of these came from my grandparents. They were big collectors. I inherited them, and I like them, so I keep them around. But if I had to choose, I'd pick a family every time."

Understanding began to dawn. "I take it you're not close with your relatives?"

"That's one way of putting it," he replied. "We exchange holiday cards. That's about it. They can't be bothered with anything more meaningful."

"But what about…? Your daughter, I mean. Surely you had support?" She hated mentioning it, but she had to know.

Pain flickered across his face. "That's a no," he confirmed. "My parents were in Europe at the time. I didn't tell them until after the funeral. They sent flowers and a card."

"That's terrible," she whispered. She placed her hand on his knee, wanting to offer comfort. What kind of people responded that way to the loss of a child?

"It's what I expected," he said. "My family has never been one for emotional displays. They'd pretty much written me off, anyway, after I decided to become a doctor rather than join the family business."

"Are you serious?" Desiree couldn't believe what she was hearing. "Most parents would be thrilled to have a son as caring and intelligent as you." She'd already known Stavros was a good man, and his earlier story about the table had proved it. Not everyone would have been so honorable about accepting such a valuable gift. The fact that he'd gone above and beyond to save his former patient's pride and do the right thing spoke volumes about his own character.

Her indignation must have shown on her face, for he smiled at her. "Yeah, well, my parents aren't most people. My family owns several hotel properties in Greece. It was always assumed I would help manage them and eventually run the company."

"But you had other ideas?"

"I did," he said simply. "I took the inheritance from my grandparents and set off on my own path. My parents were not happy, but they stopped short of disowning me."

"How generous of them," Desiree said dryly. As a mother, she couldn't imagine ever cutting ties with Danny. No matter what he did, what dreams he pursued, she would always love and support him.

Stavros laughed and placed his hand over hers. His skin was warm as he folded his fingers around the back of her hand with a gentle squeeze. The contact sent a shiver down her spine, but she held his gaze, determined not to show how he affected her.

"I won't lie," he said. "Money has made my life easier in a lot of respects. But it's not meaningful. I saw the way your family responded last night, the way they rallied around you. I wasn't kidding when I said I had a lot of calls to make once you woke up. Every person I spoke to was relieved to hear that you were okay. They all wanted to know how they could help you. That's something you can't buy." He looked around the room with a one-shouldered shrug. "So, yeah, I have a lot of expensive stuff. And I recognize that, and I don't take it for granted. But I would give it all up in a heartbeat for the kind of family you have."

Desiree's heart softened. Stavros's compassion and care for others was even more impressive now that she knew he hadn't learned it from his family. She couldn't imagine how cold and lonely his childhood must have been. Just the thought of Danny being in such an environment was enough to make her want to cry.

"What do you say we make a deal?" He ran his thumb over the back of her hand as he spoke, making it hard for her to focus on his words. "I'll move the most expensive stuff into my room and put the other things out of reach. And you and Danny won't go running off because you're worried about messing up my home. How does that sound?"

Desiree couldn't help but smile. "That would make me feel better." In truth, Desiree didn't want to leave. Stavros had a beautiful condo full of nice things to look at, true, and the ambience was peaceful. But more than that, she didn't want to leave *him*. He made her feel safe in a way that her relatives in law enforcement never had. As though he would protect her not just physically, but on an emotional level, as well. And he was so good with Danny. She'd never seen her son respond to a stranger the way he'd connected to Stavros. Even when he'd been feeling sick in the middle of the night, he'd responded to this man. Now that Danny was starting to feel better, he was even more interested in Stavros.

Not that she blamed him. Desiree found herself drawn closer to the handsome doctor with every passing moment. But she knew nothing could come of it.

He might want a family, but given the tragic loss of his daughter, it was unlikely he'd want a relationship with a woman who already had a child. Besides, he'd been nothing but courteous and polite to her from the moment they'd met. He was a decent man, a caring man, but he was helping her out of the goodness of his heart, not because he had any personal interest in her.

Stavros smiled, which transformed his face from handsome to gorgeous. Desiree tried not to stare, but it was difficult not to gape at him. She wasn't used to being so close to such an attractive man, and being on the receiving end of his dazzling grin was scrambling her brain.

"Then it's settled," he said. He took his hand off hers and stood, then reached down to pull her off the couch. She got to her feet, feeling a little light-headed from both the change in position and the man himself. "Will you help me move stuff? Some of the pieces are heavy."

Desiree nodded, a little thrill shooting through her. Not only was she going to see some amazing art, but she was also going to get to touch it. It was a surreal thought.

"It shouldn't take us too long," he said, leading her over to the Remington. "And once we're done, we can work on the sketch."

"Sounds good." The mention of Danny's would-be kidnapper was a splash of cold water on Desiree's mood. But she quickly pushed aside thoughts of the woman. She wasn't going to let that stranger detract from her enjoyment of this moment.

Getting up close and personal with some amazing

pieces of art, in the company of a handsome man, as her son slept peacefully and safely in the other room?

It didn't get any better than that.

THE CHILDPROOFING PROCESS didn't take long. Stavros had meant what he'd said when he'd told Desiree he wasn't concerned about Danny being around his things, but he could tell she was bothered by the possibility of something breaking. And, truly, the minor hassle of relocating everything had been worth it—she was now relaxed, her muscles no longer tense and her eyebrows no longer drawn together in a slight frown of worry.

They sat at the dining table again, a few papers and an eraser scattered on the surface between them. Desiree had a pencil and was busy sketching the outlines of a face.

Stavros found the process fascinating. Desiree asked him questions as she worked, prodding him to describe the curve of the nose, the line of the hair. He racked his brain, trying to recall not just the look of the woman, but a way to clearly articulate her appearance to Desiree.

"Her eyes were rounder," he said, watching Desiree's pencil move.

"Like this?" A few strokes modified the image, changing the entire look of the person.

Stavros frowned. "No, not quite." He sighed, wishing he could somehow download his memory and share the image with the police. "I guess it was more like what you had before."

Desiree erased a few lines and tried again. If she

was frustrated by the quality of his descriptions, she didn't show it.

"I'm sorry," he said. "I'm not being very helpful."

"No, you're fine." She smiled a little as she worked, but her eyes didn't leave the page. "You're doing a great job."

"How long have you been a sketch artist?" He studied her hands, marveling at how she was creating such a lifelike portrait with seemingly little effort. Her carefully controlled movements reminded him of a surgeon at work—both professions seemed to require an economy of motion he'd always lacked.

"A few years," she replied. "I studied art history in school and was on track to become a museum curator. But then I had Danny and things changed."

Her tone was matter-of-fact, but Stavros imagined there was a lot more to the story. What about Danny's father? Why wasn't he around to help her, to encourage her to chase her dreams? "Can I ask a personal question?"

"Shoot," she said absently.

Stavros took a breath. "Where is Danny's father?" He knew it wasn't really his business, but he was curious.

Her hand faltered, and he kicked himself for bringing it up. *Way to go*, he told himself. "Never mind," he said hastily. "I shouldn't have asked."

"No, it's okay." She glanced up at him, a guarded look in her eyes. "I know about your past. It's only fair I tell you about mine."

"Desiree, no." He reached across the table for her hand, needing to touch her. "This is not a quid pro quo.

You don't owe me your story, especially if it brings you pain." He'd overstepped; that much was clear. They hadn't known each other for long, and the intensity of last night's events combined with her presence in his home had created a false sense of intimacy, at least on his part. Based on her reaction, Desiree wasn't suffering from the same misconception.

To his surprise, she smiled. "I think I want to tell you," she said. "I don't really talk about it with my family, and after I had Danny, I lost touch with a lot of friends. Just didn't have the time or energy, you know?"

Stavros nodded. He remembered all too well how his world had shrunk after Sammy's arrival. It was hard to juggle a job and a baby at the same time, and he'd had his wife to help. How much more difficult had it been for Desiree? Had she been able to rely on Danny's father at all?

"His name is Jeremy," she said, taking a deep breath. "We'd been dating for almost six months, and things were going well. We'd talked about kids before, but always in the sense of maybe someday, not as anything concrete and coming soon. We were just getting ready to move in together, so it's not like we were one step away from walking down the aisle or anything."

"So Danny was a surprise?" Stavros refused to say "accident." That was a term for car wrecks and spilled drinks, not people.

Desiree nodded. "Oh, yes. I'd just finished taking some antibiotics for a sinus infection and was feeling better. But I neglected to read the fine print on the medicine bottle, and I guess I was one of the only people in the world who didn't know that antibiotics affect how well birth-control pills work."

"Trust me," Stavros interjected. "That's not the case. I can't tell you how many women I've seen in the ER get a surprise positive pregnancy test because they didn't realize antibiotics diminish the efficacy of birth-control pills."

"It was a powerful way to learn that lesson," Desiree said wryly. "I immediately told Jeremy. He wasn't thrilled, but he didn't blame me, either."

Stavros refrained from rolling his eyes. "Wow," he said flatly. "Glad to hear he acknowledged his part in the process, at least."

Desiree laughed. "It's a low bar, I know, but some men don't even come close to clearing it."

That was another thing Stavros knew to be true. Working in the ER had provided many firsthand examples of men mistreating the women they claimed to love.

"Anyway," she continued, "we talked a lot. He genuinely did not want a child at this point in his life. He was up for a big promotion at work, and they wanted him to relocate. He wasn't ready to have a baby and be tied down like that."

"So he left?" Stavros tried to wrap his brain around that idea. It would never occur to him to walk away from his child. Even if his relationship with the woman didn't work out, he simply couldn't imagine not being part of his kid's life.

"I told him to go," she said. "I wasn't going to beg him to stay, you know? I felt like my baby deserved a father who wanted to be there, not someone who had grudgingly stepped up. I knew if Jeremy stayed, he'd grow to resent me and probably the baby, too. So I cut him loose."

"And he didn't argue?"

She shook her head. "I think he was relieved, to be honest."

"Wow." Stavros tried to imagine the kind of man who would walk away from his responsibilities like that. He sounded like a coward. "So Danny hasn't had any contact with him?"

"No. Jeremy doesn't want to know anything about him. He sends child support every month, but doesn't want to see any pictures or hear any stories."

"At least he helps support Danny."

"Yeah, I do give him credit for that." Desiree shrugged. "I was surprised, actually. After he left, I only contacted him once to let him know Danny had been born and that he was healthy. A few weeks later, I got a document in the mail from an attorney. It was a proposal for child support, asking me to sign in agreement. I looked it over, and basically Jeremy had contacted a lawyer to draw up an official arrangement. It stated he wanted no claim on Danny, but he would send money every month until Danny turns eighteen."

"Better than nothing, at least." His respect for the man rose a slight notch. Jeremy might not want to be an involved father, but at least he was doing something to make sure his child didn't starve.

"It's quite a bit, actually," Desiree said. "Because of the promotion and move, Jeremy is making a lot of money. I'm not rich, but due to the support, I can afford to work part-time while Danny is still young. As he gets older and starts school, I'll be able to work more, but it is nice to be able to spend so much time with him while he's this little."

"I can tell you two share a special bond." He'd noticed it in the hospital, the way Danny had been around Desiree. The ways she responded to him in turn, practically anticipating his needs before he even started to fuss. Not every mother was so attentive to her child; Ellory certainly hadn't been.

Desiree smiled, her face seeming to glow at the thought of her son. "I'd do anything for him," she said simply. "That's one of the reasons we stayed in Grave Gulch."

"You were going to move?"

She lifted one shoulder in a shrug. "Before I got pregnant, I was planning on following Jeremy when he relocated. I was hoping to get on staff at one of the larger museums. But once I realized I was going to be a single mother, I decided to stay close to my family. As you already know, I have a lot of relatives here. I wanted Danny to have some positive male figures in his life. It doesn't make up for not having a dad, but it's better than nothing."

"That makes sense," Stavros replied. Her choice to put her career on hold for the sake of her son was just one more sign that Desiree was a special person. Not everyone was willing to put their child's needs before their own, the way she had.

"Anyway..." She trailed off, pencil beginning to lightly trace across the paper again. "That's my story. Not very interesting, I'm afraid."

"It's interesting to me." The words came out before he had a chance to think, to consider their implication.

Desiree glanced up to meet his eyes, her cheeks flushing slightly. "Thanks," she said softly. "I haven't talked about it in a long time."

Stavros held her gaze, wishing he could touch her. "I'm glad you told me," he said, hoping she could hear the sincerity in his voice.

"You're easy to talk to." She sounded a little surprised, as if she hadn't expected him to be a good listener. Or perhaps she hadn't planned on telling him so much personal information. Either way, Stavros was glad she'd opened up to him.

"Anytime," he said, meaning it. "I'm always happy to listen."

"I am, too," Desiree said. "If you ever want to talk, I'm here."

It was a tempting offer, and Stavros wanted to accept. But he was enjoying this time with Desiree, watching her work on the sketch and learning more about her. He didn't want to delve into his story right now and put a damper on things. There would be other opportunities to share his past with her.

He'd make sure of it.

Stavros glanced down at the paper on the table and felt a small shock of recognition jolt through his body. "Oh, wow," he exclaimed. "That's amazing!"

Desiree tilted her head to the side. "Is it a good likeness?"

Stavros nodded and reached for the page. "May I?" Desiree nodded and he turned it so the image was facing him. He stared at the drawing, marveling at Desiree's work. It looked like the woman from the hospital, right down to the curve of her earlobe and the glint in her eyes. Stavros half expected the likeness to frown, the way the kidnapper had just before throwing Danny at him.

"That's definitely her," Stavros said. "I don't know how you did this based on my crummy descriptions, but there's no mistaking her."

Desiree picked up her phone and tapped the screen. After a few seconds, she turned the device to face him. "Notice any similarities?"

Stavros looked at her phone; it was the same sketch she'd shown him in the hospital. In this one, the woman's eyes were obscured by a large pair of sunglasses. He studied the nose and mouth, comparing it to his memory. It was hard to tell, since the person at the hospital had worn a surgical mask, but the bit of hair he'd seen was the same and the facial proportions seemed to match.

"You think this is the same person?"

Desiree nodded. "This is the woman who tried to take Danny from the park last week." She tapped the edge of her phone as she spoke. "I can't imagine there are two people trying to kidnap my son. Can you?"

"That does seem highly unlikely." Stavros studied the two images side by side with a growing sense of certainty. "Yeah, I think they're the same woman."

"Do you recognize her from anywhere?" Desiree sounded hopeful, and he could tell she was desperate for answers. "Maybe she's been to the hospital before?"

He shook his head, hating to disappoint her. "Not that I've noticed," he said. "I'm sure the police can check the security camera footage. But now that I've seen her, I'll be sure to recognize her in the future."

Desiree nodded, then snapped a picture of the newest sketch with her phone. "I'm going to send this to Troy," she said as she typed. "He can make sure it's distributed to everyone on the case."

Stavros continued to stare at the latest image, unable to look away. There was something about the woman's eyes that bothered him. Not the way Desiree had drawn them—they matched his memory very well. No, there was something about the way her eyes had gleamed when she'd seen him, when she'd tossed Danny at him to make her escape…

"Are you okay?" Stavros looked up to find Desiree watching him. "You look like you've seen a ghost."

Her words turned on the light bulb inside his head. "Maybe I have," he murmured, a sick feeling spreading through his stomach.

"Stavros? What's wrong?"

He heard the worry in her voice and knew she deserved an answer. "Her eyes." He gestured to the page. "I've seen that look before."

"Oh? Where?"

He swallowed hard. "My ex-wife," he said, the words tasting bitter in his mouth. "Ellory had that sick expression in her eyes the last time I saw her. I thought she just hated me because I'd been awarded custody of Sammy. But, after what she did, I realized it was more than that. Her mind had snapped." He blinked, pushing back the sting of tears. "I don't want to scare you, Desiree," he said, glancing at her once more. "But this woman, whoever she is, she has that look, too."

Desiree's face went pale. "So you're saying you think this person is mentally ill?" Her voice was barely above a whisper.

Stavros wanted to reassure her, to tell her it was all going to be okay. But he couldn't make himself lie to her. "I'm not making an official diagnosis," he said. "But I don't think this woman is going to give up until she gets your son."

Desiree leaned back, seeming to deflate before his eyes. "That's what I was afraid of," she said, sounding miserable.

Stavros moved without thinking. He pushed back his chair and stood, then slid onto the bench beside her and put his arm around her shoulders. Desiree leaned into him, apparently appreciating his support.

"They're going to catch her," he said, wanting to give her some kind of encouragement. "Your brother, the other officers—they won't stop until they find her. And you know as well as I do that Grave Gulch isn't that big. She can't hide forever. The police will find her and arrest her, and then you and Danny will be safe once more. This will all be a bad memory." He ran his hand down her arm as he spoke, his fingers gliding over her smooth skin.

"You really think so?" Her voice was a little muffled, but the hope in her tone was clear.

"I do," he said. It was true; he had no doubt Desiree's family would rally around her to make sure she and her son were safe until this woman was in custody. "No one is going to take Danny away from you." And why would they want to? A pang stabbed his heart; if only he'd been able to say the same about his own daughter!

"I hope you're right."

"I am," he said, pushing aside his own memories. "And I'm here for you, too."

She pulled away and met his gaze. Their faces were only inches apart, and Stavros was suddenly very aware of the warmth of her body. He'd initially touched her to offer comfort, but now her proximity was giving his body other ideas.

He stared into her brown eyes, noting the darker flecks in her irises. He felt her breath caress his face, and with every inhalation, he drew in the light floral scent of her skin. His gaze dropped to her neck, to that small triangle formed by the ends of her collarbones. What would she do if he pressed his nose into that divot and breathed her in? How would she react if he put his hands on her body and pulled her forward, pressing her curves into his chest?

Stavros watched in fascination as the pulse in her neck started to pick up speed. Was she nervous, being this close to him? Did he affect her the same way she affected him? Or was she scared, worried that he might try something physical?

The thought that she might fear him put a damper on his growing arousal. But before he could move away, her tongue flicked out to smooth over her lips and her pupils widened. She sucked in a breath, and as she exhaled, he heard her whisper his name.

"Stavros?"

She leaned forward in silent invitation, and his body rejoiced. She wasn't afraid of him; her unconscious reactions were born out of desire, not uneasiness.

He tilted his head and met her halfway, his lips brushing across hers. The slight contact set his blood on fire, and he nearly moaned.

Desiree gasped softly. Stavros drew back and met her eyes, wanting to see her reaction. Her cheeks were flushed, her lips slightly parted and shiny. Confusion flashed across her face, but before he could ask if she was okay, she leaned forward and pressed her mouth to his once more.

There was no ambiguity here, no doubt in his mind that she wanted this as much as he did. Stavros reached up to cup her cheeks with his hands and felt the tendrils of her hair brush his fingertips. Her lips were warm and soft and fit perfectly against his own. She sighed softly and he slid one hand down to the small of her back and pulled her toward him. Her breasts flattened against his chest, and the contact caused his blood to rush south.

One of her hands rested on his chest, her fingers curling into the fabric of his shirt in an unconscious gesture of possession that sent sparks of sensation through his limbs. Her other hand went to the back of his head, tangling in his hair. He'd been meaning to get it cut for weeks, but as she tugged gently on the too-long strands, he was glad he'd put off that errand. His skin felt electric, hypersensitive to every touch.

Desiree opened her mouth, seeking more contact. Stavros didn't hesitate; he slid his tongue along her lips,

enjoying the shiver that went through her body. Then he
delved deeper, stroking, probing, learning her taste and
the feel of her tongue against his own. His awareness
of the world shrank as Stavros focused on the kiss, the
rush of blood in his ears drowning out all other sounds.

His hand drifted down to the hem of her shirt and
he tugged it up, needing to feel more of her against his
own. She shifted against him, exposing more of her
stomach. He splayed his fingers along the side of her
torso, the heat of her body racing up his arm to curl
inside his chest. She was smooth and perfect, and he
wanted more. But just as he began to slide his hand up,
she froze against him.

After a split second of confusion, Stavros dropped
his hand. Desiree pulled away and he blinked down at
her. "I'm sorry," he began, but before he could say more,
she slid off the bench and walked away.

Feeling dazed, Stavros stayed where he was. It was
clear he'd crossed the line somewhere along the way,
but for the life of him, he couldn't understand when that
had happened. Desiree had seemed like an eager par-
ticipant in the kiss and she hadn't objected when he'd
touched her. If anything, she'd made it easier for him
to put his hands on her. But she'd definitely changed
her mind, and he'd obviously missed the signals. Guilt
formed tight knots in his stomach, making him feel
sick. Maybe he was more out of practice when it came
to women than he'd realized.

A moment later, Desiree returned with Danny in her
arms. "Sorry about that," she said, briefly meeting his
eyes before looking down at her son. "I didn't mean to

run away from you, but I heard him stirring, and since we're in a new place, I didn't want him to be scared when he woke up."

A wave of relief hit Stavros, washing away his tension.

"No, I understand. I'm glad you heard him before he was fully awake."

She gave him a half smile that hit him right in the center of his chest. "Mom superpower."

"Must be." That she'd heard him at all was amazing; Stavros had been so caught up in the kiss, so intent on touching her, that a bomb could have gone off in the living room and he wouldn't have noticed.

And maybe that was the problem.

After all, he'd brought Desiree and Danny here to keep them safe. Logically, he knew the odds of the woman from the hospital tracking them to his place, and then trying to break in and kidnap Danny again, were long. Still, it was the principle of it. Stavros was attracted to Desiree—he could no longer deny it, even to himself. Unless he missed his guess, she liked him, too. But this was neither the time nor the place for him to act on it. He owed it to Desiree and her son to behave himself. Later, after this was all over, they might be able to explore this pull between them.

Stavros got to his feet and walked over to Desiree. He ran his hand lightly down Danny's back. "Hey, buddy. How'd you sleep?"

Danny stared up at him for a second, then reached out. Stavros took him easily and smiled at the look of shock on Desiree's face. "I guess he decided I'm okay after all."

"Looks like it," she said, running her hand over the boy's head.

"I'm sorry," he said. She glanced up at him, her expression questioning.

"About earlier," he began. "I, uh... I shouldn't have kissed you. I think you know I'm attracted to you, but now's not the time for me to act on it."

"Oh." She looked down without speaking. Stavros fought the urge to tip up her chin so he could see her face. What was she thinking? Hopefully he hadn't irredeemably messed up any potential chance he'd had with her...

"It's fine," she said finally, glancing up at him once more. "Don't worry about it. We'll just pretend it never happened."

Stavros nodded, glad to hear she agreed with him. Desiree smiled and tickled Danny's toe, making him giggle. "Do you mind holding him for a minute? I'm going to duck into the bathroom."

"No problem," Stavros said. "We'll be in the kitchen. It's time to start thinking about dinner."

They parted, him heading in one direction and her the other. Stavros braced himself for Danny to get upset as they traveled farther away from his mother, but the little one stayed calm as Stavros carried him into the kitchen.

"What should we make tonight?" he asked, opening the fridge to consider his options. He gazed at the shelves, but his mind was still on Desiree. Their kiss had been electric—there was no other way to describe it. He'd never experienced anything like it before. Sure, he'd kissed women he was attracted to, and he'd loved Ellory; he wouldn't have married her otherwise. But never in his life had he felt those sparks after such brief contact. It made him want more—more of Desiree and her lips, her hands, her body. And more time to explore this phenomenon. His logical side demanded he keep going, to find out if those sparks between them would ignite a flame or sputter out and die.

If she hadn't heard Danny, he probably wouldn't have stopped. He'd have been quite happy for the kiss to progress until he had her splayed, naked on his dining room table, her sketch be damned. In a way, he was glad the boy had stirred. Desiree deserved more than a frantic coupling against the nearest flat surface.

They definitely had a connection. And as soon as there was no longer a threat to Danny, they should pursue it.

Fortunately, Desiree seemed to understand. Stavros closed the fridge and walked over to the pantry, hoping to find inspiration there. Really, their conversation couldn't have gone any better. She hadn't needed him to explain his thoughts or questioned his conclusion. Clearly, she felt the same way. Knowing they were on the same page was a huge relief.

Danny reached for a box of pasta. Stavros handed it to him reflexively, then laughed as the toddler used it as a drumstick against the wall.

"Spaghetti, huh?" he asked. "Well, it's as good an idea as any other." He backed out of the pantry and set down Danny, then assembled the remaining ingredients for their meal. He'd keep his distance from her, at least on a physical level. But as long as she and Danny were guests in his home, he'd take care of them.

It was the least he could do.

Chapter Five

Desiree splashed water on her face and stared at her reflection in the mirror over the sink. Her cheeks were flushed, her pupils wide and her lips swollen. She looked like a woman who had been thoroughly kissed.

What had she been thinking?

One moment, Stavros was sitting next to her, literally offering a shoulder for her to lean on as she worried about what the future might hold for Danny. Then her hormones had taken advantage of her temporary weakness, and she'd practically thrown herself at the handsome doctor.

He hadn't seemed to mind, though.

She shivered as she recalled the feel of his lips against hers, the warmth of his tongue in her mouth and the caress of his hands on her body. His chest had been solid and strong, and she'd been all too happy to find herself pressed against him.

The man could kiss. And that wasn't her lack of recent experience talking. No, Stavros had skills. Even now, her body still pinged with the echoes of her arousal. If he could turn her on so quickly with just a touch or two, how would she respond if they actually slept together? Would she even get to enjoy it, or would she spontaneously combust as soon as she saw him naked?

"Doesn't matter," she muttered to herself, reaching for the towel. Stavros had made it clear the kiss was a one-off, a mistake on both their parts. He'd tried to be sweet about letting her down easy, but Desiree wasn't a fool. This was the only one she was going to get from him.

It was probably for the best. She finished drying her hands and placed the towel back on the hook. With everything going on in her life right now—the attempted kidnappings, Danny's strep throat, her work for the police department—the last thing she needed was to add a new relationship to the mix. It would be all too easy to let down her guard and focus on Stavros, and that kind of distraction would put Danny in danger. She owed it to her son to remain vigilant, especially while that woman was still out there. Why did she even want to take her son, anyway? There had to be an explanation, but for the life of her, she just couldn't see it.

After turning off the light, she started walking down the hall, heading for the kitchen. She heard Stavros's voice as she approached, but couldn't make out his words just yet. A large part of her was surprised Danny hadn't started fussing yet. He usually didn't care for strangers, and he generally got upset whenever she left his sight. But as she got closer, she heard the sounds of his babbling.

"You might have a point," Stavros said. Desiree

stopped just before the door to the kitchen, hanging back a bit to eavesdrop. "But I'm still going to add some more basil."

"Ba ba ba ba," Danny replied.

"Here, try it now." Desiree peeked inside to see Stavros holding a spoon up to Danny's mouth. The boy took a small taste, then opened his mouth and grabbed Stavros's hand, trying to fit the whole spoon in his mouth.

"Whoa there, little man," Stavros said. He laughed softly. "You're feeling much better, now that those antibiotics have kicked in. I'm glad you like it. But I still think it needs more basil."

Stavros tugged on the spoon, but Danny refused to surrender the utensil. "Okay, you can keep that one for now," Stavros said.

Desiree's heart swelled as she watched from the shadows. This was the kind of thing she wanted for her son. A man spending time with him, talking to him, including him. She'd hoped Jeremy would be that man, but he'd made it clear he wasn't up for the job. And while Troy and her other relatives did their best to be in Danny's life, they couldn't spend every moment with him. He was still young, so he probably didn't miss having a father in his life every day. But how much longer would that ignorance last?

She watched Stavros as he worked. He kept up a steady stream of chatter, asking Danny questions and pausing to let him respond. He listened to Danny's babbling and commented on it, making it seem as though her son was a true conversational partner. It was the same thing Desiree did at home, but she'd never expected that Stavros, a relative stranger to them, would be so natural with Danny. In her experience, people without children tended to regard little ones as curious nuisances rather than people to engage with. Not that she blamed them—toddlers weren't exactly known for their social skills. But then again, Stavros *was* a father. He just didn't have a living child.

It was clear he'd been a good dad. Desiree smiled as she watched him interact with Danny. He included the boy as much as possible, giving him things to play with and redirecting when Danny started getting upset or wandering too far afield. At the same time, he continued cooking their meal, which was starting to smell good. Desiree could tell Stavros was no stranger to multitasking, which made sense, given his chosen profession. Handling a meal and a toddler at the same time was likely small potatoes compared to the amount of information he had to juggle in one shift at the hospital. Still, she enjoyed seeing him like this—relaxed but competent, doing work that normally fell on her shoulders. In a way, it was a bit of a relief for her; he'd stepped in to take care of this chore, and she could relax knowing he had everything totally under control. In her younger days, she'd been attracted to looks and a sense of humor, but now that she was older, she was forced to wonder if there was anything sexier than a man who simply got things done without needing her input or instructions.

For a brief second, Desiree was tempted to slip away and take a few minutes for herself. She so rarely got any breaks. Even when Troy or one of her cousins watched

Danny, she spent the time cleaning or doing laundry or working on sketches. It would be so nice to just sit in peace and read a bit or play a mindless game on her phone.

But it wouldn't be fair to Stavros.

He was doing well with Danny, but she'd only asked him to watch her son while she was in the bathroom. He was already letting them stay in his home—the last thing she should do was further impose on his hospitality by making him keep up with Danny while she relaxed in the other room.

She stepped into the kitchen with a smile. "Smells good," she said.

Stavros glanced up. "Thanks," he said. "I have a good sous-chef helping." He nodded at Danny, who was sitting on the floor happily banging a spoon against a collection of pots.

"He's definitely providing the soundtrack," Desiree said, wincing as Danny made a particularly loud clang. "I can take him now. Thanks for watching him."

"No problem," Stavros said. He stirred something on the stove, then looked at her again. "Why don't you go rest in the living room? We're fine in here, and you've had a rough few days."

Tears sprang to Desiree's eyes, and she blinked hard. How had he known? Had he read her mind, or did she simply look exhausted? "Are you sure?" she asked, her voice wavering a bit.

Stavros nodded and smiled gently. "I'm sure. I'll let you know if Danny gets tired of me. Dinner will be ready in about twenty minutes. Go recharge."

"Thank you."

Desiree walked back into the living room and sank onto the sofa with a sigh. She couldn't remember the last time she'd had a few minutes to herself, when she didn't have other responsibilities vying for her attention. The fact that Stavros had even thought to suggest she take a break made him all the more attractive.

Too bad nothing was going to come of it.

She leaned back on the couch and closed her eyes, thinking back to the kiss. Something told her she was going to be thinking about that kiss a lot in the future, especially after she and Stavros had gone their separate ways once more. It was the kind of memory she would pull out at night, while she was alone in her bed. The beginnings of a wonderful fantasy she could spin about the two of them. In her imagination, they didn't stop at one kiss. No, they went further, stripping down to explore each other's bodies until they were both lying sweaty and spent on the huge table.

The sound of Danny's laughter drifted from the kitchen and she smiled reflexively. The fact that Danny had so easily connected with Stavros gave her hope that he could do the same with another man, one she might have a relationship with at some point in the future. One of her worries about dating was Danny's reaction; she had to find a man who worked not just for her, but for her son, too. Before, he'd always been shy around new people. But Danny had quickly moved past that with Stavros and was now responding the same way he did to his uncle Troy. If he could do that once, surely he could do so again?

Desiree let her thoughts drift, trying to let go of the stress and worries of the past few months. All that mattered was that right now, in this moment, Danny was safe and so was she. Tomorrow would bring a new set of issues, but for this spot in time, she was determined to relax.

She wasn't sure how long she sat with her eyes closed, half attuned to the noises coming from the kitchen, her ears ever alert for sounds of her son in distress. She must have drifted to sleep, because she didn't hear the footsteps. Didn't even register Stavros's presence until she felt his weight settle next to her on the cushions.

Desiree jumped a little and opened her eyes. Stavros smiled. "Sorry to startle you. Just wanted to let you know dinner is ready."

He was holding Danny, and the toddler showed no signs of letting go. As Desiree shook off the fog of sleep, she realized they looked good together. Like they belonged to each other. Both man and boy had near-black hair and golden skin, and they both had dark eyes. A stranger might pass them on the street and never know they weren't actually related. It was enough to send a pang of longing through her heart. One more reminder of what she couldn't give her boy.

Not yet, anyway.

Desiree got to her feet and sniffed. "It smells delicious," she said, following Stavros to the dining room.

"I don't know about that," he replied. "It's nothing fancy. I thought Danny might be willing to eat spaghetti, so that's what I made."

"He loves pasta," Desiree confirmed. She sat at the table and helped Danny get settled at her side. Stavros handed her a plate heaping with food, and she smiled in thanks. "This looks amazing." She twirled some noodles on her fork and began to blow on them to cool them off for Danny.

Stavros sat across from her and served himself. "Like I said, it's nothing special."

Desiree shook her head. "Are you kidding? I didn't have to cook it, which makes it great in my book." It was the truth—Desiree could count on one hand the number of times a man had cooked for her, and Troy didn't count, since he was her brother. "You let me rest, you fix my dinner…" She trailed off. "I feel like I'm on vacation." She deliberately kept her tone light, hoping to signal to Stavros that she'd moved past their kiss. She'd only be here a short while; once she got home, she could curl up in embarrassment over the fact that she'd made such a blatant move, only to be rejected.

"I guess if medicine doesn't work out, I could open a bed-and-breakfast?" Stavros joked.

Desiree swallowed her own bite of food. "Absolutely," she said, nodding for emphasis. The pasta was delicious. Granted, spaghetti wasn't an especially complicated meal, but Stavros had added a combination of spices and seasonings that elevated the meal from a kitchen staple to something truly tasty.

They chatted sporadically as they ate. It was hard to have a full conversation with Danny by her side. She was focused both on feeding him and keeping him from wearing the majority of his meal. He was used to sitting in a booster seat, and it was clear he was enjoying the freedom of eating without being strapped into a chair. For his part, Stavros truly didn't seem to mind the inevitable mess that accompanied a meal with a toddler.

"Can I wash the dishes?" Desiree offered when they finished. "It's the least I can do."

"Absolutely not," Stavros declared as he got to his feet. "Company never cleans."

"But I want to help," she protested. More than that, she *needed* to. It was strange, having someone else take care of her and Danny. She should just sit back and enjoy the hospitality, but truth be told, Stavros's generosity was making her a little uncomfortable. Desiree couldn't help but feel that she owed him, even though he'd never even hinted he felt the same way. In fact, he'd had the perfect opportunity to push for something more during their kiss. After all, she'd been the one to pull away first. If Stavros had wanted to, he could have easily pressured her to stay, to turn the kiss into something more. But he hadn't done that. It was yet another indication of his character and the type of man he truly was.

"Why don't you get Danny's bath started?" Stavros suggested. "Might help to keep some semblance of your normal routine tonight, to make it easier for him to rest in this unfamiliar place."

Desiree knew he was right. And as she watched him attack the pile of dirty dishes, she realized she'd lost this particular battle. It was clear Stavros wasn't going to let her assist him in cleaning up the kitchen, so she might as well get her son ready for bed.

"All right," she said. "Thank you again for dinner. It really was great."

He glanced up and shot her a grin. In that moment, standing at the sink with his sleeves rolled up and his cheeks dark with stubble, he looked like every woman's dream man. She had the absurd thought that he should make a calendar that showed him doing a different chore every month. He was the perfect mix of sexy and competent, domesticated but with a glint of mischievousness in his eyes.

Since when have I found housework sexy? Desiree asked herself as she steered Danny toward the bathroom. It was clear her hormones were out of control—it had been so long since she'd been around a man she wasn't related to that now that she was spending a little time with Stavros, everything about him was appealing to her. Once this was all over, she definitely needed to start dating again.

She owed it to Danny. But more than that, she owed it to herself. After a kiss like that, she couldn't be satisfied with lonely nights anymore.

STAVROS GLANCED AT the clock on his nightstand, squinting a little in the darkness—2:36 am.

He closed his eyes with a sigh and started a familiar set of mental calculations. If he fell asleep in the next ten minutes, he could get at least three solid hours before his alarm would go off. That was not an ideal amount of rest before a workday, but he'd take what he could get at this point. All he had to do was empty his mind and relax his body…

He focused on his breathing, kept the tempo slow and steady, drawing air deep into his lungs. The tension started to leave his muscles, and he felt like he was sinking farther into the mattress. Maybe this was actually going to work…

Then his traitorous brain fired a shot. *Is Desiree sleeping?*

That was all it took. His body perked up at the mere thought of her, and his lips started tingling with the sense memory of kissing her. He knew he needed to keep things friendly between them, at least for now. But now that he knew what she tasted like, he wasn't sure he'd be able to look at her without imagining her in his arms again.

And then there was the matter of Danny.

Ever since the accident, Stavros hadn't spent much time around children, aside from those he treated at work. Kids were walking, talking reminders of what he'd lost, of the life his Sammy never got to have. Losing her had felt like an amputation, leaving him incomplete. Being a father without a child felt like an abomination, something unnatural and wrong. And being by kids had always made him acutely aware of his situation.

But, to his surprise, spending time with Danny was different.

Maybe it was the fact that Danny was a little boy rather than a girl. Maybe it was the fact that Danny's temperament was so different from Sammy's. Or maybe it was due to the passage of time; five years had passed, and Stavros no longer felt like he was drowning in pain anymore.

Whatever the reason, the little boy made Stavros cautiously optimistic.

He'd enjoyed being with the toddler today. Cooking with Danny had been a new experience, one he hadn't expected to like. Stavros was used to silence in his home. Sure, he'd watch the news or listen to music while he got some work done. But, for the most part, he was alone. Having Desiree and Danny here made the place feel bigger somehow, more alive.

There was something about the little boy that touched Stavros. It wasn't the same feeling he'd had for Sammy; no one would ever replace his daughter, and the love he had for her was hers alone. But being around Danny, connecting with him the way he had today, made Stavros hopeful that he *could* love a child again. He'd felt the stirrings of that paternal bond once more, and it both scared and thrilled him to think he could have another baby in his life, if that was what he wanted.

In the years since losing Sammy, Stavros had begun to wonder if he was capable of having another family. If he found the right woman, would he be able to father another child? To give his heart and soul to another baby, the same way he had to Sammy? He was broken, that was true—when Sammy had died, she'd taken parts of him with her. But was there enough left behind to do justice to a new child? Could he really be a dad again?

He stared at the ceiling, searching in vain for answers. When he'd started his last shift, he'd had no idea that one of his patients would end up touching him on such a personal level. But meeting Desiree and Danny had thrown him for a loop, forcing him to rethink issues he'd either buried or ignored for far too long. And more than that, they'd given oxygen to the flame of the candle of hope that had been flickering inside him. Hope that he might connect with someone again, hope that he could be happy once more.

He still didn't know if his future included the two of them. His libido definitely wanted to see more of Desiree, but that might not be possible. She'd tried to hide it, but Stavros had caught the brief flash of hurt and disappointment in Desiree's eyes when he'd told her they should keep things professional for now. He rolled over in bed, scoffing at the memory. Who even said something like that, after such an amazing kiss? It wasn't like she'd come back to the dining room and started talking about moving in with him. He'd simply panicked about the kiss and all the things it could mean, and he'd overreacted. And, in doing so, he might have pushed her away for good.

"Figures," he muttered, rolling over again and punching his pillow into a better shape.

Even if Desiree was willing to overlook his gaffe, did he want to risk getting involved with her? He hadn't known her long, but one thing was clear: Desiree Colton was not the kind of woman to have a fling.

He didn't blame her. As a single mother, she had to consider her son. The fact that she admitted she hadn't dated since Danny's birth told him that she put her son's needs above her own. Desiree would want to make sure that any man in her life was as good for Danny as he was for her.

And while Stavros liked the boy and the toddler seemed to like him, he wasn't ready for that kind of responsibility.

His earlier words echoed through his mind. *I'm attracted to you, but now's not the time for me to act on it.*

Maybe it never would be.

He had his own set of issues to work through. It wouldn't be fair to Desiree or Danny to use them as practice for a future relationship and family. No, he needed to start in the shallow end of the dating pool, find a woman who wasn't also a mother and see how that went. Trying to have a relationship with someone who already had a kid was advanced-level stuff, something he wasn't ready to handle.

His mind knew it was the truth, but his body wasn't willing to give up on the idea of seducing Desiree so easily. She'd felt so good pressed up against him, her curves flattening on his chest. Despite the layers of fabric that had separated them, he'd felt her nipples pucker into points when he'd touched her skin. It had taken every ounce of willpower he'd possessed to keep his hands on her waist, when what he'd really wanted to do was cup her breast and draw her into his mouth.

Stavros shifted as his blood began to warm. He'd heard her sighs today and wondered what other sounds he could coax from her. Would she moan for him? Gasp? Could he make her call out his name?

His imagination caught fire and his arousal built. One hand slid south and his body tensed as he pictured

Desiree in bed with him, her scent on his sheets and her breath on his face. Stavros clenched his jaw as his pleasure mounted. He wanted to feel her against him, wanted to have her under him. Wanted to make her eyes roll back in her head, to make her see stars. He wanted to taste her—all of her.

His hips thrust involuntarily as he tightened his grip. Thoughts of Desiree took over his mind as his fantasies progressed, growing increasingly graphic. He barely had time to reach for a tissue from the box on his nightstand before his release took him. Stavros bit his lip, determined to remain silent as pleasure rolled through his body. Through it all, he saw Desiree. Her dark eyes, her full lips. The curve of her breasts, her ass. He wanted to share this with her, to connect to her on this basic, primal level. Forget about emotions, forget about commitment; Stavros needed her, even if only for one night.

His breathing slowed as his body relaxed once more. Sleep began to pull at him and he didn't try to fight it. But as he drifted off, one thought kept floating to the top of his consciousness.

Once with her could never be enough.

Chapter Six

"Wow. They're out in force today."

Stavros wasn't kidding. Desiree bit her lip as she stared at the protesters lining Grave Gulch Boulevard, one of the main thoroughfares through town. She saw lots of handmade signs decrying the police and calls for her cousin Melissa's resignation. Protests had been going on for the last few months, ever since the news had broken that Randall Bowe, the crooked forensic scientist, had corrupted several GGPD cases. But there was something different about the crowd today. They seemed more agitated than usual.

"Yeah. I've never seen so many people participating before," Desiree replied. Stavros stopped at a red light, bringing her face-to-face with a cluster of people standing on the corner who were holding up signs. One of the women glanced at her and did a double take, then nudged the person next to her. In a matter of seconds, it seemed like they were all focused on her. One of the men took a step off the curb, and for a heart-stopping second, Desiree thought he was going to approach the car. She fumbled at the door, searching for the lock.

Stavros placed his hand over hers, and she heard the locks *thunk* into place. She glanced over to find him staring at the man, his expression hard and unyielding. The protester saw it, too. He stopped, faltering a bit. Then the light changed and his friends pulled him back onto the sidewalk.

Stavros sent the man one last glare before turning his attention back to driving. Desiree relaxed into the seat as they drew away from the intersection.

"Thank you," she said softly.

"Don't mention it." His voice was gruff, but he gave her hand a quick squeeze before releasing it. "I guess you're a bit of a celebrity."

She shook her head. "For all the wrong reasons." Danny's first kidnapping and the surrounding events had helped expose Bowe's crimes and put a spotlight on Desiree and her son. Most of the time, things were normal. But every so often she'd feel eyes on her, and find people staring and whispering in the grocery store or at the park. For her child's sake, Desiree hoped the police found Bowe quickly. Lately, he'd been texting members of the police department, taunting and antagonizing them. He thought he was smarter than everyone, but he was bound to make a mistake eventually. The sooner the man was brought to justice, the sooner the scandal would pass and everyone would move on.

"There's a lot of angry people out today," Stavros remarked, eyeing some of the signs as he drove. "I guess news of the most recent murder has spread quickly."

"I'm sure it did," Desiree said. "Death and sex are two topics that never go out of style."

Stavros glanced over at her, one eyebrow raised. "I take it you don't agree with the protesters?"

Desiree shrugged. "I see their point. There's a serial killer on the loose, along with a corrupt forensic scientist with an agenda who has clearly caused a lot of pain in this town. But to say that Melissa should resign or that the police are at fault for all of it strikes me as unfair. Once they realized what has been going on, they tried to stop it. And they've been searching for Len Davison from the beginning."

"That's fair enough," he said.

Desiree turned to look at Stavros as they stopped at another red light. "You make it sound as though you agree with them." She jerked her chin in the direction of another cluster of protesters.

"Like you said, I see your point," he replied. "I'm sure it must be difficult for you to see people badmouthing your relatives. But I can understand why they are calling for your cousin's resignation. She is the chief, and ultimately, the department is her responsibility."

"Trust me, she knows that," Desiree said. She turned to look out the window once more, her eye drawn to a sign displaying a caricature of Melissa. She scanned the crowd, which was growing thicker as they approached the police station. She thought she recognized a few faces, but it was hard to tell. Just who all was out there? Were they all concerned citizens exercising their right to protest peacefully, or were there some criminals hiding in the throngs, as well, hoping to sow discord and possibly stoke violence?

Another thought made the hair on the back of her

neck stand on end. Was Danny's would-be kidnapper involved in the protests? Maybe someone was targeting her son to make Melissa seem incompetent, to send her a message? Or was she holed up at home, plotting her next move?

Desiree shivered. Stavros reached over and placed his hand on her knee. "Hey," he said quietly. "It's going to be okay. People are upset, but once the killer is caught and Bowe is behind bars, things will go back to normal."

"I hope you're right," Desiree murmured. The truth was, her world would never return to normal until the woman who was trying to kidnap her son was out of the picture. She had faith in her brother and the rest of her family and she knew the police department was stretched thin, but the sooner they found that woman, the better.

Stavros pulled into a parking spot close to the entrance of the police department. Desiree was surprised when he turned off the car. "What's going on?"

He gave her a puzzled look. "I'm going to carry the car seat in for you."

"You don't have to do that," she began. "I know you have to get to work, and I can handle it myself."

"I'm sure you can," he said, smiling a little as he unbuckled his seat belt. "But you don't have to. I'll take care of it."

Before she could lodge another protest, Stavros climbed out of the car. Desiree sighed and unbuckled herself. A man with manners. She could definitely get used to it.

Stavros circled around the trunk and met her at Danny's door. He hung back, letting her pick up the boy and lift him. Then he bent and quickly unfastened the car seat. He'd insisted on driving her to his home yesterday morning, and before leaving, they'd stopped by her car for Danny's seat. Desiree had figured Stavros would take her back to the hospital and her own vehicle this morning, but Troy had called last night and asked her to stop by the station first. It was a little annoying, this game of musical transportation. But Troy had insisted she meet him here, so he must have something important to tell her.

Stavros locked the doors and pocketed his keys. "After you," he said, gesturing with his free hand. Despite carrying the bulky contraption, he somehow managed to get to the door before she did and held it open so she could enter the station first.

Desiree smiled and shook her head slightly.

"What?" he asked, glancing at her curiously.

She waved at the receptionist manning the front desk and walked around the divider into the larger room beyond, where a collection of desks was arranged. "Nothing," she said. "You're so unfailingly polite."

"You say that like it's a bad thing," he replied, walking alongside her.

"No, it's not," Desiree said. She stopped, so he did, too. His dark eyes searched her face. "I'm just not used to it. I mean, Troy is a good guy. But he's my brother. And Jeremy wasn't rude, but he wasn't like you…" She trailed off, her cheeks growing hot as she realized the implications of what she was saying. It wasn't appropriate for her to compare Stavros to Jeremy, especially after the way he'd rebuffed her yesterday. She certainly didn't want him to think she considered him anything but a friend.

"Never mind," she said, waving away her words.

Before Stavros could say anything, Troy poked his head out of one of the conference rooms that lined the periphery of the open space. "Did I just hear my name?"

Desiree turned and smiled at her brother, grateful for his interruption. "Maybe you did," she teased. "What are you going to do about it?"

Danny squealed at the sight of his uncle and started wriggling frantically. Desiree bent to set him down before he flopped out of her arms, and he made a bee-line for Troy.

Troy knelt and opened his arms, grinning widely at his nephew. Danny launched himself into his uncle's embrace, and Troy rose to his feet.

He sauntered over, a mischievous glint in his eyes. "Does it hurt, knowing I'm his favorite?" he asked Desiree.

Desiree laughed. "Oh, is that right? I guess this means you're gonna change his poopy diapers today?"

Troy shook his head. "Uh-uh. As his mother, it's important you're aware of all his input and output. Isn't that right, Doc?" He looked to Stavros for confirmation.

Stavros held up his free hand and shook his head. "Oh, no. Don't try to bring me into the middle of this."

"Coward," Troy said with a smile.

Stavros laughed. "Call it a healthy survival instinct."

Troy jerked his head in the direction of the conference room. "I'm in here. Come set that down." He nodded at the car seat Stavros still held.

"Here, I'll take it." Desiree reached for it. "I know you have to get to the hospital."

Stavros handed her the seat, but he seemed a little reluctant. "Yeah, I should head out." He glanced in the direction Troy had gone. "Are you going to be okay?"

Desiree nodded. "I should be. Troy said he'd drop me off at the hospital to get my car. And Danny seems to be feeling much better today."

"That's why I wanted him to have the shot of antibiotics—it works quickly," he said. "Well... I guess this is goodbye, then." There was a gleam of emotion in his dark eyes, but Desiree couldn't tell what he was thinking. "Let me know if you need anything?"

"I will." She set the car seat on the floor and reached for his hand. "I can't thank you enough for what you did for me and Danny yesterday."

Stavros glanced away, and Desiree could tell her praise was making him uncomfortable. "It was nothing," he said, shifting on his feet.

"It was everything to me," she replied. She squeezed his hand and he met her gaze again. "Truly," she said.

He nodded. Before she could say anything else, an intent look crossed his face, and he leaned down.

Desiree's breath caught in her throat. Was he going to kiss her?

Just as she started to tilt her head, his lips landed on her cheek. He pressed a chaste kiss to her skin and stepped back. "Take care, Desiree."

She blinked up at him. He looked torn, as though

there was more he wanted to say. But as she watched, his expression smoothed into one of impersonal politeness, whatever emotions he'd been feeling effectively suppressed.

Before she could speak, he turned and walked away. She stood there for a few seconds, watching him go. An unexpected longing rose inside her, along with a sense that she'd missed something. Maybe it was just the heightened emotions of the last few days, but Desiree felt like they could have had a connection. Maybe even built something together. But that was likely wishful thinking. Stavros had come into her life when she was worried and scared; he'd saved her son from being kidnapped and brought her to his home so she and Danny could rest in a safe place. Was it any wonder she'd felt drawn to him? He'd quietly taken charge and given her the time and space to process the danger to her son. But that didn't mean he wanted her. After their day together, she felt like she knew him better. Stavros was simply the kind of man who helped people; he was honorable and polite and kind, and she shouldn't misinterpret those qualities as signs of his interest.

Even though their kiss had been off the charts, it was clear from his reaction he hadn't meant to take things that far. Despite the obvious spark between them, she had to respect his desire to keep things friendly between them. After all, he had his own demons to handle. She could only imagine how difficult it must have been for him to be around Danny after losing his own daughter in such a terrible way.

Troy poked his head out of the conference room. "Dez?" he called. "You coming or what?"

She shook her head and picked up the car seat. "Sorry," she said. "I was just thinking."

"Uh-huh." Troy watched her as she approached, a speculative gleam in his hazel eyes. "Did these thoughts have anything to do with the good doctor?"

Desiree shot him an exasperated look. "No," she said forcefully.

Troy took the car seat from her and set it in the corner of the room. "He seems like a nice guy."

"He is." She took one of the chairs at the table and reached for Danny. He shook his head and tightened his grip on Troy's shirt.

Troy gave her a triumphant smirk and sat across from her. She dug some crayons and a few toys out of her bag and slid them across the table.

"He's handsome, too," Troy said, his tone suspiciously casual.

"Is that right?" Desiree pretended to look at some of the papers on the table. She plucked her two sketches of Danny's would-be kidnapper out of a pile and placed them side by side, studying her work. With the one sketch showing the woman's eyes and forehead, and the other showing her nose, mouth and chin, Desiree could work on drawing a composite image of the complete face.

"You know he is," Troy said. She felt the weight of her brother's gaze and looked up.

"What about it?" Desiree asked. She was tired of

beating around this particular bush. "There's nothing happening, if that's what you're getting at."

"You sure?" Troy asked. "'Cause the two of you looked pretty cozy together when you walked in here."

His words made her stomach do a little flip, but Desiree was determined not to let her brother know she was attracted to Stavros. Especially since nothing was going to come of it.

She rolled her eyes. "You see a man hold open the door for me and suddenly you think we're together? Please." She shook her head. "I thought you were a better cop than that."

"Whatever," he muttered, handing Danny a toy car. "I know what I saw."

Desiree held up the sketches. "Did you get anywhere with these?"

"Ellie's running them through the system. So far, no one has reported any sightings of her, but we're on high alert."

A short rap on the open door made Desiree turn. Ellie Bloomberg, GGPD's resident tech guru, was standing in the doorway. She smiled when she saw Desiree.

"Hey!" she said. "Are you doing okay? I heard you had quite a scare the other day."

Desiree nodded. "We're fine," she said. "Things could have been much worse."

Ellie's expression was sympathetic as she glanced at Danny. "I'm glad it wasn't."

"What'cha got for us, Ellie?" Troy asked.

"I ran the images through the database." She turned

to look at Desiree. "Thanks for getting that sketch to us so quickly," she said.

"No problem," Desiree replied.

"And?" Troy interjected.

Ellie shook her head, and Desiree's stomach dropped. "No matches."

"What if I could sketch her whole face for you?" Desiree asked. "It's probably harder for the program to match only a few features, right? If I could give you her whole face, would that help?"

Ellie bit her thumbnail, considering the question. "It might," she said slowly. "Are you going to combine the two pictures, make a composite?"

Desiree nodded. "That's my plan."

Ellie shrugged. "It certainly couldn't hurt. I don't mind running the program again once you get it done. At the very least, we'll have a more complete image to release to the public." She glanced at Troy, who nodded.

"That would be helpful," he said. "People often have a hard time recognizing a suspect if any part of their face is concealed. Having a composite image would make it easier for the public to help us find her."

"Great." A sense of purpose rose in Desiree's chest, pushing aside her worry and disappointment. This was something she could do, an action she could take so that she didn't have to sit around doing nothing, waiting for this nameless woman to make her next move.

"Let me know when you're done," Ellie said. "I'll run the program as soon as I get the image." With a little wave to Danny, she left.

Troy handed Danny another small toy. "You want to work on it now?"

Desiree hesitated, feeling torn. She wanted to get started right away, but she knew her brother probably needed to take her to get her car so he could get back to work. "I can do it later, while Danny takes his nap."

Troy tilted his head to the side. "Don't you want to get it done now so Ellie can search?"

Exasperation rose in her chest. "Of course I do. But I know you have work to do, so I figured you'd want to take me to my car so your day is free."

"Yeah, about that…" Troy trailed off and glanced away.

A stone of dread formed in her stomach. Her brother was clearly hiding something. But what?

"Troy," she said evenly. "What's going on?"

He met her eyes and shrugged. "Nothing, really. I mean, nothing new, that is. I'd just feel better if you and Danny stayed close today."

"You want us to spend the day at the station with you?"

Troy nodded. "I know it's a pain, but I'd feel more comfortable if you weren't alone right now. At least until we have a better idea of who this woman is and where she might be."

His concern touched her, but there were some practical flaws in his plan. "But who knows how long that might take? Are you really suggesting we spend our days at the station for as long as she's at large?"

"Not necessarily," he replied, a defensive note in his voice. "Just for now, okay? Whoever this person is, she's escalating. She didn't hesitate to drug you to get to Danny. Don't you think it's possible she'll do worse next time? And if you and Danny are home alone and she incapacitates you again, or worse," he added darkly, "I'd have no way of knowing Danny was gone until it was far too late."

His words sent a jolt of fear skittering down her spine. Desiree knew he was right. She'd assumed that by locking the doors, she could protect Danny from harm. But the woman hadn't hesitated to inject her with a sedative, and in a rather public setting, too. She was naive to think a dead bolt would stop her son's would-be kidnapper.

"All right," she said, nodding. "You have a point. We'll hang out here today." Hopefully it wouldn't be too hard to keep Danny occupied and entertained. "But where is he going to nap? If he doesn't sleep this afternoon, he'll be inconsolable."

"Not to worry," Troy said. "Melissa has a cot in her office. She has meetings for most of the afternoon, so she said you can put him down there. I'll make sure you're not interrupted."

"That'll work," Desiree replied. "Sounds like you had this all planned out."

Troy stood, still holding Danny. "Yep. Almost like I'm a good cop or something."

Desiree rolled her eyes. "Where are you guys going?"

Troy grabbed a toy car off the table and handed it to Danny. "We're gonna go do boy stuff. Maybe go see the puppies at the K-9 training center, eat a few dough-nuts. Whatever we want."

Desiree chuckled. "I see. Don't work too hard."

"Oh, we won't." Troy stopped in the doorway. "Say 'bye to Mommy," he said, grabbing Danny's hand and helping him wave. "There's paper by the copy machine, and I have some pencils at my desk. Call me when you've got something."

"Sir, yes, sir," Desiree said, firing off a mock salute. Troy responded by sticking his tongue out at her, then turned and walked away with Danny. "Go easy on the sugar!" she called after them.

Smiling to herself, Desiree spent the next moment gathering the papers on the table into a neat stack. She didn't like to work on a messy surface—it was too hard to focus when she was surrounded by clutter. That task complete, she left the conference room and headed for her brother's desk, where she snagged a pencil from one of his drawers. After a quick stop at the copier for some fresh paper and a detour to the break room for a cup of coffee, she settled into her chair once more. The door to the room was shut, but she purposefully sat facing away from it so that she didn't get distracted by the view from the pane of glass set in the wood. Even though she'd sketched faces in chaotic situations, she always preferred a calm, quiet environment to work.

More importantly? This sketch was personal.

She started drawing, her eyes flickering first to one image, then the other as she roughed out the shape of the face, the general proportions of the woman's features. She tried not to let her own recollections override the process; there would be time to fine-tune the image once she was closer to being done.

Emotions swirled within her, and more than once, Desiree had to set down the pencil and take a short break. Normally, she had no problem doing her job. Even though talking to crime victims could be distressing, she was always able to set aside her feelings and focus on the drawing. But now, knowing she was trying to capture the face of the woman who had threatened her child, it was harder for her to ignore the anger and fear building in her chest. When she'd made the first sketch, after the incident at the park, she'd been running on adrenaline. And yesterday, Stavros had been there to distract her, to draw her out of her own head. This time was different, though. Maybe the quiet and solitude wasn't such a great idea after all...

"No," she said aloud. Distractions would only increase the chance that she made a mistake. She owed it to Danny to do her best work. Even if this woman wasn't in the system, someone in town had to know who she was. The more lifelike and realistic her drawing, the better the chances someone would see it and recognize this criminal.

Desiree picked up the pencil once more and leaned forward. "All right," she said softly, exhaling across the page. "Let's find out who you are..."

"Dr. Makris?"

Stavros glanced up from the computer monitor to see Stacey standing in the doorway of the small computer room he used for charting. "What's up?"

"I could use some help with the patient in room three," she said apologetically. "He won't let me examine him, and he doesn't seem to understand English. I'm sorry to bother you, but everyone else is occupied and he keeps saying 'doctor, doctor,' over and over again. I'm hoping that if he sees a white coat, he'll calm down."

Stavros pushed back from the table. "No problem," he said. "Have you called for a translator?" Stavros spoke some Greek, thanks to his family. But he wasn't fluent enough to practice medicine in it, and he didn't know any other languages.

"Not yet," Stacey replied, walking alongside him. "I was hoping you could help me figure out what language he does speak first. I tried Spanish, and I know a little French from high school. But he didn't respond to either one."

"Hmm." That was certainly going to complicate things. But Stavros was glad to have a challenge. It would help keep his mind engaged, so he didn't spend more time thinking about a certain dark-eyed woman and her toddler…

They walked into room three, and Stavros got his first look at the patient. He was an older man, tall and thin. His eyebrows were silver, but his hair was dark, and Stavros could see a few faint smudges of hair dye on the skin along his hairline. *Guess vanity only goes so far*, Stavros thought to himself.

"I'm Dr. Makris," he said. Even though the man might not understand him, he couldn't help but introduce himself.

The man pointed at his leg, and Stavros saw dark spots on his jeans. Blood. *"Eto vredit,"* he said. He looked at Stacey and repeated himself, as though pleading with them to understand. *"Eto vredit."*

Stavros turned to Stacey. "That sounds Slavic to me," he mused. He turned back to the man. "Are you Russian?" He searched his brain for the right term. *"Russki?"*

The man's face lit up and he nodded. "Now we know," Stavros said to Stacey. "Request a translator, will you?"

She nodded and left the room.

Stavros gestured to the man's leg. "All right, let me take a look." He walked to the small counter in the corner and reached for the gloves. "I'll just need you to get on the gurney." He turned back, realizing he was going to have to pantomime his explanation, since the man didn't understand him. But, to his surprise, his patient was already sitting on the bed.

Interesting.

"Let's roll your pant leg up." The patient reached for the hem of his jeans, but Stavros interrupted him. "On second thought, I'll just have you take them off so I can see better."

Without missing a beat, the man reached for his belt. Stavros waited in silence as the man peeled his jeans down to expose his thigh.

So he does understand me, he thought. Feigning a lack of fluency in English was a trick his grandmother used to pull when she didn't want to be bothered with talking to someone. But why would someone in need of medical attention do that? Was this man trying to hide something?

As an ER physician, Stavros knew some patients were reluctant to seek care for accidents or injuries that occurred while they were doing something illegal. Those patients were always harder to treat, as they were usually less forthcoming with information. But he'd never encountered someone who pretended not to understand English.

His suspicions grew deeper when he saw the man's leg. Bite marks marred his thigh and shin—it looked as though he'd been attacked by a dog.

Stavros recalled Troy's warning from the other night—the police had found blood at the scene of Len Davison's latest victim. Since Davison liked to attack men walking their dogs, was it possible a pet had gone on the offensive in a bid to protect its owner?

Stavros eyed the wounds critically. The marks on the thigh were especially deep, and the edges of the wounds were puffy with inflammation. Scabs had already formed over the shallow punctures, and the lack of fresh blood made it clear these injuries had not just occurred. Whoever he was, this man would soon be feeling the effects of an infection.

His mind racing with possibilities, Stavros pushed gently on the edges of the marks. The man winced and sucked in a breath. "That hurts?" Stavros asked.

"Eto vredit," the man repeated.

"Are these dog bites?" Stavros pointed at his teeth and made a pinching motion with his hand. Although he was convinced the man understood him, he was willing to play along until the translator showed up.

"Da. Sobaka."

Stavros didn't understand him, but he was willing to bet his lunch the man had just said the Russian word for *dog*. He nodded and peeled off his gloves.

"I need to get supplies," he said, pointing to his patient's leg. "These need to be disinfected, and the deeper ones need stitches. You'll also need antibiotics and a tetanus shot." He pantomimed giving himself a shot in the arm.

The man nodded, apparently satisfied. Stavros forced himself to walk out of the room calmly, but as soon as the door shut behind him, he jogged over to the nurses' station and grabbed a phone.

Melissa Colton picked up on the third ring. "Chief Colton."

"This is Dr. Makris, from Grave Gulch General ER."

There was a hesitation, as if she was trying to place him in her memory. Then Melissa spoke. "Dr. Makris. What can I do for you?"

"It's probably nothing, but…" He relayed his suspicions about this new patient, and the possible connection to the latest park murder victim. "I know we got a bulletin about it yesterday, but I don't know where it is, which is why I called your direct number."

"That's fine. I'm glad you did," she said, brushing aside his apology. "Is the man still in your ER?"

"Yes," Stavros confirmed. "I'm about to go back in to treat him."

"Stall as long as you can," Melissa said. "I'll dispatch units there now. Get hospital security to the ER, but have them hang back. We don't want to spook him. Don't let anyone go in the room."

"Will do," Stavros confirmed. He hung up and dialed hospital security, warning them of the need to stay quiet. Then he glanced around, looking for Stacey. They'd need to intercept any translators before they entered the room.

She wasn't at the nurses' station, and he didn't see her in the hallway. Maybe she was in with another patient? But a quick glance at the board showed him there were only two other occupants, and he confirmed with another nurse that she hadn't gone to attend to either one.

Concern mounted as he intensified his search. Was she in the break room? No, it was empty. The bathroom, maybe? He stuck his head in the women's room and called her name, but his voice echoed off the tiles.

A knot of dread formed in his stomach as he realized there was only one place left to look: room three.

His steps slowed as he considered his options. If he burst into the room and grabbed her, the man would know something was wrong and might bolt. If this man really was Len Davison, Stavros couldn't let him get away. No, better to walk in calmly and pretend like nothing was amiss.

He made a stop for supplies—might as well treat the patient's injuries while he was in there. Even if the man was a killer, Stavros had taken an oath to care for the sick. Besides, if he was seeing to these wounds, the patient might be less likely to suspect something was going on.

He rapped on the door and pushed inside. Sure enough, there was Stacey, standing next to the bed with her phone out. She glanced up when she saw him walk in.

"I know it's not policy, but I'm using this translation website until our official translator arrives," she said. Then she spoke into the phone. "Help is on the way." Her phone spoke the Russian equivalent in a disembodied female voice. She studied the man's face hopefully, clearly looking for a sign of recognition. He smiled absently and nodded.

Stavros wanted to tell her not to bother, but he didn't want to give anything away. "Good thinking," he said carefully. He grabbed a small rolling cart and pulled it over to his stool, then began unloading his supplies.

"Need some help?" Stacey asked.

"Maybe," Stavros said, thinking quickly. If he could send her on an errand, she'd leave the room and he would know she was safe. "Actually, yeah. Can you bring some more gauze? And maybe a few extra syringes of saline?"

"Sure thing." She started to move, but before she could take a step, the patient's hand shot out and grabbed her by the wrist. The man started babbling, tears tracking down his cheeks. He looked terrified, but Stavros wasn't buying it. Unless he missed his guess, this was all an act designed to keep Stacey in the room and close to him.

So he can use her for leverage? Or protection? Stavros mused.

Stavros stood, wanting to pull Stacey free. But she was focused on the patient, speaking in a soothing voice. "I'll stay," she said into her phone, the translation coming a few seconds later. She shot Stavros an apologetic look. "Sorry, Doc."

"It's okay." Stavros wasn't sure what to do. He normally intervened if he saw a patient touch a nurse, but in this case, he was worried about spooking the man. A sudden, ominous thought struck him: What if this guy was armed?

For her part, Stacey didn't seem distressed. It wasn't unusual for patients to grab a hand or seek a comforting touch, and based on the man's demeanor, it was clear she thought this was a distraught patient who needed reassurance.

Stavros slowly sank back onto the stool and resumed organizing his supplies.

"Should we wait for the translator?" Stacey asked. Standard policy was to hold treatment in nonemergency situations until it was clear the patient totally understood what was to be done and why. But, in this case, Stavros knew the translator wasn't going to arrive.

"You fix," the man said, speaking English for the first time. "Now."

Stacey's eyes widened and she glanced at Stavros.

"Sir, we need to wait—" he began.

The man muttered an expletive and reached behind him. Before Stavros could react, the man was pointing a gun at Stacey. "Enough," he said, all traces of confusion gone. "Fix my leg. Now."

Stavros's heart threatened to pound out of his chest. Stacey opened her mouth to scream, but the man poked her in the ribs with the muzzle of the weapon. "Don't even think about it," the man said harshly. He tightened his grip on her wrist and yanked her even closer. Stavros saw the fear on her face and tried to reassure her.

"It's okay, Stacey," he said, hoping he sounded calmer than he felt. "You're going to be okay."

"Not if you don't get to work."

Stavros forced himself to look at the man's wounds again. He pulled on his gloves and took a deep breath. "This is going to hurt a little," he warned.

"Don't care," the man snarled. "Just hurry."

Stavros set to work cleaning the puncture wounds as best as he could, under the circumstances. His hands shook a bit as he moved. "You're Len, aren't you?"

"What if I am?"

That confirms it, Stavros thought. But he took no satisfaction from knowing he'd guessed correctly.

He reached for the syringe of lidocaine. "I'm going to numb this so I can put in a few stitches."

"No," Len said shortly. "No stitches. Just give me the meds."

"It'll heal better if I repair some of this damage." In truth, Stavros was trying to stall. It would take only a moment to inject antibiotics, and then Len would make his escape. If he could keep him here a few more minutes, though, the police might arrive…

"No." Len punctuated the word with another yank on Stacey, which made her yelp. "Just the drugs."

The threat was clear. Ultimately, Stavros wasn't willing to risk Stacey's life on the chance of helping the police. "All right," he agreed. "Here you go." He injected Len with the antibiotics.

"Now bandage me. Quickly."

Once again, Stavros did as Len instructed.

Len kept hold of Stacey's wrist as he climbed down from the gurney. He tugged her over to the far wall and kept the gun trained on her while he pulled on his pants. Then he eyed Stavros. "We're gonna walk out of here," he said. "And if you try to stop me, I'll shoot her. If you raise any kind of alarm, I'll shoot her." He turned to Stacey, who was quietly sobbing. "And if you give me any trouble, I'll kill him and then you."

Stacey nodded and sniffed, trying to pull herself together. Len eyed him expectantly, and with a sense of resignation, Stavros stepped aside so that Len had a clear path to the door. Impotent rage filled him, but he knew if he made any kind of move, Len would make good on his threat to hurt Stacey.

He held his breath as Len and Stacey stepped out of the room, bracing for the sound of an approach from a security guard or, even better, the police. But aside from a surprised gasp, he heard nothing.

Stavros poked his head through the door in time to see Len yank Stacey around a corner, headed for the exit. In their wake stood a few stunned nurses and one shocked housekeeper, all frozen in place. Stavros trotted after Len, determined to keep an eye on Stacey. Watching her wouldn't save her from the killer, but he felt responsible for the situation. He refused to simply abandon her.

More cries rang out as he followed them, and he saw people jumping out of the way. Len pushed through a set of glass doors at one of the side entrances to the hospital and headed for the parking lot. Stavros followed, careful to keep a distance so that Len wouldn't feel provoked into hurting Stacey.

He led her to a car parked on the edge of the lot. For a second, Stavros thought Len was going to drag her inside. But he shoved her away, then climbed inside and started the engine.

Stavros tried to get a look at the license plate of the car, but he was too distracted by Stacey to focus on the small piece of metal on the back bumper. He broke into a run and reached her in a few strides.

She was curled up in a ball, leaning against the wheel of a car. Stavros knelt next to her, scanning her body for signs of injury. "Hey, Stacey," he said, keeping his voice low and calm. "You're okay. He's gone."

After a second, she glanced up at him. Her eyes were brimming with tears, and Stavros could tell she was still terrified. "Dr. Makris?" Her voice shook.

He smiled. "I think, under the circumstances, you should call me Stavros."

Stacey sniffed, then launched herself at him. Stavros wrapped his arms around her in a hug as she sobbed against his chest.

"It's okay," he said. "Everything is fine now."

Her body shook with terror and adrenaline. Stavros did his best to comfort her. There was nothing sexual about the embrace; there had never been the spark of attraction between them, and even though they were now pressed against each other, he felt nothing but a friendly affection for her.

So much for his theory that he was drawn to Desiree because he hadn't been close to a woman in too long.

If that was the case, he'd be having the same response to Stacey right now.

"Did—did he hurt anyone?"

"I don't think so," Stavros replied. He was impressed that, despite everything that had happened to her, Stacey still had the presence of mind to think about others.

"Are you ready to go back inside?" he asked. The police should be arriving soon, and he wanted to make sure he was able to talk to them right away.

"Okay," she said. She sounded stronger; the shock appeared to be wearing off.

He helped her to stand and they made their way back inside the hospital. As soon as they returned to the ER, they were surrounded by worried nurses and other staff.

Stavros left Stacey to the care of their coworkers and made his way to the men's room. Once inside, he splashed water on his face and took a few deep breaths. His heartbeat was returning to normal, but his stomach still felt wobbly; it wasn't every day he treated an armed serial killer who'd also taken one of the nurses he worked with hostage.

At least Desiree and Danny weren't here…

The thought gave him pause. If Danny's symptoms had come on this morning instead of the day before yesterday, Desiree might have very well brought her son in for treatment at the same time as Len.

Just the idea of Len pointing a gun at Desiree or Danny was enough to make his stomach lurch. How was it possible he'd grown so attached to her in such a short space of time? It didn't make sense, but there was one thing he did know: he needed to see her again.

He grabbed some paper towels from the dispenser on the wall and dried his face. Hopefully the police were here; if not, he'd simply go to them.

And if he happened to find Desiree at the station? So much the better.

Chapter Seven

Something was going on. She just had to figure out what it was.

Desiree softly closed the door to Melissa's office. Danny was sacked out on the cot inside, snoozing peacefully. It hadn't been difficult to coax him to sleep, despite the unfamiliar location; he was worn out from his morning adventures with Uncle Troy. True to his word, Troy had taken Danny to the K-9 training facility behind the police station, and the pair had spent a few hours playing with the puppies. They'd come back sporting huge grins, and Desiree wasn't sure which of the two of them had had the most fun.

She'd finished the composite sketch of the unknown woman and given it to Ellie. Unfortunately, the program once again failed to turn up a match, but Ellie had released the image on all the police social-media channels and distributed it to the officers. Hopefully someone, somewhere, would be able to put a name to the face.

Desiree walked over to the coffee station and poured herself a cup, then sauntered over to Troy's desk. He'd been sitting there for the last hour, muttering into his phone, typing on his computer. She could tell by his frown that something was bothering him. Time to find out what.

He didn't look up when she took a seat across his desk. Fortunately, he was close enough to Melissa's office that she could hear Danny if he woke up anytime soon.

"You gonna tell me what's going on, or do I have to guess?"

Troy looked up with a scowl. "What do you mean?"

Desiree took a sip of her coffee. "Come on, brother. I'm not stupid. You came back with Danny in a great mood, and in the space of the last hour I've watched you turn grumpier by the minute. You've been pacing the floor, muttering something into your phone, and when you're not doing that, you're sitting here typing rather aggressively."

His eyebrows shot up. "Typing aggressively?"

"You know what I mean." She gestured to the computer. "Pounding the keys like you're trying to punish them for something. It's a wonder you haven't broken the keyboard yet."

"Everything's fine," he said.

Desiree merely looked at him.

He shifted in his chair. "Okay, fine. There is something going on. But it's police business."

She tilted her head to the side. "Then I guess it's a good thing I work for the department," she replied evenly.

Troy stared at her for a moment. "You're not going to let this go, are you?"

She shook her head. "Nope."

He sighed and ran a hand over his head. "All right. Fine. We've had a couple of texts from Bowe come in, and a sighting of Len Davison today. Sent a couple of units out there to apprehend, but he took a nurse hostage and got away."

Desiree leaned forward, shocked. "Oh, wow. Is the hostage okay?"

Troy nodded. "Yeah. He ditched them in the parking lot to get away."

"Where was this?"

Troy glanced away. "Doesn't matter."

Alarm bells started ringing in her head. Why was he being so evasive? "Troy…"

He glanced back, then sighed. "The hospital," he mumbled.

Desiree sat straight up in her chair, feeling as though she'd just been doused with a bucket of ice water. "The hospital?" She practically screeched the words. Was Stavros okay? Had he been the hostage? She had to see him, had to know for herself that he was fine. "I need to go there."

Troy looked at her like she'd lost her mind. "Absolutely not," he said firmly. "Stavros is all right, as far as I know. He's been talking to the officers on the scene. He was the one who called us in the first place. And besides—" he glanced to the door of Melissa's office "—you really think it's a good idea to leave Danny alone while you run off on this fool's errand?"

"Of course not," she snapped. Now that she'd had a second to think, she knew she couldn't head for the hospital. But she did want to see Stavros again, just to verify that he was truly okay.

Troy was silent for a moment, watching her. A knowing look entered his eyes, and when he opened his mouth, she knew exactly what he was going to say.

"Thought nothing was happening between you two."

Desiree ground her back teeth together, determined to hold on to her temper. If she protested too much, Troy would know she had feelings for Stavros. And while she might, she didn't want to discuss that with her brother right now. She was still trying to understand her emotional response to this man for herself. Talking about it with Troy, or anyone else, would make it harder for her to figure out how she felt and what that might mean for her future.

"I just want to make sure he's okay," she said evenly. "He was very kind to me and Danny, and Danny responded well to him. Is it so bad that I want to make sure he's all right after encountering a serial killer?"

Troy opened his mouth to respond, but a commotion at the front desk made them both turn.

"Sir, I need you to calm down."

"I have to speak to an officer!" The man's voice grew louder, his desperation clear. "Please, I need to know who is in charge of this case."

"Sir, please have a seat and I'll call someone to help you." The front-desk sergeant was trying his best to get the man to sit, but it was clear the new arrival was too agitated for that.

"No. I need to talk to the person in charge. My sister

would never hurt that boy. Do you understand? I need them to know that."

Desiree glanced at Troy as a chill washed over her, making goose bumps pop out on her skin. *"That boy?"* she said softly.

He nodded. "On it." He got to his feet and walked over to the desk. "Sir, I'm Detective Troy Colton. What can I help you with today?"

Desiree watched from a distance as the newcomer stared up at her brother. "Are you the one in charge of the attempted kidnapping case? The little boy?"

"I am," Troy confirmed. "Do you have some information for me?"

Even from her spot at Troy's desk, she saw relief wash over the man's face. "Yes. Is there somewhere we can talk?" He was clutching a piece of paper to his chest, but from where she was, she couldn't tell if there was anything written on it.

"Right this way." Troy opened the gate and ushered the man through. He glanced meaningfully at Desiree as he led the man past his desk and into one of the interrogation rooms.

Desiree waited a few seconds to let them get settled. Then she walked into the small observation room attached to the interrogation room. From this vantage point, she could see through the one-way glass and hear everything he and Troy were talking about.

"All right," Troy said, settling into a chair across the table from the man. "Why don't we start with your name?"

"I'm Stephen Douglas." Desiree studied the man's

face as he spoke. He was calmer, now that he was speaking to Troy. But she saw the lines at the corners of his eyes and mouth and knew he was still upset.

"Okay, Stephen," Troy said easily. "You said you had some information for me on the attempted kidnapping case?"

Stephen nodded. "Yes." He extended his arms and placed the paper he'd been holding on the table. He ran his hands over the surface, trying to smooth out some of the wrinkles.

Desiree gasped. It was her sketch, the composite of the face of the woman who'd tried to take Danny.

"I saw this online today," Stephen said. He tapped the image with his forefinger. "That's my sister. I'm sure of it. Her name is Dahlia Douglas."

Desiree's heart leaped into her throat. They finally had a name!

"Okay," Troy said. He jotted the name on a notepad. "Where is your sister now?"

Despair flickered across Stephen's face. "That's the thing. I don't know."

Desiree fought back the urge to scream. They were one step closer to finding this woman, but still so far away from apprehending her.

"When was the last time you saw your sister?" Troy asked.

Stephen frowned. "It's been about a month. I've been searching for her, trying to find her so I can bring her back home." He shook his head. "She's not well, you see. She stopped taking her medication, and then she disappeared."

"What kind of medication does she take?"

Stephen reached into his pocket and withdrew another piece of paper, which he handed to Troy. "Here's a list from her doctor. It's all to help her function, to keep her grounded in reality. She's always had trouble staying in the present, even as a little girl."

Troy tucked the paper under his notepad. "I see. Has she ever tried to kidnap a child before? Or had any violent outbursts?"

"No, never." Stephen shook his head. "The thing is, I think I know why she's fixated on this little boy."

Desiree leaned forward, her forehead almost touching the glass.

"When we were kids, we had a little brother. I was eight and she was six, and our mother asked her to watch Jacob while she took me to baseball practice. Jacob was two at the time. She told Dahlia they could play at the park, and we would pick them up after practice. But when we got to the park, Jacob was gone and Dahlia was hysterical. She said a man had taken Jacob."

Desiree frowned. Apparently, Troy was skeptical, too. "Your mother left a six-year-old in charge of a toddler?"

Stephen nodded. "I realize now it wasn't a good idea. But this was thirty years ago, you see. Things were a little different back then."

Not that different, Desiree thought to herself. Even though she and Troy were the oldest in their family, her father and stepmother would have never dreamed of leaving them in charge of their younger half siblings at such a young age. It sounded like Stephen and Dahlia's childhood had been very different from her own.

"I see," Troy said. "Did your mother file a missing-person report?"

"Oh, yes," Stephen replied. "It was a huge story. I'm sure your department still has the records. I don't know what the statute of limitations is on kidnapping, but we never found Jacob. It's possible the case might still be open."

Desiree's stomach dropped. It was all too easy for her to imagine what it must have felt like to lose a child that way. The unanswered questions, not knowing if he was alive or dead. She'd nearly gone insane when Danny had been taken from her, and he was found quickly. But to spend years in that kind of limbo? To never find closure? She shuddered, her heart going out to Stephen's family.

"I'll definitely check into it," Troy said. "But tell me why you think your sister is attempting to kidnap this little boy now."

A look of sadness crossed Stephen's face. "She always blamed herself for Jacob," he said. "I tried to tell her it wasn't her fault—everyone tried to tell her that. But she never believed us."

"Your mother didn't blame her?" Troy asked.

Stephen shook his head. "No. She blamed herself. She pulled away from us after that. Went to work, came home and made dinner, then went to bed. I don't think I ever saw her smile after that."

"What about your father?" Troy persisted.

"Long gone," Stephen replied. "He left soon after

Jacob was born. I don't know where he went. We never saw him again."

Sympathy welled in Desiree's chest. Yes, Stephen's mother had made a terrible mistake. But as a single mother of three young children, she had to have been feeling worn thin. Letting the youngest two play at a nearby park while she focused on her oldest boy had probably seemed like the best option at the time. How would she have known her life would forever change?

"So Dahlia felt responsible for Jacob's kidnapping."

"Yes," Stephen confirmed. "And after that, her mind was never the same. She'd always been a flighty kid, but before Jacob, it had been sweet in a way. Like she was living in her imagination all the time, and she liked it there. After Jacob was taken, though, there was a darkness about her that worried me. I begged my mom to take her to the doctor, but she said she couldn't afford to."

"Did Dahlia ever harm any other kids? Or animals, maybe?"

"No," Stephen said. "I told you, she was never violent toward others."

There was something about the way he said "others" that pricked Desiree's curiosity. There was something Stephen wasn't saying…

Fortunately, Troy seemed to have heard it, too. "What about herself? You said she blamed herself for Jacob's disappearance. Did she ever self-harm?"

Stephen hesitated, and Desiree knew her instincts had been correct. "There was one time," he said. "I came home from school to find her in the bathroom."

He swallowed hard. "It was horrible." He shook his head. "I thought she was dead for sure."

"But she wasn't?" Troy said gently.

"No." Stephen blinked a few times, then lifted his gaze to Troy's face once more. "I got her to the emergency room. They patched her up. She was put on a psych hold. That's when she got access to medications. They said she had PTSD, and some kind of dissociative problem." His smile was crooked. "They helped her. For a time, it seemed like she was going to be okay."

"How long has she been taking her pills?"

"Ten years," Stephen said. "She was doing really well. She had a job at the grocery store, and she was still living with Mom. I knew she was never going to be able to live on her own, but Mom absolutely refused to consider a group home. I think she felt guilty about the way she'd changed after Jacob, and she wanted to do what she could to help Dahlia."

"Any idea why your sister stopped taking her medication?"

Stephen's lips pressed together. "Mom died six months ago," he said. His voice wavered a bit. "I brought Dahlia to live with me. My plan was to talk to her, find out what she wanted to do long-term. I have the room and would have been happy for her to stay with me, but if she wanted more independence, I wanted her to have it."

"I take it Dahlia didn't adjust well?" Troy's voice was kind as he probed for details. It was clear Stephen was upset, and who could blame him? No wonder he'd been so desperate to talk to an officer.

Stephen shook his head. "It was really hard on her. Then when the news broke about that little boy's kidnapping back in January, his picture was everywhere."

"Which reminded her of Jacob," Troy ventured.

"Yes," Stephen confirmed. "The thing is, he looks like Jacob. Same dark hair, hazel eyes, olive complexion. The first time she saw his picture she called him Jacob."

Desiree gasped. No wonder Dahlia had been trying to take Danny!

"I told her this little boy was not Jacob," Stephen continued. "But as time passed, I could tell she didn't believe me. She started talking about Jacob all the time, claiming that she needed to save him."

"Was she still taking her medication at this point?" Troy asked.

"Looking back on it now, I don't think she was," Stephen said. "I thought she was still going to work, but after about a week, the grocery store called me to check on her. That's when I realized she hadn't been going in. I left my job early that day, but when I got home, she wasn't there."

"When was this?"

"Two months ago," Stephen replied. "I've been looking for her ever since."

"Did you file a missing-person report?"

"Yes, I did." Stephen nodded. "But since she's an adult, I was told there wasn't much that could be done."

"That's partially true," Troy said. "If there are no signs of foul play, it can be difficult to determine if an adult is missing because they want to be or because something happened to them."

"Well, in this case, I don't think Dahlia knows what's going on. I'm certain she's back in her imaginary world. She's convinced this boy is Jacob, and if she takes him, she can bring our brother back to our mother."

Desiree rocked back on her heels and hugged herself, her mind racing. She heard Troy's voice asking additional questions, but she didn't focus on his words.

Dahlia Douglas. Now she knew the woman's name.

Feeling a little dazed, Desiree quietly left the observation room and wandered over to Melissa's office door. She stood there for a moment, hand on the knob, warring with the impulse to peek inside and check on Danny. Logically, she knew he was still fast asleep on the cot. But on an emotional level, she needed to see him, needed confirmation that he was still safe and here with her.

Moving quietly, she eased the door open and caught a glimpse of her little boy, sleeping peacefully. The sight soothed her troubled heart, and she closed the door once more. Then she walked over to the break room and poured herself a cup of coffee. She didn't really need one, but it gave her hands something to do. The familiar routine helped her feel grounded as her mind wandered.

Desiree sat in one of the empty conference rooms close to Melissa's office. Emotions swirled within her, making it hard for her to focus.

A large part of her was thrilled to have this new information. Now that they had a name and a face, it would help in the search for Dahlia. Grave Gulch wasn't a huge metropolis—someone would know where she was.

But now that Desiree knew more about Dahlia, an unexpected feeling was clouding her thoughts: sympathy. Never in a million years had she thought she would feel sympathy or pity for the woman who was trying to kidnap her son. It seemed wrong on some level to think of her as anything less than a monster. But she couldn't deny that Stephen's story about their childhood and Dahlia's mental health made her more real, more human. She was no longer a one-dimensional bogeyman, now that Desiree knew she was a person in pain who had spent most of her life grieving and feeling guilty over the disappearance of her brother. Desiree couldn't imagine what a burden that must have been, and to feel it from such a young age! If what Stephen had said was true, it seemed Dahlia's actions were motivated by the desire to right this old wrong. It was a noble impulse, even if her actions were wrong.

She heard Troy's voice and realized he must have finished asking questions and was probably escorting Stephen to the entrance of the station. "Let me know if you think of anything else..." he said, his voice growing fainter as he walked past.

Desiree didn't move from her spot. She knew if she saw Stephen, she wouldn't be able to keep her mouth shut. And while she technically was an employee of the police department, watching the interview from the observation room wasn't the most kosher thing she'd ever done. She was reasonably sure Troy had known she was there, but Stephen had not. She wanted to make sure

Stephen trusted Troy and would come to him again if he learned anything new about his sister's whereabouts. If he realized she'd spied on their conversation, it might make him reluctant to talk to Troy in the future.

After a few minutes, Troy poked his head into the conference room. Desiree met his gaze, her hands wrapped around her still-full coffee cup.

Troy nodded at the cup. "You gonna drink it or just hold it?"

"Haven't decided yet."

He took a chair across from her. "Well, don't let it go to waste."

"You want it?"

He shrugged. "Wouldn't say no."

Desiree carefully slid the cup across the table and watched as Troy took a sip. He sighed. "Perfect temperature."

"So what happens now?"

Troy eyed her over the rim of the cup. "We keep looking."

She stared at him, unsatisfied with his response. "That's it? That's the plan?"

He narrowed his eyes slightly. "What were you expecting?"

Desiree shook her head. "I don't know. Something a little less passive, I suppose."

Troy raised one eyebrow. "You think continuing to search for this woman is passive?"

Desiree pushed back from the table, needing to move. She started pacing the room, her frustration building. "We have a name now, a history. Surely, her brother told you where she used to like to go? Can't you get Melissa to send officers to check all those locations?"

Troy's gaze was level as he watched her move. "No, I can't."

Desiree whirled on him. "What do you mean you can't? More like you won't. This is *Danny*! Your nephew! Why aren't you moving heaven and earth to find her?"

A look of shock and hurt crossed Troy's face, and Desiree immediately wished she could take back the words. She knew he was doing everything he possibly could to find Dahlia. It wasn't fair for her to imply otherwise.

"Troy, I'm—" she began. But he held up his hand to cut her off.

"I know you're upset right now," he said quietly. Desiree sank down into her chair, recognizing the tone of his voice. He was angry and trying hard not to show it.

"May I remind you that we have quite a lot going on right now?" he continued. "We're still untangling the mess that Randall Bowe left behind, and we're searching for him, as well. There's a serial killer on the loose, and he slipped through our fingers earlier today. Not to mention the other crimes and issues we deal with on a daily basis. So although the department does want to find Dahlia Douglas, we can't be everywhere all the time."

"I know," Desiree said softly. Her face felt hot and she looked down, unable to meet her brother's eyes.

"Dammit, Dez, don't you think I would do anything in my power to keep Danny safe?" Emotion crept into

Troy's voice. She glanced up to find his eyes shiny with tears. "I love that little boy like he's my own son. How dare you imply otherwise?"

"I didn't mean to," she said. She reached across the table, but her arms weren't long enough to touch his hand. "I'm so sorry, Troy. I know you're doing everything you can. I didn't mean to accuse you of dropping the ball. I'm just worried and scared, and I took it out on you because you're here and you're an easy target."

"I know," he said. The emotion had left his voice and his shoulders slumped. "Believe me, I understand your frustration. I wish I had more resources. But I have to work with what I've got."

Silence descended in the room as their emotions settled once more.

"I feel sorry for her," Desiree said softly.

Troy sighed. "I know. Me, too. It was easier when she was 'the bad guy.' Now that I know her story, I can kind of understand her actions." His phone buzzed and he pulled it from his pocket. He glanced at the screen and sighed. "What fresh hell is this?" he muttered.

"Everything okay?" Desiree asked as he got to his feet.

"I hope so," he said. "The front-desk sergeant just texted that there's someone at the entrance looking for me."

"At least this one's not making a scene," Desiree joked.

"True enough." Troy left the room but returned a moment later with a funny look on his face.

Desiree opened her mouth to ask what was wrong,

but before she could speak, she caught a glimpse of the person standing behind Troy.

It was Stavros.

Relief slammed into her as her heart leaped into her throat.

He followed Troy into the conference room and offered her a shy smile.

"You're okay," she said. She ran her eyes over him, searching for any signs of injury. But from what she could see, he was fine.

She dug her fingers into the tabletop, rooting herself in the chair. The urge to throw herself against him and wrap her arms around his body was strong, but she felt Troy's eyes on her and knew what kind of signal that would send. Besides, she didn't know if Stavros would appreciate such a blatant display of affection.

"I am," he replied. He took the chair next to her while Troy sat across the table once more. Part of her was irritated that her brother was sticking around, but she wasn't about to tell him that.

"What happened?" she asked. Before he could speak, she held up her hand. "Wait—why are you here? I thought your shift didn't end until seven. Is something else wrong?"

He chuckled. "I take it you already know about Davison's visit to the ER?"

She nodded. "Troy told me about it. Is the nurse he took hostage okay?"

"Yes, Stacey is fine. She's still a bit shaken up by it all, but she'll cope."

"And you?" Troy asked. "How are you handling things?"

Stavros glanced across the table and shrugged. "It definitely wasn't a typical day at the office, I'll tell you that. I'm just glad no one was hurt. Things could have taken a nasty turn, if Davison had acted differently."

"I can only imagine how scary that must have been for you and Stacey," Desiree said.

Stavros sat back and ran a hand through his hair. "It was a pretty wild ride. I spent the last few hours talking to police and hospital officials. I told the higher-ups I'd be happy to finish my shift, but they insisted I go home. Told me to take the week off and decompress."

"Wow." Desiree was surprised to hear that. "Are they usually so generous with time off?"

"Hardly," Stavros said dryly. "I think they want me home so it's harder for the press to find me. You should have seen the number of news cameras set up by the time I left."

"That might not be such a bad thing," Troy mused. "I'm sure the hospital wants to avoid bad publicity, but if the public knows Len is still hanging around town, we might get lucky with a sighting." He pulled his phone from his pocket and stood. "Excuse me a minute," he said, stepping through the door.

Stavros looked at Desiree. There was a warmth in his eyes that made her stomach flutter. "How was your day?" he asked.

Despite knowing he was just being polite, Desiree got the warm fuzzies. "Interesting," she replied, "though not as dangerous as yours." She filled him in on the composite sketch and Stephen's visit. Stavros's eyes grew large as she relayed what she knew about Dahlia.

"Wow," he said when she was done. "That's quite a windfall. Do you feel better, knowing more about her?"

"In some ways." Desiree shrugged. "But I also feel sorry for her, if that makes sense?"

Stavros nodded. "Yeah. It's a complicated situation, that's for sure."

"Do you know what kind of condition she might have? What would cause her to break from reality like that?" She'd been curious ever since Stephen had mentioned it. He hadn't said what her official diagnosis had been, or rather, if he had said it she'd missed it.

Stavros frowned. "Without seeing her chart or knowing what medications she's taking, it's hard to say. There are several diagnoses that could explain her issues."

"I can help with the medication." They looked up to see Troy returning to the room. "Stephen gave me a list of her drugs. I put a call into her doctor's office, but in the meantime..." He sat at the table and pulled the paper from his notepad.

Stavros took the page and scanned the list. "Well..." He trailed off, then slid the paper across the table. "I'm not a psychiatrist. But these look like medications that are generally involved in the treatment of PTSD."

Troy frowned. "But Stephen said Dahlia was always living in her imagination, even before the kidnapping. You think this all stems from PTSD and not an underlying condition?"

Stavros leaned back and put up his hands. "Like I said, without seeing her records, I have no way of making an accurate diagnosis. It's quite common for young children to have active imaginations and a rich fantasy life. It's impossible to determine if her prekidnapping behavior was abnormal. But the loss of a brother, particularly if she blamed herself, and the mother's subsequent withdrawal would be an incredibly traumatizing experience. Children's brains are still forming—an event like that would forever shape how Dahlia understands the world. I know some people with PTSD experience dissociative episodes. That might be what's going on here. The death of her mother would be another wound to her psyche, and if she's no longer taking her medication, it will be harder for her to cope."

Desiree pressed her lips together, her worry growing. "How long do these episodes usually last?"

Stavros shook his head. "Everyone is different."

"Do you think she might wake up one morning and forget about Danny?" Maybe she would come out of her fugue, return to reality. Even if it only lasted for a few minutes or hours, she might be able to find her brother and get the help she needed.

"It doesn't work that way," Stavros said sadly. "Her brother's kidnapping was the defining moment of her life. She doesn't just think Danny looks like her brother. She thinks he *is* her brother. In her mind, taking him is the only way to restore her family. I don't think she's going to forget that or suddenly move on."

A chill went down Desiree's spine. "So until we find her, Danny will be in danger."

Stavros nodded. "I think so, yes."

"That's it, then," Troy said. She glanced at her brother, who was wearing a determined look on his face. "You can't be alone until we have her in custody."

"And how are you going to ensure that?" she challenged. "Not even an hour has passed since you sat in that chair and told me you don't have enough manpower. You're telling me you want to divert officers who could be out searching for Dahlia or Davison or Bowe and put them on babysitting duty?" She shook her head. "I don't think so."

"We'll make it work," Troy said, practically spitting the words out.

Desiree shook her head. "We'll just go." She wasn't willing to risk Danny's safety, but she knew the police were stretched too thin to help. "Danny and I can get out of town for a while, until you find Dahlia."

"Who knows how long that could take?" Troy said. He crossed his arms over his chest, looking thoroughly frustrated.

"It won't take as long now that you don't have to divert resources to watch me," Desiree said smugly.

Stavros emitted a strangled laugh, and she and Troy turned to look at him. He cleared his throat and held up a hand. "I have a suggestion. If I may?"

"Let's hear it," Desiree said. Troy angled his head to the side, but didn't object.

"You and Danny can stay with me," Stavros said. "It worked well yesterday. And now that I have the next week off, you don't have to worry about being alone while I'm at work."

Desiree sucked in a breath, feeling like the bottom had just dropped out of her stomach. Stay with Stavros? Again? She wasn't so sure that was a good idea…

"That's perfect," Troy said. "You really don't mind?"

"I don't," Stavros replied. But he was watching Desiree, his eyes on her face as she considered his offer.

Her first instinct was to say yes. The thought of spending more time with him sent warm tingles through her limbs. And he was so good with Danny!

But could she risk it? It had only taken a few hours in his presence before her defenses had eroded to the point where kissing him had seemed like a good idea. Now that she knew what Stavros tasted like, could she really spend the next week in close proximity to him without making a fool of herself again?

On the other hand, she didn't have much of a choice. There weren't enough police officers to spare, and while she could take Danny and head out of town, her bank account wouldn't appreciate an extended stay in a hotel. And what if Dahlia followed them? She didn't want to be alone in a strange place if Dahlia tried to take her son again...

No, Stavros had presented her with the only viable option. She knew staying with him was the best way to keep her son safe.

Even though it was going to put her heart in danger.

Chapter Eight

It was getting harder to control the urge to touch her.

Stavros sat on one end of the sofa, watching Desiree as she spoke on the phone to her brother. It had been two days since she and Danny had come home with him, and once again, he was shocked at how easily they'd fit into his life here.

They'd spent most of the time in his condo. It was so nice to have someone else here, someone to talk to. Their conversations had ranged from the serious to the silly, and he smiled to himself as he recalled their discussions over favorites—favorite food, color, music, movie, book, all of it. There was just something about talking to Desiree that made him feel whole again, that patched over the broken places of his heart. In the back of his mind, he knew he shouldn't get used to this. After all, she and Danny wouldn't be here forever. At some point, they were all going to return back to their normal lives. But right now, he was determined to enjoy this break from reality. It felt as though they were creating their own idyllic cocoon, and he didn't want to emerge anytime soon.

Desiree ended the call and gave him an apologetic smile. "Sorry about that."

"Don't mention it. Did Troy have any updates?"

The corners of her mouth turned down. "They're still looking for Dahlia. Someone thought they saw her the other day near the hospital, but by the time police arrived, she was gone. If it was even her in the first place."

"They'll find her," Stavros said. He didn't like to see Desiree worried or upset, but he understood her frustration.

She reached for her wineglass and took a sip. "I know you're right," she said with a sigh. "I just want this to be over with. I want to go back to when my son was safe and I didn't have to look over my shoulder all the time."

"He seems to be doing okay here," Stavros said, changing the subject slightly. "Has he had any trouble sleeping?"

Desiree shook her head. "Not at all. He fell asleep quickly tonight, and he's been sleeping through the night since we got here."

"Is that unusual for him?" Stavros asked.

"Not really," Desiree said. "Sometimes when we're at home he wakes up once, but he usually drifts off again without my help. I'm just surprised he's doing so well here, since this is a new place."

"Maybe that's helping," Stavros suggested. He took a sip from his own glass and smiled over the edge. "There's so much new stuff to look at and explore here and it's wearing him out for bedtime."

She laughed softly. "Could be. Whatever the reason, I'm not going to complain." She lifted her glass in a toast and took another sip. Then she leaned back against the sofa and closed her eyes.

"This is so nice," she said. "I haven't really had an opportunity to relax like this in ages. Good wine, good company," she said and glanced over at him. "You're spoiling me."

There was a sultriness about her that sent tendrils of heat through his limbs. Stavros reached for the wine bottle and topped off his glass. He gestured to hers and she held it out for him.

"It's nice for me, too," he admitted. "I like wine, but I don't like drinking alone. It's been great having you and Danny here—you make the place warmer, if that makes any sense."

"It does." She smiled, her lips dark from the wine. "At home, it's just me and Danny. And while I love him more than anything, I miss having an adult around."

"You're close with your family," he pointed out. They'd been checking in with her on a near-constant basis over the last two days. If Troy wasn't calling, Melissa or Grace or any number of her siblings and cousins were texting. It seemed like a lot of attention and contact, but then again, his reference for comparison regarding family communication was complete radio silence, save for the annual Christmas card he received from his parents.

"I am," she conceded. "But it's not quite the same. After Danny was born, my siblings and some of my cousins would take turns spending the night with me, to give me a chance to sleep. I was grateful for their help, but in some ways it made me feel more alone."

"How so?" Stavros thought he knew what she meant, but he enjoyed listening to her talk.

She lifted one shoulder in an elegant shrug. "I think having someone there with me made it even more obvious that Danny's father was missing. A lot of people have a partner when they bring a baby home—not necessarily a spouse, but someone who will be there every day, someone who's also going through the life-changing experience of becoming a parent." She shook her head. "Don't get me wrong, I'll be forever grateful for my family's help, but I was always aware that they were just visiting. They got to go home, back to their normal routines. But my life had changed forever. Things were never going to be the same for me."

Stavros was quiet a moment, considering her words. Becoming a parent had been hard for him, as well, but not in the same ways. As a father, his adjustments hadn't been nearly as difficult since he hadn't had to give birth or deal with postpartum hormones. But there was another experience that had left him isolated and alone…

"Believe it or not, I know what you mean." He took another sip of wine for fortification, but realized it was time to talk about Sammy. Desiree was a good listener, and he knew her well enough now to feel safe talking to her about his daughter.

"After the accident…" He trailed off, his throat growing tight. He shook his head and tried again. "I'd never felt so alone before in my life. Like you, I had a few friends come by. Some insisted on staying with me—I think they were afraid of what I might do if I was alone."

"Did you ever...?" Desiree's voice was quiet. "Did you harm yourself?"

Stavros stared into his wineglass and shook his head. "No. I wasn't capable of it. Not because I didn't feel anything—I think it was because I felt *too* much. I was so overcome with grief that it paralyzed me and made it so I couldn't do much more than breathe."

"Maybe that's a good thing?" she ventured. He glanced up and saw the empathy and understanding on her face. "If you hadn't felt frozen, who knows what you might have done?"

He nodded. "I've wondered that myself at times."

"I'm glad you had friends who were with you." A frown crossed her face. "Especially since I know your family wasn't."

"I was lucky, in that regard. But, like you said, having them here forced me to face the fact that my daughter was gone. When I was alone, I could pretend like she was just out with a sitter or sleeping in another room. But my friends being here was a constant reminder that she was dead. I felt like I was under a microscope, being watched all the time. They were so kind to me, so good about not intruding or forcing me to talk. But I knew they were keeping an eye on me, making sure I wasn't going to hurt myself."

"Are we...?" Desiree swallowed, then spoke again. "Are Danny and I staying in her room?"

Stavros shook his head. "No. I sold that house and moved here. I couldn't live there anymore. It wasn't a home to me. It was a tomb for my old life."

Desiree exhaled and he saw the relief cross her face.

"I don't blame you. If something happened to Danny I'd have to move, too."

He smiled. "My friends helped me with that, too. They packed up her things for me, so I didn't have to do it."

"Do they live in Grave Gulch?" asked Desiree.

"No." He took another sip of wine. "These are friends from medical school. Everyone matched to residencies in different locations, so we're all scattered across the country. But we've all stayed in touch."

"And you're obviously still close," Desiree said. "The fact that they dropped everything to support you shows you how much they care about you."

"It does," he admitted. "I know I'm lucky to have so many people care about me. In a way, they're like the family I never had."

She smiled. "So you do know what it's like to have a big family like me."

"It's not quite the same." He tilted his head to the side. "We text each other, but not nearly to the same degree as your family. I can go weeks without a new message. I don't think you've gone more than an hour without contact since you've been here."

She pursed her lips in an expression that was part rueful smile, part frown. "Yeah, we definitely keep in touch."

"Does it ever bother you?" Stavros appreciated her family was a part of her life, but in some respects, he thought having that much interaction would feel suffocating.

Desiree shrugged. "I'm used to it at this point. It's

how we've always been, so if we stopped talking to each other so often I would be worried something was wrong."

Stavros laughed. "Fair enough. Better the devil you know than the one you don't, is that it?"

She smiled and nodded. "Pretty much." The smile faded from her face and a serious expression took its place. "Can I ask you a personal question?"

He drained the last of his wine, feeling pleasantly warm and loose. Talking with Desiree was easy and effortless. And while he didn't usually like to share the details of his life, in this case, it felt right. He made a mental note to tell his therapist; the man had complained before about Stavros's reticence during appointments.

"Sure," he said, leaning forward to set the empty glass on the coffee table. "What's on your mind?"

Desiree took a deep breath, as though to fortify herself to ask the question. "What happened with you and your wife? Do you know why she took your daughter?"

Stavros didn't respond at first. The question didn't surprise him—on some level, he'd known the subject would come up between them. They were getting to know each other, and she'd shared lots of personal stories with him already. It only made sense she was curious about his past, too. Losing Sammy had been the defining moment of his life, so it wasn't exactly a topic he could just ignore or sweep under the proverbial rug.

Still, he wasn't sure how to start telling her this particular tale. It was so messy, so big, he struggled to find a place to start.

Apparently, Desiree mistook his silence for refusal. "Never mind," she said, leaning forward to reach for his empty glass. She stood, clearly ready to leave. "I shouldn't have pried. I'm sorry. I'll head to bed now." She turned in the direction of the kitchen.

"No."

Desiree paused and turned back to look at him. "I'm sorry?"

Stavros shook his head. "I said no. I want you to stay." He reached up and took their empty glasses from her hands. He placed them back on the table and gestured for her to sit next to him once more. "Please," he said. "If you want to."

She slowly sank onto the cushion, her expression guarded. "I don't want to cause you pain," she said. "I just want to know more about you, and that's been a huge part of your life."

He snorted. "To say the least." He waved his hand. "It's okay. I don't mind you asking the question, and I don't blame you for being curious. I'm simply trying to figure out the best place to start, you know?" He shook his head. "You'd think after all the times I've talked to my shrink I'd have this part down, but it's hard every time."

She reached over and placed her hand on his knee. "Take your time," she said softly. "I'm not going anywhere."

Her touch was warm through the fabric of his jeans, and he focused on the sensation as a way to ground himself in the here and now. It was all too easy to get lost in these memories, but having Desiree next to him would help.

"Things started out okay in the beginning," he began. "I mean, I wouldn't have married her if I'd had any doubts about my feelings for her or her feelings for me. I had just started medical school, and she knew what she was signing up for. Her dad and brother are both doctors, so she understood I wasn't going to be around much in the beginning."

"Lots of time studying?" Desiree asked.

"Oh, yeah. And doing clinical rotations, and taking exams, all of it. I made it a point to have date night every two weeks—I'd shut everything off and we'd focus on each other for an evening. It kept us close as I worked on med school and she made a name for herself at her job. She was the manager of a clothing boutique," he said, anticipating Desiree's next question.

He reached for his empty wineglass and poured the dregs of the bottle into it. He wasn't drunk—he and Desiree had taken hours to finish one bottle of wine between them—but he wanted to hold something.

"Anyway, she didn't complain when I matched to a residency in Grave Gulch. She knew it was part of the process. But in hindsight, I think that was the beginning of the end for us."

Desiree frowned. "How so?"

"It's hard to pack up your life and start over in a new place. In our case, we were several states away from her family. She had to leave her job, and it took her some time to find a new one where we landed."

Desiree brushed a strand of hair behind her ear. Stavros tracked the gesture, wishing he could touch her. *No*, he told himself. If he touched her, it would be hard to stop.

"So she started to resent you?"

He nodded. "I think so. It's one thing to say you'll be okay with a nomadic life, and quite another to actually have to do it."

"But I thought residencies only last a few years?" Desiree frowned slightly. "Couldn't you have planned to move back after your training was over?"

"Theoretically, yes," he said. "But it's common to stay in a place once you've finished residency. This is where I have professional relationships and contacts, so it would be hard to move somewhere again and start over."

"I see," she said. "So this was more of a permanent move." She reached for his wineglass and he smiled a bit as she took a sip.

"Basically, yes." She handed the glass back, and he resisted the temptation to put his mouth on the spot where her lips had been.

"To make matters more complicated, Sammy was about a year old at the time. So not only were we stressed about the move, we had a toddler to deal with, as well."

"I can imagine," Desiree murmured.

Stavros took a deep breath. This was the part of the story that hurt the most. "Ellory had postpartum psychosis after Sammy's birth. It was a bad case, and it took months for me to convince her to get treatment for it."

"Oh, no." Genuine sympathy washed over Desiree's

face. "I was so grateful I didn't experience that, but I've read how hard it can be."

Stavros nodded. "In her case, it prevented her from bonding to Sammy. And by the time she got help, she felt very disconnected from our daughter. I think she always loved Sammy, but she didn't like being a mother. It's not exactly something you can rehearse before diving in, so when her expectations didn't match her reality, that made it even harder for her to recover from her depression."

"I can understand that," Desiree said. Then she covered her mouth with her hand and let out a small gasp. "Oh, I'm sorry. I don't mean to imply I don't blame her for what she did or for what happened."

She looked stricken at the thought he might misinterpret her words. Stavros reached for her hand with a smile and laced their fingers together. "I know what you mean," he said. "If I could change things, I'd go back and make sure she got help sooner. Her depression is not to blame for what she did, and I don't think you're saying it excuses her actions."

Relief washed over Desiree's face. "I'm guessing her job was very important to her, then. It gave her an escape from the responsibilities of motherhood."

"Exactly," Stavros said, impressed with her insight. "So you can imagine that moving here and losing her job made things doubly hard."

"Is that why you divorced?"

For a few seconds, he was quiet, remembering their arguments, the fights that dissolved into screaming matches and the nights he'd rocked Sammy back to sleep after their yelling had woken her up. His heart hurt with the knowledge that for the last months of his daughter's life, their home had not been a happy one.

"That was a big reason, yes. She wanted to move back home. I couldn't leave. She hated me for leaving her home alone every day with a toddler. I couldn't magically conjure up a job. I told her we could put Sammy in day care so she would have more time to herself, but Ellory refused. I think on some level, she was trying to punish me."

"That's terrible," Desiree said softly. She squeezed his hand and he squeezed back, thankful for her support.

"Anyway, we got divorced."

"And you got custody of Sammy?"

"I did." Stavros closed his eyes, remembering the hearing. He'd been so afraid the judge would reject the agreement the lawyers had drawn up. "Ellory didn't want custody of Sammy—she was happy to just have visitation. I think in a lot of ways, the divorce was a relief for her. She could have her life back again."

"But if she was pleased with the arrangement, why did she take Sammy?" He heard the note of confusion in Desiree's voice and opened his eyes to find her frowning. He sighed, steeling himself for the next part of the story.

"She saw me having lunch with a coworker a few months after the divorce." His heart grew heavy at the memory. "There wasn't anything going on between us, but she thought there was. And it made her angry." He could still hear the accusations she'd flung at him when she'd come to visit Sammy, the anger in her eyes as she claimed he'd never loved her and had been cheating on her throughout their marriage. None of it was true, but she hadn't listened when he'd tried to explain. If anything, his denials had only made her more convinced that he'd already moved on.

"Oh." A look of understanding crossed Desiree's face. "I think I see where this is going," she said sadly.

Stavros nodded. "Ellory wanted to punish me. She knew Sammy was my world, so she was going to take her from me and move back home. In her mind, I didn't deserve Sammy because of the way I'd hurt her."

"Oh, Stavros…"

He pushed ahead, needing to finish his tale. "Ellory knew my schedule. She picked a night I was working and used her key to get inside the house. The sitter was dozing in a recliner. She only realized what was happening when Sammy started to cry. She woke up and confronted Ellory, but Ellory sprayed Mace in her face and took off with Sammy in the car. She hit a patch of ice just outside of town, and the car rolled down a steep embankment and slammed into a tree."

Desiree made a small sound of distress, but he kept going. "Ellory was dead at the scene, but Sammy was still alive. They brought her to the hospital, and I jumped in to run the case before anyone knew it was Sammy." He stared into space, but instead of seeing his living room, he saw the hospital bed and the small body of his daughter lying limp and broken on the blue sheet.

"I froze when I saw her. I just couldn't believe it. The rest of the team started working on her, but it was clear she couldn't be saved. I shoved my way to the bed and grabbed her." He lifted his hands to his chest, his movements an echo of the way he'd held her for the last time. "She died in my arms."

He heard a sniffle and looked over to see the sheen of tears on Desiree's cheeks. She reached up and cupped the side of his face with her hand, stroking her thumb across his cheek. He felt wetness on his skin and realized he was crying, too.

Without thinking, Stavros leaned over until he was lying on his side, his head in Desiree's lap. She placed one hand on his shoulder and the other in his hair. He closed his eyes, letting the pain of his memories wash through him. Experience had taught him that fighting his feelings was a losing battle, so he surrendered to the moment.

It didn't take long. A few minutes, that was all. Then he was ready to speak again. He wasn't sure if the transition was due to experience or because of the fact that, this time, he hadn't been alone.

He sat up and met Desiree's eyes. She was still emotional—he could see her empathy and sadness. But relief flashed through him as he realized there was something he didn't see in her eyes: pity.

Before he could second-guess himself, Stavros closed the distance between them and pressed his lips to hers. It wasn't a passionate kiss, one born from lust. No, this was a kiss of connection, of joining. Of understanding.

Her lips were soft against his, and as he drew back, he tasted the wine they'd both had on his mouth. Stavros touched his forehead to hers, and for a moment, they breathed the same air.

"Thank you," he said quietly, his voice barely above a whisper. "I haven't told many people this story. But I wanted you to know it."

"I'm the one who should be thanking you," Desiree replied softly. "I'm honored that you trusted me enough to share."

Stavros ran his hand down her arm as he leaned back, putting some space between them once more. He didn't know what to say to Desiree now, wasn't sure how to transition to a lighter topic.

But looking at her now, he realized maybe he didn't have to speak. Desiree wasn't the type of person who seemed uncomfortable with silence. She appeared to be content to sit next to him and let the heaviness of their conversation ease as the minutes ticked by. It was refreshing, spending time with someone who wasn't in a hurry to rush to the next task or jump into a new conversation while the words of the previous one still hung in the air. Even better, Desiree didn't seem uncomfortable with his emotional display. In the past, Stavros's grief had bothered people—it was one of the reasons he didn't talk about the accident much. He hated to see that gleam of pity in someone's eyes, or the way a person tensed up when Stavros displayed emotion. It was hard to find support when he felt like he had to comfort the person listening to him or to assure them that he was okay.

But Desiree was different. She listened without centering herself, so that he could talk without worrying how he was affecting her. It was wonderful, to say the least. And it made him feel closer to her. Knowing that he could open up and share his deepest pain and worst memories brought a sense of peace. He trusted her enough to be vulnerable, and she seemed to recognize that, which was another kind of gift.

Stavros sat next to her, waiting for the emptiness to take over. Usually, he felt hollowed-out and brittle after releasing his emotions. But, to his surprise, that sense of vacancy didn't appear. Instead, he became aware of a gentle warmth in his chest, as though a banked fire was smoldering inside his heart. Instead of feeling alone and broken, he was soothed.

He looked at Desiree, marveling at how her presence had changed everything about this experience. She hadn't needed to do anything—just having her here, listening to him, had made all the difference.

He wanted to tell her, to share his surprise and wonder at this development. But what could he say? How could he possibly convey what he was feeling right now? If he started speaking, he wouldn't be able to control his emotions, and he'd wind up sounding like some kind of zealot in a fervor. She was probably completely unaware of the effect she'd had on him. The last thing he wanted to do was scare her or make her feel uncomfortable. She'd given him a beautiful gift tonight, one he would always treasure. It wouldn't do to repay her by making things awkward between them.

"It's getting late," she said quietly. He glanced at the clock on the wall and realized she was right; it was past one in the morning.

She reached for their empty glasses, but he placed his hand on her arm to stop her. "I've got this," he said. "You go on to bed."

Desiree didn't protest. She stood and glanced down at him. Then she bent at the waist and kissed his cheek. "I hope you sleep well," she said.

The corner of his mouth turned up in a half smile. "You, too."

He watched her walk away, down the hall toward the guest bedroom. Part of him wanted to follow her, to stay in her company. How much better would he sleep if she was pressed against him all night? If her scent could perfume his dreams?

But Stavros knew if he followed her now, they wouldn't spend the next few hours sleeping.

So he waited until he heard the door to the guest bedroom shut. Then he got to his feet and picked up the glasses and empty bottle of wine. He left them on the kitchen counter and trudged to his room to crawl into bed, alone as usual.

DESIREE COULDN'T SLEEP.

She reached for her phone on the table next to the bed and pressed a button on the side. The screen lit up, displaying the time—3:18 a.m.

Two hours since she'd left Stavros in the living room, his hair mussed and his lips stained with the wine they'd shared.

She hadn't wanted to walk away. Quite the opposite, in fact. If he'd asked her to stay, or to come to be with him, she'd have skipped down the hall to his room.

The way he'd opened himself up tonight, shared his story and told her about his past and his daughter... It made her feel special for him to trust her with his story. She knew he didn't talk about his past much—he'd told her so. But the fact that he'd done so tonight was a sign of how much their relationship had changed in the time they'd spent together.

And when he'd laid his head in her lap, seeking comfort from her touch... Her heart ached at the memory. She'd wanted so badly to hold him, to rock him, to take away his pain. But she'd settled for running her hand through his hair, letting the strands trail between her fingers. She'd never seen a man surrender to his emotions before, never been around someone so secure in himself that he let her witness his pain and struggle. It was both beautiful and powerful to share that moment with him. On one level, it was the most intimate experience she'd ever had with a man.

And it left her wanting more.

She flipped onto her back with a sigh, then winced. Danny was sleeping next to her, and she didn't want to wake him. Maybe she should just go back to the couch, so her restlessness didn't disturb her son.

Moving carefully, Desiree slipped from the bed and tiptoed across the room. She left the door ajar so she'd hear Danny if he stirred. Then she headed down the hall, her thoughts still on Stavros and the evening they'd shared.

It had been difficult to hear his story, to learn about his relationship with his ex-wife and the things she'd done. Her heart went out to him and she wished there was some way she could help him heal from the loss of his daughter. Desiree knew she should just focus on supporting him and being a good friend. But in many ways, the deepening emotional connection she was feeling with Stavros made her want to explore her physical attraction to him, as well. It was as though learning more about him had simply whetted her appetite for all of him.

Guilt speared through her as she quietly made her way toward the living room. It felt wrong to want Stavros physically when he'd been so vulnerable with her. It was clear he still carried the loss of his daughter, and probably always would. He'd lowered his defenses tonight to share that part of himself with her, and it was greedy for Desiree to hope for more.

Distance would help. Once Dahlia was caught and she and Danny could move home again, she wouldn't have to be around Stavros so much. It would be easier to control her attraction when she wasn't literally bumping into him in the kitchen.

Lost in her thoughts, she didn't notice anything unusual until one of the shadows in the room moved. She let out a strangled squeak and jumped back, her heart pounding out a thunderous rhythm in her chest.

"I'm sorry." His voice was deep and gravelly in the stillness of the room. "I didn't mean to scare you."

Desiree took a deep breath and smiled, though he couldn't see her. "It's okay," she said. "I just wasn't expecting anyone to be out here."

"Can't sleep?"

She shook her head. "No."

He shifted, patting the cushion next to him. "Me, neither."

Desiree walked over to the sofa and sat, acutely aware of the fact that her nightshirt left most of her legs exposed. Her thigh brushed his, and the hair on his leg tickled her skin. She glanced over at him and felt a small, jolting shock as she realized he wasn't wearing a shirt.

The moon peeked around some clouds, brightening the room a bit. She tried not to stare, but it was difficult to think of anything else while she was so close to him. Her gaze tracked over his broad shoulders and flat chest, taking in the triangle of hair that tapered to a narrow line bisecting his stomach. The path disappeared under the hem of his boxer shorts, and she swallowed, forcing her eyes back up to his face.

Stavros was staring straight ahead, showing no sign of awareness of her frank perusal of his body. Desiree shifted, feeling like some sort of Peeping Tom.

"Thirsty?" He leaned forward and picked up a mug from the table. He held it in front of her and she took it, the glass cold against her skin.

"Thanks." She brought the mug to her lips, but the strong fumes of whiskey shot up her nose and made her sputter.

"Sorry," he said, turning to her. "I forgot what it was."

"How much have you had?" Desiree coughed a bit as she studied him. Stavros didn't look drunk, but he did seem...removed, somehow, as though he was in his head and not really here.

"Not much." The warmth was coming back into his voice as he spoke. "When I can't sleep, I have a little bit. Just enough to take the edge off and help me relax."

"That sounds like a good idea." She reached for the glass and caught the flash of surprise on his face as she took a sip. It burned her tongue and throat, but a pleasant warmth spread through her as the alcohol made its way to her stomach.

She leaned forward and set the cup back on the table. Stavros put his feet on the table, stretching out his body like a graceful panther. He was all lean lines and golden skin over trim muscle, and Desiree wanted nothing more than to climb onto his lap and take advantage of him.

Did he have any idea how he affected her? Likely not, she decided. He wasn't the type of man to tease, at least not like this.

She sat there, feeling like a flock of butterflies was taking flight in her stomach. She had to do something, say something to break the tension she was feeling.

"Is it my fault you can't sleep? Because I brought up your past?"

A faint smile crossed his face and he glanced at her. "No. And yes."

"Oh." Guilt descended, crushing her nervous awareness of him. "I'm sorry."

"Don't be." He turned his head to look at her fully now. "Sammy is never far from my mind. In a lot of ways, it felt good to talk about what happened. It was a release I didn't know I needed." He reached over and placed his hand on her knee. His touch was warm and sent zings of sensation through her body.

"I'm—I'm glad," she stuttered. It was hard to concentrate while he was touching her, watching her with those dark brown eyes. Her heart started to pound again, making her body flush.

"Can I ask you a personal question?" His index finger began to move on her knee, tracing imaginary patterns across her skin. Desiree swallowed hard, torn between the impulse to ask him to stop so she could focus on his words, and the desire for him to keep going, to move his hand up her leg and over her thigh.

"Sure." Could he hear the quiver in her voice?

"When was the last time you were with someone?"

Even in the dim moonlight, she could see the intensity in his gaze as he looked at her. "Ah…" Her brain scrambled, trying to decipher the meaning of his question. "You mean romantically?"

He nodded, his finger still gliding across her knee.

"Well." She searched her memories, trying to come up with a date. But with Stavros's hand on her leg, she could barely remember her own name.

"Not since Jeremy left." The confession probably made her sound pathetic, but it was the truth. She hadn't been interested in finding someone new while she was pregnant, and after Danny's birth, she'd been overwhelmed with the transition to motherhood. While the idea of a man was nice, the reality was lacking.

"What about you?" She bit her lip, determined not to squirm.

"It's been a while," he said. "I've dated a bit, but nothing serious."

"I see." Why was he telling her this? Was he just trying to make conversation, or did he have something else in mind…?

Please, her hormones pleaded. *Let it be something else!*

"I wish…" He stopped, sighed. "I wish we had met under different circumstances." He pulled his hand away and she immediately missed his touch.

"Oh? Why's that?" Did he regret inviting her and Danny to stay with him?

He met her eyes, the moonlight casting one side of his face in darker shadow. "I wasn't lying the other day when I told you I find you attractive. But it wouldn't be right for me to act on it while you're here."

"Why not?" She blurted the question before she realized she was speaking. "What's wrong with acting on it?"

"I don't want to take advantage of you," he replied.

No, please, she thought. *I want you to take advantage.*

"Why do you think you would be?" She was genuinely curious to hear his thoughts. It was thrilling to know her attraction wasn't one-sided, but why couldn't they explore it while they were together?

"I don't want you to feel beholden to me. That you owe me in any way for having you and Danny stay here."

"I see." That made sense. She did feel grateful to him for opening his home and keeping her and her son safe.

But she had no intention of using her body to repay his generosity. Maybe there was a way they could both get what they wanted, without complications.

"What if I told you that while I appreciate what you're doing for us, my attraction to you has nothing to do with it?"

"Oh?" Stavros raised one eyebrow, a note of hope in his voice. "Is that right?"

Desiree nodded. "I liked you in the hospital, before you ever mentioned bringing us here."

"Really?" He shifted, leaning against her a bit. The sides of their bodies were pressed together from shoulder to ankle now, and warmth was radiating off him like a furnace.

"It's true," she confirmed. "As soon as you walked into the room, I thought you were handsome. And you were so good with Danny."

He leaned over and nuzzled the side of her neck with his nose. "He's easy to get along with." His breath was hot against her skin. One of his hands began to trace along her leg, the light touch making her shiver.

"So you see," she continued, trying to ignore the tingles of sensation sparking through her with his every move, "this attraction between us has nothing to do with any feelings of gratitude I might have."

"I'm glad to hear it." He nipped at her shoulder, his stubble scraping gently against her skin. "What do you propose we do, then?"

"I think we owe it to ourselves to experiment," she said, getting the words out with some difficulty. His hand was on her hip now, his fingers playing with the waistband of her panties. "That is, if you want to."

He chuckled softly and the sound went straight to her gut. "I could be persuaded." He pulled back a bit until he could meet her eyes. "But only if you're certain."

Desiree nodded, appreciating his obvious need for her consent. "I am," she said.

A shadow of doubt crossed his face. "I don't know if I can give you what you deserve. What Danny deserves."

Desiree reached up and ran her hand through his hair. "I'm not asking you to." She didn't want to think right now, to analyze all the ways this might be a mistake. She just wanted to feel, to connect with Stavros physically and let go of her worries and stress, if only for a little while.

He leaned over and kissed her, shifting so that he could guide her to lie back on the sofa. He moved over her but kept their bodies apart, his hands planted on either side of her neck. Despite the inches between them, Desiree felt the heat of him soak into her muscles, softening them.

Stavros broke the kiss. "Stay here," he commanded.

"Where are you going?" Desiree tilted her head up, confused. Had he changed his mind already?

But no sooner had she asked the question than she had her answer. Stavros moved down her body and slid her panties down her legs. He sat up and pulled them free from her ankles.

Desiree put her knees together, waiting for him to crawl over her again. But he didn't. He circled her ankles with his large hands and slowly slid them up her legs.

"Stavros?" His hands were on her thighs now, gently coaxing them apart.

"Shhh," he replied. Desiree tried to relax, but she trembled as he ran his fingertips along the inside of her thighs. Was he going to—?

Every muscle in her body clenched as she felt his touch and then his tongue against her. The stubble on his chin rasped against her sensitive tissue and she bit her lip to keep from crying out.

Over the rush of blood in her ears, she heard him make a small sound of approval. One of his large hands traveled up her body to cup her breast, squeezing gently. She writhed against him, unable to control her movements as he pleasured her, taking his time to explore the most private parts of her body.

Time seemed to stop as her awareness of the world shrank to this man and what he was doing to her. She was reduced to being overcome by sensations, incapable of rational thought. Stavros seemed to anticipate her every desire, his lips and breath and tongue sending her to the edge of release in a matter of minutes.

Desiree's back arched off the sofa as her orgasm rolled through her. She cried out, her breath heaving as the rhythmic contractions spread warmth throughout her body. Stavros made a humming sound, the vibrations of it prolonging her climax.

Gradually, her body relaxed back onto the cushion. A drowsy satiation washed over her, making it hard to move. Her muscles were languid, her limbs heavy.

She felt like she was floating in a warm pool, totally at peace.

Stavros slowly began to work his way up her body. The stubble on his chin dragged lightly over the skin of her belly, her ribs, her breasts. He moved deliberately, carefully, lavishing attention on every part of her. By the time he made it up to her neck, Desiree's desire was building again.

She ran her hands over his shoulders, down his back. The flex and play of his muscles under her touch thrilled her, a potent reminder of his leashed strength. He covered her completely, his body long and lean over hers.

His arousal pressed against her, a reminder that they were just getting started.

Desiree's hands found the elastic band of his boxer shorts and she tugged them down, freeing his erection. Stavros stiffened as she wrapped a hand around him and gently squeezed.

"Not yet," he rasped as she began to stroke his length. "I need to get a condom."

"Okay," she whispered. "I'm on the Pill, but better safe than sorry."

He reached for the coffee table drawer and fished inside for a few seconds.

Then he kicked his boxers free and helped her tug off her nightshirt. She helped him with the condom, and they came together again.

Desiree shivered at the feeling of Stavros all along the length of her body. It had been so long since she'd enjoyed the weight of a man on top of her, soaked up the heat of a body larger than her own. The contact alone was enough to make her sigh.

She continued to stroke him as they kissed, their tongues exploring each other. Her need grew as the minutes ticked by and her hips shifted restlessly, instinctively.

Desiree guided him into place, wrapping her legs around Stavros's waist. He began to slowly push inside her body.

A sharp pain made her stiffen, and she bit her lip to keep from crying out. Stavros immediately stopped and withdrew, his eyes searching her face.

"What's wrong?"

She shook her head, embarrassment making it hard to meet his eyes. "Nothing. I'm fine. Go ahead."

Stavros pressed his forehead to hers. "Did I hurt you?"

"A little," she admitted. "But it's not your fault. It's just been so long. I guess I'm out of practice."

"Then we'll stop."

He moved as though to get up, but Desiree grabbed his shoulders. "No, please. I want this. I want you."

A look of indecision flashed across his face. "I don't want to hurt you."

"I'm fine, I promise." And she was, or would be shortly. She wanted this connection, and she wasn't going to let a little discomfort get in the way. "Please," she added, hoping to convince him of the truth of her words.

She tightened her legs around his waist and kissed him. He gradually relaxed against her again, falling back into the moment. Desiree's arousal built until she was writhing underneath him. Stavros positioned himself, but before he moved again, he met her eyes.

"Tell me to stop and I will." His voice was a deep rumble that she felt as much as heard.

"I don't want you to stop," Desiree whispered.

She held her breath as he entered her, but this time, there was no pain. He moved carefully, giving her body time to stretch and adjust to this welcome intrusion.

"Okay?" His breathing was jagged and she felt the subtle trembling of his muscles as Stavros forced himself to remain still.

"Better than okay," she said, pulling his head down for a kiss. She started to move her hips, encouraging him to do the same.

He groaned as he started to thrust, slowly at first, gradually picking up the pace. Desiree wrapped her arms around him, needing to feel more of him as they moved together.

Stavros's breath was hot on her neck. The feel of his chest hair against her nipples sent zings of sensation to her core. She placed her mouth on the curve of his shoulder and bit down lightly, smiling as Stavros grunted and thrust harder into her body.

With every motion, Desiree's need climbed higher until she was on the precipice, about to fall. She sucked in a breath, wanting to hold on until Stavros was ready to go with her.

"Faster," she murmured, encouraging him. She planted her feet on the cushion and moved her hips to meet his thrusts. He picked up the pace, his muscles tight under her hands.

That was all it took. She threw her head back as her release took control of her body, her core clenching around Stavros with an intensity that made him groan.

Stavros went still, his hips jerking slightly as he climaxed with her. She felt him kick inside her, the sensation prolonging her own orgasm.

As the seconds passed, he sank onto her, slowly giving her more of his weight until he was lying fully on top of her. Desiree wrapped her arms around him and hooked one leg over his waist to keep him in place. She knew the moment wouldn't last forever, but she wanted to stay joined with Stavros for as long as possible.

Gradually, their breathing returned to normal. She idly ran one hand up and down his back as satisfaction filled her.

Eventually, Stavros lifted his head to look at her. He smiled. "That was…"

"Yeah," she responded. "It was."

She debated if she should tell him it was the best sex she'd ever had. Jeremy had been okay in bed, but the connection she felt with Stavros was electric, like holding a bolt of lightning. It would be far too easy to spend the rest of her life chasing this high.

The cold air of the room began to register, making her shiver slightly. Stavros slipped free of her body and sat up. He pulled a blanket off the back of a nearby chair and placed it over her. "Don't go anywhere," he instructed. "I'll be right back."

He headed in the direction of his room. Desiree did

as he asked and remained on the sofa, closing her eyes and smiling to herself as aftershocks of the pleasure they'd shared zinged through her. Even if she'd wanted to, she couldn't have followed him. She felt like her body had melted into the furniture.

Stavros wasn't gone long. He returned wearing pajama pants.

"How are you feeling?" His voice was gentle as he pushed a strand of hair off her face. It was still dark, but the sky outside the windows was starting to lighten with the signs of the impending sunrise.

Desiree's heart flip-flopped in her chest and she smiled. Stavros made her feel cherished, as though she was a special treasure. It made her hope that, despite what they'd said before, maybe they did have a chance together.

"I'm great." She stretched, enjoying the way his eyes darted to her breasts as the fabric shifted over her chest. "How about you?"

A slow, satisfied grin spread across his face. "This has been one of my better nights." He gestured to the couch. "Is there room on there for me?"

"Of course." Desiree lifted the edge of the blanket and scooted over, making space on the cushions.

Stavros slid next to her, his legs intertwining with hers. "My bed is bigger, but this is warmer," he said, pressing his nose into her hair.

Desiree rested her head on his chest and closed her eyes. A sense of peace filled her, her mind drifting off as her body relaxed against Stavros. *This is perfect.* She let out a small sigh of contentment and surrendered to the pull of sleep, feeling safe in Stavros's embrace.

Chapter Nine

Two days later

"Are you sure it's okay for me to go with you?"

Desiree glanced up from changing Danny's diaper and rolled her eyes. "For the zillionth time, yes, I'm sure. The more, the merrier." She pulled the last tab into position, then yanked Danny's shorts back into place. "Unless you don't want to come?"

Stavros shook his head. "No, I do. I just don't want to make things awkward." If he was being honest, he wasn't totally comfortable going to a Colton family function. But Desiree had assured him that her aunt Verity would be happy for him to attend her birthday party. He wasn't so sure about that, but he didn't want to be away from Desiree and Danny. Even though the whole Colton clan was expected to attend the party and Stavros knew the two of them would be safe, he'd quickly grown accustomed to spending time with them.

They hadn't left his condo since he'd brought them home four days ago, save for a quick trip to the grocery store. And while under normal circumstances Stavros would chafe at the thought of spending all his time at home, he hadn't minded it. It felt like the three of them had been hibernating together, blocking out the wider world as they focused on each other. In some ways, it was as if they'd made their own cocoon, just the three of them.

He and Desiree had only slept together the one time but it wasn't a lack of desire keeping them apart. Danny was going through a sleep regression, so they'd taken turns getting up with him in the middle of the night and soothing him back to sleep. It was a bit of a novel experience for him; when Sammy had been going through the same thing, Ellory had been the one to take care of her, since he was usually at work.

Even though they hadn't been intimate again, they'd shared dozens of little moments, fleeting connections that made him feel closer to her.

But now it was time to break free, to jump back into normalcy. Objectively, Stavros knew they couldn't stay like this forever.

But emotionally? It sounded nice.

As soon as Desiree released him, Danny got to his feet and made a beeline for Stavros. He held up his arms and said, "Up! Up!"

Stavros smiled and picked up the little boy. He was a special kid; that much was clear. And the more time Stavros spent with him, the more he liked him.

He caught Desiree watching them, saw the small smile she tried to hide when she saw the two of them together. Stavros knew how much she wanted to find someone who would be a father to Danny, and he remembered from their earlier conversations that Danny didn't connect with just anyone.

But as much as Stavros cared for Danny, he didn't think he could fill that role.

His heart ached at the knowledge that he was going to disappoint Desiree. Even though she hadn't asked him for anything, he could tell by the look in her eyes that she still had hope something might come from their relationship.

And for one special moment, when he'd woken with her in his arms, their bodies entwined, Stavros had hoped the same.

Their physical chemistry was undeniable. Off the charts, never been better. But a relationship needed more than excitement between the sheets. There was no doubt that Stavros trusted her and enjoyed spending time with her. But their lives were so different. It was hard to see how they could join together.

Desiree's phone rang as she added a few spare diapers to her bag. She fished it out of her pocket and frowned at the display.

"Is something wrong?"

She shook her head. "It's just Troy, wanting to bug me." She answered the call and continued getting ready while she spoke to her brother.

Stavros sighed and turned his attention to Danny. He truly didn't understand how Desiree could stand the level of contact with her family. It seemed that someone was always calling or texting her, wanting updates on how she and Danny were doing, asking if she needed anything. In some ways it was nice—her relatives clearly cared about her and Danny, and he was glad to know she wasn't alone. But most of the time, it seemed like an exhausting degree of communication.

He knew he was biased, since his own family hardly ever spoke. But Desiree's was clearly on the other end of the spectrum, and in many ways, it made him uncomfortable. He didn't like the idea of someone always wanting to know where he was and what he was up to. However good their intentions, it felt too much like surveillance. And if Stavros was being completely honest with himself? It was another reason he was hesitant to start anything with Desiree.

Desiree finished the call and walked over to where he was standing. "Ready to go?"

"Do we have permission from your brother?" Stavros knew he sounded snarky, but he couldn't stop himself.

Desiree looked taken aback. "I don't need his permission to do anything."

"If you say so." Stavros started to walk toward the door, but her hand on his arm stopped him.

"What's that supposed to mean?" There was an edge to her voice that made it clear he'd upset her.

Stavros shook his head. He truly hadn't meant to pick a fight. "I don't mean anything. It's just that your family calls you a lot. Like they're trying to keep tabs on you or something."

"They're just worried about me," she said, the irritation fading from her tone. "They want to make sure Danny and I are okay."

"I guess they don't trust me to keep you both safe." Stavros snorted, feeling a little slighted.

A look of understanding flashed across Desiree's face. "That's not the case at all," she said. She ran her hand down his arm, trying to comfort him.

Stavros shook off her touch, frustrated with himself for sharing his thoughts. He'd sounded insecure and whiny, which embarrassed him. "It doesn't matter. Let's get going."

They rode the elevator to the parking garage in a silence that was punctuated by Danny's occasional babbling. It didn't take long to secure him in the car seat, and then they were on their way.

Desiree gave him directions to Verity's home, but otherwise didn't speak. Stavros spent the drive wishing he'd kept his mouth shut. It wasn't his place to criticize her family, and if the constant calls and text messages didn't bother her, why should he care?

After parking in the driveway of Verity's house, he cut the engine and turned to face her. "Look, I'm sorry for what I said earlier. I shouldn't have snapped at you."

"It's all right," she said slowly. "The past few days have been strange and stressful. You're entitled to lose your cool."

"Not if it means taking my frustration out on you," Stavros replied. That was no way to treat a friend, much less a woman he had feelings for.

Sleeping with Desiree had been both the best and worst decision he'd made recently. Now that he knew what they were like together, it was going to be harder to resist the pull of attraction he felt for her. But Stavros couldn't give her what she needed, what she deserved. And while she hadn't asked him for any promises, Stavros's own conscience wouldn't let him off the hook. Their hours together had been amazing. But it was all they'd ever have. He couldn't stand the thought of hurting her or Danny when they realized he wasn't the right guy for them.

Oblivious to his thoughts, Desiree leaned over and kissed him softly. Coward that he was, Stavros did nothing to stop her. The brief contact made his heart flutter, but he quickly tamped down the reaction.

"Apology accepted," she said, smiling. Her eyes shone with affection, making the breath stall in his chest. She was so beautiful, inside and out. Was he being a fool to reject the idea of a future with her before really knowing what it would mean?

The wall of his resolve began to soften. But before he could fully consider the thought, a rap on the window made them both jump.

Stavros looked past Desiree to see Troy standing beside the car, bending at the waist to peer inside.

Here's our chaperone, Stavros thought sourly.

Desiree turned and caught sight of her brother. She shot Stavros an apologetic look as she unbuckled her seat belt.

Stavros climbed out of the car and nodded a greeting to Troy. He didn't dislike the man; he just didn't appreciate his sense of timing.

"Hey, sis." Troy greeted Desiree as she stood. He wrapped his arms around her in a hug. "You guys doing okay?"

"Always," Desiree said. "Stavros has been taking good care of us." She glanced at him and he smiled faintly.

Troy eyed him, then his sister. "Glad to hear it." He made no mention of Desiree's kiss a few seconds ago. Was it because Troy hadn't seen it happen, or because he didn't approve?

Desiree retrieved Danny from his car seat and the four of them headed up the walk toward Verity's house. Troy reached for Danny, but the little boy refused to let his uncle pick him up. Instead, he ran to Stavros and lifted his arms.

Stavros obliged him, feeling Troy's eyes on him the whole time.

"Okay, little man," Troy said. "I see how it is." He cast a meaningful look at Desiree, who glanced away.

Troy nodded thoughtfully but didn't say more.

Fortunately, the awkwardness didn't last long. The front door opened as soon as they set foot on the porch, and the chief of police herself stood on the threshold.

"Issy!" Danny lunged for Melissa, a huge smile on his face.

She caught him and snuggled him close. "Hi there, bug. How's my favorite boy?" She stepped back and traded greetings with Troy and Desiree as they filed past. Then she turned to Stavros.

"I understand you've been watching over them?" Her tone was friendly, but he saw the questions in her eyes.

Stavros nodded. "My condo's building is locked twenty-four-seven, and there's a doorman always on duty. Seemed like the safest option at the time."

"I really appreciate it," she said. "I didn't like the thought of Dez and Danny being alone, with Dahlia still unaccounted for. But we don't exactly have officers to spare right now."

"I understand," Stavros said. "You're working a lot of cases."

"Speaking of which." Melissa bent to set Danny on his feet and he made a beeline for his mother. "Are you okay after what happened at the hospital? I was told Len didn't hurt you or the nurse he took hostage, but I know sometimes it takes a while to process an event like that."

Melissa's concern seemed genuine, and Stavros was touched she would think to ask after his mental health. "I'm fine," he said, glancing in the direction Desiree had gone. In truth, he'd been so focused on her and Danny, he hadn't given much thought to Len and his escape from the ER. "I exchanged messages with Stacey the other day—she's the nurse Len took hostage. She was given some time off, too, and she's handling things well. She told me she's ready to get back to work." He understood her desire all too well. After Sammy's death, his job was the only thing that kept him going. He hoped Stacey was truly fine and not using work as a means of ignoring her feelings, a mistake he knew he'd made for far too long.

Melissa nodded and led him deeper into the house. "I'm glad to hear it," she said. "The last thing I want is for Len to hurt anyone else." She shook her head. "I can't wait to bring him to justice."

Stavros scanned the large room, which was full of people. He recognized many of the Coltons, having seen them at the police station. But there were some faces he didn't know. "I'm sure your officers will find him," he said.

A shadow crossed Melissa's face. "I hope so. But not every killer." Her gaze fixed on someone to the side, and Stavros followed her eyes to see she was watching Desiree and Troy, who were talking to Grace Colton.

Curiosity demanded he ask. "What do you mean?"

Melissa glanced at him. "Amanda. Desiree and Troy's mother. She was killed in a home invasion when they were small. Troy was not much older than Danny when it happened."

Dread filled Stavros's chest, making him feel heavy. "My God," he murmured. His heart ached for the children they'd once been and for the innocence they'd lost far too early. How had she felt when she'd become a parent herself? Did her mother's death affect her relationship with Danny?

"GGPD never found him," Melissa continued. "It's still considered an open case."

Understanding began to dawn as Stavros watched Desiree and Troy from across the room. No wonder the two of them were so close. After losing their mother, was it any surprise they'd turned to each other for support?

Some of his irritation toward Troy faded in light of this new information. But even as his understanding of the family dynamics increased, part of him was hurt that Desiree hadn't told him about her mother herself. Hearing about this part of her past from her cousin made him wonder why she hadn't brought it up. After all, they'd had no shortage of time to talk and had spent much of the last several days growing closer. Did she not share this story because it was too painful? Or because she hadn't thought to bring it up?

Desiree looked over and caught him staring. She gave him a questioning smile. Stavros shook his head slightly. He'd ask her about it later; now was not the time to put her on the spot.

"Oh, there's Grace. I need to ask her something. Will you excuse me?" Melissa moved away even as she spoke, leaving Stavros alone.

He walked over to Desiree. "You doing okay?" she asked. "I didn't mean to abandon you."

"I'm good," he said. "Melissa was just filling me in on some family history."

"She's helpful that way." Desiree didn't seem at all concerned over what her cousin might have said, so Stavros gathered the long-ago murder of Desiree's mother wasn't a still-gaping wound. Still, he had questions and he hoped Desiree would be willing to talk to him later.

"This is quite a gathering," he said, scanning the room.

Desiree nodded. "We don't know how to have a small party. Come on. I see Verity over there. I'll introduce you." She took his hand and began to lead him through the crowd.

Stavros glanced down, searching for a pair of little legs. "Where's Danny?" He couldn't have gone very far and Desiree didn't seem alarmed, but the boy's absence made Stavros worry.

"My brother Palmer took him," she replied. "He's

going to feed Danny mass quantities of sugar and then bring him back once he starts to get grumpy."

"That's not very nice," Stavros observed.

Desiree shrugged. "It's not as bad as I made it sound. Palmer loves to play with Danny, and he does give him a few forbidden treats, which Danny thinks is great. It was only the one time he overdid it and Danny threw a huge tantrum because he was hopped up on sugar and overtired. Palmer learned his lesson, though he still likes to tease me."

"I remember talking to him on the phone at the hospital," Stavros said. "You'll have to introduce me."

"I'll introduce you to everyone," Desiree said simply.

True to her word, Desiree spent the next half hour making the rounds, stopping to talk to pretty much everyone at the party. She made it a point to introduce Stavros to all her relatives and their significant others, and soon his head was spinning from the sheer number of new names he'd heard. How did Desiree manage to keep them all straight?

Desiree took him to the kitchen and poured him a cup of punch. "You look like you could use some of this."

Stavros took the cup and tried a cautious sip. It was good; not too sweet, with a slight kick from some kind of alcohol. "That's nice," he said. "But I don't think I should drink too much or else you'll be driving us home later."

Desiree smiled and reached for a bottle of water. "So now you've met the family," she said. "What do you think?"

"Honestly? I didn't realize there were so many Coltons in Grave Gulch."

"Yeah, we don't have to go far for the reunions."

Stavros tilted his head, trying to gauge Desiree's mood. "Melissa told me about your mother," he said softly. "I'm so sorry."

A shadow crossed Desiree's face. "Thanks," she said. She glanced down at her shoes, then looked up with a sigh. "I probably should have told you myself, but to be honest, it didn't occur to me to talk about it."

Stavros was a little surprised by her response, but part of him was glad to know she hadn't withheld the information because she didn't trust him. "It sounds like you were very young when she died."

Desiree nodded. "I was. So was Troy. I hate to say it, but I don't have many memories of our mother. Our stepmother, Leanne, was really the one who raised us. She and my dad were always sure to talk about our mom and show us pictures and things like that, but unfortunately, we didn't know her long enough to form solid, long-lasting memories."

"How do you feel about that?" Stavros wanted to pull Desiree into his arms and hold her close. Only the fact that they were surrounded by prying eyes kept him from embracing her.

Her smile was sad. "I wish things were different, but I've made my peace with it. Right after Danny was born, I got really emotional about the whole thing. It broke my heart to know that if something happened to me, Danny would have no recollection of who I was or how much I love him. But I talked to my dad about it, and he helped me understand that my mother wouldn't be upset that Troy and I don't know her. She'd just be grateful that we were spared during the attack. I think he's right. I might not have a lot of memories of her, but whenever I try to think of her, I'm filled with a sense of safety and love. She left her mark, even if I'm not aware of it." She gestured to the people nearby. "I mean, just look at how many Coltons went into law enforcement."

Stavros smiled, as he knew she'd meant him to do.

"It's the same for you and Danny," Stavros said. "Children know when they're loved. And they thrive when they feel safe. Looking at you and Troy now, I'd say your mother laid a great foundation for your lives, and your father and stepmom nurtured and built on it."

Desiree blinked, her eyes shiny. "That's a nice way to think of it," she said softly.

Stavros lifted his hand to touch her arm, but before he made contact, a deep voice boomed throughout the house. "Burgers are done! Grab a plate and come get one off the grill!"

He inclined his head toward the backyard. "Hungry?"

"Getting there," she said. She put the cap back on her bottle of water. "I'd better track down Danny first and start a plate for him."

The jingle of her phone rang out. She pulled it from her pocket and frowned. "Who's texting me now? Practically everyone I know is here."

Stavros moved to set his now-empty cup in the sink. Desiree's hand clamped onto his arm, the ferocity of her grip making him wince. He looked down to see her face had gone deathly white, and her eyes were fixed on her phone screen.

"Desiree? What's wrong?" He slid his cup onto the counter and put his hands on her shoulders. A knot of tension formed in his stomach and he got a sour taste in his mouth. "Talk to me," he urged, bending his knees so he could get on her level.

Desiree met his gaze, her eyes filled with terror. "Danny," she said, her voice a harsh whisper. "Where is Danny?"

Stavros shook his head. "I'm not sure. Probably with your brother or one of your relatives. What's wrong?"

Desiree didn't answer him. Instead, she lunged forward, intent on joining the stream of people heading for the backyard. "Danny!" she cried out. "I need to see my son!"

She slipped out of his grasp and darted into the group, her movements frantic as she searched.

A wave of dread washed over Stavros, gluing his feet to the ground. There was only one reason Desiree would be acting like this.

Someone had threatened her boy again.

DESIREE HAD FOUND Danny with Palmer, and now held him tightly as Troy and Melissa stared at her phone screen. She didn't need to see the words to remember the message. It was burned in her brain, the letters glowing bright every time she closed her eyes.

I see your little brat is in danger again. You're lucky I haven't taken him to pay you back for causing me all this trouble. Sleep tight!

Desiree shuddered, her heart still pounding.

Danny didn't appreciate her tight grip. He began wiggling, his protests at being held growing louder by the second.

"Hey, buddy." Stavros's voice was calm and soothing. "It's okay."

Danny reached for Stavros. Desiree passed him over without hesitation.

"Can I take him to get some food?" Stavros asked. "I think he's hungry."

Desiree nodded. "But bring him back here, please," she said. "I need to be close to him." Even though they were surrounded by family and friends, she couldn't let down her guard. After all, the first time Danny had been taken was at a function full of Coltons.

Stavros ran his hand down her arm as he walked past her. "Of course," he said.

His touch was brief, but comforting all the same. Desiree hugged herself and turned her attention to her brother and Melissa.

"Well?" she asked. "What do you think?"

Troy handed her the phone. Desiree couldn't bear to put it back in her pocket while those hateful words were still on the screen, so she placed it on the counter. Troy ran a hand over his head and exchanged a glance with Melissa.

"I think this is from Randall Bowe," he said.

"Bowe?" Desiree repeated. She glanced at Melissa, who nodded her agreement. "I don't understand. Why would he text me? I have nothing to do with him—I think I've met him maybe once at a GGPD holiday function, if that!"

"Think about it, though," Melissa said. "You don't know him, but it was Danny's kidnapping back in January that made us realize what Bowe had been up to. If Danny had never been taken, we might still be in the dark about Bowe's crimes."

"So that's why he mentioned payback," Desiree said, the message starting to make sense.

Melissa nodded. "Exactly. Even though you weren't directly involved, it sounds like he blames you and Danny for exposing him."

"Do you think he's in contact with Dahlia?" Desiree asked. Maybe Bowe was egging her on, goading her to take action.

Troy frowned. "I doubt it. From what Dahlia's brother told us, she's convinced Danny is her little brother. Bowe would have no way of knowing that, and I doubt she'd respond to him anyway, given her current mental state."

Stavros returned to the kitchen with Danny, a plate of food in his free hand. He moved some things out of the way and let Danny sit on the counter to eat. His attention was focused on her son, but Desiree knew he was hearing everything they said.

"Do you think he'll come after us?" The thought of another person trying to take her child made Desiree want to vomit. How could she keep him safe in the face of all these threats? They couldn't stay with Stavros forever.

Troy frowned. "I don't think so. At least, not right now." He must have seen the hope in her eyes because he held up one hand. "I can't be certain, mind you. But Bowe is a fugitive and he knows we're searching for him. He also knows we're looking after you and Danny because of Dahlia's actions. If he were to try anything, it would be a huge exposure, and he has to know he'd likely be caught. My guess is he'll lie low. He might continue to taunt you, but that's probably all he's willing to risk right now."

"I agree," Melissa said. "Randall has been sending texts to some other GGPD officers over the last few months. He's angry and lashing out, but he's not rash. It's easier to hide behind a phone screen than to take a chance on being found."

"Can you trace the messages?" Desiree asked. "Maybe Ellie can find out where he is?" The thought was a bright spot in her otherwise dark mood. Ellie had a gift when it came to technology. Bowe was smart, but Ellie was on another level with regard to cyber issues.

Troy shook his head. "We've tried that," he said. "Every time, we come up empty-handed. Ellie thinks he's using an untraceable burner and bouncing the signal off several cell towers to boot."

"But with your permission, we'll have her try to trace this message," Melissa said. "Who knows? We might get lucky this time."

"Of course," Desiree said. "Whatever you need."

Stavros spoke up. "I can take you to the station after Danny finishes eating. Will Ellie meet us there?"

Melissa snorted. "She's probably already there. That girl works more than anyone else I know."

"I'll text her," Troy said. "Let her know what's up." He pulled his phone from his pocket and began typing.

Desiree flashed Stavros a grateful smile. It was like he'd read her mind. And the fact that he was willing to drop everything and help her once more…well, if she wasn't careful, she was going to fall in love with him.

The thought made the breath stall in her chest. *Oh, no*, she thought. *No, no, no.* Liking was fine. Liking was good, even. Liking him and being his friend was the way to go. The safe choice. Because Stavros had made it clear that was all they could ever have. If she allowed her heart to think otherwise, she was going to wind up disappointed and hurt. And with everything else going on in her life right now, a broken heart was the last thing she needed.

Three days. That was how much time they had before his week off was over and she and Danny would have to go back home. Surely Desiree could keep her heart under wraps for another three days?

But as she watched Stavros with Danny, saw the way her son responded to him, she knew she was fighting a losing battle. Desiree had told herself and Stavros that she didn't want any promises from him. But after their night together, she knew she'd been lying. She did want it all—and she wanted it with him.

"Okay." Troy's voice interrupted her thoughts. "Ellie was already on her way in to the station. She said she'll see you there."

"Great." Knowing she was going to do something about this disturbing message made Desiree feel a little less helpless. Ellie might not be able to trace the message, but at least they were trying.

"I wonder why Bowe is hanging around here," Melissa mused.

Desiree frowned. "What do you mean?"

Melissa gestured to Desiree's phone on the counter. "He mentioned Danny's attempted kidnapping. As far as I know, that story only broke in Grave Gulch. I know the *Grave Gulch Gazette* reported it, but I don't think many regional or national news outlets picked it up. So if he knows about it, that means he's probably sticking close."

"His other messages to officers have referenced current events, as well," Troy said. "It's almost like he doesn't want to leave because he wants to keep tabs on what we're doing."

"Shouldn't that make it easier to find him?" Stavros asked. "I would think it narrows your search area."

Melissa shrugged. "Theoretically, yes. But if he's hiding out in the forest on the edge of town, that makes things difficult. We simply don't have the manpower to do a thorough search of such a densely wooded area."

Stavros tilted his head in acknowledgment. "I understand. Could you ask for outside help?"

Melissa bit her bottom lip. "Not yet. Once the Feds get involved, we lose control of the investigation. Right now, Bowe hasn't hurt anyone physically, and we're still untangling his cases. My first priority is apprehending Davison. Once we get him off the streets, we can turn our full focus to finding Bowe and bringing him to justice."

Desiree watched Danny munch on a piece of noodle from a pasta salad. Even though she knew Melissa hadn't forgotten about her son, it stung a little to hear that finding Dahlia was low on GGPD's list of priorities.

Stavros caught her eye and flashed her a sympathetic glance, as though he knew exactly what she was thinking. "You about done, little man?" he asked Danny, who was reaching for the last strawberry slice on the plate. "We need to get going so we can make a stop before your nap time."

Desiree smiled faintly. Did Stavros even realize how quickly he'd adjusted his life to accommodate Danny's schedule? In the space of a few days, he'd gone from a single man who owned his time to one who planned his days around the sleep habits of a toddler. He'd made the change seemingly effortlessly and without complaint, another testament to his calling as a father.

"Want me to go with you?" Troy asked. Desiree saw the concern in her brother's eyes and knew he wanted to help. But there was nothing he could do, and she knew Stavros already felt stifled by her family. Asking her brother to tag along would only make Stavros uncomfortable. Besides, she could use a break from her relatives, as well.

"Nah, we're good," she said. "Can you do me a favor, though? Give my excuses to Verity?" The thought of navigating the crowd and talking to Verity was exhausting. Her aunt would want to know what was wrong, and then she'd have to talk about the text message, and it would turn into a whole thing. Better to sneak out while she could and avoid the attention of her extended family.

"Of course." Troy pulled her in for a hug. "It's going to be okay," he said softly.

Desiree nodded and turned to Melissa while Troy said goodbye to Danny. "We're going to get Bowe," Melissa said. "You don't have to be afraid."

"He's not the one I'm worried about," Desiree said.

Awareness dawned on Melissa's face. "We're going to find her, too," she promised.

Desiree nodded, unable to speak. What could she say? It was clear that GGPD was stretched thin, and despite what Troy had led her to believe, finding Dahlia seemed almost like an afterthought. It made sense, from a logical standpoint. Dahlia hadn't successfully taken Danny, so compared to a serial killer on the loose and a corrupt forensic scientist, a near-miss kidnapping wasn't as much of a threat to the community. But Danny was Desiree's world, and she'd hoped that, given the family connections, the search for Dahlia would have rated a bit higher for the police.

Stavros carried Danny as they made their way out of the house and back to the car. Now that he had a full tummy, Danny didn't mind leaving. He let Stavros buckle him into his seat without protest, and Desiree was grateful. With her own emotions in such turmoil, she didn't think she'd be much use trying to help Danny manage his own.

Stavros took her hand after they were in the car. She turned to look at him to find him studying her, his eyes bright with concern. "I'm here," he said simply. "Whatever you need."

Desiree nodded, but inside, her heart ached. He said he was here for her, and in many ways, that was the truth. Stavros had stepped up to keep her safe, to help her protect her son. They'd shared an amazing night together. But despite all of that, there was still a separation between them, a divide she knew he didn't want to cross. It was a special kind of torture for her to be around him—the feeling that they connected in all the right ways, but knowing Stavros didn't want to take the leap with her.

"I think…" She swallowed hard, tried again. "I think Danny and I should probably go home today." She deliberately kept her head turned to the window so she didn't have to look at him.

"What?" Stavros sounded surprised. "Why do you want to leave? Have I done or said anything to make you feel uncomfortable?"

Desiree closed her eyes, cutting off the sight of the buildings flashing past outside. "No, nothing like that. It's just that we can't stay with you forever. We'll have to be on our own again eventually. We might as well get started now, so you can have a little time to yourself before you have to go back to work."

"I don't understand." Stavros sounded genuinely confused. He placed his hand on her knee, his touch warm. "I know you're worried about Dahlia still being on the loose. Why do you want to leave before she's apprehended?"

"Because I don't think she will be," Desiree said. She turned to look at Stavros as he drove. "It's very clear to me now that the police aren't going to find Dahlia unless she literally runs into an officer. They're too busy looking for Davison and Bowe."

"I'm not sure I agree—" Stavros began, but Desiree cut him off.

"I get it. I really do. Dahlia isn't a violent offender, so it's more important to stop the people who are—Davison and the others in Grave Gulch who commit crimes. But that means this thing could drag out for weeks, maybe even months." Just the thought of it sent a wave of fatigue crashing over her. How much longer would she have to live in fear?

"We can't stay with you forever," she repeated. "You need to go back to your normal life, and we do, too. Aren't you tired of having us in your space all the time?"

"No," Stavros replied without hesitation. "Being with you and Danny has been good for me. You've made my condo feel like a real home."

Desiree was quiet, mulling over his words. It was nice to hear Stavros wasn't sick of them yet, but that didn't change the fact that this arrangement was never meant to be a permanent solution.

She glanced out the window, noticing the number of protesters increased the closer they got to the police station. There was a large crowd gathered outside the station, blocking the closest parking spots. The cops had a perimeter set up with sawhorse barricades, and several were on duty, keeping a watchful eye. The sight did nothing to soothe Desiree's nerves.

The officers who could have been searching for Dahlia. Or Davison. Or Bowe.

It was enough to make her want to scream. If they would all go home, GGPD could devote more time and effort to fixing the issues they were upset about in the first place.

Stavros parked about a block away from the police station. Before Desiree could unbuckle her seat belt, he placed his hand on her knee and turned to face her.

"Look, I understand if you want to take Danny and go home. And I won't argue with you about it. But can you at least wait until tomorrow? I'd feel much better if you let me come with you so I can check everything out and make sure it's safe."

Desiree nodded. "That's fair."

He breathed a sigh of what might have been relief. "Okay. Do you have an alarm system? Enough locks on the doors? A security camera set up?"

She hadn't expected so many questions, and for a second, doubt began to creep in. She didn't have an alarm system or any cameras. Maybe she should. Home had always felt like a safe place before, but now she had to consider her circumstances had changed, and not for the better…

"I guess there are some things I should get," she admitted.

Stavros nodded. "I'll help you," he said. "We can easily get some cameras to monitor your doors, but some things will take a little more time to have set up. We can start looking at your options tomorrow." He sounded supportive, but there was an odd note in his voice she hadn't heard before. It almost sounded like he didn't want her to go but was trying to put on a brave face or something.

Before she could reply, Stavros turned to the crowd assembled in front of the police station. "Are you ready to run the gauntlet?"

Desiree took a deep breath. "I suppose so. I hope the noise doesn't upset Danny too much."

"Would you rather I stayed in the car with him? I can drive him around town while you talk to Ellie."

Desiree didn't need to consider his offer for very long. "Would you? If you really don't mind, I think that would be best. I'd rather the protesters didn't catch sight of him."

"It's not a problem," Stavros confirmed. "Are you sure you'll be okay going in by yourself? I hate to make you walk in alone."

Desiree nodded. "I'll be fine. I'd rather go solo than risk Danny getting upset. Besides, who knows who's actually in the crowd?" She scanned the faces, but didn't recognize any of the people on the edge of the protest. No matter. The crowd was large, and it was impossible to tell if they were all friendly faces or potential threats. Better to keep Danny hidden as much as possible.

"I understand. Hopefully it won't take too long for Ellie to work her magic. Call me when you're done and I'll pick you up right here."

"That sounds good." She unbuckled and twisted around in her seat to smile at Danny. "'Bye, baby. I'll see you soon."

He grinned at her and then returned to staring out the window, apparently fascinated by the scenery.

Desiree glanced at Stavros. "Thanks," she said.

Before she realized what he was doing, he leaned in close and pressed a kiss to her mouth. "Be careful," he said, his dark eyes drilling into hers.

Desiree's stomach did a flip-flop at the unexpected contact, and she fought the urge to thread her hands through his hair and pull him in for another, deeper kiss. Why did things have to be so complicated? She wanted him; he seemed to want her. If only her emotions would stay out of it!

Instead, she nodded and pulled away. She shut the car door carefully behind her and walked toward the police station, away from the boy she loved and the man she wished she could.

STAVROS DROVE AIMLESSLY, his movements on autopilot as his thoughts drifted. Danny sat in the back seat, babbling happily at the passing scenery. The sound of the toddler's voice curled around his heart, stirring memories of Sammy. He'd loved to listen to his girl chatter. She'd been like a little parrot, repeating everything she'd heard. She'd kept up a running commentary of everything she'd seen, which he'd found charming and also a little exhausting.

Danny was different. He talked, but not as much as

he remembered Sammy doing. Danny was shy compared to his girl, though now that they'd spent more time together, Danny had really come out of his shell around Stavros. It touched Stavros to know the boy trusted him and enjoyed his company. He realized what a gift it was to get to see the silly side of Danny.

He turned right at the light, heading past one of the elementary schools. Sammy would have been a student there now, if not for that unfortunate twist of fate. Stavros felt the familiar ache in his heart, but it started to fade as soon as it appeared. That was new—he was used to the pain sticking around. But ever since talking to Desiree and sharing the details of his past, he felt lighter, freer somehow.

Just the thought of her leaving to go back to her own home was enough to put a damper on his spirits. In the back of his mind, Stavros had realized the arrangement wasn't permanent. As soon as he'd brought her to his place, the proverbial clock had started ticking. But he'd figured she and Danny would stay the full week with him, until he had to return to work. Hell, a small part of him had even hoped they'd stay longer than that, until some undetermined date in the future.

It was a nice fantasy, but one not rooted in reality. Desiree and Danny had their own lives, and he had his. It was nice to play house like this for a while, but at some point, things had to go back to normal. It might as well be sooner rather than later.

After a few blocks, Stavros made another right turn. His plan was to circle Grave Gulch until Desiree called and told him she was ready. Not the most exciting route, but it was a journey he'd taken many times before at night with Sammy in the back seat, the motion lulling her to sleep on difficult nights.

He glanced in the rearview mirror, noting with satisfaction that Danny was still awake. That was good; hopefully he'd stay that way until they got home so he'd take a normal nap.

No, not home, he thought. *My place.*

Despite the fact that Desiree's presence had elevated the condo from a place to sleep into a home, he knew she didn't see it that way. She saw herself as a guest, not a resident. And while part of him wanted desperately to know what it would take to convince her to change that status, a larger part of him was afraid.

Being with Desiree, talking to her, sharing this time with her—all of it had given Stavros a glimpse of what his life might be like. He could be with a woman, trust her. Grow to love her. And, yes, maybe even have a family with her.

But while he wanted that happy ending, the voice of doubt still rang in his mind. What if it didn't work? What if he lowered his guard and let someone into his heart, only for her to leave? After what he'd been through, Stavros didn't think he could bear to have his heart broken again. He'd barely survived the first time. If something happened again, he wouldn't be able to cope.

So as much as he wanted Desiree, as much as he cared for Danny, Stavros knew he wasn't the man for them. They deserved someone who wasn't broken. Someone who wouldn't spend the rest of his life holding his breath, waiting for the other shoe to drop. A man who had a full heart to give them, not the chipped, cracked, fragile thing he possessed.

Maybe it was better this way, he mused. The time he and Desiree had spent together had been intense. But after Dahlia was in custody and the threat to Danny gone, it would be good for Desiree to move on with a clean slate. Having him around would only serve as a constant reminder of this unhappy time when her son had been at risk.

Another right turn, this one taking them close to Mason County Prison and the forest beyond. Was Bowe hiding in those trees, as Melissa had suggested? From what Stavros had heard of the man, he wasn't the type to go camping. "What do I know?" he muttered to himself. He glanced in the mirror at Danny. "I should stick to doctoring, don't you think?"

Danny grinned and tried to mimic Stavros, but it came out as "tockering."

Stavros smiled. "You'll get there, buddy. *D*s can be tricky."

Wherever Bowe was hiding, hopefully Ellie was having success tracing his location from the text he'd sent Desiree. It took a special brand of cockiness to taunt the police the way Bowe had been doing, and Stavros hoped the bastard soon got what was coming to him.

His phone rang as he made the last right turn, back onto the main thoroughfare into Grave Gulch.

He punched the button, and Desiree's voice flooded through the stereo speakers.

"Hey."

Just one word, but Stavros could tell from her tone that Ellie's attempt had been unsuccessful.

"Stay put," Stavros said. "I'm on my way."

Chapter Ten

Desiree sat next to the bed, watching the sleeping face of her son. Danny looked so peaceful, his lips slightly parted, his hair mussed. He was lying on his stomach, one hand curled in a loose fist near his face and his legs tucked under his body, pushing his little rump in the air. He was the most beautiful thing she'd ever seen, and her heart ached with love for him.

She knew she should climb into the bed next to him and close her own eyes, but she was too unsettled to try to sleep. The events of earlier that day were replaying on a constant loop in her mind, demanding her attention as she relived the moments.

First, the text message from Bowe, ugly and cruel. Then the realization that, despite Troy's assurances otherwise, finding Dahlia was not a major police priority. And, finally, the disappointment of watching Ellie try—and fail—to track Bowe.

It wasn't her fault. Ellie had done everything in her power to trace the text message. She'd run it through several different programs, searching for an angle that would reveal its secrets. Desiree had watched her work, fascinated by how quickly her fingers had flown across the keyboard. Ellie's mind worked faster than the computer; no sooner had one digital door shut than she was trying a window or a back exit to get the information she wanted.

Unfortunately, nothing had worked. "He's not stupid, unfortunately," she'd said with a sigh. "And because he worked for us, he has an understanding of the ways we'll try to track him. He's got an insider's advantage, which makes things harder for us."

Desiree had nodded, trying to mask her disappointment. "I knew it was a long shot," she'd said.

Ellie had passed her phone back with a small smile. "It was worth a try. One of these days, he'll slip up and we'll get him."

"Can I delete the message?"

"Absolutely."

Desiree had wasted no time erasing the hateful words from her phone. But they lingered in her mind, his venom coming through loud and clear, despite the distance between them.

She leaned her head back against the edge of the mattress. Was now really the best time to go home? They had to, eventually—she recognized that, of course. But now that she knew Danny was on Bowe's radar, maybe it wasn't so smart to leave the relative safety of Stavros's condo before his week off was up.

Except…he'd offered to help her shore up the security at her home. If she wanted his aid, they'd have to start now. He wouldn't have time once he went back to work. She sighed. The bottom line was, at some point, Desiree was going to have to start living her life again, threats be damned. She couldn't spend all her time holed up inside, afraid of the world. That wasn't fair to Danny. Or to her.

No, best to move forward. Take Stavros's offer of assistance and get some security cameras installed and an alarm system put in. Then she could feel as safe as possible, knowing she'd done everything she could to keep both her and Danny secure.

And as for the rest? Dahlia couldn't stalk them forever. Hopefully she would grow to realize Danny wasn't her brother. With her own brother searching day and night, Desiree had to believe he'd eventually find her. Maybe even before the police did.

So that settled it. She and Danny would go home tomorrow. Stavros could have his place back to himself and prepare to return to the ER. And she'd have to relearn what it was like to be alone.

It was shocking, how quickly she and Stavros had settled into a routine. Desiree hadn't lived with a man since Jeremy left, but there had been no awkwardness between her and Stavros, no uncomfortable moments or feelings of annoyance at the new person's presence. They'd simply meshed, joining together like well-choreographed dancers. He helped out with Danny without being asked, and she pitched in with the chores. The conversation had flowed between them, sometimes serious, but mostly lighthearted and fun. Stavros hadn't hesitated to play with Danny, getting down on the floor to build blocks or push cars, or even give horseback rides on his back. There'd been no self-consciousness, no uncertainty. Danny had blossomed under Stavros's attention, becoming more talkative and smiling more. Desiree had always known her son was happy, but these last few days he'd seemed to glow whenever Stavros was around.

The fact that she was taking her boy away from this man made her heart ache. But what choice did she have? Stavros cared for Danny; that much was clear. But he didn't want to be a father figure. It was all well and good that he played with Danny, but as her son got older, he was going to need more than a playmate. No, better to move on now, before Danny got irrevocably attached to Stavros and felt let down later.

And *her* heart? Well, she'd dealt with pain before. In many ways, she was lucky. Stavros had been clear from the beginning about what he could and could not offer. She'd taken him at his word, but her emotions had hoped for a different outcome. That would teach her.

Still, part of her felt like there was something unfinished between them. That even though they'd shared both their bodies and their painful pasts, there was more they needed to experience together. In the grand scheme of things, they hadn't spent much time with each other. But the experience had been intense, and Desiree wanted to mark the end of it with a proper goodbye.

What did that mean, though? Sex? She rejected the thought as soon as it popped into her head. Sex with Stavros was amazing, and under any other circumstances, she'd jump at the chance to sleep with him again. But she knew it would be a mistake. If they were together again, there was no way she'd be able to keep her heart out of it. Leaving him tomorrow was going to be hard enough as it was; if she added intimacy to the equation, it would be nearly impossible.

There had to be some other way. Something they could do to help her say goodbye, to help her walk away from this moment in her life and the possibilities she'd never get to explore…

Before she knew what she was doing, Desiree was on her feet and walking out of the room. She moved down the hallway, her steps light, until she came to Stavros's closed bedroom door. Hesitating only a moment, she knocked lightly on the wood.

Her nerves started to tingle as she waited. Maybe he was already asleep. Maybe he didn't want to see her? This was a mistake… She should go—

The door opened and Stavros was there, standing in front of her. His hair was mussed but his eyes were clear, making her think he'd been awake.

"Can't sleep again?" He lifted one arm and propped it on the door frame, then leaned forward into her space. Desiree's body rejoiced at his nearness, but her mind refused to acknowledge the effect he had on her.

She shook her head. "You?"

"Nope. Was just thinking about getting a drink. Do you want one?"

It was a tempting offer, but she was already struggling to maintain her self-control. Adding alcohol to the mix wouldn't be helpful. "No. I was hoping we might… That is, can we…?" She fumbled with the words, trying to figure out how to articulate what it was she wanted from him.

Emotions flashed across Stavros's face: desire, longing, regret. "Dez, I'm not sure—"

"Will you just hold me? Please?" She searched his eyes, wishing he could read her mind. "It's been a really long day, and I don't want to be alone right now. I know I have no right to ask this of you, but I could use some support." How could she explain her fears, her disappointment, her worries? Talking was probably the best way to work through everything, but right now, she was too tired to search for the words. She just wanted Stavros to wrap his arms around her and pull her close. To make her feel, if only for a moment, that things were going to be okay.

His face softened. "Of course." He reached for her hand and pulled her inside his bedroom, leaving the door open. It was a thoughtful gesture, one that made sure she'd be able to hear Danny if he woke and missed her.

She trailed behind him, squinting to see in the dark room. He led her to a large bed against the far wall and helped her climb onto the mattress.

The sheets were soft and cool. She slid across a warm patch where Stavros must have been lying. He climbed into bed next to her and reached for her.

Desiree fit her body against his and laid her head on his shoulder. He wrapped one arm around her and reached across his stomach with the other to place his hand on her arm. He was warm and strong and solid, and the steady rise and fall of his chest under her hand was a peaceful rhythm that made her feel grounded. She sighed and closed her eyes, soaking up the feel of him.

Stavros idly stroked her arm with his fingers. He turned his head so that his mouth was in her hair. "Dez? I just want you to know I'm sorry—"

"Shhh," she said, interrupting him. This was not the time for apologies, for explanations of why things couldn't be different. She didn't need that. "Not now, okay?" All she wanted was to be held, to feel like someone was taking care of her. Tomorrow, she was back to being in charge. But tonight? She just wanted to feel like Stavros was looking out for her, one last time.

"Okay," he whispered. He pressed a kiss to the top of her head and then rested his cheek on the spot.

Desiree focused on his breathing, letting the warmth of his body soak into hers. Her muscles relaxed and her mind quieted, her worries silenced for the time being.

They weren't going anywhere. Her mind knew that, and her heart was working on accepting it. This was the end of the road for them. And as Desiree sank into sleep, she felt a sense of peace wash over her. At least she was getting her goodbye.

THE BED WAS empty when he woke.

Stavros stretched his hand across the mattress, touching the space where Desiree should have been. The sheets were cool, but they still smelled faintly of her skin. It was cold consolation.

He couldn't remember ever sleeping so well. Holding Desiree last night had been the best solution for his insomnia. Feeling her against him, breathing in the smell of her shampoo, hearing the soft sighs of her breathing—it was a potent combination that had knocked him out. Having her in his bed had allowed him to relax, as though her presence made him feel that all was right with the world. It was an experience he could all too easily get used to, but one he knew would never happen again.

It didn't take long to shower and dress. He walked into the living room to find Danny playing with some toys on the living room floor, while Desiree stood a few feet away, her phone to her ear.

Stavros could tell by her expression she didn't like what she was hearing.

"Are you serious?" she asked. She caught sight of him and gave him a little wave of acknowledgment. He nodded back, then turned his attention to Danny.

"Hey, buddy. What are we doing this morning?" He knelt next to the boy and started playing with him, but kept half of his attention on Desiree. Who was she talking to? And why did she seem upset?

"Troy, I have plans today," she said.

Well, that answered one of his questions. Stavros should have known her brother had something to do with the situation. Based on the number of calls she got from her family, the laws of probability practically ensured Troy was involved.

"No," she continued, an edge to her voice. "Stavros and I are going to get some security cameras set up at the house and make sure the locks are good."

Oh, boy. Troy wasn't going to like that.

"Because we can't stay with him forever," she said, her tone icy.

He felt a twinge of sadness in his chest at hearing her words. Even though they were true, he still wished things might have been different...

"If I do this for you, you owe me. Big-time."

It sounded like they were coming to some kind of arrangement. Stavros handed Danny another block, his curiosity well and thoroughly piqued.

"Fine. I'll be there as soon as I can."

Desiree ended the call and shoved the phone into her pocket with a huff.

"Trouble in paradise?" he asked lightly.

She rolled her eyes. "Troy wants me to come in and revise a sketch I did a few weeks ago for a robbery suspect. He says some new witnesses have come forward with more information on the person's appearance, so he wants me to do an update."

"And I take it you're not happy about that?"

She shook her head. "We had plans, remember?"

"I do." But there was no reason why they couldn't have their cake and eat it, too. "How long do you think it will take you to edit your original sketch?"

She shoved a hand into her hair and sighed. "Hopefully not too long, but it all depends." One shoulder lifted in a shrug. "I don't know what these witnesses are going to say or how off the mark the original was. It might take thirty minutes. It might take a few hours."

"Tell you what." Stavros handed a toy car to Danny and smiled as the boy rammed it into the block tower he'd just finished constructing. "I'll keep Danny entertained while you go to work. When you're done, we'll go shopping for security cameras. Sound good?"

Desiree smiled faintly as she watched her son play. "You really don't mind?"

Stavros shook his head. "Not at all. We'll go to the park. It's too pretty to stay inside all day, don't you think?"

At the mention of "park," Danny's face lit up. "Sideside," he jabbered. He got to his feet and started searching for his shoes.

Stavros looked at Desiree. "I guess that settles it?"

"I suppose so," she replied. "Give me just a minute to get ready."

Stavros helped Danny with his shoes and filled a sippy cup with water for the boy while Desiree headed for the guest bedroom. She returned quickly, her hair pulled back and her purse in hand. She grabbed the diaper bag and checked inside. "There's two diapers in here," she reported. "Hopefully you won't need more than that."

"I'm sure we'll be fine," he said. He took the bag from her and reached for Danny's hand. "Come on, little man. Let's get going."

"Don't you want to bring a snack?" Desiree called from behind them. "And what about sunscreen? Or bug repellent?"

Stavros fought the urge to roll his eyes. "If he gets hungry, I'll feed him. And a little sun never hurt anyone. The boy needs his vitamin D."

He heard Desiree grumbling under her breath, but she followed them out the door and into the elevator.

"We're going to have fun today, aren't we, buddy?" he asked Danny.

The toddler looked up at him. "Side-side," he replied.

Desiree smiled. "He has a one-track mind."

"It's good to know what you want," Stavros said quietly.

The drive to the police station didn't take long. The usual protesters were out in force, so he dropped Desiree a block away, like he did yesterday. "I'll hurry," she told him as she climbed out of the car.

"Take your time," Stavros called after her. "Danny and I will be fine." It was true. He didn't mind taking care of the little boy while she worked. If he was being totally honest, he was actually looking forward to going to the park. He hadn't been in years, and it would be fun to watch Danny on the playground and push him on the swings. They'd all been inside for too long—fresh air and sunshine were exactly what they needed right now.

Their destination was only a few blocks away from the police station. He found a parking spot easily and climbed out of the car. Even though he couldn't see the protesters, the faint sounds of their chants against police incompetence drifted through the air. If he could hear them from this distance, it had to be incredibly noisy in the station itself. Hopefully Desiree would be able to work amid the chaos.

Danny grinned as Stavros unbuckled him from his car seat. He started running as soon as his feet hit the ground, making a beeline for the playground. Stavros trotted after him, smiling as a breeze wafted across his face. The boy's enthusiasm was contagious.

Danny showed no fear as he launched himself onto a swing. "Push! Push!" he called. Stavros plucked him off the big-kid swing and deposited him in the bucket swing a few feet away. Then he pulled back the chains and released them, sending Danny arcing through the air.

Stavros moved around to the front, so he could see Danny's face. The child was delighted, his teeth on full display as he giggled and chattered. Stavros took his phone out and snapped a few pictures to show Desiree later. She'd be glad to know her baby was having so much fun.

After a few minutes of the swing, Danny decided he'd had enough. Stavros lifted him out of the bucket and set him down, only for the little one to take off running for the slides.

Stavros jogged to keep up. This was definitely one of the more entertaining ways to work out.

He lost track of time as Danny explored the playground, climbing, sliding, bouncing. The child had no fear, and more than once, Stavros had to stop him from climbing too high or running too fast. Other kids had started arriving, as well, and Danny was excited to see them. Stavros could tell the little one wanted to play with the bigger kids, but he didn't think that was a good idea. If Danny got hurt on his watch, Desiree would never forgive him.

"C'mon, Danny," he called, beckoning to the boy from his spot at the top of a slide. "Slide on down and we'll go for a walk." There was a flat trail that made a large loop nearby, and he knew from experience it was a nice walk. There were trees and flowers along the way, enough to hold the attention of even the most distracted child.

His phone buzzed in his pocket, and Stavros pulled it out. Was Desiree done already? A glance at the display told him otherwise. This was a hospital number.

"This is Dr. Makris." He glanced at Danny, who was still at the top of the slide.

"Sorry to bother you on your time off," said the voice on the other end of the line. It was a fellow doctor, calling about a patient Stavros had seen last week. The individual was back in the ER, and the doctor had a few questions for him.

It was difficult to hear with all the children squealing and laughing around him, so Stavros took a half step back and used his free hand to plug his ear. He kept his eyes on Danny, watching the little boy gather his courage. He sat and peered down the slide, his expression uncertain. Stavros walked over and held his hand up. Danny smiled and took it, then launched himself down the slide.

His exhilarated squeal was loud enough for the other doctor to hear. "Sounds like quite a party."

"We're at the playground," Stavros explained.

"I won't keep you, then," the man replied. "Thanks for your help."

"Anytime."

Stavros ended the call and laughed to himself as Danny went running up the stairs to go down the slide again. Now that he'd gone down the long slide once, it seemed he was no longer worried about it.

Danny had just made it to the bottom a second time when a cry split the air. "Help! Please, someone help us!"

Stavros turned to see a mother and a boy standing on the edge of the playground. She had her hand pressed to his head, and there was blood welling around her fingers.

Moving on instinct, Stavros grabbed Danny's hand and half pulled, half carried him along. He pushed through the growing circle of people and made it to the woman's side. "I'm a doctor. What's going on here?"

The mother, obviously distraught, launched into a story about a rock hitting her son in the head. He turned his attention to the boy, who looked to be about five or six years old. "Hey, buddy," he said calmly. "Can I take a look at your head?"

The kid nodded, but seemed dazed. Stavros gently pried the mother's fingers off her son's head and took in the large gash along the hairline. His forehead was already swelling, but the good news was the gash didn't look to be too deep.

"I called an ambulance," said a voice from the crowd.

Stavros nodded. He didn't think the boy's injury was too severe, but it wouldn't hurt to get a full workup to make sure. Besides, that gash was going to need a few stitches.

He worked quickly, doing a basic neurological exam to look for signs of a concussion. The surprise was starting to wear off, and the boy was getting upset now.

Stavros glanced up at the mother. "I think he's going to be okay," he said. "Head wounds tend to bleed a lot. A few stitches should take care of that."

The ambulance roared into the nearby parking lot as he spoke, and a look of relief flashed over the mother's face. "Thank you," she said. "I can't believe someone would deliberately throw a rock at a child."

Stavros frowned. "Was it another kid?"

She shook her head. "No. It was an adult. I saw her pick up the rock and pull her arm back, but she threw it before I could get to Alex." She pressed her lips together, visibly upset. "If she hadn't hit him, I would have gone after her for that."

A chill went down Stavros's spine. He stepped back to give the paramedics room to treat the little boy. They were accompanied by two uniformed officers, who started talking to the mother.

Why would someone deliberately hurt a child? He glanced down, expecting to find Danny standing nearby. But to his shock, he didn't see the toddler.

Oh, God.

A sick feeling started in Stavros's stomach and began to spread throughout his body. "Danny!" he shouted. A few people shrank back from the volume of his voice, but he didn't care. He had to find the little boy. "Danny! Where are you?" He scanned the thinning crowd, searching for signs of his dark hair or a flash of blue from his shirt.

"No," he muttered, starting to jog around the playground. "No, no, no. Not again!" His heart pounded a thunderous rhythm in his chest, his ears filled with the sound of rushing blood. "Has anyone seen a little boy?"

One of the uniformed officers approached him. "Sir? Is there a problem here?"

"He's gone." Stavros heard the despair in his own voice. "Danny is gone. He was with me here when I helped the boy, and when I looked down, he was gone."

The other officer approached, and Stavros recognized her. "Grace," he said urgently. "Danny is gone."

Her face drained of color. "Are you sure?" she whispered.

Stavros nodded, afraid that if he tried to speak, he would scream. Panic clawed at his throat, making it hard to breathe.

"She took him," he gasped. The puzzle pieces clicked into place, and he swallowed hard to push down the bile rising up from his stomach. "Dahlia. It has to be her."

"Did you see her?" Grace asked.

He shook his head. "But don't you see? She threw the rock at that boy. She knew I'd help, knew I'd be distracted. Then she took Danny while I was focused on the other child."

Grace turned to her partner. "Start looking. You take the east side. I'll go west. What was he wearing?"

Stavros rattled off a quick description of Danny's clothes. "She's got to be carrying him," he said. "He wouldn't have gone with her if she didn't force him."

Grace nodded. "Let's go," she instructed her partner. They began to move in opposite directions. Stavros started for the trail, intending to search there. Grace noticed his movement. "You stay here," she instructed.

"Like hell I will," Stavros snapped. He wasn't about to just stand around and twiddle his thumbs while Dahlia took Danny farther away. There was a lot of ground to cover, and until the other officers arrived, Grace and her partner needed all the help they could get.

She shot him an exasperated look. "Fine. But if you see Dahlia, don't approach. We don't know what she might do if she feels cornered."

The warning made the hairs on the back of his neck stand on end. He hadn't thought about the possibility that Dahlia might hurt Danny. Based on what her brother had told the police, he figured she saw Danny as her long-lost brother. But Grace was right—who knew how she would react if she realized her warped view of reality was wrong?

He set off down the path at a jog, his heart in his throat. A growing feeling of helplessness dogged his every step, but he pushed forward, determined not to succumb to his despair. "I'm coming, Danny," he muttered to himself.

Sammy's face flashed through his mind as he moved, and he blinked back tears. He hadn't been able to save his daughter. But he was damn sure going to do everything in his power to save Desiree's son. She would see her boy again—he had to believe that.

The alternative was too frightening to consider.

Chapter Eleven

Desiree was putting the final touches on the revised sketch when the door to the conference room flung open with a bang.

She jumped, the pencil dragging across the image in a garish line.

"Dammit," she muttered. She glanced up to glare at her brother. "I was just about finished with this, Troy! Now I have to fix it."

He stared at her, eyes going wide. "Dez."

She froze, the tone of his voice making it instantly clear that something was horribly wrong.

"What is it?" she asked quietly. Her thoughts immediately turned to Danny, but surely Stavros would call if something had happened?

"She got him," Troy said. He swallowed and ran his hand over the top of his head. "Dahlia took Danny again."

"No!" Desiree shot to her feet, propelled by shock. "No, that's not possible," she said. "Stavros is watching him. Stavros would never let anything—"

"There was an accident," Troy interrupted. "Dahlia

threw a rock at a child, hitting him in the head. When the mother called out for help, Stavros and Danny went rushing over. That's when she took him."

Desiree shook her head. "But Stavros wouldn't forget to watch him…" Disbelief and denial warred for dominance. Stavros was responsible, caring. He wouldn't let Dahlia take Danny, especially after what had happened to his own daughter.

Troy put his hands on her shoulders and shook her gently. "He didn't forget," Troy said firmly. "He was distracted helping the other boy. Dahlia took advantage of it."

Desiree blinked at her brother, his words penetrating the fog of her thoughts. "She really has him?" Her voice wobbled as her eyes filled with tears. "My baby?"

Troy nodded in grim confirmation. "Grace and another officer are on the scene now, searching. I just heard the call come in."

"Take me there." Desiree straightened and turned toward the door.

"Dez, I don't think that's such a good—"

"Take me there, now!" she screamed. Troy flinched, but quickly nodded.

Desiree followed him out of the station, her body trembling. She was shaking so badly she thought she might fall apart as they climbed into Troy's car. The park was only a few blocks away, and if the laws of physics didn't apply, she felt like she could fly there powered by rage alone. But the car was faster, and soon they pulled into the nearby parking lot, already filled with police cars and blinking sirens.

She climbed out of the car before Troy had come to a full stop and ran to the playground. A knot of officers stood there, apparently waiting for some direction.

"Where is he? Where is my son?"

"Ma'am, please step back," one of the officers said. "Try to calm down."

Desiree fought the urge to punch him. "Calm down?" Hysteria seized the muscles of her throat, making her voice unnaturally high. "My son is gone and you want me to calm down?" She clenched her fists, her entire body as taut as a coiled wire.

Large hands grabbed her upper arms, pulling her away. "Dez, they're searching," Troy said behind her. "Let them do their job."

She tore away from her brother's grasp. "This is your fault," she said, practically spitting the words. "If you hadn't insisted I come redo the sketch, Danny would have never been on this playground."

Troy looked stricken. "You know that's not true—"

"Yes, it is! And I know for a fact your department wasn't working hard enough to find Dahlia."

Her brother's face twisted in confusion. "Why would you say that?"

"I didn't say it," she snapped. "Melissa did. At the party. She said you were focused on finding Bowe and Davison because they were violent. Well, what about now?" She spread her arms wide to encompass the playground and the gathering of police. "Is this violent enough for you?"

"Desiree—"

"And where is Stavros?" she continued. "Why isn't

he here?" In her heart, she knew Troy was right and that he wasn't to blame. But her emotions weren't interested in logic right now.

"Sorry to interrupt, but is this the boy's mom?"

Desiree whirled around at the new voice to see a redheaded man standing nearby. He was wearing jeans and a T-shirt, but the badge he wore on a chain around his neck made it clear he was part of the GGPD. She frowned, recognizing his face, but couldn't recall his name. "I know you," she said.

He nodded. "Brett Shea."

"The new guy," she said.

"Um, yeah. That's right."

"What do you need?" Desiree knew she was being snippy, but she was too scared and worried to care.

"Do you have anything that belongs to your son?" Brett asked. He gestured down, and Desiree noticed for the first time the black Lab sitting by Brett's feet. "I was off duty when I heard the call go out, and I figured my partner and I might help with the search. But it'll go a lot faster if I can give her something to track."

Desiree's heart dropped to her toes. "I don't have anything here. I left my bag at the station." She turned to Troy, her eyes filling with tears once more. "We have to go back." But that would take time—time she wasn't sure her son had. Oh, God, what if this delay cost her everything? It was enough to make her want to sink to the ground.

"Hang on, man. I think I have something in my car." Troy spun on his heel and took off, running back to the parking lot.

Desiree kept her gaze on the dog, whose tail was thumping gently against the cement path surrounding the playground. "What's her name?" she said numbly.

"Ember," Brett replied.

"Can I touch her?"

Brett hesitated, then spoke. "Yeah, okay. We're not working yet."

Desiree knelt and extended her hand for the dog to sniff. Ember looked up at Brett, as if asking for permission. Desiree saw him nod and the animal stretched forward, her nose cold against Desiree's skin.

"I, uh, couldn't help but overhear what you were saying to Troy."

Desiree ran her hands over the soft fur, the feel of it silky and smooth. "What of it?"

"I know it's not really my place to say so, but he's been working hard to find Dahlia. We all have, but Troy especially."

Desiree looked up to find Brett watching her, his blue eyes kind.

"He'd never tell you this, but he's been working late pretty much every night since you were drugged at the hospital."

Desiree's prickliness toward her brother faded somewhat. "I didn't know that," she admitted.

"Nobody wanted this to happen, Ms. Colton," Brett said gently. "And we'll get your son back."

Ember's form blurred as Desiree's eyes filled with tears once more. "I hope you're right." She heard pounding footsteps approaching and Troy appeared again, panting slightly.

"I had this stuffed bear in the trunk—he left it behind a few weeks ago. Will that work, or is the scent too old?"

Brett took the bear and held it in front of his dog. "It's better than nothing. Okay, Ember. Track."

The dog sniffed the bear intently for a few seconds, then lifted her nose to the air. Her nostrils flared delicately as she sampled the surrounding odors. Then she started moving, heading for the playground equipment.

Desiree watched with fascination and impatience as Ember carefully sniffed the swings and then moved to the slide. The playground was obviously empty, but she knew from experience those were Danny's favorite things to do. She closed her eyes, easily picturing him running from one to the other and back again.

"She's on the move," Troy said quietly. Desiree opened her eyes to see the canine leading Brett down the path that started close to the playground. It looped into the park and around a duck pond located about a mile into the trail. It was normally a peaceful, enjoyable walk, but right now all Desiree could think about were the potential dangers lurking around every bend.

She started to follow Brett. "Whoa," Troy said, placing his hand on her arm. "I know you want to go with him, but we need to give them some space. If we crowd them, it might make it harder for Ember to do her job."

"Fine." She stood in place, watching Brett's form grow smaller as he and his partner traveled down the path. Soon, they were obscured by the trees and vegetation along the edges.

"Can we go yet?" She turned to find Troy standing a few feet away, his phone to his ear. Who was he calling at a time like this? It seemed all of the police department was already here.

He finished the call and stepped over to her. "That was Stephen," he said, answering her unspoken question. "I told him what was going on, asked if he has any idea where his sister might have taken Danny."

Hope flared to life in Desiree's chest. "And does he?"

Troy shook his head. "Not really. He repeated the places she used to go, and some units have already been dispatched to check them. But he didn't have any new suggestions for us."

"Then the dog is our best option." She wanted to laugh at the absurdity of the situation. Was a *dog* really going to be the one to save her son? But her thoughts turned dark with her next breath: Was he even still alive to be saved?

"For the moment," Troy replied.

"Then let's go," she said, starting for the trail without waiting to see if Troy would follow. If she didn't do something, she was going to lose it. For a few seconds, her mind flashed to Stavros. Was her story going to have an equally unhappy ending? She'd gotten lucky once—her boy had been found before, safe and whole. Maybe this time she wouldn't be so fortunate…

Troy trotted to catch up to her and she felt his presence at her back.

"We'll find him," he said softly, and Desiree wasn't sure if he was talking to her or trying to reassure himself.

"We'll find him."

WAS THAT...SINGING?

Stavros stopped, straining to hear. A breeze rustled the tree branches overhead, but once the air stilled, he caught another snatch of sound. It was a light tune, cheerful and rhyming.

A nursery rhyme, he realized with a small shock.

He set forward again, stepping carefully. He didn't want to go charging ahead and scare Dahlia. If he spooked her, there was no telling what she might do to Danny.

Please, let him be safe.

The thought kept circling in his mind, an endless loop that was part prayer, part mantra. He had to find Danny. There was no other option. If he walked out of here without that boy, there was no way he could keep going. Bad enough that it was his fault the child had been taken. His only hope for some kind of redemption was in getting him back.

He saw water through the bushes and knew he must be getting close to the duck pond. The grass was shorter here, and there was a bench set up near the water's edge. Stavros hung back a bit, scanning the area. He didn't see Dahlia or Danny, but the singing was getting louder, so they had to be close.

A flash of color caught his attention and he turned, trying to focus on it. A clump of reeds waved in the breeze, and he saw it again—a patch of blue fabric.

They're at the water's edge, he realized.

His blood turned to ice as he crept forward, straining to see. As he got closer, he saw Dahlia sitting on a large rock on the other side of the reeds, hidden from view. She was holding Danny in her lap and rocking as she sang, but from this angle, Stavros couldn't see the boy's face. He was still in her arms, though.

Because he was calm? Or because she'd hurt him?

There was only one way to find out.

Stavros stopped a few feet away from the rock and started to sing along with Dahlia, softly at first, then gradually increasing the volume of his voice. She didn't seem to notice him right away—she kept singing until she reached the end of the song. Then she turned and looked at him, her eyes growing wide when she saw him.

"You're real!" She gripped Danny to her chest as she clambered to her feet, staring down at Stavros with shock.

He held up his hands, palms facing out, trying to show her he meant her no harm. "I'm real," he said. It was clear Dahlia wasn't in touch with reality right now—he needed to be careful what he said so as not to trigger her into running away or hurting herself or Danny.

"I like that song," he said, trying to get a glimpse of Danny's face. The boy began to wiggle in Dahlia's arms, but she kept him clutched to her chest with his back to Stavros. *At least he's moving*, Stavros thought with some relief.

Dahlia seemed to relax a bit. "It's Jacob's favorite," she said.

"I can understand why," Stavros replied. "You have a lovely voice."

She smiled shyly. "I'm the only one who can get him

to calm down sometimes. Mama doesn't like it when he cries so much. She needs her sleep."

She thinks she's a child, he realized. In her mind, Dahlia was six years old again, taking care of her baby brother. No wonder she'd thrown the rock at the other boy—it was the action of a child.

"I bet you take good care of your brother," he said.

Dahlia nodded, her expression proud. "I do," she confirmed. "I have another brother, Stephen, but he's older. Jacob likes me better."

Stavros smiled despite his worry and fear. Right now, Dahlia didn't seem violent or threatening. She seemed like a small girl trying to make her brother feel better.

"Where's your mom and brother now?"

Uncertainty flashed across Dahlia's face. "She took him to baseball practice. She said we could play at the park, but there were a lot of kids there and I kept losing him. So I got Jacob away from the crowd and we took a walk."

"I see." He had to be careful here, had to help her realize that the boy she took was not her brother. But he didn't want to harm her, either. As a doctor, he could tell that Dahlia's mind was betraying her, through no fault of her own. As long as she didn't hurt Danny, there had to be a way to get him back peacefully.

Danny was struggling now, clearly unhappy with being held. "Do you think your brother wants you to put him down?"

Dahlia looked at the boy and frowned. "I can't. We're too close to the water."

"I can help you watch him," he offered.

She studied him a moment, eyes narrowing. "No, that's okay." Her lips pressed together. "I shouldn't be talking to you. I'm not supposed to talk to strangers."

"That's smart," Stavros said, taking a step back. "But I'm not a stranger. Do you remember seeing me at the playground?"

Doubt flickered across her face. "I think so…" Then she gasped. "You had Jacob!" She took a step back, closer to the edge of the rock.

This was not going well. "No, I didn't have Jacob," Stavros said. "I was playing with a little boy named Danny."

"Danny?" She sounded uncertain, as though she'd never heard the name before.

"Yes, that's right," Stavros said. He heard a rustling behind him, and then a black Lab bounded up. What the hell? He glanced behind him to see a man approaching, holding the leash. He wore a badge around his neck on a chain, and Stavros realized he wasn't an owner chasing after his wayward pet. He was with the police.

The officer saw Stavros and his eyes flicked to Dahlia and Danny. "Ember, rest," he commanded softly, his voice too low to carry far. The dog immediately sat, tail thumping against the ground. Her eyes were fixed on Danny and her body trembled, but she didn't try to get closer.

Dahlia saw the animal and stared, clearly trying to figure out where she'd come from. Fortunately, the officer was obscured by the reeds, and he didn't try to approach. Not yet, anyway. Stavros didn't know how much time he had before the police had to make a move, but he hoped he could talk Dahlia down before then.

"Is that your puppy?" she asked.

He glanced back at the officer, who nodded. "Yes, it is," he said. "Does your brother like dogs?"

"I do," she replied. "Does she bite?"

"I've never seen her bite anyone," he said truthfully. The dog in question was undoubtedly well trained, and currently showing no signs of aggression. Hopefully she wouldn't be alarmed if Dahlia moved closer.

"Can I pet her?"

"Yes," Stavros said. "Would you like me to hold your brother while you pet her? He seems upset." That was an understatement—Danny was loudly protesting his confinement and wiggling like mad to escape Dahlia's arms.

She glanced down at him. "He's not usually this grumpy," she said. She took a hesitant step closer. "But I don't know if I should let a stranger hold him."

"My name is Stavros," he said, thinking fast. "What's your name?"

"Dahlia," she replied.

"Nice to meet you," he said. "Now we aren't strangers anymore."

Her face brightened and she nodded. "That's true."

"Can I help you climb down from the rock?"

She shook her head. "No, I can do it. What's your puppy's name?"

"Ember," he said, recalling the name the officer had used moments before. His heart thumped hard against his breastbone. Was she really going to come down? Danny was close, so close…

"That's a funny name." Dahlia crouched and sat on the rock, hanging her legs over the edge. She slipped down to the ground, still clutching Danny to her chest. Danny turned his head and caught sight of Stavros. He immediately squealed and reached for him.

Stavros felt his heart crack. He desperately wanted to grab the boy and hold him tight, but Dahlia was still too close to the water for his liking. If he moved suddenly, she might fall into the water or, God forbid, throw Danny into the pond. He just couldn't risk it, not when he was on the verge of getting the boy back.

Dahlia tightened her grip on Danny and eyed Stavros warily. "Why does Jacob want you to hold him so bad?"

Stavros swallowed, hoping he was doing the right thing. "Because that's not Jacob you're holding," he said gently. "His name is Danny."

She shook her head, fear tightening her face. "No— no, he's not. He's my brother. Not your Danny." She looked down at the squirming little boy and Stavros realized the instant she snapped out of her episode. Her expression changed from confused to horrified, and she looked up, her mouth open in a silent scream.

Stavros held out his arms, and Dahlia released Danny. He knelt just in time to catch the boy as he plowed into him. Stavros wrapped his arms around Danny, pressing his little body against his chest. Relief made him feel light-headed, so he stayed close to the ground, unsure if his legs would support him in this moment.

Dahlia crumpled against the rock, tears streaming down her face. "What did I do? What did I do?" she moaned, over and over again.

Stavros felt the officer move past him and looked over to see the man approach Dahlia.

"Please don't hurt her," he said. Dahlia's actions were wrong, but she needed medical help.

The man shot Stavros an offended look over his shoulder. "Wasn't gonna," he said shortly. He crouched by Dahlia and put his hand on her shoulder. "Can you stand for me, miss?"

She nodded, gripping his upper arms for support as she got to her feet. "That's good," he said. "Turn around for me, okay?"

Dahlia did as she was asked, and the officer placed handcuffs around her wrists. "We're going to walk this way now." He led her past Stavros and glanced down. The dog was still sitting a few feet away, her eyes locked on Danny. "Let's go, Ember," he said.

The Lab stood and trotted over to Danny. She nosed him once, swiped her tongue along his cheek, then turned and loped after her partner.

Danny stared up at Stavros, clearly confused. Stavros couldn't help but laugh. "You got a doggy kiss," he said.

There was a shout a few feet away, and then Desiree tore around the clump of bushes. "Danny!" Her voice was frantic, her eyes wide.

"Mama!"

Stavros released his hold on Danny and the child shot forward, into his mother's arms. She closed her eyes, swaying back and forth as she held her baby once again.

Troy arrived a few steps behind her, his face softening when he saw his sister and nephew.

Stavros slowly stood, watching the reunion with tears stinging his eyes. Some stories had a happy ending after all, and he couldn't imagine anyone who deserved it more.

Troy glanced over and saw him standing a few feet away. *Thank you*, he mouthed. Stavros nodded, but gratitude was the last thing he deserved right now. If he'd been paying more attention, Dahlia wouldn't have gotten close enough to take Danny in the first place.

He started walking, intending to get back to the path. Desiree hadn't noticed him yet, and he didn't want to interrupt her reunion with Danny. Even though he was overwhelmingly happy the boy was safe, seeing them together was a visual reminder of the outcome he'd never experienced.

Stavros had just made it to the path when someone came up behind him. He turned and saw Troy walking after him.

"Hey, man, hold up a minute."

Stavros stopped, though he wanted nothing more than to slink away. He couldn't face Desiree right now, not this soon after letting her down. "What's up?"

Troy stared at him for a few seconds, as though he was trying to decide what he wanted to say. "I owe you. Big-time."

Stavros shook his head. "No. You really don't."

Troy ignored his objection. "Yeah, I do. You took in my sister and nephew and kept them safe when I couldn't. And you got Danny back. That's the second time you've saved him."

"I wouldn't have had to save him at all if I hadn't let myself get distracted today." Stavros kicked at a rock, emotion making his chest tight. He didn't want to talk about this, especially not with Troy.

"Don't even go there," Troy said. "You weren't neglecting him. You were helping someone else. Dahlia took advantage of your instincts as a doctor. You can't blame yourself for that."

Stavros snorted. "Sure. If you say so."

"I do. And I know Desiree will, too."

He jerked his head up fast to see Troy watching him, his expression sincere. The absolution in the other man's eyes made the pressure of his guilt lessen somewhat, but it was still there…

"What's going to happen to her? To Dahlia, I mean," he added, seeing Troy's confusion.

"We'll take her to the station, book her in. She'll get a psych consult right away."

Stavros nodded, happy to hear they were going to get her the help she needed. "That's good. I know it's not my place to forgive, but from what Desiree told me about her and the behavior I saw here today, I think a psych hospital would be a better place for her than prison."

Troy shrugged. "It's not my call to make, but I think most of us feel the same way. We'll do what we can to advocate for her."

"Let me know if I can help," Stavros offered. He wasn't sure what Desiree would think about him helping Dahlia's defense, but did it really matter? They were going to go their separate ways now, so it wasn't a personal conflict of interest for him.

"I might hold you to that," Troy said. "I'm going to go back and get Desiree and Danny. Want to join me?"

Stavros recognized the gravity of the invitation. The fact that Troy had asked him to take part in this family moment was a mark of respect and a sign that he no longer considered Stavros an outsider. It should have made him happy. Instead, it only made him feel worse about the situation.

"Nah, I don't want to intrude," he replied. No sense in dragging this out, either. It was going to be hard enough to adjust to his life without Desiree and Danny. Might as well start now, before the emotion of the moment sucked him in too deep.

Surprise flickered across Troy's face. Apparently, he hadn't expected Stavros to refuse. "Oh. Okay, sure. I guess we'll see you later?"

Stavros nodded, his throat aching with the words he wished he could say. He gave Troy a wave, then turned on his heel and started down the path.

Alone once more.

The way it had to be.

Chapter Twelve

Two weeks later

"Okay, spill it."

Desiree glanced at Troy, frowning slightly. "Spill what?"

"What's bothering you," he replied.

They sat at her kitchen table, sipping coffee and eating pie. Danny was in bed, worn out from a day of playing with his uncle. It was one of Troy's rare days off, and he'd taken Danny for most of the afternoon so Desiree could get some errands run and chores done without interruption. She'd paid him back with a home-cooked meal and a slice of apple pie, which they'd saved to enjoy once the toddler was asleep. Eating dessert was a lot easier without a demanding little boy around.

"I don't know what you mean."

Troy shot her a knowing look. "Uh-huh. You've been moping around for the last two weeks. I want to know why."

Desiree shrugged, trying to deflect. She thought

she'd done a better job of hiding her emotions. Apparently not.

"Everything's fine," she said. "Danny is safe. Dahlia is in custody. Our lives are getting back to normal."

Troy nodded. "But it's a new normal now."

"Yes, that's true." She took a bite of pie, wishing he would do the same. If he was eating, he couldn't talk.

"How's Stavros?"

Troy's tone was innocent enough, but Desiree saw the glint in his eyes and knew there was more to the question than simple curiosity.

"I don't know," she said. The mention of his name made her heart clench, but she shook off the unpleasant sensation. They'd made no promises to each other, and she'd always known they would go their separate ways once Dahlia had been found.

That didn't make the reality hurt any less, but that was just life, wasn't it?

Troy's eyebrows shot up. "Are you serious?"

She nodded. "Yes. Why is that so surprising?"

"Dez, you and Danny stayed in his home. He saved Danny from Dahlia. How have you not been keeping in touch with him?"

She shrugged. "I did speak to him, shortly after the event. I stopped by his place to get some of the things we'd left there. But that's it."

Troy shook his head. "Wow. That's cold, sis. I really thought you cared about him."

Her temper flared to life. "What the hell is that supposed to mean?"

"So you just dump him after you don't need him anymore?"

Desiree felt her jaw drop. "How on earth did you draw that conclusion from what I just told you?"

"All I know is I saw him right after Brett arrested Dahlia. He was blaming himself for what had happened. I told him it wasn't his fault and asked him to walk back with us, but he said no. Didn't want to intrude."

"That sounds like him," she said quietly, imagining the scene all too easily.

"Did you at least tell him you don't blame him for what happened?"

She blinked at her brother. "Not in so many words, no." A sense of unease began to unfurl in her stomach. Did Stavros think she was upset with him? She missed him terribly, but how many times had he told her they couldn't have a relationship? Even though it was difficult to be apart from him, her heart wasn't ready to try for a platonic friendship. "I thanked him for saving Danny, but he seemed uncomfortable, so I didn't press the issue."

Troy gawped at her. "Dez! What is wrong with you?"

"It didn't come up, okay?" She shifted in her chair, feeling uncomfortable. "I didn't know he blamed himself. Otherwise, I would have said something."

"Well, it's not too late. Maybe you should call him."

Desiree eyed Troy suspiciously. "Since when do you care about Stavros's feelings so much?"

He shrugged and took a sip of coffee. "I just want you to be happy, that's all."

"And you think Stavros is connected to my happiness, is that it?"

"Don't you?" he retorted.

The question made her sit back. For a brief, perfect moment, she'd thought Stavros might be the one. The man she could build a family with, the man she could love. But he hadn't shared those dreams with her, and so in the end, she'd woken alone. And even though her heart ached with missing him, she couldn't spend the rest of her life wishing for something she'd never have. She owed it to herself and Danny to move on.

She shook her head. "It doesn't matter what I think. It takes two to have a relationship, Troy. And he doesn't want that."

"Are you sure?" her brother asked. "Because I saw the way he looks at you."

Desiree stood and picked up her plate and cup and took them to the sink. She didn't want to look at Troy right now. Didn't want to see his earnest expression.

Didn't want to hope that maybe he was right about Stavros's feelings for her.

"It doesn't matter," she said. She ran some water over her dishes and put them in the dishwasher. "I'm not about to go chase after a man and beg him to love me. To choose me. Stavros may have all the feelings in the world, but he made it clear he doesn't want to be in a relationship. I'll never forget what he did for Danny. But that doesn't mean he wants to be with me."

She heard Troy get to his feet behind her. "All I'm saying, sis, is that I don't think you'd have to beg." His voice was quiet as he brought his dishes to the sink.

Desiree kept her hands on the edge of the sink and looked down. She hadn't expected this conversation from her brother. Troy generally didn't have much to say on the subject of her love life—he seemed to prefer a don't-ask, don't-tell policy. But from the start, he'd been curious about Stavros and the way she felt about him. And if she was being honest with herself, Troy's opinion meant a lot to her. The fact that he was going to bat for Stavros meant he must like the guy.

But it was too little, too late. Troy's approval was nice and all, but it had no bearing on her relationship with Stavros. Or lack thereof. She hadn't walked away from him because she feared the disapproval of her family. She'd turned her back because he'd made it clear he couldn't give her what she needed. And despite Troy's naive assertions about the way Stavros looked at her, as far as Desiree knew, he still wasn't ready or willing to commit.

"Thanks for taking Danny," she said finally, deliberately changing the subject.

Troy took the hint, but she knew from the set of his mouth she hadn't heard the last of his thoughts about Stavros. "Sure. Anytime. You know I love hanging out with him."

She nodded. "I do. And I've been thinking… I owe you an apology."

He leaned back, crossing his arms over his chest. "Oh, really? This ought to be good."

Desiree swatted at him, but there was no force behind it. "I'm serious. I said some not-so-nice things to you that day at the park. I shouldn't have."

Troy shook his head. "I've already forgotten them," he said. "I know you were out of your mind with worry. I didn't take it personally."

She gave him a small smile, knowing he was letting her off the hook more easily than she deserved. "Thanks, brother mine."

He started for the door. "Sure thing. I'll let you know when I figure out how you can make it up to me."

Desiree laughed softly. "I thought you said it was forgotten?"

"It is," he said, stopping in her living room. "But I know you still feel guilty about it. So I'll let you do me a favor so you can feel better."

"I see," she said. "How generous of you."

He nodded, but his eyes were on the television she'd accidentally left running. The nightly news was on, and they were showing a clip of the protesters outside the police station from earlier in the day.

Desiree watched for a few seconds, shaking her head. "Is it just me, or are the crowds getting bigger?"

"It's not just you," Troy replied absently.

She watched as a tall woman with long dark hair broke free from the crowd and started walking up the steps of city hall. She wore an expensive-looking suit, but kept her head down. "Who's that?"

"The assistant district attorney," Troy said. A picture of the woman's face flashed on the screen, the news anchor obviously talking about her. But the volume was too low for Desiree to hear the story.

"They don't look happy with her," Desiree observed.

She glanced at her brother, but his eyes lingered on the screen and the image of the woman's face.

Interesting...

It was only after her picture disappeared and the anchors moved on to another story that Troy turned to her. "I'm sorry—did you say something?"

"I said the crowd doesn't look happy with her."

He shook his head. "They're not. She's under fire right now because Bowe's fraud resulted in innocent people getting convicted and guilty people being set free."

"Yeah, but that's not her fault," Desiree pointed out. "She had no way of knowing the evidence had been tampered with."

"You and I recognize that," Troy replied. "But a lot of people out there are running on emotion. They're not exactly thinking clearly." He started for the front door again, and Desiree followed him.

"Well, hopefully now that Dahlia is in custody and getting the help she needs, you'll have more time to devote to finding Bowe and setting things right."

Troy smiled, but it didn't reach his eyes. "I'll keep trying."

Desiree hugged him at the door. "Take care of yourself, okay? Get some rest."

He rolled his eyes. "Yes, ma'am."

"Hey, I'm your big sister," she said. "You have to listen to me."

Troy just laughed as he walked to his car, keys in hand. Desiree waited until she heard the engine turn over before shutting the door.

She clicked the lock into place and wandered back into the kitchen, then sat at the table. It had been nice having Troy over for dinner. She'd gotten so used to being around Stavros that the last two weeks without him had made her life feel empty. But Troy had been good company tonight; a nice, if temporary, fill for the space Stavros had left behind.

She wondered what he was doing now. Working? Maybe. Or was he home, sitting at that huge wooden table? Or the couch where they'd made love? Did he miss her as much as she missed him? Or was he too busy to think about her?

Desiree picked up her phone, her fingers itching to dial his number. But what could she say? *Hey, my brother said he thinks you care about me more than you're letting on. Is that the truth?* Hardly a good way to start the conversation. And again, did it really matter? His feelings weren't the issue—it was his aversion to a relationship that had set them on separate paths. He'd saved her son, and she'd be forever grateful to him for that. But that didn't mean he wanted to be with her. As much as she hoped things were different, Stavros hadn't said anything about a relationship. In fact, maybe helping Danny had brought him pain? He'd saved her son when he hadn't been able to save his daughter. Perhaps being around them was too hard for him now?

She sighed and put down the phone. No, like she'd told Troy earlier, she wasn't going to beg. Stavros was a grown man who knew his own mind. Even though she felt in her gut they were good together, she couldn't force him to agree with her.

Desiree got to her feet and walked out of the kitchen. It was time to start moving on. She wasn't sure how long it was going to take before she could hear Stavros's name and not feel that ache in her heart, but she had to keep going until she found that place.

Hopefully tomorrow would bring her one step closer.

Two days later

"Dr. Makris? There's a detective here to see you."

Stavros looked up from the computer in the dictation room and frowned. "A detective?"

Stacey nodded. "He's in the patient counseling room." She tilted her head to the side. "I didn't realize we had any problem cases tonight."

"We don't," Stavros said shortly. It wasn't uncommon for the police to come to the ER—sometimes they brought people who'd been injured, sometimes they arrived to help victims of assault or domestic violence. But they generally didn't stop by just to say hi. If a detective was here, there was a reason for the visit. And as the senior doctor on shift tonight, Stavros should already know what that reason was.

He finished typing in his note and logged out, his mind whirling. What was this about? The ER had been quiet since Len's visit a few weeks ago, at least from a crime perspective. So why was one of GGPD's finest waiting to speak to him?

He rapped his knuckles on the door to the counseling room and opened it to find Troy Colton standing inside.

Ah, Stavros thought to himself. *Figures.*

He stepped inside and closed the door behind him. "Detective Colton. What can I do for you today?" He had a feeling he already knew. Troy had called him a few times recently, his messages saying he needed to talk to Stavros about a personal matter. Stavros hadn't felt up for any such conversation, so he'd ignored the messages. He was still sorting through his own feelings where Desiree was concerned. Adding her brother to the mix was the last thing he wanted to do.

But it seemed Troy wasn't going to take his silence for an answer.

"You can start by returning my calls," Troy said easily.

"Sorry. I've been busy," Stavros said automatically.

Troy nodded. "Sure you have. Still, if Muhammad won't come to the mountain…"

Stavros nodded and pulled out a chair. *Might as well get this over with.* "Indeed. Well, you're here now. Why don't you tell me what's going on?"

Troy took the chair opposite him and regarded him with a level stare. "What are your intentions regarding my sister?"

Stavros laughed. He couldn't help it—the question was so off base, there was no other way to respond. "Really? This is what you wanted to talk to me about?"

Troy didn't reply. He sat across the table, silently watching.

Stavros shook his head. "Look, I get you're protective of Desiree. But you don't need to worry about me. Now, if you'll excuse me, I'm busy."

"We're not done talking," Troy said.

Stavros felt his temper flare to life. "Yes, we are. I'm not one of your suspects, Detective. And I don't appreciate you trying to pry into my personal life. I'm sure your sister doesn't, either. Does she even know you're here?"

A guilty expression flickered across Troy's face, telling Stavros all he needed to know. "That's what I thought," he said. He pushed back from the table and stood. "We're done here. If you need me in an official capacity, let me know. Otherwise, I have nothing more to say to you."

He made it to the door before Troy spoke. "She needs you."

Stavros froze, his hand still reaching for the doorknob. "What?" A stone of dread formed in his stomach. Was Desiree hurt? Was she in danger again? Or, worse, had something happened to Danny?

He turned around, needing to know more. "What happened to her? Are she and Danny okay?"

Troy held up his hands. "They're fine. Physically."

The tension in his muscles eased a bit. "Then what's wrong?"

The chair dragged across the linoleum tile as Troy got to his feet. He planted both hands on the table and leaned forward. "Look. Desiree doesn't know I'm here. And if she found out...well, let's just say she wouldn't be happy about it. But I'm tired of watching my sister mope around. It's been two weeks and she's not getting any better. I don't know what went on between you, but I do know you care about her and Danny. And I can tell she has feelings for you. So why don't you two do something about it?"

A small shock zinged through Stavros, rendering him temporarily speechless. He missed Desiree terribly. Danny, too. It was one of the reasons he'd thrown himself back into work. But he'd never expected to hear that Desiree was similarly affected by their separation. She'd seemed fine when they'd last seen each other a few days after Dahlia's arrest. Stavros had figured that, with Dahlia gone, Desiree would be relieved to have her life get back to normal. And while she hadn't explicitly blamed him for Dahlia taking Danny that day, she hadn't been her usual self when they'd said goodbye. It had stung a bit, but he'd actually been a little grateful for the distance. It had made it easier for him to let her go. As much as he cared for her, he knew he wasn't good enough for her. Better to let her go so she could find happiness. His heart cracked at the thought, but it was for the best. Stavros had thought Desiree was ready to move on, but what if he'd been wrong?

Troy was watching him, waiting for a response. Stavros sighed. "It's not that simple," he began.

"I don't see why not," Troy replied. "Do you care about her? Do you care about Danny?"

"Of course I do," Stavros said. He was tired, so tired. Not just on a physical level, but emotionally, too. These last few weeks had been like a roller coaster, and he was ready for the ups and downs to stop.

"Then what's stopping you two?" Troy shook his head. "I really don't get it. You, of all people, should know that life can change in an instant. Why are you guys wasting time when you could be together?"

"Because it's more complicated than that!" The

words came out a little louder than he'd meant, so Stavros cleared his throat and tried again. "Yes, I do realize nothing is guaranteed. But I also know that Desiree and Danny deserve someone who is whole and unbroken. Someone without a truckload of baggage to deal with."

Understanding dawned in Troy's eyes. "And you think you're not that guy." It wasn't a question—more like a statement of fact.

Stavros smiled, but there was no humor in it. "How could I be? I've spent the last five years mourning my daughter and trying to forgive my ex-wife. I know now that I'm never going to get over losing my kid—it's something I'm going to have to live with for the rest of my life. I don't know if I'll ever really feel whole again. It's not fair to ask Desiree or Danny to put up with that." He blinked hard as tears stung his eyes. He didn't know why he was telling Troy all of this. But hopefully his confession would help Troy see that Stavros wasn't fit for his sister. Desiree and Danny deserved better— surely, Troy would agree with that?

Troy straightened and ran his hands down the front of his shirt. "I think I get it," he said. "You think there's some perfect guy out there. But you should know better than that. Nobody's perfect."

Stavros shook his head. "No, that's not what I mea—"

"It's okay," Troy interrupted. "I hear what you're saying. And I realize I was wrong to come here. I thought I could help the situation, but now I realize you aren't the right guy for my sister. You clearly don't respect her enough to let her choose for herself."

"Wait—what?!" Stavros felt like his head was spinning from Troy's rapid about-face.

Troy walked to the door and stopped a few inches away from him. "You have your issues. We all have issues. But don't you think Desiree deserves to make up her own mind? She's the one who has to deal with you. But you're not even giving her the option of deciding if she wants to take you on, warts and all." He cocked his head to the side. "I thought doctors were supposed to be smart?"

Stavros stepped aside to let Troy pass. He was dimly aware of the door snicking shut behind him, but he was too wrapped up in his own head to pay much attention to the rest of the room. Troy's accusations echoed in his mind, making him profoundly uncomfortable. Was there any truth to what the detective had said?

His knee-jerk reaction was to dismiss Troy's words. What did he know about Stavros's situation and how it related to Desiree and Danny? And how dare he show up to the ER unannounced so he could nose his way into Stavros's personal life? It was rude and inappropriate, and Stavros should shake it off and get back to work.

Except…a small voice in the back of his mind piped up. *What if he's right?*

Stavros grabbed the nearest chair and sank down onto the seat. Ever since Desiree had come into his life, Stavros had been focused on all the reasons why they couldn't be together, why he was wrong for her and Danny. But he'd never stopped to ask her what she thought or how she felt. He'd been so preoccupied by his worries and insecurities that he'd forgotten to take into account Desiree's feelings. And he'd been so convinced he wasn't good enough for her that he'd failed to even consider her viewpoint.

Troy was right about one thing: no one was perfect. After their time together, Stavros had no secrets from Desiree. She knew about his past, was aware of the ways in which he still struggled to deal with his loss. And she hadn't judged him or pitied him. She'd supported him, made him feel whole again. If what Troy said was true, did her feelings extend beyond friendship? Had she been willing to give him a chance, despite knowing about his demons? A chance he'd wasted?

His head spun as his world tilted on its axis. The bottom dropped out of his stomach and a sick feeling of fear washed over him. Had he really thrown away his best shot at happiness? Had he been too stubborn and shortsighted to see that Desiree was willing to try, if he would only take her hand?

"I'm such an idiot," he mumbled. As a doctor, Stavros usually prided himself on his ability to assess a situation and make the right call. But the more he thought about Desiree and what Troy had told him today, the more he had to admit he'd thoroughly mucked things up.

He leaned forward and cradled his head in his hands. Okay, he'd blown it. That much was clear. What could he do about it now? How could he convince Desiree he deserved another shot with her?

Would she even listen to him? Or would she slam the door in his face? He had no way of knowing, but one thing was certain: he had to try.

The sooner, the better.

SOMEONE WAS KNOCKING on her door.

Desiree cracked open one eye and peered at the clock on her nightstand. Ugh. Why was someone trying to visit so early in the morning?

She rolled out of bed and reached for a robe, then tiptoed down the hall. Whoever was on the porch wasn't knocking loudly enough to wake up Danny, but if they kept it up or decided to escalate to the doorbell, all bets were off.

Desiree pulled aside the thin curtain that covered the glass pane inset in the door and saw her visitor. For a second she just stood there, unable to believe her eyes.

Stavros offered a sheepish smile. "Hi."

His voice was muffled through the door, but it was enough to shake her back to full awareness. She unlocked the door and held it open. "Stavros?" She looked him up and down, searching for a clue as to why he was here. She hadn't stopped thinking of him since her brother's visit two days ago, but she hadn't expected to see him, either. He was dressed in green scrubs, his hospital badges still clipped to his hip. His hair was mussed, and based on the stubble on his face, he hadn't shaved in days. The dark circles under his eyes were a testament to his fatigue, but there was a buzz of nervous energy around him, as though he was charged up about something.

"I know I should have called, but I needed to see you."

"Is everything okay?" Desiree took a step back and gestured for him to come inside. She led him to the kitchen table and started filling the coffeepot with water. Might as well get the day started.

"Yes. I mean, no. I mean…it's complicated." He sighed and ran a hand through his hair. "Can I sit down? Maybe start over?"

Desiree leaned against the edge of the counter as the coffee maker started percolating. "That sounds like a good idea if it'll help you start making sense. I haven't had my caffeine yet and I don't really follow what you're trying to say."

Stavros huffed out a laugh. "Fair enough. I'm not sure I get it myself." He sat and put his forearms on the table, clasping his hands loosely together. He took a deep breath and looked up at her once more.

"The thing is, Desiree… I owe you an apology."

She frowned. "What for?"

"Lots of things. For not paying close enough attention to Danny—"

"Yeah, about that." She shifted, seeing an opening. "A little birdie told me recently that you feel guilty about what happened. Like it was your fault Dahlia took Danny. But it wasn't your fault, and I hope you know I never thought that. And I'm so grateful you saved him, too."

A look of relief crossed Stavros's face, and Desiree realized she should have told him that a long time ago. "I appreciate it, but that's not the only thing I'm sorry about."

Desiree crossed to the table and took the chair opposite him. She'd never seen Stavros look so flustered before. What was going on with him?

"I realized something while I was at work last night," he said. "I miss you. I miss Danny. And I miss our time together."

Desiree swallowed the sudden lump in her throat. "We miss you, too," she admitted softly. "But I walked away because I thought that was what you wanted. You'd told me we couldn't have anything more than that one night together."

"I know," he said. "But I've realized something. When you both were with me, my life didn't feel so empty," he continued. "I started to feel whole again, and my condo became a home. Despite that, I spent my time thinking of all the reasons why it couldn't last. Why you wouldn't want to be with me."

Desiree felt her breath catch. Never in a million years had she expected Stavros to talk like this. He'd made it clear from the start he couldn't make any promises. What had changed?

"I told myself that even though I had feelings for you, I didn't deserve you. That you and Danny needed someone better. Someone who didn't have a sad past clinging around his neck."

"You know I want to support you," she said, unable to keep quiet any longer. "That night you told me your story... I only wanted to help you, to make you see that you're not alone."

"I know." He offered her a wobbly smile. "And you did. It meant a lot to me to talk to you about Sammy and what happened to her. But I convinced myself that you were being a good friend, and I shouldn't hope for anything more because I didn't know if I could love again. I didn't want to practice on you and find out I was too broken to heal."

Desiree sat back in her chair, considering his words. Leave it to Stavros to want to protect others, when really, he was the one deserving of help.

"You're not," she said quietly. She reached across the table and put her hand over his. "I know you, Stavros. You're one of the strongest people I've ever met. You're not too broken to love again. You just have to let yourself try."

He flipped his hand over so they were palm to palm. His fingers curved gently around the edges of her hand, and his touch sent tingles up her arm. "See, that's the thing," he said. "I think I do love you. And Danny. But I spent so much time worried that you wouldn't want a man like me, I pushed you away."

Desiree gasped, his words washing over her like a warm rain. "Stavros, I—"

He looked up at her, eyes shiny with emotion. "Desiree, I know it was wrong for me to run from you. I should have given you the choice. You know me. You know my past. You know my present. I should have let you decide if it was enough for you."

"I—" she began again.

"And I know I don't deserve it," he continued. "But I'm here today because I want to ask if you'll consider giving me another chance. I want you and Danny to know that you fit in my life. You make it better. I just hope there might be room in your lives for me."

He went quiet, watching her. She waited a few seconds, nerves fluttering in her stomach like a flock of butterflies. "Can I talk now?" she asked.

Stavros smiled. "Sorry about that. Of course."

Desiree squeezed his hand. "You do fit with us," she said. "And I don't need to give you a second chance. You're still on your first one."

Hope flickered across his face. "Really?" His voice was filled with wonder, as though she'd just shown him a magic trick.

Desiree nodded. "Really. Danny already loves you. I do, too. So if you want to take a chance and see where we end up, we're happy to go on the ride with you."

Relief washed over Stavros, the tension seeming to drain out of his body. "Oh, Dez." He got to his feet and pulled her up with him. He pulled her close and brushed a strand of hair to the side of her face. "I don't deserve you."

"Sure you do," she said, smiling up at him. "But I'm going to remind you that you said this when you leave your dirty socks on the floor."

Stavros laughed, his brown eyes sparkling with joy. He dipped his head and kissed her.

Desiree relaxed against his chest, loving the feeling of being pressed against him once more. They did fit together, in all the ways that mattered.

Warmth spread through her body, and as Stavros's hands moved over her, the heat inside started to grow. If she wasn't careful, they'd wind up naked on her kitchen floor in no time.

With no little effort, she pulled back. They were both

breathing faster, and Stavros stared at her mouth with a hunger that sent zings straight to her core.

"Here's the thing, though," Desiree said, determined to get this out before her thoughts melted into a puddle. "If we're going to do this, I need you to promise to talk to me."

Stavros nodded. "Of course."

"No more working everything out in your head without asking me what I think, too," she continued. "Especially if it's something that will affect both of us."

Stavros shook his head. "I've learned my lesson." He leaned in and nipped at her chin, making her gasp. "I have some concessions for you, too."

"I'm listening," she said. His fingertips were gliding up her torso, so she placed her hand over his, stopping his exploration.

Stavros leaned forward until his mouth was at the level of her ear. "I'm going to want to marry you." His voice was low and husky. "And I want Danny to be mine, as well."

Desiree pulled back, needing to see his face. "Really?"

He nodded. "Really. Not right away. But soon."

Her heart pounded against her breastbone. "What's your hurry?"

"I've wasted enough time already. I don't want to waste any more. Not where you and Danny are concerned."

A lightness washed over Desiree, making her feel almost giddy. Even in her wildest dreams, she'd stopped short of imagining this. She'd been too afraid to even hope, feeling it would only make it harder to move on.

But now she didn't have to. She was getting her happy ending, despite all the odds.

She and Stavros and Danny were going to be a family. And maybe, in time, they would have more children together, a brother or sister for Danny. Whatever final form their family took, she knew it would be perfect.

She opened her mouth to reply, but the muffled sound of Danny's voice drifted into the kitchen.

"Ma-a-a-m-a-a-aa!" he called.

Stavros chuckled. "Sounds like someone's awake."

Desiree nodded. "And he'll be hungry. Give me a second to get him?"

Stavros shook his head. "I'll come with you."

She smiled, her heart feeling so full it might burst. "I'd like that. He will, too."

Stavros grinned. "That's good, because from now on, we'll be doing lots of things together."

"Promise?" she asked.

He nodded, the look of love on his face so intense it nearly took her breath away. "Promise."

* * * * *

COMING SOON!

We really hope you enjoyed reading this book.
If you're looking for more romance, be sure to
head to the shops when new books are
available on

Thursday 13th May

MILLS & BOON

THE HEART OF ROMANCE

A ROMANCE FOR EVERY READER

MODERN

Prepare to be swept off your feet by sophisticated, sexy and seductive heroes, in some of the world's most glamourous and romantic locations, where power and passion collide.

HISTORICAL

Escape with historical heroes from time gone by. Whether your passion is for wicked Regency Rakes, muscled Vikings or rugged Highlanders, awaken the romance of the past.

MEDICAL

Set your pulse racing with dedicated, delectable doctors in the high-pressure world of medicine, where emotions run high and passion, comfort and love are the best medicine.

True Love

Celebrate true love with tender stories of heartfelt romance, from the rush of falling in love to the joy a new baby can bring, and a focus on the emotional heart of a relationship.

Desire

Indulge in secrets and scandal, intense drama and plenty of sizzling hot action with powerful and passionate heroes who have it all: wealth, status, good looks…everything but the right woman.

HEROES

Experience all the excitement of a gripping thriller, with an intense romance at its heart. Resourceful, true-to-life women and strong, fearless men face danger and desire - a killer combination!

To see which titles are coming soon, please visit

millsandboon.co.uk/nextmonth

MILLS & BOON
MEDICAL
Pulse-Racing Passion

Set your pulse racing with dedicated, delectable doctors in the high-pressure world of medicine, where emotions run high and passion, comfort and love are the best medicine.

MILLS & BOON
Desire

Indulge in secrets and scandal, intense
drama and plenty of sizzling hot action
with powerful and passionate heroes who
have it all: wealth, status, good looks…
everything but the right woman.